WITH DESIRE . . . FOR HIM

All too crystal clear, she realized that it wasn't the company of strangers in Teddie's diner that she needed—she wanted to be near Cole Dumont. She wanted to feel the strength in those large hands, to buoy her up from her despair. She needed him to be her comfort and her family. But more than that, she desired him!

When she captured his gaze, Cole knew what he'd suspected from the first time they'd locked eyes days ago—that Ava, in all her smoothness and denial was a woman in desire . . . for him. What that knowledge did to him just now threatened to take away his resolve to leave her alone—she wasn't a plaything for his immediate sexual healing.

But here, in an unguarded moment, she was telling him differently. He held her gaze for an interminable moment, and then stepped onto the porch and came toward her. The second he moved, the spell was broken and she was standing on her porch, hand on her doorknob with him standing beside her.

"Ava," Cole said.

"Hello," she said easily. She had control now, was the master of her voice and body.

Also by Doris Johnson

Hello Again

Goodbye Heartache

Doris Johnson

KENSINGTON PUBLISHING CORP.
http://www.kensingtonbooks.com

DAFINA BOOKS are published by

Kensington Publishing Corp.
850 Third Avenue
New York, NY 10022

All Kensington titles, imprints and distributed lines are available at special quantity discounts for bulk purchases for sales promotion, premiums, fund-raising, educational or institutional use.

Special book excerpts or customized printings can also be created to fit specific needs. For details, write or phone the office of the Kensington Special Sales Manager: Kensington Publishing Corp., 850 Third Avenue, New York, NY 10022. Attn. Special Sales Department. Phone: 1-800-221-2647.

Dafina Books and the Dafina logo Reg. U.S. Pat. & TM Off.

ISBN 0-7582-0900-2

First Printing: February 2006
10 9 8 7 6 5 4 3 2 1

Printed in the United States of America

*For my granddaughter, Shaneva Bryant,
and Lois Highe and Gloria Black*

Chapter One

"Walden Pond it's not, but it's *my* solitude." Jogging into her yard, Ava Millington cut a disgusted look at the dusty black SUV sitting in the driveway of the house next door that had been vacant since she'd moved in two years ago. The attraction for her purchase of the small three-bedroom house was its isolation. When the Realtor told her not to worry about anyone moving in next door she'd been delighted. The family had deserted the place years ago and were not expected back. She'd had her doubts about that though since once each spring and fall the place was maintained by a crew who came and went as quietly as Santa's elves, leaving the grounds swept, cleared, and cut and the house looking lived in with newly washed windows. And each time she expected to see a van drive up with a load of furniture and people to boot. But none ever came. After the first three times she stopped looking. So when yesterday she stepped off the porch for her early-morning jog with the roosters crowing, she was startled to see the big Chevy Tahoe with California plates parked in the yard on the black-topped driveway. It hadn't moved since she'd seen it, nor had she seen its driver.

Feeling betrayed that her blessed peace was about to be disturbed by neighbors, she reached her porch and before going inside, did cool-down stretches, then began jumping in place. When she turned, swinging her arms in half circles, she stopped abruptly as she met the dark eyes of the stranger with a days-old scraggly beard ruining the outline of his mustache and goateed chin, looking at her from his front porch.

Ava's heart skipped a beat, and the scowl she'd had for the SUV was replaced by an involuntary smile that moved her lips to form a surprised "Oh." The sound escaped softly and she flamed inside thinking that it sounded like the shot heard 'round the world. Flustered for thinking in clichés, she straightened and stiffened her shoulders and returned stare for stare. *It's nice to be neighborly, Ava. Where are your Southern manners, Georgia girl? People are no different here in South Carolina.*

Dutifully she said, "Good morning." She nodded as he had but she wondered if the man was punch-drunk or mute because after that minute movement of his handsome head he continued to stare. His body was as still as the two-hundred-pound boulder it emulated. Oh, well, so much for welcoming new neighbors. She turned to go inside, muttering, "So be it. I did my part."

"Good morning."

Ava stopped and watched as the man left his porch. In the still-early, misty morning light of the last days of May, she watched him walk through a natural opening of the neatly trimmed row of hedges separating their properties. He grimaced as the bushes swung back, scratching his bare arms and shoulders that weren't covered by the white tank top he wore. Her lips curled thinking how a big, muscled man, at least six feet of him, would even notice the light touch of the branches. Her insides acted funny again when she took in the length of him, his shirt tucked inside unbelted jean cutoffs. She scanned the muscular calves, even noticed the shape of his feet pushed into backless tan sandals. She swallowed and silently watched his approach.

"I'm Cole Dumont. You're the doctor?" He had one foot on the bottom step.

Startled, she automatically extended her hand. "Ava Millington, Ph.D."

His dark eyes snagged hers and ignoring her hand, he stepped back. "Oh, *that* kind of doctor." After a long look he said, "Sorry to have bothered you."

Ava watched in disbelief and unneighborly relief as he walked away, but her surprised cry when she saw his bloodied shirt made him stop and turn around. He waved a hand as if to say "No problem" and proceeded through the hedge opening. When the branches tapped his back again she heard him grunt and swear, and seconds later she saw him stumble up the steps and then disappear inside.

The calm Ava had felt for the last two years in Minuet, South Carolina, a midsize suburban town outside of Florence, was fading fast. She hurried into her house and stood with her back against the door as if to keep at bay a sense of foreboding that caused her chest to rise and fall. It was as if she'd always feared that the past tragedies of the empty house would somehow sidle over in a reptilian manner and ensnare her in chilling chaos, disrupting her peace. Was this coming to pass in the person of Cole Dumont?

What was it her friend Teddie Perkins had said?

"Trouble just followed Cole Dumont. His brother's death was an accident, but no one believed Cole wasn't at fault." *No one believed.* Those words had cut through Ava, causing her to shrivel up inside, dying a thousand deaths as she had in the past. No one had believed her either.

Ava shivered and hurried up the stairs, tearing her clothes off as she ran. In the shower she stood under the gushing spray as hot as she could stand it, as if trying to scald away her memories of the past and to keep her from being tainted by this stranger's own tainted history. Misery seeks company and she was so close to his. Did one's past. forever jump up to bite one in the face?

Twenty minutes later, lying on the bed, staring at the ceiling, calm and acting sane now, she thought of the quietly strange man next door and her reaction to him. He was a chocolate dream walking, as raunchy as he'd looked. He'd have to do much more than sport an unkempt beard to keep the sisters at bay. But his penetrating dark eyes screamed danger and she was willing to bet that it would take a crowbar to pry those full luscious lips into a big, genuine smile.

He'd come looking for the doctor, and from the look of the blood staining the back of his shirt, he'd needed one badly. Why hadn't he just driven that big monster of a truck into town? she wondered. What had made him think she was a medical doctor?

She sat up and walked to the window and stared over at the still house. There was no sound of music breaking the quiet of the morning, no lights that she could see, and she wondered if he was in an upstairs bedroom staring back at her through those lacy curtains. She frowned. What was happening in there? Had he passed out? Surely he was able-bodied

enough to seek out some medical help. Common
sense should have had him hightailing it to town
after learning her doctorate was useless to him.

Teddie's words bothered her. Was Cole Dumont another victim of misunderstood circumstances as she
had been? Innocent of whispered accusations? She
shook off her Florence Nightingale cloak. She wasn't
getting involved, neighbor or not. And if he had good
sense he'd find his way to some help, she rationalized.
She got up, shed her robe, and began dressing for
church. Somehow she had to go today, be surrounded
by a host of others sending out good vibes and uplift-
ing messages. Maybe, just maybe, the ominous feelings
would have dissipated when she returned.

Cole Dumont was sprawled on his stomach on the
living room couch, his feet dangling to the floor.
He'd peeled off the shirt, pulling scab and stitches
with it. Using mirrors in the bathroom he'd seen the
damage he'd done to the wound. The doctor had
warned him about taking that long drive from Los
Angeles. Two weeks hadn't been long enough for
the wound to heal. Now the oozing pus was a sure
sign that he'd picked up an infection.

Besides his fellow officers on the L.A.P.D. force,
Cole's older brother, Graham, had been his only
other visitor in the hospital. It was Graham who'd
given him the keys and told him it was time to go
back home because the mean streets of L.A. would
do him in. If not the jailed gang member who'd
tried to kill him, another would be waiting to finish
the job. Weary of his years-long effort as a detective
in the Youth Gang Unit, to convert gang members to
another way of life, Cole had halfheartedly agreed.

Spending time in Minuet right now was probably the best way to clear his head and think about his future. But he knew his stay would be short-lived. Too many ghosts still left to be put to rest here. He sent a baleful look in the direction of the kitchen where his pain had started all those years ago.

"Damn, Graham, I thought you'd heard a doctor had bought that old house," he muttered. He groaned as pain shot through his shoulder when he moved. He'd been wrong to think a few hours of sleep would do magic after finding out the stranger next door wasn't the quick cure-all he'd gone looking for. His head was still pounding and he felt feverish. He had to get out of here and go get some relief before his foolishness helped to finish the job that that little L.A. hoodlum had started on him.

In the kitchen he dashed cold water on his face, and then dried it with a towel he found in a drawer. Inevitably his glance went to the spot on the floor he tended to avoid when in this room. Though he'd arrived in the wee hours of Saturday morning, Cole had yet to feel at ease in the home where he'd grown up. It was almost as if the nightmare he'd lived with for eighteen years was happening all over again, reruns flickering on and off before his eyes.

Curtis. Graham. Mama, stop screaming!

Skirting the dreaded spot, Cole left the kitchen. In the living room where his bags still lay, he found a button-front shirt and eased into it, and then grabbed his keys off the table by the front door and left the house.

Ava didn't know whether it was the good reverend's sermon about loving your neighbor that did it or whether her conscience had gotten the better of her as she drove home. Her surly manner earlier was as uncalled for as was the kind of selfish, uncaring person that she despised. So what if she was feeling annoyed that her peace was shattered? There was nothing written that said one act of kindness would thrust her forever into the kind of sharing-the-cup-of-sugar neighbor that she didn't want to become, but she didn't have to act uncivilized. Going over to see if he needed help would have only been the humane thing to do. She swore the reverend's eyes were boring into her soul when he was preaching, and she had to actively prevent herself from sliding down the pew out of his sight.

It was almost one o'clock when Ava pulled into her driveway in time to see Cole leave his house and stumble to his car. Feeling the reverend's eyes on her, she breathed a silent prayer and went through the opening in the hedges.

"Can I help?" she said, her eyes scanning the back of his shirt where it was beginning to stain.

Cole turned his head to look at the beautiful woman who'd earlier clearly shown that she didn't want to be bothered. What changed her mind? he wondered. His eyes traveled up from the tip of her shoes to her fine deep beige shapely legs to the delectable curve of her hips to the small waist to the ample bust and to that gorgeous round face with the full kissable lips, and finally her flashing, pretty maple-brown eyes. She pushed a wisp of that long, silky dark brown hair from her forehead and put her hand on one hip and stared at him. He'd take a bet that she was just waiting to hear a no and she'd make like a rabbit and scurry back home.

"You got it in church?" he rasped, assuming that's

where she'd been, dressed as prettily as she was. His eyes bored into hers.

"What are you talking about?" Ava snapped, impatient with the man and flustered after the undressing of her he'd just done. She wondered if he now knew that she was wearing lacy lavender lingerie under her black silk suit.

"Your medical license. You already know what kind of doc I need."

Ava's jaw dropped. "Well . . ." she sputtered. "You know what? Why don't you just dial 911?" she said, and turned on her heel.

"Dr. Ava Millington," Cole said.

Turning back, she waited with a raised shapely eyebrow, suddenly concerned about the beads of sweat forming on his upper lip and realizing he really was in pain.

"Yes, I can use your help," Cole managed, trying not to wince like a wimp. "If I plaster my back against this seat for fifteen minutes, they'll have to pry more of my skin off with my shirt. If you would drive me to the hospital I can lean sideways. I'll forever be in your debt."

Ava looked for signs of humor but saw none. She didn't think the man *could* joke. She gave his car the once-over and rolled her eyes. "We'll leave the monster here. I can do better in my own ride. Can you make it?" Was that a glimmer of a smile on his lips?

She opened the door of her Toyota Camry and he grimaced, eyeing the smaller vehicle. "If you don't mind I'll take a back seat," Cole said. She watched him settle himself, leaning on his good shoulder, his long legs stretched sideways. With a twinge of conscience she realized he would have been more comfortable in the monster vehicle.

Minuet Hospital was a five-minute drive past town

and it normally took seven minutes to get to the hubbub of activity. When Ava jogged she usually took this same route, ending up at the diner where she stopped for breakfast. She could make it in fifteen to twenty minutes most times.

She glanced in the rearview mirror. Cole had his eyes closed and he appeared to be sleeping, so she was startled when those piercing dark eyes opened to meet hers.

"Monster?" he said.

"Monster?"

"So you don't like driving my type of car, Doc?"

"It's Ava," she said, hating that word when applied to her. "And no, I do fine without having to feel like I'm sitting on top of the world. Gets me to the same places in the same amount of time and less gas," she said with emphasis on the last word.

Cole closed his eyes, inwardly smiling. He liked when she flipped her head in annoyance, and though he couldn't see, he knew she was pursing those lips in what she thought was a scowl but only made a guy want to kiss that mouth until she opened up to some serious kissing.

"Mr. Dumont?" Ava was alarmed that he'd fallen silent so suddenly.

"It's Cole," he said, "and I'm just fine." He looked out the window and noticed they'd passed town. "We're not going to the one in Minuet?" he asked.

"Yes, we are. The old hospital was closed years ago and is now a tourist hotel. The new place is just up ahead. We'll be there in two minutes."

Two hours later, Ava was still sitting in the lobby waiting for news of Cole. She was flipping through a magazine wondering if he was worse than either of them had thought he was.

"Ava?"

"Fiona?" Ava said and tossed the magazine on the table, looking at the doctor curiously. "You're working today?" Fiona Fitzgerald never went out of her way to speak to her unless it was beneficial to her in some way. For some reason that's the way it'd been ever since Ava arrived in town two years ago. The woman was gorgeous and some thought, the town beauty, with her flawless beige skin and hazel eyes. Her naturally light brown hair was highlighted with blond, but it suited her and was as gorgeous as she was. Now those changeable green eyes glittered and Ava wondered what was coming.

"On call," Fiona said. She sat as if settling in for a long conversation, crossing her long shapely legs and folding her hands comfortably in her lap. "So you brought Cole in, he told me."

"You're his doctor?" Ava asked. Somehow that bit of knowledge rankled.

Fiona shrugged. "Emergency room. I get everything." She eyed Ava. "I didn't know you knew each other," she said. "I hadn't heard he was back after all these years."

"We're neighbors, Fiona. You know the house I bought. He arrived yesterday." She felt smug telling the beauty something she didn't already know. "He was hurt and asked me to drive him here. Being neighborly, you know?" She smiled then said, "Is that why you're here? To tell me how he's doing?"

Fiona eyed the other woman before speaking. "Yes, he wants to go home. That stab wound was deep and on the way to healing." She clucked her tongue. "Those L.A. gang members really tried to kill him. Just as well he did come home. Don't know why those cops out there continue to try and make a difference. It'll

never do any good." She smoothed the already perfectly tousled hairdo. "Anyway, he showed good sense
in getting here before the infection worsened. I want
him to stay overnight until the fever goes down but
he's insisting on going home. The wound is cleansed
and stitched again and the antibiotic should be working now. He's in the pharmacy having a prescription
filled." She stood, smoothing her brief royal blue skirt
showing shapely legs. "He'll meet you here when he's
finished."

"I'll be here," Ava said. *So he's a cop.* She felt a
strange sense of settling and readjusting going on in
her brain that was comforting.

"Hmm, I wonder why Graham didn't come, knowing his brother was hurt like this. Uh, did Cole say
whether Graham was on the way?"

Ava knew about the older brother from Teddie
and wondered about Fiona's interest. "I don't know
anything about that," she answered. "You'll have to
ask Cole."

"Oh, I thought you'd have spoken on that."

"I told you I was being neighborly, Fiona," Ava said
firmly. "Anything else you want to know about the
family you'll have to ask somebody other than me."
She saw Cole walking toward them and she couldn't
help but smile. He looked revived, walking with
vigor, almost strutting. Oh, the wonder of a little miracle drug. "Like I said, ask somebody who knows."

Fiona gave her a look and walked away, saying
something briefly to Cole before she disappeared
around a bend.

They were quiet on the way back home, the car
smelling of sterile hospital, and Cole in the passenger
seat, resting back gingerly, bandages bulging beneath
his shirt.

"So, who did that to you?" she asked. "You were on duty?"

"A very bad boy," Cole answered briefly, recalling that Fiona always was a talker. "Yes, I'm a detective with the L.A.P.D. and I was on the job." He spoke quietly, remembering that when he'd trusted he should have been wary.

"You were lucky," Ava said.

He didn't respond to that but said, "What's your field?"

"History professor at Floyd Compton University in Florence."

Cole thought that she appeared young to have gotten her doctorate so early. She didn't look past twenty-five but guessed she could be close to thirty. "Professional student?"

Ava frowned. "I was fortunate enough to be able to go straight through." Yes, and to keep on running.

"Okay, case closed," Cole said.

"What?"

"It's obvious you don't want to talk about yourself, so I'm not pushing it." He stared ahead. "It's rather warm for May, don't you think?"

Ava smiled. He did have a sense of humor though his lips never parted in a smile. "When all else fails, weather, huh?"

"Something like that," he said.

She pulled into her driveway, parked and went around to the passenger side. "Can you get out of there okay?" she said, ready to stick out a hand if he wanted it. To her surprise, he reached out.

"Thanks," Cole said when he caught hold and hoisted himself out. He held tightly, liking the feel of her. She had small hands but they were strong and firm and bracing, holding him steady. He lurched against her and he quickly reached out to steady her in her black high heels, wondering at the sound she made as he held her shoulders. They were firm and solid beneath the black silk, yet soft, and he wondered what her skin would feel like under his touch. He inhaled the scent of her—that reminded him of a freshly scrubbed infant—so clean! When he looked in her eyes he was surprised to see a glimmer of fear. He released her.

Ava's senses were heightened when she grasped his hand. When his body brushed hers, she stiffened, unable to do a thing about the sudden change in her body temperature. As she'd imagined, he was rock-hard, his hands on her strong and protective.

"You okay?" Cole asked, staring at her curiously. She was afraid of him. Or something.

"Fine," Ava breathed, stepping away. "I think maybe you'd better take the long way around," she said, gesturing toward the walkway. "Those bushes slapping you can't be a good thing."

"You're probably right," Cole said, and began to walk away, when her voice stopped him. He waited.

"If you need anything, let me know if I can help."

After a moment he said, "Thanks, I'll remember that. I'm already in your debt and I'll remember that too," he said quietly. He lifted a hand and walked away.

She turned and walked toward the house. From her porch she watched him go up the steps, but he stood watching her unlock her door. He lifted a hand and she waved and went inside.

For the first time since he'd arrived home, Cole felt human. All he needed now was a hot shower but would have to settle for a shallow, butt-covering soak in the tub. Better than nothing, he thought, and safer in keeping his wound dry. He grabbed one of his bags and went upstairs.

An hour later he was shaved, smelling good but starving to death. Food had been the last thing on his mind for the last few hours but his stomach was talking to him now. He wondered if there was such a thing as food delivery on a Sunday evening in Minuet. But from where? He didn't know the place anymore.

Downstairs in the kitchen he opened the fridge and pulled out what was left of the carton of orange juice he'd traveled with. He emptied the contents but that only whetted his appetite. Through the kitchen window he stared at his neighbor's house. *If you need anything . . .* "Yeah, a home-cooked meal would go over big right now," he grumbled. Dare he? Cole shook his head. Even he didn't have that much nerve. He hated like hell to go back out. All he wanted to do was eat and hit the sack. Startled at the ring of the phone he should have known that Graham would have had the service turned on.

"Hello."

"So, how's it going? Thought I'd give you some time to rest up before checking in."

"Hey, Graham. Thought you Ohioans were in bed by six on a Sunday."

Graham laughed. "Nah, it ain't like that, but I am crashing early. Rough week making lots of dough. The realty market is running haywire. Can't build houses fast enough. So you ran all over checking out the old town?"

"Yeah, I wish," Cole said.

Alert, Graham said in a quiet voice, "What's wrong?"

"Just like the doc warned, the drive opened up my back," Cole said.

"What? You okay?"

"Yeah, got to the hospital today, got fixed up."

"The hospital? There's a doctor living right next door, for Christ's sake," Graham exclaimed.

Cole grunted. "Next time get your facts straight, man. Looked like a fool going over there for help and her looking at me like I had two heads."

"Whoa, back up," Graham said. "He's a she and not a doctor?"

"She's a she, all right, and with a doctorate in history."

"So much for gossip from back home. You sure you're okay?"

"Infection, but I'll be fine." Cole heard the concern in his brother's voice and he had a sudden feeling of belonging to someone—that someone cared. He sat down at the kitchen table and explained the happenings of the last two days.

"Man, what a mess. Look, just take it slow. I expect you to be shipshape when I come down there."

"You're coming?"

"Yeah, see how you're settling in." He paused, and then said seriously, "So how is it?"

Cole knew what he meant. "I—it's not bad. Getting used to . . . things."

There was a short silence as the brothers reflected on memories.

"Yeah," Graham said. "After I thought about it, I should have been there to meet you. Might have been a little easier."

"You *were* there, man. In L.A.," Cole said. Graham, listed as next of kin, had been with him in the hospital until he was out of danger. Cole would never forget that. It'd been years since he'd felt as if he were part of a family. It was Graham who'd insisted on keeping in touch during the last eighteen years, tracking down Cole to every new address, a new police district, trying to maintain that brotherly tie. It was Graham who'd said it was time to go home.

"I was there because I wanted to be," Graham said quietly. "You're my brother. You're where you should be now. Just give it some time."

Cole silently agreed. He didn't mention that he didn't have the courage to occupy his old room. That was where he'd awakened to the screams of his mother and brother, yelling Curtis's name. Curtis should have been in the bed with him.

"What is it?" Graham said, sensing his brother's discomfort.

"Why?" Cole blurted. "Why didn't you sell the old place?" But in his heart he knew.

"You know how Dad loved the old farmhouse," Graham said quietly. "We all loved it. I didn't have the heart to get rid of it, and Mama didn't care one way or the other. She told me so, and said to do whatever I wanted with it. I thought that one day she might want to come back."

"That wouldn't have happened," Cole said bitterly. "*I* might have shown up." But Graham was right. Their father had loved the old farmhouse that had been gentrified even before he'd bought it for his wife, Patrice, who once she saw it refused to look at another house. *Cole! What did you do?* The screams in his ear caused Cole to flinch and he gripped the phone.

"You're thinking about them."

"Yeah, sorry, man." Cole's gaze went from a spot on the floor to the ceiling. "Can't help it."

"I know. They were great together. *Dad* was great." Graham breathed heavily. "It took a long time to fathom that he was gone. But we made it past that, so don't relive it all now. We've moved on."

"Yeah, we have." Cole's voice was dry.

"Look, just take it slow like I said. I've got some time and will be shooting down there soon as I can." He paused. "So, a lady Ph.D., huh? Maybe I'll get down there sooner than later."

Cole took a moment to answer then drawled offhandedly, "Sure. Suit yourself."

"Hmm. You make a move?" Graham asked.

"The lady's got claws, and the only move I made was to the hospital and back. Besides," Cole said with a grin on his lips, "I don't think Fiona would like you checking out any potential competition." He laughed and hung up on his brother's sputters.

His laughter died as taking his circuitous route from the kitchen, he went upstairs, and passing the bedroom that had once been his, stopped and looked inside. It was as he'd left it, looking for all the world that it was still inhabited by a boy on the verge of leaving his teens to become a man. But, he thought grimly, at seventeen he'd grown up fast. For those four months after his three-year-old brother, Curtis, lay dying in his arms on the kitchen floor, Cole didn't know how he'd managed to continue living in the same house as his mother. He used to wonder who was going to bolt first. As it happened, his mother, leaving the house in the care of her sons, left for Las Vegas one week before Cole graduated from high school. The day he graduated, only Graham was in the audience for him. The next day Cole enlisted in the navy. He was eighteen.

Cole had believed that you couldn't go home again. Not and expect things to be as they had been. His mother was gone, disappearing from their lives running to a faraway place to live with her grief, never to lay eyes on her second son again. Graham had told her of Cole's near-death experience but she never came, never called the hospital.

Mama, you should have come.

For you? You caused the death of my baby! Curtis is dead. Dead!

Cole banished the voices from his head, but as he entered the guest bedroom and closed the door, he remembered Graham's words.

"No, Graham," he said in a ragged voice. "I'm not sure I'm past anything. Not in all these years."

Chapter Two

Ava liked to eat and she loved to cook. Sometimes on a Saturday during the school year she'd start her cooking and finish up on Sunday making different dishes to freeze and eat for days ahead. Since Friday had been the last day of school and she wasn't due to start her summer lecture series for a week, there was no need to prepare so far ahead. But yesterday she'd made peach dumplings and a dark chocolate cake with mocha filling.

Over the years she'd learned that cooking was her therapeutic way of dealing with her problems. She was fine with that as long as she didn't fall into gluttony. She found it satisfying that her solitary life offered the latitude to eat what she wanted when she wanted. In pursuing her studies she'd traveled extensively, tasting and learning how to prepare regional dishes. Some she enjoyed and some were relegated to the trash straight from the stove.

Earlier, after closing the door on Cole Dumont, she'd felt the need for some therapy, especially after experiencing long-dormant sensual emotions. Feelings she hadn't experienced since her early college

years. At thirty-one and engrossed in her career she
was indifferent to subtle and some not-so-subtle ad-
vances of men she encountered.

She'd undressed and donned white shorts and a
light blue T-shirt and spent the rest of Sunday afternoon in the kitchen. While she washed, pared,
chopped, sliced ingredients for her special paella Va-
lencia with saffron rice, she let her mind wander.

For as long as she could remember she'd never
wanted to do anything else but study faraway places
and things of the past. She'd pursued her love of history accepting grants and fellowships that had
enabled her to travel worldwide, feeding her hunger
to know and learn. She'd made her home wherever
she'd been studying at the moment, happy to always
have a place to go to besides returning to her Collier,
Georgia, hometown.

A quick wrinkle of her forehead was meant to
chase away the bad memories. But she knew she'd
never forget. Her throat closed up sometimes when
they encroached upon her, stealing her peace. How
could anyone who knew her think she'd steal a precious artifact? Her passion for the old and the
mysteries surrounding them had been a joke among
her family, her father teasing her unmercifully. He
couldn't understand why a kid with such a sunny dis-
position went crazy over relics. But researching them
was all she'd ever wanted to do.

*Miss Millington, under the circumstances it's best that
you leave.*

Ava shook off the voices as she finished preparing
her cucumber vinaigrette salad with Boston lettuce
and put it in the fridge to chill. Before closing the
door, she poured a glass of lemonade and took it to
the living room where she sipped. The shade was

half-raised and she pushed aside the sheer white cotton curtain and peered out the window.

It was almost six thirty. She wondered if her neighbor had gone out to eat, but she could see that the SUV hadn't been moved. She listened for sounds coming from his place but all was silent. There were no houses on either side of them, and her nearest neighbor was the equivalent of two city blocks away. Across from them was a new single-family home complex that was hidden from view by a forest left intact after development, and Ava was only aware of the houses at night when a twinkling of lights could be seen through the dense branches. She loved the quiet and the fact that while on her porch there was no one facing her on theirs, wanting to come over to chat.

Moving away from the window she returned to the kitchen. The salad was chilled and the paella's savory smells with its chicken, clams, shrimps and spices filled the kitchen, making her realize it'd been hours since she'd eaten. She began preparing her plate, when she stopped, put a hand on her hip, and frowned down at the food. After a moment of thought, Ava reached in the cabinet and pulled out a casserole dish, then filled it with paella. When she finished she took a large basket from atop the refrigerator and stuffed it with the casserole and other accompaniments for a meal.

Ava shifted the basket on her arm and rang Cole's doorbell. In seconds she almost regretted what she was doing. Wasn't she the one who swore never to play the intrusive neighbor? The man had probably eaten and fallen off to sleep she reasoned and bent to lower her burden to the porch. When the door opened she had started down the steps.

Cole stared at the woman taking flight like a startled bird. The legs he'd admired this morning in a skirt were even more admirable with shapely deep beige thighs disappearing beneath her shorts that covered a sinfully curvaceous derriere.

"Ava?" He glanced down at the basket from which delicious smells emanated, and then raised a brow at her. His stomach grumbled like an angry furnace being awakened for the winter. "Smells great," he said, and picked up the basket. "You've come to my rescue again." He cocked his head. "My debt to you is growing."

Stepping farther away from the porch, Ava hadn't realized she'd been holding her breath until she heard the expulsion. He wasn't the same man she'd left earlier. He stood tall, confident, as if the world was his, almost challenging her to deny the bold desirous look in his eyes. He'd changed into a bright yellow T-shirt that seemed to make his skin gleam like copper and loose-fitting chinos that slouched down to his feet. Gone was the scraggly facial hair, including the mustache that had defined the mouth that she'd stared at before, thinking that it was even more inviting to look at and to kiss. *Lord, help me,* she thought. She raised a hand. "Not a problem," she finally breathed. "Just thought you might not have had any food in the house. You can set the basket on my porch when you're done."

Cole studied her, and then opened the lid of the basket, releasing mouth-watering smells, and looked inside. "Thank you." He paused. "So, you've already eaten?"

"N-no . . . not yet. I wanted to get that over here while the food is still hot." She gestured. "But the salad tastes best cold so I suggest you take it out now before it wilts," she said, and started to go but was stopped by his voice.

"Looks like more than enough for two. Why not join me?"

"Uh, no, I don't think so. I'm sure you'd like to be alone. . . ."

"Are you?" Cole asked.

"What?"

"So sure about my wanting to be alone," he said brusquely. Briefly he shuttered his eyes as he thought about eating in the kitchen. His voice softened. "Come on, Doc, I'd really like your company." His look was intense.

Ava saw and heard the silent plea that caused her to wonder. *He really doesn't want to be alone,* she guessed. Sighing, she walked up the steps. "Well, if you're going to stand out here and let my food be ruined, I'll join you, Cole." She gave him a look. "And it's not Doc," she said firmly.

When she sauntered by him, he caught her fresh clean scent and he drew in a breath, wanting to reach out and finger the warm delicate softness of her throat. Hard to think about ghosts with her sitting across from him, he thought.

She paused before following him down the long hall, glancing into the living room. Shirts and luggage were where Cole had apparently dropped them when he arrived. A blanket was strewn over the long beige leather sofa and she realized that he must have been sleeping down here. She saw him watching her.

"This way," he said without explanation.

In the kitchen, Cole rinsed out plates and utensils, dried them, and set them on the table while Ava lifted the carefully packed dishes from the basket. He watched her frown as she felt the bottom of the casserole dish then looked around and spied the microwave.

"This is best piping hot," she told Cole as he watched her moving quickly. Ava set the dish in the handy appliance and turned the knob. Nothing happened and she made a small sound.

Cole reached around her and plugged the cord into the outlet. He inhaled, wondering just when squeaky clean had started to have such an effect on him. "Just about everything was unplugged except for the refrigerator," he said. He stepped away from her. "My brother Graham's been looking after the place."

Ava swallowed, and then nodded. "I've seen the maintenance crew coming every so often," she said. "They're very efficient."

The microwave pinged and Ava quickly spooned out the food, taking care that every ingredient in the Spanish dish was heaped on his plate.

Minutes later when the first bite of the delicious food slid down Cole's throat and hit his stomach, he thought he was in heaven. He didn't speak for several mouthfuls, savoring the different tastes sweetly assaulting his taste buds.

"How does a history professor find the time to learn how to make paella like this?" Cole asked after taking another mouthful.

"I'm glad you like it," Ava said, smiling at his appreciation. She wasn't shy about people enjoying her food. Her friend Teddie had been the only one in her house raving over her fancy dishes and made her promise to call whenever something exotic was on the menu.

"You're going to keep it a secret from me?" Cole asked as he ate more of the yellow rice.

"I traveled a lot," said Ava. "In Spain I lived with a family. I picked up a few things."

"Where did you study?"

"A few schools. Finished up in Philadelphia," she said, as if closing the topic.

Cole noticed the shadow flicker so quickly he could have been mistaken and he wondered if she was keeping secrets. "Did you grow up in Florence?" He stood, rinsed out glasses, and ran cold water from the faucet and handed her a glass. He took a long swallow. "Sorry I can't offer you anything else," he said, sitting back down and finishing his meal.

"This is fine," Ava said after she drank. "I'm from Collier, Georgia. A suburb outside of sprawling Atlanta."

Cole raised a brow. "You opted for all this quiet? Must be quite a change after seeing the world."

"I like it here," Ava said, lifting her chin. "Suits me. It's not so big you're lost in a crowd, yet not so small that you know every face you pass by on the street. Then again, it's not so different from you coming back after living in L.A." Again her tone implied enough.

He could see that her hackles were rising. *So she does have a secret,* he mused and watched as she removed plastic wrap from the dessert.

"I brought two kinds. A lot of people don't like chocolate."

A hint of a smile touched the corners of his mouth. "Never met *that* species in my travels."

For the first time, Ava believed him capable of smiling, and what with the sudden racing of her pulse she hoped the real thing wouldn't turn her to mush. She busied herself with separating the dumplings. She'd made six and brought him two. "These should be warm," she said, and got up to put them in the microwave. Seconds later she returned to the table.

Cole surveyed the delicacies. "Choices, I'm not used to," he said, pulling the dumpling toward him first. He savored it and closed his eyes in pure ecstasy. He made short work of it and then cut a slice from the generous half of the chocolate cake. When he finished he pushed back his chair and looked at Ava who'd eaten a dumpling and was watching him with pleasure.

"You like that I liked that," he said, looking at her curiously.

Ava flushed and nodded. "I like to cook," she said simply.

"To my benefit today," Cole said. "Thank you." He wondered if her Sundays were always spent cooking meals that'd turn the coldest brother into a pool of melted butter. The thought occurred to him that maybe there was a brother in the picture.

"No problem. Happy you enjoyed it."

He gave the empty plate a rueful look. "The likes of that I won't be seeing too often, so I'm doubly grateful."

"The kitchen is a foreign world?"

Cole grunted. "No interest, but I do okay when I'm not being lazy about putting a few pots together. Besides, with my hours it was easier to grab something wherever I happened to be. More often than not, fast-food joints."

Ava rolled her eyes upward. "No telling what your cholesterol level is like. Don't they make you guys take regular physicals?"

With a shrug, Cole began to gather up the dishes and Ava helped. "I'm fine," he said. Then he gave her an amused look. "But one thing I can do is put a hurtin' on some real down-home Southern fried chicken. I'll repay the favor sometime if you're willing."

Smiling at his sudden enthusiasm and the sincerity

in his eyes, Ava said, "I'm up for that. Something you picked up in L.A.?"

"No, my mother . . ." Cole paused. "My brother and I picked that up at home," he said.

Ava saw the light go out of his eyes and she picked up the bad vibes from the mention of his mother. There's more to his long absence than Teddie had ever mentioned, she thought.

The dishes were washed and dried and Ava packed hers in the basket.

Cole didn't want her to leave. It was nearly eight o'clock, the sun was gone, and it was too early for him to turn in. Far too many hours left of the night for him to sit and listen to the sounds of the house. "I wish I could offer to make some coffee for you." He opened the cupboards and made a grand sweep of his hand. "Bare. Looks like the diner for me in the morning." He cast a rueful eye at her. "It *is* still there, isn't it? Otherwise I'm going to starve until I go back home."

Home? Ava thought. A disturbance in her stomach didn't surprise her. "Perk's Diner?" she said. "Of course. Teddie runs it like a fine restaurant."

"You know Teddie?" He frowned. "What happened—Hank and Billie retired?"

"Her father, Hank, died in a plane crash, and her mother, Billie, remarried and moved away."

"Whoosh," Cole said with shock, remembering the good-natured man Hank, who if he'd bothered, could have made his mark in the best of restaurants. "So much for coming back to the old."

They were at the door and Ava reached for the basket but he held on to it as they stepped out onto the porch. "The least I can do is carry it back," he said, wanting to prolong his time with her.

They walked in quiet across the yard. At her porch

steps Ava said, "Would you like coffee?" He didn't
answer and she saw him looking strangely up at the
house. He almost took a step backward. "Cole?"

Handing her the basket, Cole looked at her. "No,
I'm fine." He nodded toward the door. "Go on up.
It's chilly."

At the door, which she hadn't locked thinking that
she was coming right back, she turned to say good-
night but Cole was already backing away. He waved
and hurried to his yard. On his steps he motioned
for her to get inside.

When she closed the door, as she had this morning, Ava leaned against it with a sudden pounding in
her chest. She had the eerie feeling that she'd been
right. Years before, the Dumont tragedy had somehow touched this house.

On Monday morning, out of habit, Ava awoke early
as if planning for work. She usually jogged a mile, returned, showered, and dressed, which never took long
because she disliked dressing up. Her professional
wardrobe was very casual, consisting of separates and
pantsuits in basic neutrals and black and white that she
mixed and matched all year. For school dinner func-
tions she owned two gowns, a red and a black, and two
dresses, a red and a black. For church when she went,
she owned three suits; black, red, and white. Off-hours
she lived in a rainbow of shorts, T-shirts, and jeans. Her
lack of clothing style was a source of anguish for
Teddie, but only amused Ava.

She was standing at her bedroom window that
faced the right side of the Dumont house. Nothing
stirred. Unexpectedly she was beset by that same
eerie feeling of last night, causing tiny prickles to

dance on her skin. Backing away from the curtain she finished dressing in a pale yellow T-shirt and white shorts and went downstairs where earlier she'd put the coffeemaker on. The rich, strong aroma filled the kitchen and she poured an oversize mug of the dark brew and carried it to her back porch.

As she sipped, her curiosity about Cole and his past gave way to an increasing sense of disquiet. More than ever she felt as though her peaceful world was about to shatter all because she'd acted like the Good Samaritan yesterday. The hospital thing was charitable and humane and so was giving bread to a hungry man, but did she really need to stay and break it with him, she asked herself. She liked the closeness of sharing a meal with a man in a setting other than the school dining hall with her male colleagues. She liked *this* particular man. The one with the past so hurtful to him that it had kept him away from his home for years. She loved a mystery. Wasn't she all about delving into the mysteries of the earth? Researching the strange and the unfathomable? But she feared Cole's mystery, when revealed to her, would touch her soul.

She set her cup down and began stretching and marching in place before she hopped off the back steps and rounded the front of the house to start her jog. It was just past six-thirty, damp with the morning chill, and quiet. There was some traffic on the road, those cars heading toward town to the highway that would take folks to their jobs and whatever other business people were about.

During her jog, Ava loved to look for the rare subtle changes in her neighborhood. Nothing changed, yet it did, especially with Mrs. Lansdowne, her nearest neighbor, a widow for many years who lived alone except for two dogs. The change this spring was the new pastel-colored doghouses sitting to the side of the house. Ava saw the woman who was waving and walking toward her at a brisk pace. Ava stopped, hopping in place.

Ellen Lansdowne was a tall woman, about five foot ten. Her large frame carried a good amount of flesh that suited her carriage.

"'Morning, Ava."

"'Morning, Mrs. Lansdowne. How are you today?" Ava withstood the scrutiny from the startlingly gray eyes that were never still. When she'd first seen the widow from a distance, Ava had thought that she was waving to a white woman. But Mrs. Lansdowne was a pale African-American with the tiniest tinge of beige to her skin, and very prominent blue veins. Her long white wavy hair was pulled away from her square face in a long braid that swung down her back and was caught with a thick blue rubber band. A to-the-point woman, the widow didn't respond to the mention of her health.

"Things okay down at your place?" Ellen Lansdowne asked. Her two dogs, Scout, a mixed German shepherd with a black snout, and Twister, a liver-colored cocker spaniel, sat at her heels, watching Ava, deceptively quiet.

"Just fine, Mrs. Lansdowne," Ava said in surprise. "Why?" She made the mistake of touching the fence and the two dogs immediately stood and growled with that low rumble in their throat that signaled danger. Ava promptly removed her hand.

"Hush, you boys," the widow said, and they quieted but continued to stare down their owner's visitor. "Saw Cole Dumont hunched over in your car yesterday like he was hurting bad. Heard Fiona stitched him up. Saw you go by again and haven't seen Cole since." Her penetrating gaze didn't miss the younger woman's look. "Oh, don't look so surprised, you been here long enough to know word gets around," she said. She peered at Ava. "So, young Cole is back. Here to stay, is he?" She clucked her tongue. "Well, sure hope he's not carrying that big chip on his shoulder that he left here with. Time that boy knew who his friends are, and were, back then."

Mrs. Lansdowne was eagerly awaiting her answer but Ava didn't know herself whether he was staying. Not when only last evening he'd referred to L.A. as home.

"I'm not certain what Cole's plans are, Mrs. Lansdowne," she said.

"Cole?" Ellen's mixed gray brows lifted. "Friendly so quick, huh?"

"We're neighbors." Ava continued swinging her arms. "I'm cooling down, Mrs. Lansdowne. Gotta go," she said, and waved. She picked up her pace and jogged briskly down Pine Road toward town.

The widow lifted her brows again but continued to stare after Ava who was still "new people" in her mind. She watched until the younger woman was out of sight, then with narrowed eyes she said, her voice grim, "That girl is keeping secrets."

Later, Ava was sitting in the cozy corner diner on Center Street. It was on a block filled with other small businesses and was centrally located. During the summer, travelers visiting Myrtle Beach or Fort Sumter often stopped in Minuet after touring the two nearby large wineries. In town and also dotting the countryside were many antique shops that drew the serious collector. In the spring Florence celebrated with a floral festival that drew thousands who eventually found their way to the midsize town. Just like the tourists, Ava had also wondered why such a busy street wasn't named Main Street as in many other sister cities in the U.S.A.

The activity inside Perk's Diner, where she sat at nearly seven-thirty, was still bustling. Ava had sat at the counter nursing a tomato juice until the traffic let up, not wanting to hog a booth by herself. Finally seated in the back by the window sipping coffee and waiting for her breakfast, she watched her friend, who was the owner-manager, busily helping her staff deliver orders and seating customers.

Teddie was the first person in Minuet who had warmly welcomed Ava. The same age, their friendship had grown firm when Ava learned that Teddie was as genuine as the real McCoy. Honest. At times she wondered what her friend's reaction would be if she knew that Ava had once been accused of theft. That thought brought a twinge of worry when she thought about the meeting she had to attend at the university tomorrow morning.

The president of the university, Charles Howell, had told Ava that she was the university's choice to monitor the traveling slave archives exhibit during its temporary stay from June through October. After all, precious artifacts were her specialty, they'd all agreed, and she'd be the first to know if anything was amiss. Although there was a curator on the staff, it was Ava whom the president had chosen as overseer.

"Uh-oh," Teddie Perkins said, watching her friend. She set the plate of food and a mug of coffee down in front of Ava. "You only get that look when your thoughts are in overdrive," she said, sliding into the booth. A waitress appeared with another plate and a mug of coffee for Teddie. "What's wrong?" Her big brown eyes were searching as she drank her black coffee. "Where's that beautiful smile that my male customers look for? Their day isn't complete without a friendly smile from the Doc."

Ava blushed as usual at the familiar banter from her friend. She looked around in mock horror. "My public is here?" But she felt good about the teasing, especially since she was nervous about handling the exhibition. It was true that she had a friendly smile, if only because she was acting in kind. Some might call it small-town nosiness, but Ava welcomed the nods and hellos.

"For somebody who likes their privacy and is a regular homebody you'd think you were Miss Congeniality in a beauty pageant."

Ava laughed. Teddie made that happen often.

"Seriously. What happened this morning?" Teddie said. "I saw that frown. Regret you signed up for that summer lecture series instead of flying off to Greece or one of your other exotic destinations?"

"Nothing happened," Ava answered evasively. "But I probably will take a short trip when the series is finished."

"Summer school in this heat is no joke," Teddie said. "It'll go quicker than you think, though."

Ava smiled at her beautiful friend who'd never married. Teddie's son, Royce, was a cutie and in the years that they'd been close, Teddie had never mentioned her five-year-old son's father. Before Ava's and Teddie's friendship, some people had shared some gossip. It was rumored that Teddie had gone away one summer looking for the love of her life. She must have found him, they quipped, because she'd come back with a love child. Now people know better than to share any such ill news about her friend.

She glanced at Teddie's mysterious smile and said, "What?"

"You know I was out of town for the weekend and got back last night, too late to call you, my friend," Teddie said. "So I hear Cole Dumont is back. When were you going to tell me that you two met, driving him to the hospital and all?" She feigned hurt. "I just know you cooked dinner for him seeing as how he was in no condition to mess around in the kitchen." Her mouth twitched. "You know, being neighborly and all."

"Lord, have mercy," Ava said grabbing her chest and raising her hand heavenward. "You're psychic as I always wondered."

"No, I live in Minuet," Teddie said, then laughed with her friend. "And Fiona was in this morning," she said, the smile going out of her voice.

"Oh," Ava said. She never knew the story behind the two women's dislike for each other. For that matter she never knew the reason Fiona disliked *her.*

Dismissing her thoughts, Teddie said with a bright smile, "Is he still a dream walking, stab wound and all?"

"You'll see for yourself," Ava said. "He has no food in the house, and he'll be stopping by here."

"No food in the house, huh? You know this for a fact?"

"His cupboards are bare, Teddie," Ava said, and then broke into a laugh at the look on her friend's face. Then she followed her friend's gaze out the window.

"Now, *there's* the dream," Teddie said.

Cole was walking toward the diner.

"Brothers under the skin," Teddie murmured, staring at the tall man.

"What?"

"Nothing," Teddie answered. "Just thinking out loud."

Ava noticed her neighbor walking tall and straight and wondered if the pain medication was working its magic. Undetected, Ava stared, and she was almost overwhelmed by the same magnetism she'd felt while with him last night, feeling now as though her insides were being flushed with warm soothing water. He wore a navy shirt tucked in, washed out, well-fitting jeans, and white sneakers. The sleeves were rolled halfway up his arms, and she remembered the feel of his strong hands on her shoulders. He was ruggedly handsome and as she'd thought yesterday, the thin, pockmarked line on his high forehead and another tiny scar near the corner of his left eye did not mar the dark copper skin so that one would want to look away with disinterest. Instead, he impressed as an intriguing figure.

Teddie was watching Ava and a smile touched her lips. "Hmm, I see," she said.

"What?" Ava stared at the woman who stood, taking her plate and coffee mug.

"The stories revealed in glances can be almost criminal," Teddie said. She laughed softly. "We'll talk later. Got a hungry man coming." She winked and walked away.

Ava met Cole's glance when he entered the diner and they traded pleasant smiles. Even amid startled calls of "Well, well" and "I'll be" from old-timers and longtime staff who knew him, he continued to stare boldly at her until she flushed. As heads turned her way, she bent her head to study her check, then reached for money in her fanny pack. When her cheeks cooled she looked up to see that she was no longer the center of everyone's curiosity and she slid out of the booth. She wondered if people would hear the rat-a-tat-tat of her heart as she passed by.

Her thoughts raced. Yesterday was one day out of her life and today was a clear morning. Being thrown together as they were had been a necessity. Accepting the bold challenge in Cole's eyes that he'd just thrown her—to get something started between them—was not in her orderly equation. She knew they were attracted to each other; there was no denying that. Acting on lustful impulses would bring drastic change to her world. For years she'd searched for peace and a home she could be happy in. She'd finally found it in Minuet. Why have it disrupted by a man with a past who was only making this his refuge until his wounds were healed? Then he'd be gone and she would have to start all over again to heal the scars left behind. Would that mean leaving Minuet and Teddie, other friends, and her job? She shrank from the pictures flashing before her and she frowned. No, it was best to get any thoughts of a mild flirtation out of Cole's head . . . and hers.

Cole smiled and greeted people, careful not to let anyone slap his back. All the while he kept an eye on his neighbor. He raised a brow at the quick smile she'd given him and at warp speed he saw her go through a complete turnaround. When their eyes locked when she passed him on the way to the cashier, he felt as though he were looking into the frozen depths of a golden-brown glacier.

"Cole!" Teddie, too short to even think about reaching his shoulders, threw her arms around his waist, and hugged him. "Welcome home, stranger," she said with warmth, her eyes almost brimming with tears.

Cole bent to hug the woman who had been his childhood friend and kissed her cheek. "Hello,

Theodora," he said, and hugged her again. "Can you hold on a minute?" he said, and released her.

"Good morning, Ava," he said as she turned to look at him. "Would you stay for a while?" he asked quietly. "Have another cup of coffee with me?"

"Good morning, Cole," she answered. Behind his back, she could see Teddie gesturing toward the back booth. So, she's trying to fix me up? "I don't think so!" She saw Cole's eyes darken, and then realized she'd spoken aloud.

"As you wish," Cole said, and turned on his heel only to bump into Teddie.

"You sure you can't stay, Ava?" Teddie said. She looked at Cole. "With you two being neighbors, I can fill you in on just what mischief this guy used to get into." She put an arm around Cole's waist. "What about it?"

Ava turned to the cashier and paid her bill, then snapped on her fanny pack. "I don't think so, Teddie. I'm going to start back. The sun's high in the sky now."

"You're telling me?" Teddie said. "Since you jogged here, the temp's gone up nearly fifteen degrees. It's got to be over eighty. You can't jog back in that heat. Cole wouldn't mind driving you back home."

"The lady knows what she wants, Teddie," Cole said, giving Ava a cold look. "Obviously coffee and conversation aren't it." He turned on his heel and strode to the back booth, the same one Ava had vacated. When he sat, he could feel her warmth and he steeled himself against the flames licking at his loins.

He flexed his shoulder gently and thought that he couldn't heal soon enough and return to L.A. There, only his body was assaulted. Here, he didn't know what he'd been hit with, but he couldn't get that woman out of his mind since he'd left her last night. Now, she'd knocked him in the solar plexus with that ice-woman's stare. What stories had she been told about him? he wondered. He snatched up the menu and saw nothing but Ava's big beautiful brown eyes looking at him with disdain—and fear?

Chapter Three

Cole looked amused as he watched his old friend boss her staff with authority. He saw Theodora Perkins, the pretty young girl who'd grown into a beautiful woman. Her folks had owned the diner and everyone had treated her like their kid sister. When she was fourteen, Pop Perkins had warned everybody away from her and he'd meant business. But as young as she was, Teddie'd had a crush on older brother jock Graham Dumont, who hadn't known she existed. Cole noticed her left hand free of rings and he wondered if he was looking at that oddity, a one-man woman—and if she was still carrying a burned-out torch left over from her teen years for his long-absent brother.

Teddie slid into the booth across from Cole with a big sigh. Then she took both his hands in hers and squeezed. "It sure is good to see you again, Cole," she said, releasing him as he began to eat.

"Me too, Teddie," Cole answered. Then he touched her hand briefly. "I'm sorry to hear about Pop."

"Thanks. I miss him though he's been gone since I was sixteen," she said. "My mother remarried and is living in Pennsylvania."

The news was surprising but Cole remarked, "This was always a good business."

"Wasn't after Pop died." She wrinkled her nose. "Enough about me," she said. "You've moved back?" Teddie gave him an impish grin. "I can think of at least one good reason why you should and you've gotta agree she certainly is a looker." She glanced outside and saw Ava hesitantly look up and down Center Street and then put her hands on her hips.

Cole turned to look outside to see his neighbor squinting up at the sun. He looked back at Teddie and winking said, "You're right, but have you ever been to L.A.?"

Smiling, Teddie said, "Don't play that game with me. I know and you know if it was like that back there, you wouldn't be sitting across from me now, all wounded up. She'd have kept you close to home." She grew serious as she studied him. "You've changed. Haven't you, Cole?" She reached over and smoothed the scar on his forehead. "There are more of these still on the inside." Before he could speak she dropped her hand and looked over at her cook, Roonie, who was signaling for her from the kitchen. "I'm glad you're back home." She stood and pecked Cole on the forehead. "Gotta go," she said. "But don't leave without seeing me. We've got to catch up." She hurried away.

Cole looked after the woman who was no longer the bubbly young girl he remembered. How could he have missed that she was so introspective? Or had she had to grow up fast after her father died and her mother left her? Home. Minuet hadn't been home for the last eighteen years. What makes everyone think that he's here to plant his feet? If not for his brother's talk of home, putting ideas in his head that he could live here again, he would have been laying up in his L.A. apartment nursing his wounds. There, he wouldn't be playing dodge with a certain spot on his kitchen floor and listening to the screams in his head. No, there were no ghosts in L.A. He continued to eat but had suddenly lost his appetite.

After leaving the cool temperature of the diner, the oppressive warmth swept over Ava in a whoosh. Teddie was right, she thought. There was no way she could have an easy time of walking for even ten minutes with stifling bands of heat encircling her. It had to be close to ninety already.

"Okay, what was that all about?"

She turned to see her friend giving her a searching look. "I think I should be asking you that question, Ms. Matchmaker," Ava said. "I don't need hooking up and especially as you put it, with a man who never knew how to keep himself out of trouble. He's even *returned*, running away from trouble that could have killed him. I like my life the way it is, thank you very much. I certainly don't need the drama of a Cole Dumont messing it up."

Teddie pursed her lips. "You didn't understand what I meant or you're taking it the wrong way," she said. "Cole is one of the most generous and the kindest person I've ever had the pleasure of knowing and if you keep him at arm's length you'll be doing yourself a disservice. A better neighbor you can't have, living as isolated as you do." She took Ava's arm and pulled her to the shade of a big oak tree ringed with backless benches. They sat and she turned to Ava. "Look, my friend, you need a reality check."

"I do?"

"Yes," Teddie said firmly. "I don't know what other stories you've heard around town about the

Dumonts but I'm going to tell you what I know, and it's not gotten cloudy over the years."

"What do you know?" Ava said softly. Had they been such tight friends? she wondered.

"Cole suffered a lot when he was younger. Home is where he should be able to find some peace."

Peace, at home. "How true that is," Ava murmured.

"I told you there were three brothers—Graham the oldest, Cole in the middle, and Curtis, the baby. When Cole was seventeen, his three-year-old brother died in his arms. Because it happened in the house there was an investigation."

"Of course, there would have been," Ava said sadly, knowing what excruciating pain that must have been for a teenager.

"Mrs. Dumont was hysterical and she blamed Cole."

"Why?"

"Because there was no one else. She . . ."

"Teddie, you're needed in here!" A waitress waved, and then disappeared back inside.

She stood, touched Ava's arm. "I've got to go, but I'll call you later. Listen, why don't you rest out here and let me call a taxi? It won't take but a second. You really shouldn't jog back in this heat." She studied her friend. "I hope it wasn't what you ate at my place, but you suddenly look washed-out. Are you sure you're feeling okay?"

"I'm fine, Teddie, but I think I'll take you up on that offer. Thanks, I'll call you later."

While waiting, Ava sat digesting all she'd heard. His mother had blamed him? *It's no wonder the man doesn't call Minuet home anymore.* Just as she didn't call Georgia home. Her father's angry, bloated face, floated before her and the memory of his harsh words stung her ears.

Don't lie, Ava. If you stole it, admit it, and return it. I hate thieves, but liars are worse than the dirt beneath my feet and will never earn my trust!

The baritone she tried to forget over the years but still remembered so well that it pierced her ears even now caused her to sway and clutch her stomach to soothe the sudden flutters. How alike her past was to Cole's—young people enduring the hatred of a parent, she thought. Her mouth twisted in a wry grin. Some match-up her friend was trying to get off the ground. *If you only knew, Teddie.*

Feeling deflated, Ava turned to see Cole standing by his car watching her. She saw him shake his head in disgust, get in the big Tahoe, and pull off. Her stomach roiled and she rubbed it again.

The screech of brakes made her look up at an angry Cole who was getting out of his car and marching toward her. He stood arms at his sides, fists clenched. "You're a fool," Cole said, staring down at her. "But I heard once that God loves all fools and babies and he sent this fool back for you because he's in your debt. Get in the car." He unclenched his fists. "So you won't faint from fright, you have my word that I'm not planning on causing anyone's death today."

Stunned, Ava just stared at the unmovable block of granite before her. Finally she blurted, "I don't faint!"

Minutes later, Ava gave the silent driver a sideways glance. Neither had spoken since she'd climbed in beside him. Her thoughts had stabilized and she was breathing easier. Conversation and coffee, that's all he'd wanted. Shouldn't she have stretched her neighborly act a bit longer and done that? she asked herself. She took a deep breath and looked at him again.

Cole felt her stare. "You nearly keeled over back there on that bench. What's wrong with you? Are you sick?"

"I'm fine."

"Sure you are," he said in disgust.

After a moment, Ava said, "Thanks."

Cole nodded and kept his eyes on the road.

"How are you today?" she asked mildly.

"Fine. Antibiotic is working." He clamped his lips. *Oh, great,* she thought. *I've reduced him to caveman lingo. Okay, Professor, undo the harm you've done. You can admit you jumped the gun with your conclusions.* Wrong, wrong, wrong, for a history major who dealt in facts, not necessarily always the truth. His voice made her jump.

"Whatever you heard," he rasped, "maybe I can help you get the story right. Especially if the gossip involves my bro . . . family." His voice was hard and his jaw tight.

"I'm not asking you to explain your life to me," Ava said. "It was rude and unneighborly to act the way I did. Making assumptions is not usually what I do."

"Is that a fact?" Cole said dryly. He stopped in his driveway and cut the engine. "Home," he said as he got out of the car. Ava was out on her side before he came around.

"Can you make it from here?"

"Just fine. Thanks for the ride."

Cole watched her push through the hedges. When he saw her turn the knob and open her door without unlocking it, he shook his head in amazement, wondering where in the world she thought she was living.

After showering, Ava dressed in loose-fitting chino slacks and a navy sleeveless blouse, intending to do some badly needed gardening before the sun overtook this side of the house. Afterward, she really needed to get inside to her study and look over the meeting agenda the assistant provost, Winifred Whidby, had given her, and the packet that the president had special-delivered to her at the university. She was due to give her expert opinion on the precious items in the slave archives exhibit, which was arriving at the end of the week. She was both thrilled and apprehensive about the artifacts being housed at the college for so long. A historiographer well-versed in the study of old slave narratives, she was always pleased to share her knowledge on the topic. Her summer research lecture series for eager research students was always a favorite and her session filled fast. She could handle but so many projects so the class was limited. She'd brought home synopses of some of the students' intended projects. Intrigued by them all, one in particular, a historic narrative written by Gustavus Vassa, fascinated her, and to her surprise had captured the interest of her friend, Winifred. That was most curious to Ava, but she'd yet to dwell on the significance of it.

Stepping out the back door and walking to the small shed where she kept her gardening stuff on one side of the house, she frowned at one of the toppled clay flowerpots, which bordered the flower beds under the window. Clucking in dismay, she bent over to right the pot. She was annoyed, because not being the best of gardeners she was doubly pleased when the fruits of her labor grew so prettily. She looked around, suddenly realizing that maybe Scout or Twister had gotten loose. Never friendly toward her, she straightened and warily listened for sounds of the dogs scrambling around in the dense forest on this side and in back of her house. It was so quiet, and she walked all around looking for more damage. Strangely enough there was none. Perplexed, she stood looking out past the driveway and toward the road. Nothing else looked out of place. She walked around to the side of the house again and bent down on one knee staring at the deep rich brown soil. Frowning at what she thought was a footprint, she reached down to touch it and then drew her hand back. Silly. It had to be hers.

A sudden chill coursed through her as she remembered forgetting to lock the door. It was a habit that she knew she should get out of but sometimes the peace and serenity of her small space in the universe belied the cops-and-robbers stuff of the real world, somehow bypassing Minuet. Becoming friends with Winifred after meeting years ago while she was studying in Italy had led to Ava's discovery of Minuet and her present position at the university.

More frowns creasing her forehead she was standing in the doorway of the room that she'd made her study in the old farmhouse, her sharp gaze scanning every inch of the room. Something was not right. The walls and tables were filled with artifacts, some historic—the result of years of travel during her studies. She walked to the long table along one wall and stared. Her brow smoothed and her breaths came easy as she reached down.

"Now how did you get over here?" she said. She picked up an iron stand holding a glass-encased square of fragile parchment and switched it with a Navajo Indian Kachina doll. She smoothed the white-and-red feathers of the full headdress and placed the figure of the native dancer at the edge of the table where the feathers were untouched by other objects. "There," she said. "Now you can stay unruffled. And stop giving me the evil eye." She patted the figure's head.

At the desk where she'd placed the school materials, Ava picked up the packet that the president wanted her to see before anyone else. He'd said to report any discrepancies to him in what was supposed to be coming and what was actually shipped and due to arrive at the university on Friday. Because of the nature of the exhibit and her expertise, he was giving her full responsibility of overseeing the exhibit over the duration, although the university curator would be working closely with her. Her stomach knotted as she fingered the packet.

When had she opened it? she wondered, staring at the loosened flap of the large envelope. It'd arrived before she left the building on Friday and she'd dropped it on the desk as soon as she reached home, with intentions of having a relaxing weekend before diving into work.

Ava felt the chill at the nape of her neck. She stared at the packet. Had she opened the envelope and didn't remember? Had she been distracted and dropped it to attend to something else? She stared at the Kachina doll. Why would she have moved it to where its feathers would be crumpled? Feeling unnerved and just a little silly, Ava dropped the envelope and left the room. Maybe she was just wired after the hectic drama of encountering her intriguing new neighbor. In the kitchen she poured a tall glass of cold lemonade and took it to the shade of the back porch where she intended to get a grip.

Except for the Dumont property on her right, surrounding her was nothing but an expanse of green, land she'd learned that had been farmed by a Harper family. Though others, including the Dumonts, had resided on the property, she wasn't surprised that longtime residents such as Mrs. Lansdowne and other folks called the two houses the Harper place. The ways of the South are long, she thought.

The Dumont house had been the Harper homestead. Her small house had been built for relatives but was later sold as a separate property. When farming had stopped, the earth had been allowed to return to its natural growth pattern and the result was uneven splotches of greenery dotting the land. Someone had planted a row of dogwood trees along the edge of the forest, and an old oak tree offered welcomed shade in the center of the backyard.

Ava liked to look at the open space and often worked from the porch. The seclusion was what she relished and it was here in this space that after so many years she was content. At times in her aloneness, especially on gray days, she felt as though the warm rains driven by warm winds were bringing her strength—and peace. A peace that had eluded her since she was seventeen, a disheartened young woman betrayed by her family.

But now she shuddered at the thought of that peace being disturbed. In her heart she knew she hadn't opened that envelope. Who had? Was that really a footprint outside that window? Thinking back, she knew she would have noticed if the envelope had been opened while in her unlocked office. Or would she have? She'd been all too anxious to leave same as everyone else to begin a leisurely weekend in the oppressive heat.

"What's wrong?"

Her pulses jumped at the sound of Cole's voice as she turned to see him staring at her. Puffed with irritation because she hadn't heard his approach she said, "What could possibly be wrong?" and then took a long swallow of her lemonade. "I'm sitting here minding my own business, enjoying what is going to be a blister of a day. Would *you* like some?" She held up her glass.

Ignoring the sarcasm Cole said, "From the looks of it I thought you were assessing the value of the property, the way you walked around scrutinizing the place. Putting it up for sale already?" He stood, rocking back on his heels with his hands in his jeans pocket. "New neighbors are a bitch, huh?"

When he was turning away, Ava realized the shrewlike sound of her comments and she stood. "It's hot, Cole," she said, suddenly too weary to spar with him. "There's more lemonade inside. You're welcome."

Cole looked in surprise at the sound of defeat in her voice—instinctively knowing that that was not her—and the worried look in her eyes. Something was wrong. He took the three wide steps up to the roomy back porch. "Yes, a long cold one would be fine," he said. He watched her leave and return with the pitcher and a glass. He helped himself. After swallowing he said, "But my question stands. What's wrong?"

She looked at him. "Still the cop?"

He rolled his good shoulder. "Ingrained. So why the surveillance?"

She stepped off the porch. "Come look." Cole followed her around to the side of the house facing the woods. Ava pointed to the clay pots. "One of those was overturned. I didn't do it," she said almost defensively. She pointed again. "Can you make that out?" she asked him.

Cole's glance dropped to the earth. He saw the long flat markings of a sports shoe, possibly a sneaker, and the imprint of the toe disappearing where the stone of the house began. "A sneaker print." He stared pointedly at her feet. "Not yours."

"Exactly."

He turned his attention to the house and studied the scratches on the vinyl window, then turned to Ava. "It looks like you've had a visitor who might have gotten in by this window."

Ava remembered the Kachina doll and the opened envelope. As she stared at the footprint and the scratches, she knew. Someone *had* intruded into her home. Her hand went to her throat as she digested that information.

"That was totally unnecessary, though," Cole said dryly.

"What?" She looked at him as if he'd suddenly spoken in tongues. "What do you mean?"

"I've been here over two days and on at least two occasions I saw you walk inside without using your key," Cole said, throwing her an accusing look. "Anybody could walk right in the front door anytime they please." He waved at the dirt. "Guess this poor sucker didn't know that or he'd saved himself the trouble."

His eyes followed her hand on the delicate, golden skin of her neck, and he swallowed the lump in his throat. The tip of her tongue darted out as she nibbled nervously on her bottom lip. Inner warning bells clanged and he heeded them. He wasn't sticking around Minuet *that* long. Cole sensed the inner stress that the prideful woman was trying to hide from him, and he backed off his lecturing. "Any idea of what's going on?" he said, giving her a chance to recover.

Ava, dizzied by the discovery, needed to sit. She walked to the front of the house where guiltily she opened the front door without a key. "Come inside, please?"

"Sure," he said. But at the door, Cole hesitated and took a step back, shuttering his eyes. For a second he was a teenager. He and Graham knew every inch of this house. They'd camped out here, played foolish games, experimented with smokes, and had brought dates here. Countless times they'd played hide-and-seek with Curtis. His squeals of laughter when he found them rang in his ears.

"Cole?"

He opened his eyes to Ava's inquisitive look.

"Are you okay?"

He looked at the house. Damn. It was bad enough that he avoided a certain spot in his kitchen and couldn't sleep in his old bedroom. Was he going to go through this every place he'd ever been with Curtis? If that was the case, he might as well leave town as fast as his ride could take him.

"I'm okay." He nodded curtly at the door. "Let's go inside."

Ava led the way to the study, which had windows facing Cole's house. Whatever had shaken her neighbor must have passed because he now looked recovered, but she didn't question him. Instead she watched as he looked around with interest.

"You've done some traveling."

"For many years. Since I was eighteen." *Traveling? Or running?* She shushed the voices. "These are the result," she said, surveying her treasures.

Cole didn't miss the shadow that had darkened her face and he wondered what secrets she held. *Running.* That was the first thought that had entered his mind. *Like me.* He smoothed the intricately carved black wood of a seated figure holding a bowl. His keen eyes noted the theme in like pieces. "Museum-quality stuff."

"Many could be," Ava agreed. A student of art? she wondered. She knew so little about him. This morning she'd wanted nothing to do with him thinking that he'd soon be gone from Minuet and from her life before she allowed her errant thoughts about him to come to the fore. And now he was in her house where she hoped his sleuthing skills could help solve this sudden crazy mystery.

He fingered an animal carved from ebony. "That, like some of the bowls, is from the Congo. I interned there one summer." Then in a rush, Ava said, "Cole,

something's going on here that I don't understand."
She sat down in a chair and gestured for him to sit.
He sat on the straight-back turquoise-and-white ab-
stract motif sofa.

Cole watched her eyes dart around the room and
then fixate on her desk. He said, "Whatever happened occurred since we got back from town. Right?"
Her eyes left the desk and caught his stare. She
nodded. "You found something missing?" he asked.

"No," Ava said. "I haven't checked, but I don't
think so," she said as she absently drew her fingers
across her throat.

As before, Cole looked away from that delicate
skin. He stood and walked around the room exam-
ining the many pieces of art. Some he recognized
and some were alien. During his stint in the navy
he'd traveled extensively. He'd begun to collect
pieces, and when he realized he'd had no one to
shower with his gifts he'd stopped, giving away what
pieces he owned.

He waved a hand. "You shouldn't be surprised that
someone would be anxious to carry out some of this
stuff." He saw her look. "But that isn't it, is it?"

"No, I don't think so." Ava walked to the long, art-
laden table. "Before, I found this over here." She
reversed the positions of the Kachina doll and the
iron stand holding the glass-encased parchment.
Cole came to stand beside her. Close enough that
she felt his warmth. She moved as if her aim was to
reposition the items, which she did.

Cole didn't miss the body language but he remembered why he was there. "You're so certain that you
didn't do the moving?"

"I am." Ava shifted away from the close space that
they shared. At the desk she sat down and eyed the envelope, her sixth sense causing a rare edginess. She

looked up at Cole. "I think if someone wanted something in here, it would have been inside this envelope." She lifted the flap. "I didn't break the seal," she said, and then frowned. "At least I don't think I did."

"What's in it?" Cole asked. "Something worth more than any of this?" His sharp gaze swept the room.

Ava didn't know where to start. To reveal to him her feelings of what she really thought would be to reveal her past. How could she do that with this stranger who was poised to flee from his own past? Even Teddie didn't know her secrets. She flipped her hand as if to dismiss the envelope, and sent him a look. "It's complicated, Cole, and I don't really know that I can explain it so that anything would make any sense to you."

His eyes glinted. "You've the doctorate. Break it down to my level."

She flushed. "You know what I meant." But she sensed his brimming anger. She did invite him in to help clear up the puzzle and he deserved better than her prudish remark. In consternation she dumped the contents of the envelope on the desk, shuddering with what she knew she'd find—or not find. "I need a few minutes."

She quietly leafed through sheets that held small photographs of many numbered items, carefully comparing them to an accompanying identifying list, and placing each sheet in a pile when she was finished. Ava picked up a sheet she'd already examined and frowns appeared. She shook her head, and after a second dropped the page on the pile with the others. She looked over at Cole. "Nothing is missing," she said, pushing the papers away, but her glance flickered over the last sheet.

"How can you be so sure if you didn't know what was in the envelope?" Cole asked, keenly observing her. He'd seen that brief look of consternation. If she'd spotted an irregularity, why didn't she say something? But she didn't speak on it and neither did he.

Holding the list of items up she said, "This would be the only thing worth stealing. Photographs mean nothing." Seeing his perplexity, Ava explained. "The university is a participating host in a national tour of slave artifacts," Ava began. "I'm well-versed in historic documents, including slave narratives and that period in our history. Last year, a list of hundreds of artifacts and art, borrowed from all sorts of institutions to make up the exhibit, was sent to participating hosts. It was a split tour. Not all hosts would be receiving the same objects. Sometimes, for whatever reason, something is removed from the tour. The president of the university didn't disclose his list, except to the head of the security team who'd be safeguarding the exhibit. He recently received a final, updated list sans photographs. He had the total package sent to me. The fewer people involved, the better the security."

"Why you?" Cole asked.

"I'm responsible for validating the authenticity of the items in the tour, seeing that nothing has been replaced or tampered with." She tapped the photos. "I know exactly what was actually shipped, and that will arrive at the university on Friday. I'm to compare my list with the president's, and then together with the curator and security, we'll inspect the actual shipment." She caught his look then said, "Someone looked at the list and then just left," Ava said, returning his stare and imagining she looked as confused as he did at the moment.

"Doesn't make sense," Cole said, frowning at what seemed too simple to contemplate. "Appears someone just wanted to know what you know. Went to a whole lot of trouble when they could have done that at the university when you got back with the envelope." He shrugged. "I think you had a punk prowler who was being nosy—somebody who doesn't appreciate your taste in art and doesn't know the value of what's in this room. I can bet that he won't be back."

"Cop's assessment?" Ava said, giving him an uncertain look.

Cole eyed her. "For now," he answered with a quirk of a brow. "You can always get a second opinion."

Ava wondered if he was making fun but there was not a hint of a smile on his face or in those dark eyes. "Sheriff Thompson?"

Cole nodded.

"You remember him?" Ava said, wondering what the young, wild, Cole's relationship was with the lawman.

"Very much," Cole answered.

Ava stared at him. "I'd feel a fool. What a ridiculous thing to bother the law with. A footprint. An opened envelope. Nothing taken. I like Sheriff Thompson, but there must be a limit to the man's patience. He's so level-headed."

Cole looked away. "He is." Years ago, Sheriff Jack Thompson had been one of the few adults in town who hadn't treated him as if he were a villain straight out of a Dean Koontz novel. He'd been the one to talk some sense into him when Cole went around town just begging anybody to knock the chip off his shoulder. Any little bad look his way or perceived whisperings as he passed, caused him to confront any and everybody, lashing out at anyone who crossed his path. He wanted to corner his mother and plead with her to give him back her love. Sheriff Thompson had seen his pain and had been there. It was the sheriff who'd driven him to the induction station in Florence and had waited with him until the time came for him to board the bus with the other recruits.

"He is a friend?" Ava sensed his inner turmoil.

"Yes. A long time ago," Cole answered. "He's the reason I became a cop." He studied her face. "I guess from what you've heard, the town hood could never get into the law enforcement and life-saving business, huh?" He stood. "The good townsfolk thought that I was *up* in somebody's jail instead of the one filling it."

"Well, you can't blame them after what you did!" Ava said, suddenly annoyed with his victim attitude. She was instantly chastened when Teddie's words pierced her brain. *Cole suffered a lot when he was younger—home is where he should be able to find some peace.* What exactly *did* he do? she questioned, realizing she didn't know a thing about this man, yet she was judging. He became like stone all except for his dark eyes that glittered like shards of black ice. She stood as he advanced on her.

Very softly Cole said, "And what was it that I did, Ava?" He was so close to her that he felt her warm breath on his throat.

Ava took a step back. "W-why did your mother blame you for Curtis's death?" It took barely a second for her to realize that her words had stabbed him in the heart. Her own heart stopped for a beat.

Time stood still as Cole stared at the woman in front of him. His brother's name on her lips sent him reeling back in time at the speed of light. He was in his kitchen rocking Curtis in his arms, willing him to speak. The gurgles in the toddler's throat were deafening as Cole kept calling his brother's name.

Trancelike, Cole started to walk from the study. He heard the soft giggles coming from the hall closet where Curtis had often hidden from his older brothers. His hand was on the knob. "Curtis?"

Ava jumped at the soft whisper as chill bumps covered her arms. "Cole?" she said, staring in wonderment. Her voice softened as she sympathized. He was in so much pain.

Cole focused on Ava. Realizing what had happened, he snatched his hand from the doorknob and backed away from his startled neighbor. Without a word he opened the front door and once outside inhaled deeply. He looked at his house and slowly began to make his way through the hedges. Inside he went straight upstairs to the guest bedroom and closed the door. No screams in here, he thought, and unmindful of the new stitches in his back, he lay down and closed his eyes.

Chapter Four

The house seemed strangely quiet after Cole left and Ava was thoughtful as she stood watching him from behind the curtains in her study. Hadn't she only yesterday fumed within at the appearance of Cole disrupting her peaceful existence? Now she was feeling suddenly bereft of his presence that had lit the room. His troubled background so mirrored her own that she was nearly spooked by the similarities in their early lives. His leaving left her with thoughts of the family she left back in Collier, Georgia, the place where before she turned eighteen, she'd been so happy. While planning for college, she'd been ecstatic and could hardly wait to finally embark on a journey she'd only dreamed about. But then her world had shattered like a fragile glass globe. So when she did at last leave home on that dreamer's journey, she'd never gone home again. Not in thirteen years.

Her glance fell to her desk and the scatter of paper beneath which lay the letter. She spied the tip of the envelope and pulled it from under the pile, staring at her sister's curlicue handwriting. It'd arrived a week ago and Ava had yet to respond either by hand or phone. *Come home, Sunny. It's long past time. We love you,* Dahlia had written.

Sunny. She hadn't been called that in years, that nickname given her by her father, when she was just a tot. He'd said that she was the happiest kid he'd ever seen but couldn't understand why his youngest daughter had a passion for relics and dead things. No one in her family had shared her love of delving into the mysteries of things long past.

Ava lifted the flap and the picture fell out. She stared at all the family she had left in the world. Dahlia Jenrette and her husband, James. Trevor and Aaron—nephews she'd never seen and who at twelve and nine were strangers to her. Dahlia at thirty-four now was as tall and pretty as Ava remembered. *They want to meet their aunt, Ava. What happened in the past was wrong. If Dad were here he'd ask your forgiveness. Please come home.*

Ava breathed, "I am home, Dahlia."

Returning the picture, she set the envelope aside as if that simple action would take care of all the hurt that surfaced with reminders of her childhood. Minuet was the place she'd discovered, and she'd never been more at peace than in the last two years, living her quiet life among neighbors and new friends who respected her privacy. Her work world was the same. In academia she was known and liked by those who knew of her love and vast knowledge of her subject. There was never a time that she wished that she was anywhere else. All her exotic travels did not beckon and call to her, trying to draw her out as they once did to see what was on the other side of another mountain. She'd been there, done that, and she was content now.

We love you. Love? Ava hadn't felt loved in years,

not ever since her mother had sided with her husband and turned her back on her youngest child, giving in to her husband's disgust and shame for his baby girl.

For months after her father had turned his back on her, Ava hadn't liked what she'd seen in the mirror. Self-loathing and low self-esteem had plagued her. She looked for someone to love her, and to show her that she hadn't lost that ability. She thought she'd found him one summer in Greece. She was his Venus as he was her Adonis. So she'd thought. In their hearts they knew the lie they were living. But she was young and wanting. He was mature and deceitful. When the two months had ended so had the blush of their false romance, as reality was uncloaked. Ava returned to the States and her lover returned to his wife and child in Spain. Sex. That's all it'd been. Stark, delicious lusting of the flesh. How she'd ever begun to equate that with love was even now so laughable after so many years.

Stirring, Ava felt a tug at her insides and in her warm womanly places. Why now after all this time? She knew it wasn't the words in Dahlia's letter that had awakened long-dormant emotions. It was the dark, hungry look of a stranger she'd met barely forty-eight hours ago. She'd seen in his eyes the desire and she'd felt her own body react to the unspoken invitation. What was she running from? she wondered.

But she knew. It was to be left alone again, unloved, and with an empty heart. That was her all-consuming fear when he'd had enough of her and Minuet and returned to wherever he came from. No, she decided, she wouldn't go there. Her life was good and sane now and she'd move mountains to keep it that way.

Ava left her desk and went to a floor-to-ceiling bookcase and searched the shelves. Her fingers skimming over volume after volume, she found what she wanted and pulled the book from the shelf and returned to the desk. The book was worn, and as she skimmed the pages, she stopped to read some of the notes in the margins that she'd written while a student. Slave narratives had held her interest from the first time that she'd ever read about their existence while she was still in high school. Years later, she'd made them the topic of her master's thesis, with an emphasis on one: *The Interesting Narrative of the Life of Olaudah Equiano, or Gustavus Vassa, The African, Written by Himself.* She'd been fascinated by the very name, her tongue getting tied up whenever she tried to pronounce the Ibo name, and she found the title bewitching. She learned that many of the slave narratives were so entitled: written by himself or herself. Olaudah Equiano was given the name of one who had been the king of Sweden, and for which he could see no rhyme or reason, but used both names throughout his life.

Ava thumbed through the volume, knowing automatically where the information she sought would be. Memories of poring over this book and many others like it came back with lightning clarity, almost as if she were a student again, struggling through a three-hundred-page paper that her mentor whittled down to a mere ten pages.

At first, when she'd spotted the letter on the list, she'd been confused, as if her mind was playing tricks or she'd doubted her own research. How could she have possibly missed something so important? The asterisked-marked item indicated that such an artifact was already at Floyd Compton University and

should be included in the exhibit, after which it
would remain when the exhibit moved on. How
could that be? Ava wondered. *There was no such artifact in existence.* As far as she knew, Gustavus Vassa and
his enslaved sister had never communicated in writing. So how could there be such an historic
document? And housed under her very nose in her
university's archives? Impossible!

She found the small section of the narrative that
had her baffled and began reading, giving careful attention to each paragraph. Transfixed, it was two
hours later before she put the book down, having
decided to read the complete slave narrative. More
perplexed than ever, she felt a slight chill. In all her
years of study and research, no information was
found on Vassa other than in his narratives—so how
could there be such a letter in existence?

On Tuesday morning, the first day of a heat-bear-
ing June, Ava sat in her office at the school's
administration building, having arrived early. She
hadn't slept well last night, the narrative being the
last thing on her mind as she tried to fall to sleep.
Her mind had been a mass of confusion, as if a thousand voices were vying for equal time in her head
and she could make sense of none of their babble.

The envelope sat in the middle of her desk where
she'd placed it after studying the contents so stu-
diously, as if the asterisked-marked item would
miraculously disappear. Then she wouldn't have to
address it. Something was trying to get through
though, and she mentally cleared the cobwebs long
enough to get a picture in her mind's eye. It was a
conversation she'd had with her friend Winifred. At

the time Ava had placed no significance in her friend's curiosity in the exhibit. Ava had teased her knowing that Winifred had no more interest in dead things than had a lovesick sixteen-year-old in knowing who had split the atom, and least of all wanting to know why.

But last week Winifred had more than once sauntered into Ava's office casually making references to the anticipated arrival of the artifacts and the beefing up of university security. It hadn't bothered Ava then, but now, she wondered. Why?

Ava picked up the phone and dialed a number. When the president's secretary answered, Ava spoke quietly, and then waited. Moments later she left her office.

Forty minutes later, Ava was back in her office, her head spinning crazily after listening to the beleaguered president's astonishing story.

The document did exist! But days ago it had been stolen!

She felt weak, ignorant, and befuddled when she'd listened. But she was in disbelief. How could she have missed so important a part of the history she'd studied for so long and so meticulously? Why had the president, Charles Howell, chosen to keep the theft a secret from her, who would be overseeing the safety of the exhibit? She could very well understand his reluctance to report the theft. Institutions were notorious for keeping thefts under wraps for various reasons. Yet his words had stabbed her in her heart. "It was an inside job, Ava, and we hope to catch the thief before long."

Thief! Her knees were weak when she'd stood and wobbled to her office, where she sank down on the chair behind her desk. Did the university president know about her past? Her hands shook and she

clasped them in her lap. But how could he? Does he
suspect her? Did he have her friend Winifred innocently question Ava about the traveling exhibit, hoping
to catch her up in something? And no wonder. The
historic document, the communication between Vassa
and his sister, had been Winifred's own discovery years
ago, and the university family had been proud to claim
Dr. Winifred Whidby as their own. *It just can't be,* Ava
thought wildly, looking about as if the answer was
somewhere on the cream-colored walls.

"What's happening in my life?" she murmured.
Ava thought she'd asked herself that question a zil-
lion times in the last few days, ever since a big black
car had transported a darkly handsome man from
the other side of the country, practically dropping
him in her front yard. When she'd left this morning
she'd been surprised to see the car missing and had
wondered where Cole had gone. Was he okay? she
worried. *Oh, stop, Ava,* she'd remonstrated. *He's not
your concern. Didn't he make that plain enough last night?*
During the drive to the school, she warred with herself thinking about Cole, Gustavus Vassa, and
whether she was going just a little bit nuts. "Maybe I
am," she said while worrying her bottom lip.

"Uh-huh. Just as I thought," a male voice interrupted. "We're talking to ourselves now? Told you a
vacation is imminent after a long school year. I'll be
leaving at the end of the sessions and you should
too, after your lecture series is over. The invitation's
still open, Ava. A week in the Bahamas with a group
of us. How about it?"

"Hale, you startled me. Don't do that," Ava said an-
grily. "You move like a cat and it's unnerving."
Unperturbed, the handsome man closed her door
and then placed one hip on the edge of her desk,

dangling a sharply creased khaki pant leg. She pushed her chair back and stared up at him. Any other time she would've been amused at Hale Trotter and his attentions toward her, but today, dark, brooding eyes filled the space in front of her eyes so that Hale's and Cole's images merged. She drew in a sharp breath and tried to erase her neighbor from her mind.

"Hmm, rough weekend? You look a little peaked. Told you cooped up with your ancient stuff every day is not the way to go. You've got to get out more, enjoy life." He leaned his face toward her. "With me."

Ava could have laughed as she usually did, though inwardly, at the good-looking man's attentions to her. He was forty, never married, childless, and lived a bachelor's life in an upscale condo community in Florence. He was educated, pleasant, and good to look at, with heavenly brown eyes, rugged, dark caramel-colored skin, and soft black hair with a tinge of gray around the temples. His oval face sported a thin mustache and a hint of a dimple dented his chin. His smile was commercial bright with sparkling white teeth.

So why was it so hard for her to fall for a catchable guy like Hale? she wondered. Instead she was having lustful thoughts about a man who wanted her to butt out of his life.

"Does that thoughtful pause mean you're thinking about it?" Hale said.

"What?"

Hale frowned. "What's wrong, Ava? You've been gone since I entered the room." He slid off the desk and sat in the chair across from Ava's desk. Serious-voiced, he asked, "What happened to you this weekend?"

In a light voice, Ava said, "You didn't by any

chance sneak into my home to try and get your
hands on that Kachina doll that you've been covet-
ing, did you?"

His frown deepening, Hale said, "What are you
talking about?" When he saw her face, he exhaled.
"You had a break-in?"

Ava nodded, and feeling helpless, she spread her
hands while giving him an apologetic look. "Please
excuse the bad joke, Hale. It's just that something
weird is going on."

"Weird, how? What was taken?"

"Nothing."

Ava explained, ending with her discussion with the
president about the Vassa theft. When she finished,
she said, "It's baffling." Her eyes slid to the envelope.
"I really believe that the mystery lies in there."

Hale gave a low whistle. "I see what you mean."
After a moment, he said, "You know Winifred is a
basket case about this whole thing."

Ava shook her head. "No, I don't," she said firmly.
"I never knew that paper existed! She never, not
once, mentioned her discovery, even though she
knew I was a student of the narratives." She held his
gaze. "Why do you suppose she kept something like
that from me?"

"Possibly because she figured you being the expert
historian, would have already known of its existence
and she didn't want to toot her own horn."

She looked at him in disbelief. "Now, you know
that even *you* don't believe that."

A lazy grin appeared and Hale said, "This is true."

Ava laughed. "Right." Winifred Whidby not patting
herself on the back several times in a day would have
been like a day when the sun didn't rise in the east.
When they first met years ago as members of a travel

group to Italy, Ava had taken a liking to the older academic who would probably lay claim to being about
forty-eight, but no more. Ava had known Winifred
was a vain, take-charge person, who had made herself
the unofficial spokesperson of the group to the angst
of the tour guide. But Winifred had a charming wit
and an infectious smile that won over many a dis-
gruntled person.

"So, what do you think about all this?" Hale asked.
"It really is a shame that Winifred's one claim to fame
is lost." He shrugged. "Yet it makes no sense that that
and only a few other manuscripts were stolen, especially since I heard that items of more value were left
behind."

"Yes," Ava said slowly, "it is a mystery. But I hope to
get to the bottom of it before the exhibit opens."

"I'm sure with the help of security, and Dr. Howell
on the warpath, you will," Hale said, standing. "Don't
let this mess take the smile out of those beautiful eyes."

After Hale left, a coldness clamped Ava's heart like
strong icy fingers trying to strangle the life from her.
The suspicions that had begun as a little acorn early
this morning had grown into a giant mushroom as
she'd listened to Dr. Howell. His pride in Winifred's
discovery was evident as he spoke of her rare acqui-
sition bringing prestige to the institution.

Unable to think logically, Ava, to unfreeze her
brain, began jotting down her thoughts. Just to be
doing something she felt would take the edge off and
warm her insides. Ten minutes later she looked at
what she'd written. So many questions. Not one
answer. Why was Winifred so interested in the slave
narratives? Had she a particular interest in the former
slave Gustavus Vassa? Exactly who verified and authenticated the document? Was he or she an accepted

authority on the subject? If this communication had ever existed, why was there no reference to it in all the essays and critiques on the veracity of Vassa's life and narrative? As far as studies went, the narrative was complete and judged to be the only document in existence on the African, Olaudah Equiano's adventures from capture to freed man and author.

Disturbed, Ava made mindless doodles on the paper. Her head throbbed from trying to clear up the doubts forming in her mind. She was a student of fact and it was fast becoming clear to her that something was horribly wrong. And she was smack-dab in the middle of it. She jotted down some more questions, the answers lying ominously in her subconscious. Where was the supposedly precious document? Who had stolen it and why?

"Winifred, what have you done?" Ava whispered, unable to deny what was a stark truth.

Later, time could not have passed quickly enough for Ava as she rushed from the building, grateful that the usually long-winded academics had a touch of spring fever and were just as willing as she was to end the boring meeting and make a quick getaway. In her office, she'd made a hasty phone call and was relieved to be added to the calendar for an afternoon appointment.

Palms sweating as she drove toward Minuet, Ava meditated, hoping to appear calm and unperturbed when she arrived. But two thoughts kept intruding on her endeavor to be at peace. Where was Winifred and what emergency could have kept her away from the required meeting? The other was the one word that instilled fear in her soul. *Thief!* Dr. Howell had never noticed her reaction to that spoken word but she'd feared that her body and mind had been zapped with a magic wand, transporting her back to a time when another esteemed man of letters had so branded her.

Now, years later, older, wiser, she knew what she had to do to begin a paper trail of proving her innocence, of clearing her name of any wrongdoing, for as sure as her heart beat, she felt that the gray clouds of doom were hovering just overhead.

Ava parked in the lot behind the courthouse, which also held the jail. Her palms were dry now, as she had a clear purpose. She refused to be a victim this time. But images of her father swam before her eyes as she got out of the car, his stern, thin-lipped grimace as he glared at her, threatening to weaken her resolve. *Thief!* She straightened her shoulders and walked firmly toward the three-story, white stone building and was directed to the first-floor office of Sheriff Jack Thompson.

From what Ava had seen of the sheriff since she'd lived in Minuet, she liked. He appeared to be a warm, friendly, get-to-know-you kind of man. He knew everybody and had a kind word for young people and the elderly. Ava judged him to be in his early sixties and he always joked that he was retiring next week or next month or next year. People just smiled because he'd been a fixture for as long as anyone could remember. She knew that he would listen to her and report the facts when and if there would ever be a need to do so. She took a deep breath and entered his office.

"Hello, Sheriff Thompson," Ava said as she walked forward with extended hand. "Thanks for fitting me in your busy day." She took the seat that he gestured to, across from his desk, and sat as he did, facing her with a curious expression.

Sheriff Thompson said, "No problem, Dr. Millington. Just hope that I can be of service." He eyed the young woman, calm and unwavering in her look at him. Forthright. Honest. That was how he'd thought of her when she first came to town two years ago. He listened and heard what people said. They liked her. He used to ride past her house some nights when she first arrived. It was quiet out that way, and he wanted to assure himself that none of the bored high school boys would get it into their heads to try and scare her with their foolish pranks. He liked the professor and now sat, waiting for her to begin. He saw her sudden indecision just for a moment, as if she were having second thoughts about her visit. "I think it would help to just start at the beginning, don't you?"

Ava smiled, and relaxed her shoulders. "I think someone entered my house a few days ago. I'm not sure which day over the weekend it was but it was probably on Sunday while I was away in church." She took a deep breath. "That's it." Before he could speak, she said, "And would you please call me Ava? I'd like that." It was a while before he spoke and she waited and watched the man's face in fascination. He had a long widow's peak and each time he raised his bushy brows she thought the three points of hair were going to tangle.

"On Sunday?"

"Yes, I'm pretty certain. I was home most of Saturday and would have seen or heard anything unusual."

Jack Thompson had been writing and he stopped and looked at her. He'd been in the people business for more years than he cared to remember and he felt he knew a little something about human nature. The professor was either extremely nervous about her surroundings or she had another agenda. He was willing to bet on the latter. "Why do you *think* someone entered your house?" he said, pushing away from the desk and moving his swivel chair from side to side. "Just tell me everything you saw or heard that concerned you enough to come here today. Take your time, and remember that the smallest detail could be important."

Ava felt the warmth in her cheeks. What would the man think about an envelope that she did or did not open, some scrapes on her vinyl window frame that could have been there since before she moved in, and a barely discernible footprint? She looked at him squarely and began her story, including meeting and helping Cole, and ending with her discovery. When she finished she sat back, thinking that she'd just wasted some of the man's precious day. But the strange look that passed over his face when she mentioned Cole had her wondering just what was it about Cole Dumont that people came to his defense? As if they wanted to protect him. She'd gotten the same feeling from Teddie.

"That it?" Jack asked after putting down his pen. He was looking at her expectantly.

"Yes," Ava answered. "At least all that I can remember." She gave him stare for stare.

"So neither you nor young Cole was going to report the incident?" His dark brows shot up wrinkling the deep brown of his forehead.

Ava started as she turned away from his intense look. She'd known that the sheriff was a precise, thoughtful individual but was still surprised at how quickly he'd sensed something was not altogether on the up and up. "Cole doesn't know I'm here," she said.

"You didn't want him to know?"

"Well," Ava replied after hesitating. "At the time he did suggest my coming in to see you but now I-I think it best that I report it alone."

Jack looked sharply at her. "You don't trust him?"

"I don't know him well enough to answer that, Sheriff," Ava said. "I told you we just met and . . . and, well, I don't know him," she ended.

Jack Thompson was quiet, absorbing all she'd said. What she wasn't saying about Cole Dumont bothered him. It'd been years since he'd seen that young man, but he was willing to bet any gambling man that honesty and trustworthiness was still an integral part of Cole's makeup. Something had happened to make the professor think otherwise.

"Did Cole say or do something to make you suspect he had anything to do with your suspected break-in?" he asked.

"What?" Ava was taken aback. "I didn't say any such thing, Sheriff Thompson."

"Then why don't you just tell me what's bothering you about your new neighbor? Then maybe we can make some sense out of what might have happened out at your place."

Ava didn't know what to say or how to begin. She'd come to cover her bases, not to snoop into a man's background. Yet she knew she wanted to know more about the mysterious Cole Dumont, and who better to find out from than the man who'd befriended Cole years before? But she felt as though she'd be prying into a very private man's past. If he'd wanted her to know, he'd have told her himself, wouldn't he?

"Ava?"

"Did Cole Dumont kill his baby brother?" The words shot from her mouth so unexpectedly that she gasped.

Sheriff Thompson relaxed in his chair, slowly swiveling back and forth while holding his visitor's gaze. *So, that's it,* he thought. Gossip scaring her senseless. "That was a long time ago," he finally said.

"I know," Ava said quietly. "He said as much."

"What happened?" the sheriff said just as quietly.

Ava explained about Cole's strange behavior when he uttered his brother's name.

Sheriff Thompson, eyes closed, rocked and listened. When she stopped talking, he opened his eyes and stood. He drew two paper cups of water from the cooler and handed one to his visitor, drank and tossed his cup in the basket.

"That boy's still hurting," he said as he sat back down. "Lots of folks around here don't know the truth of what happened to that family." His look was direct. "Cole, as I remember him was an all-right guy. Unless he's done a complete about-face after all these years, you don't have anything to fear from him." He saw her relax. "Well, seeing as how you helped him when he needed it, you're entitled to hear something more than the gossip you've been getting."

Sheriff Thompson smiled briefly at something he'd thought of and then grew serious. "Richard and Patrice Dumont were the only two real live lovebirds I've ever met in my whole life. Had two sons and they acted like newlyweds, holding hands and mooning over each other in Perk's Diner on Saturday afternoon, their two boys whooping and cutting it up over cheeseburgers and fries."

"Two sons?"

"Then," the sheriff said. "Curtis came later. Every-

body called him their love child. Rich was crazy
about that kid and Patrice was just as bad. They'd
lost two babies trying to enlarge their family, and
when Curtis got here you couldn't tell them that he
wasn't a miracle baby. Cole and his older brother,
Graham, loved that boy just as bad as their folks.
Took him everywhere and got teased by their friends
when they had him in tow. But that little boy wound
everybody around his little finger. Had a laugh that
tickled your funny bone. Was never still and loved to
tease anybody bigger than him. He was a great kid.
He favored Cole in looks. Had those same round
black eyes that penetrated your soul." The sheriff
paused and a grim look shadowed his face.

Ava saw the man's anguish. "What happened?" she
said.

"Rich was killed." He stopped.

"You were friends?"

"Yeah. They were new to town back then. Moved
here when the two boys were little things. When
Rich saw the old farm he just had to have it for his
wife. We became friends then." He sniffed. "He died
a horrible death. Alone in an elevator when it mal-
functioned when he was getting off. Crushed
between the car and the floor."

"Oh, no," Ava murmured.

"Patrice wasn't herself for weeks. But she had
Graham and Cole and Curtis. She would lie in bed
for hours hugging that youngster to her chest,
moaning her husband's name. My wife had to pry
the boy from her arms to feed and bathe him."

"How old was he?"

"Curtis was three when his father was taken from him.
Graham was nearly nineteen and Cole was seventeen."
The sheriff shook his head in disbelief. "After all these

years it's still a crying shame," he said. "Six months after Patrice buried her husband, she was back in the same cemetery burying her baby son. It was something you'd never want to see again."

Ava waited until he looked at her. "How did Curtis die?"

"Patrice wasn't well. She was under the doctor's care and she was doped up a lot of the time. Graham and Cole did more for Curtis than his mother could. My wife was there when the boys were in school. Patrice rarely let Virginia bring the tot home with her so Patrice could get some rest. But then the whole family came down with the flu." He paused, remembering. "The whole town had it. It was bad. There were two deaths. The schools closed to help stop the spreading. Graham was so sick, Patrice worried about his constant vomiting. She was afraid that he'd caught something worse. Cole was drugged up himself with meds but Patrice didn't want to expose Curtis who'd gotten better, to becoming infected again. She left him in Cole's care while she took Graham to the hospital in Florence."

Ava felt a pang in her chest as she guessed what had happened. She didn't speak.

Jack Thompson said, "It was an accident. Curtis got out of Cole's bedroom and went wandering around the house. Cole never woke up from the stupor that he was in. He was practically delirious himself. He never heard the tot open and close the bedroom door. Later he woke to his mother and brother screaming. When he got to the kitchen, Curtis was limp and barely breathing. Cole couldn't believe his eyes. His pills were all over the floor. He pushed his mother aside and held his brother, trying to breathe life into him. His mother was hysterical.

She pushed him away from her baby. By the time the ambulance took Curtis to the hospital, he was gone." The sheriff blinked. "That family was never the same. Patrice turned into a cold fish, blaming Cole for her baby's death. She didn't want anything to do with him. Treated him like he wasn't there, speaking to him through Graham. Was a wonder the older boy didn't bolt, leaving them two to butt heads. Months later, Patrice left town. Graham had started at the university in Florence and Cole was soon to graduate high school."

"She just left them?"

Jack nodded. "She left them provided for. The settlement from Rich's accident came quick, giving them a nice chunk of change. Their college money was there. The house and land was left to them. But Cole left town after he graduated high school and never came back—until a few days ago."

Ava was perplexed. "I don't understand why everyone says Cole killed his brother." She looked at the sheriff. "It was a tragedy. Somehow Curtis got hold of the pill bottle. Wasn't it ruled an accident?"

"Yes, it was." The sheriff grunted in disgust. "Don't know how that story got all twisted around. Cole was cleared of any wrongdoing. But he never forgave himself. In Cole's mind his brother would still be alive if he had stayed awake to watch him like his mother asked him to."

"Sort of hard when you're all drugged up," Ava said wryly.

"Very hard," Jack agreed. He splayed his hands. "But it was what it was and nothing can change history. If Cole hasn't forgiven himself after all these years then it'll never happen." His brows rose. "I didn't know he was still that tortured."

"I believe he still is," Ava murmured. "What about Graham?" she asked. "Does he hate Cole, too?"

The sheriff shrugged. "Those two were closer than any two brothers I've ever seen. Afterward, there seemed to be a little edginess when you saw them together. But then, neither of them stayed around long enough. After Graham finished at the university, he left." Thoughtfully, he said, "Hate? I doubt it. Graham has stayed in touch over the years. Maintains the property through a service. Used to come every couple of years or so to look after the place. Doesn't stay long. Told me once that his father would turn over if the place was sold. Think the last time he was here was about two years ago."

"I remember seeing a car with Ohio plates that first week I moved in," Ava said. "But I never saw anyone and I haven't seen it since." She remembered thinking how upset she'd been at the thought of having neighbors.

Ava stood. "Well, I appreciate your candidness, Sheriff," she said. "I think I understand my neighbor a little better now. Thanks." After a moment, she said, "Will you make a report of what I told you?"

Jack eyed her. With her quiet ways he could see the sharp intelligence in those pretty brown eyes. He saw a lot more than she intended for him to see, he thought. He stood and took her outstretched hand. "Consider it done," he said. "Let me know if there's something else I can help you with." He watched her leave, head down as if in deep thought. He was still watching out the window when her car exited the lot and moved slowly down Center Street.

Chapter Five

Cole sat in the diner waiting for Jack Thompson. Earlier when he'd stopped by the station he'd found it a madhouse—at least for Minuet—he thought. He supposed that years ago he'd never given any thought to what kind of activity went on in a jail-house. Now he was all too familiar. It'd been years since he'd lain eyes on the sheriff, much less had a conversation with him. Little guilt feelings gnawed at him when he realized that back then the sheriff was the only one in town who hadn't looked upon him as some kind of evil wizard that would taint the town and its children. He liked and respected the man and knew that staying in town another day before seeking him out would be to appear ungrateful. Any meeting was unthinkable in that chaos and Cole had left after Jack suggested meeting at the diner late in the day.

"Sheriff Jack's going to have the usual. I might as well take your order so it can be ready when he gets here." Teddie stood over the booth ready to write on her pad. "Should you be out? Back not bothering you?"

"Back's healing fine, Teddie. Thanks for asking,"

Cole said. He handed the menu back to her. "I'll have whatever Jack's having."

Teddie eyed him. His countenance was one of underlying sadness. "You sure you're okay, Cole?" Her eyes softened as she looked at her old friend. She was sure that his back wasn't the only hurting thing on him.

"I'm okay, Teddie." He smiled at her. "I know we still have to get together to hash over our lives. Suppose you let someone else close up tonight and we'll go get some real food." He gave her a solemn look.

"Of all the nerve," Teddie huffed. "You'd better watch your mouth. You haven't eaten yet!" She grinned. "Okay, it's a date. But for that remark, I get to pick the place, so stuff your wallet."

"Ouch," Cole said. "Guess I deserved that, huh?"

"Yeah, you did." Teddie gave a passing waitress the order pad and then sat in the booth across from Cole. "I'm glad you're back," she said. "It's been a lot of years."

Cole nodded. "Almost too many to feel like calling it home," he said slowly. He shook his head. "I didn't know what to expect but it's not what I thought it'd be."

"I wish you'd at least said good-bye," Teddie said. "I felt I'd lost my big brother when I heard Sheriff Jack had driven you to Florence. For weeks I expected at least a postcard. Minuet felt so lonely. You left and Graham stayed in Florence going to school. We hardly ever saw him, and then he moved away." She smiled. "The town was pretty quiet without the Dumont brothers."

"Yeah," Cole said, a shadow crossing his face. "That was a long time ago, almost another world," he said quietly.

"So, you never met the woman of your dreams and married, Cole?" Her eyes twinkled. "Time's passing by."

Cole grimaced. "No, never met her," he said. "And at this point in my life who'd want an old beat-up detective who can't watch his back?" He gave her a quizzical look. "So what about you?" he asked. "How many hearts have you broken over the years?" He knew that Teddie was around thirty or thirty-one and her fingers were bare. *I can only guess,* he mused.

Teddie glanced away before answering, but then stared at him. *"I* haven't broken any." They both saw the sheriff's car pull up. Teddie stood. "Let's take a rain check on dinner tonight, Cole. I remembered I have an appointment to keep."

"Not a problem," Cole said easily. "We'll set another date." He watched her walk away and somehow he knew that her talking to him at length would inevitably lead to talk about Graham. He'd been right, he thought. She'd never gotten over his brother.

Jack Thompson made an impressive presence as he strode through the diner toward the end booth where Cole was waiting. At sixty, he didn't fit the stereotypical image of the small-town sheriff, short, squat, paunch and jowls to match. He was tall, lean, and walked ramrod straight. That mean glint in his eyes was just a cover-up for the putty inside. He'd confided to Cole once that he didn't need to bare all his secrets.

Cole watched him approach and thought that if not for this man no telling where he would have wound up.

"Sorry, took longer than I expected," Jack said. "Had an unexpected appointment." He sat, after waving to Teddie, and stared at the younger man. "Back still bothering you?" Jack never used more words than he needed to make conversation. He always thought direct was the way to go. He eyed his old friend. "No, that's not it, is it?"

"Back's doing okay, Jack," answered Cole.

"You want my job?"

"What?"

"My job. You look restless, like you're ready to bolt, and you haven't been here long enough to give your old hometown a good long look. It's a good place to be, Cole, and what's wrong with being the sheriff?" He was quiet as a waitress placed identical plates of food in front of him and Cole. Sizzling steaks, hash browns, corn on the cob.

After a while, Cole said, "You're retiring?"

"Don't you think it's about time? Time for me to take Virginia on that cruise she's been talking about forever." He chewed some steak. "Election's coming late next year. That's plenty of time for folks to get to know you. The fool who wants my job is a lazy flake. Never get reelected. Might as well get the right man in first time around."

Cole busied himself with his own steak. Finally he said, "I don't plan on staying around, Jack. Probably move on after the summer."

"Why? You going back to that job in L.A.?"

"No. Not really. Something will turn up."

Jack squinted at Cole. "Think you're too old to become a beach bum. That's for younger folk than you." He finished off his steak and swallowed some iced tea. When the dishes were cleared and dessert set down he dug into a slab of peach pie.

"Well, while you're waiting for my job," Jack said, "there're a couple of openings for deputies. Think about it." He didn't speak again until he finished his pie.

A deputy in Minuet, Cole mused. Is *that* a joke! He

finished his pie and sat mulling over Jack's words. Just what was he going to do and where was he going to do it? Damned if he knew, but staying in Minuet hadn't been in the plan. Especially now, since he couldn't lie down in bed without thinking about the gorgeous woman lying yards away. He swallowed and shuttered the image that came to mind.

"Pardon?"

"I just asked have you seen or heard anything else that appeared suspicious around the professor's house," Jack said.

"What? At Ava's?" Cole said thoughtfully. "So she did call you."

"Visited me. Before I came here." Jack sat back. "You didn't think it was important enough to make a report, but apparently she decided it was."

Cole frowned. "I'd told her to get a second opinion," he said. "But she never gave any indication that she would—at least she hadn't made a decision to make a police report. What did she say?"

Jack related Ava's story and when he finished, said, "She appeared to be pretty intense about the whole thing. Just surprised that she waited until today to come in." He stared at Cole. "Without telling you."

"What's that supposed to mean?" Cole asked, wondering at the tone in the sheriff's voice.

"Apparently, she was upset by whatever you did or did not do." He shrugged. "Matter of trust, I think. What did you do to make her suspicious of you?"

"Of me?" Cole was stupefied. "She thinks I know something about her prowler?"

"Do you? Seems like with her away and you laid up you might have seen or heard something." Jack shrugged again. "Just a thought."

Cole's eyes darkened. "Well, I didn't hear a damn

thing. I told her that. What makes you think she doesn't trust me? What'd she say?"

"It's nothing she said," Jack answered. "More like what she didn't say was what I picked up on. She'd heard all the wrong stories about you." He saw Cole's dark look. "You like her?"

Startled, Cole stared. "What do you mean? I just met the woman who doesn't care a whoop about me. Thinks I'm slime."

Jack shook his head. "Not anymore."

Silence.

"You told her."

"Only the truth."

After a while Cole said, "At least now she's got the story straight. Thanks." He turned from Jack and stared out the window.

"No problem." Then Jack smiled. "Don't worry. Everybody will know the truth before the election next year. Can't have a smear campaign going on, now can we?"

Cole grunted. "You don't give up, do you?"

"No," the sheriff said softly. "And I know you don't either. Coming back here will make you see things as they are, not as they were. You've got some bones to lay to rest and no better place to do it than here. Your home."

"You think so, huh?" Cole stared at the serious look on the older man's face.

"Yes, I do," Jack said. He studied Cole. "You know that a body needs help from a friend every now and again, don't you—one that only means to do you good?" He acknowledged Cole's nod. "I think that the professor, now that she knows a little more about you, will be in your corner, son. I saw that before she left my office today." He smiled. "Nothing like the soothing hand of a good woman to help soften life's hard blows. Be it to the head or to the heart. A woman knows."

Cole only stared at his friend the philosopher.

"Let her help, Cole. You won't be sorry." He dropped some bills on the table and stood. "My treat this time. Come and see me when you want to talk. And when you're ready, come on out to the house. Virginia's dying for an excuse to cook up a storm for a change. Don't get to do that too much since the kids are all gone. Bring the professor too."

After parking in his drive, Cole sat on the front porch thinking about the sheriff's observations. How does a body get so smart? Must come with age, he thought. Cole guessed that Ava couldn't have been in the sheriff's office for more than an hour, and yet he'd seen so much. He even got a peek into Cole's soul, pinpointing the source of his anguish. A wise man was Jack Thompson.

He stared at Ava's house and thought about how he'd left her last night. The way she'd looked at him, her eyes full of caring, her voice so soft. And he'd blown her off.

Jack's words crowded his mind. *Let her help, Cole.*

"But she's hurting too, Jack. Just how are we going to help each other?" Cole's voice was soft and a lazy summer breeze carried his words away.

It was nearly five o'clock when Cole looked up at the sound of his neighbor's car entering her driveway. He sat watching as she got out of her car and began walking toward the house. She didn't look his way, her head down as she reached her steps. For the first time since he'd met her she looked as if she was in a daze. Uncertain, no, defeated. What could have happened at work? he wondered. Or was it the visit to the sheriff that had changed her whole demeanor?

Ava unlocked her door. Sensing his stare, she looked and saw Cole watching her. When he waved, she stood for a moment before waving back, and then went inside and closed the door.

She didn't know what to say to the man who'd borne such a weight throughout his life. How could a parent turn on their own child that way even in the loss of another? *Your father?* She stilled the inner voice. This wasn't about her, she reasoned. The young Cole must have been an angry teen who'd carried his hurt into adulthood. Yet, even in the brief meetings with him she'd seen something in his nature that belied those half stories she'd heard. How could she have played into that? Wasn't she all about getting the facts before making a judgment?

Ava couldn't get Cole off her mind, nor could she push away the disturbing day at work and her meeting with Dr. Howell. She undressed and changed into shorts and short-sleeve top and went into her study where she picked up the phone. Seconds later she hung up in bewilderment. Winifred had missed a very important meeting; now she'd turned off her answering machine. Her suspicions darkening, Ava reached for her phone book, and then called a long-unused number. Someone had to explain things to her before she went nuts.

Forty minutes later she reached hastily for the phone.

"Hi," she said breathlessly. "What did you find? Please don't tell me I'm going a little crazy." Her palms were sweating as she waited and listened. Mixed emotions washed over her like a soothing, and then fierce wave. *Why,* she wondered, *would someone do that?*

"Are you certain? You covered everything?" Her

heart plummeted though she wanted to feel elated that she'd been right. "Thanks so much," she said. "No, no, I'm okay. I really appreciate you for taking the time to clear things up. Yes, yes, I agree that it was a stupid thing to do, especially since it is so simple to investigate. Yes, I'll be in touch. Bye."

As she'd felt in her heart, her own expert on the subject had been surprised, and stumped about her story, finally confirming that there had been no such letter in existence, and that no one had ever documented any communication between Olaudah Equiano and his sister.

What Ava couldn't understand was why a savvy, intelligent woman like Dr. Whidby would fabricate such a lie. An awesome thought struck Ava as she wondered, *Did Charles Howell know?*

Weakened by the inner turmoil, she could only fall limply back against her chair, staring into space. She was unaware of the chill that crept down to her toes.

Teddie Perkins left the diner at six, leaving the evening hours of operation until closing in the capable hands of her night manager. As she drove toward her home, about two miles away, she thought how glibly she'd lied to Cole earlier. There was no appointment that she had to keep. A small smile played against her mouth. At least none other than the standard one she kept every day when she left work.

As she pulled into her driveway, she got out of the car, and for the first time in years she felt an old pang of hurt right smack-dab in the middle of her chest. She looked at the old house where she'd grown up with her father and mother. An only child, she'd wished for siblings. She'd felt that the house was so quiet and so she often had friends over. When they left, the house turned quiet once more while she kept her own company. Her father was always at the diner and so was her mother most of the time. There was a time when she felt that she lived alone in the three-bedroom house. She smiled. Now there was laughter, parties once a year, and the house seemed happy. A door slammed and she looked at the reason for her happiness and also her reticence in having Cole come here.

"Mommy, you're home."

"Yes, I am, Royce, honey," Teddie said, reaching out to hug her five-year-old son. "Miss me?"

"Yes, Mommy, but Miss Renee took me to the swimming pool after I ate my lunch so I didn't miss you too much today."

"Hmm, you didn't?" Teddie said after laughing and pulling a curl on his head. They walked to the house where her friend and his babysitter, Renee Bonner, sat waiting.

"You two had the right idea," she said, sitting next to the older woman. "Today was a scorcher." Royce had dashed back inside and she could hear the sounds coming from the TV where he was watching his cartoons. "How was he today?" she asked.

"Just fine as usual," said Renee. "The swim class starts tomorrow and he's raring to learn. It'll be good for him to know especially with that old pond so close to your house. I never did like that thing being there."

Teddie couldn't help chuckling. "It's been there for as long as you or I can remember, Renee. We all used to jump in there on days like this. That's why we learned to swim. Our parents probably did the same thing." She looked affectionately at Renee who was in her mid-fifties. She lived with her husband who

was a trucker and who was away a lot. They had one
son who had married and moved with his wife to
New Jersey. When Teddie had needed a steady
babysitter for her small son, she found Renee who'd
been a godsend. Royce had known her now for three
years and loved her to pieces.

Renee stood. "He's already eaten supper and had
his bath so you can put him to bed and relax for the
rest of the evening. I'll see you in the morning." At
the bottom of the stairs she turned. "You look tired,"
she said. "Everything all right at the diner?"

"Everything's okay, Renee," Teddie said. "But I am
a little tired. There was a busload of tourists in town
today so we were pretty busy."

"Okay," Renee said. "Well, don't stay up half the
night sewing more fancy duds on that supersonic
machine of yours. Good night."

Later, Teddie sat in her son's darkened bedroom
rocking gently in the green plaid glider, watching
him sleep.

She didn't wonder why she'd avoided having
dinner with Cole, because she knew he'd pick her up
and bring her home and there was no way of hiding
the truth. One look at her son and Cole would have
known that he was looking at a Dumont. There
would have been no denying that dimpled chin and
those round dark eyes that were so much like Cole's.
Royce was the mirror image to Cole and to his de-
ceased uncle, Curtis Dumont, the impish little boy
that she used to babysit. If Cole had turned accusing
eyes on her, could she have denied that his brother
Graham was Royce's father?

When Royce stirred, she kissed his forehead and
quietly left the room.

Teddie loved her son fiercely. She often wondered

if this intense feeling of motherhood was normal. She had no point of reference, because as an only child she'd learned early that her mother, Billie, wasn't the hugging kind. Teddie didn't hold back on her hugs and kisses for her son. She pooh-poohed his boyish dismissal of her sneaky kisses to his head when he wasn't looking. She couldn't remember such moments in her mother's house.

Her father was too busy making a living, keeping the diner a viable business to spend much time lavishing affection on a sleepy daughter who'd waited hours for him to come home. When she was sixteen, Hank Perkins was killed in a plane crash. Her mother held on to the diner, but by the time she was twenty, Teddie was practically running the place and at twenty-two it was all hers, after her mother married and moved to Pennsylvania.

"Mommy."

Teddie didn't hear Royce come into her room but she held out her arms. "What's the matter, sweetie?"

Royce settled himself in his mother's arms. "I heard something in my room," he said sleepily. "Can I sleep in your bed?"

Teddie smiled and kissed his curly head. She'd often thought that Royce had inherited his uncle Curtis's thick, soft hair, unlike his uncle Cole and his father who wore their hair well-groomed and cut close to the head. She couldn't remember what Mr. Dumont's had been like. Vaguely, she recalled Mrs. Dumont having lots of wavy hair that fell to her shoulders. Her son had the hair of a grandmother he'd never know, she thought. She hugged him and got up, taking his hand.

"Come on. Let's go see what's scaring my baby."

"I'm not a baby, I'm a big boy," Royce said indignantly through a big yawn.

"I know you are, sweetie, but you're Mommy's baby."

Once in his room, together they checked behind the curtains, looked in the closet, peered under the bed, and finally satisfied, Royce climbed into bed, his eyes closing sleepily. "Nothing's here, Mommy. I can sleep by myself," he said drowsily.

"Of course you can." Teddie smiled because he was already asleep. She turned off the light and left the room, leaving the door ajar.

It was past eleven and Teddie was feeling sleepy herself. She almost regretted not having dinner with Cole because she would really like to know more about what his life had been like since he'd left Minuet. She liked him—had always liked him—and she wished he would want to stay now that he'd returned, even though she realized the inevitability of her secret being revealed. She missed the big-brother relationship that they'd once had. Her heart had gone out to him during the short moments they'd spent together these past few days at the diner. Though they never mentioned the tragedies in his life she knew that he was still a haunted man.

Life is so strange, she thought. He'd traveled around the world while in the navy, lived in metropolitan Los Angeles, and he was still living in a tortured world. She, with the exception of two memorable weeks in Ohio, had spent her whole life in Minuet.

It had been her dream to go to college to study fashion design in New York City. But at eighteen her mother had had other ideas for her. Billie Perkins had claimed that there was no money for college, that the diner was a steady income, and that Teddie should be grateful to be handed a ready-made career.

Teddie laughed, remembering how she'd been given her "career." When Billie moved, the diner was in the red. Only because Hank Perkins had been a hardworking respected businessman did the bank help Teddie. With her family home as collateral, the loan helped Teddie to shore up the business. If it hadn't been for Roonie Hodges, her father's longtime friend and cook, and his son Allan, Teddie would have turned tail.

They helped her learn the business and in four years she'd turned the diner into a money-making operation. She'd remodeled, hired more staff, and reaped the benefits of steady traffic—regulars and visitors. She'd been worried that the new malls springing up everywhere would be a problem, but she'd been wrong. Word of mouth sent customers from as far away as Florence who wanted the experience of soul-satisfying food.

Teddie's life was in order, or so she thought. She was a successful businesswoman, had a lovely home, and was raising a beautiful son. Her friends were supportive and cared about her.

So why was the arrival of Cole Dumont in town disturbing her so?

She stared in the mirror as she slowly creamed her face and neck. In a strained whisper she answered her silent question.

"Because if Cole stays around town, there's no keeping him from recognizing Royce Curtis Perkins as his nephew."

Hearing the truth frightened her and her dark brown eyes widened in fear. Her chest constricted as she spoke another truth.

"Graham will come for his son."

* * *

The next morning, Ava arrived at the university's administration building bent on seeing Winifred before the day started. Although there were no sessions with classes starting next week, Ava had no intention of letting another day of bewilderment go by, especially with the arrival of the exhibit in a few days. She'd tried until late into the evening to contact Winifred by phone to no avail, and short of paying her friend a visit in the dead of night, she'd gone to bed, unfulfilled, nervous, and angry.

With faxed copies of her correspondence from her former mentor in her hand, Ava went in search of Winifred. She'd decided that as painful as it would be, confronting her friend was only another step in her plan of action. She was not going to sit complacently as she did when she was a teenager and become the victim of another's vicious scheme, whatever that might be. She found the assistant provost in her office. For a moment, Ava stood unnoticed in the doorway studying the woman who had become the closest thing to a friend that she'd had in her adult life. Her heart was heavy with the new knowledge of a person who was held in such high esteem among her peers.

"Ava?" Winifred Whidby looked surprised to see her colleague standing so quietly in the doorway watching her. She smoothed her tinted jet-black stylishly cut short hair and leaned back in her chair. "Come in," she said in a light voice.

Ava saw the wary look leap into Winifred's light brown eyes when she eyed the papers in her hand, and her heart sank. Was the administrator hiding something more than the authenticity of a scroll?

"What's going on?" Ava said, closing the door and taking the chair alongside the desk. When she saw her friend waver, she lost the last bit of hope that nothing had gone wrong in her tidy little world.

"What do you mean?" Winifred said, her eyes narrowing. "You mean, why have I been among the missing and absent from such an important meeting in order to recover?" She waved a hand with bright-tipped nails that matched her tinted-red lip color. "You of all people should understand how I'm feeling. Wouldn't *you* be in a quandary about such a theft if it were your baby?" She studied Ava and her hands moved absently across the front of her blouse smoothing nonexistent wrinkles from the crisp white cotton.

"Of course I would, Winifred. If I were you, I would definitely be."

"What's that supposed to mean?" Winifred's eyes narrowed to tiger eye slits.

Ava said, "You must have forgotten that I studied Gustavus Vassa. Otherwise you would never have begged me to join the staff here. Didn't you think that it would only be a matter of time before I learned of your 'find'?" She saw the dismay in the other woman's eyes. "Your discovery is just that, a discovery of your own making." She tapped the papers in her hand. "I know that now." Her voice was calm, yet sad. "Why did you do that, Winifred?"

Her chuckle was soft. "You have no idea of what you're talking about," Winifred said. "And I don't know what you think you have there."

"Did you get a look in that envelope Dr. Howell left for me before I left here last Friday, or did you help yourself to a peek inside after stealing into my home sometime over the weekend?" Ava said. "I'm just curious. It would help to know that I'm not losing it if you just told me the truth." It hurt her to say such things to the surprised woman, but she knew that she was in a battle for her future. She knew that deep in her heart. If Winifred Whidby could prove her claim and that she had nothing to do with the theft of the scroll from the archives, then Ava would do a dance and be the first to apologize. But for now she was standing her ground until she heard some semblance of truth and could make sense of the whole matter.

Winifred's mouth twisted cruelly as she stared aghast at Ava. "You have nerve, don't you?" she said, her long fingernails rapping a sharp cadence on the desk. "Just where do you think you are? You think you can come in here and speak to me that way? Making accusations that you can't prove?" She smirked as she looked at the papers clutched in her colleague's hand. "You don't know what you're talking about, Ava, and if you think you do, then if I were you, I'd bury it before it buries you."

Ava only stared at the incensed woman who was seething inside like a steaming pot ready to spill over. As if sensing she would lean over and snatch the papers from her hand, she held them tightly. She was about to stand when Winifred's voice stopped her.

"Look at you," Winifred said. "You're so young, a learned scholar, beautiful, and with eligible bachelors falling at your feet. Why should you care about any of this? Some bit of paper that the rest of the world wouldn't lose sleep over!" She sneered and rolled her eyes in disgust. "I should have known the minute I learned last year of the impending exhibit that you would be trouble."

"Then it is true," Ava said flatly.

"I don't know what you're talking about," Winifred said. "But I do know I doubt now whether we'll know what's real and what's not. Your expert, whoever you sought to confide in, doesn't have a clue." She looked triumphantly at Ava.

"You're wrong," Ava said. "The truth always manages to surface. Sometimes it just takes a little longer, but you'll be found out and your hoax uncovered. Then where will you be?"

Winifred stood. "I'd be careful if I were you about making any accusations that you can't prove," she said. "You'll be the one out of here so fast, people would forget you ever existed." She waved a hand. "See yourself out, Ava." As she sat back down she said, "I guess after this petty disagreement, my young friend, we won't be meeting for lunch and sharing our views of the world, will we?" Her smile was thin. "That's too bad. I was really looking forward to our trip to Italy next year."

When the door closed with a firm click, the smile left Winifred's face. The hands clasped in her lap were clammy and the once-crisp material of her blouse was dampened and clinging, moving gently with the erratic rise and fall of her chest.

Chapter Six

It was late in the day when Cole stood in the doorway of the kitchen giving it another once-over. He was satisfied with his accomplishments of the morning and the smells emanating from the stove tantalized his nostrils. He thought that he hadn't lost it after all. His glance slid to the repositioned table. Now he could walk around without having to circumnavigate like a man without a purpose. Common sense had told him that he'd had to get a grip on himself before he did more damage to his head. For some reason he couldn't fathom, the fact that his neighbor knew the true story had somehow scratched away some of the veneer that was scarring his soul. He knew that there were more layers to go but for now at least it was a start.

He couldn't get out of his mind the desolate look he'd seen on her face yesterday. She'd only waved and then disappeared behind the closed door. There had been such finality to that soft click that he was momentarily baffled. The slump of her shoulders was something he'd never seen before on the woman he thought to be strong, fearless, and resilient. But his detective instinct had sensed something was not right, and he would be willing to bet that it had nothing to do with him and his past, but what had happened at her job. Something or someone had sent her rushing to the sheriff's office to make a delayed report on a suspicion that had no substance, until now.

Cole felt that now it was his turn to play good neighbor and offer his help. A favor for a favor, he thought. *Stop kidding yourself, my friend.* He nearly swore at that inner voice. He knew his feelings had nothing to do with being neighborly, and all to do with his libido. He was lusting after Ava Millington and his body knew that better than his brain. That same inner voice held a warning: *Back away if you won't stay and finish whatever you start.*

When Ava left the university, she felt as down as she'd ever been in a long time, at a loss to even remember the last time she'd felt so helpless and inadequate. A mental image of her family brought frowns to her face. She thought that at troubling moments like this a person went flying into the bosom of family members who would take her problems and make them theirs. But she had no one. The loved ones she'd once had, had abandoned her during the most dreadful days of her life. Her family now held all of two people: Teddie Perkins and Royce Perkins. If she'd had to extend it she would count Teddie's good friend and now hers, Monique Anderson, who was also a single mother with a five-year-old son, Drew.

She thought of the times that she'd called Teddie who'd known instantly that she wanted company and Teddie would forgo a night of designing and they'd meet for a few hours, having dinner and drinks in nearby Hudson. Sometimes Monique would join them, and after a satisfying evening of female company Ava would awake the next morning rejuvenated.

But somehow she knew that a night spent with her friends would not do it for her this time. With their nudging they'd want to learn who or what had put such fear in her that she was walking around tossing furtive glances over her shoulder. Ava was not ready to divulge her past to her close friends. She didn't want to see the look of disbelief in their eyes when they learned the secret that their scholarly friend hid.

Teddie and Monique had expressed their regret for not pursuing higher education and both had often told her that they admired her spunk to set out on her own to accomplish so much so early in her life. Ava could have laughed at them, neither friend knowing that she'd been drummed out of the family fold like the worst pariah. She often wondered what course her life would have taken had it not been for those drastic events that had marred her young life. Would Teddie and Monique even allow her to be the surrogate aunt to their sons if they knew the truth? She didn't have the courage to test the friendships. Those women wanted the best for their sons and were striving as single parents to give them the world.

Teddie worked hard running the diner and Monique had busted her butt to make the town's only consignment store a booming business. Unlike Teddie, who had no one but Roonie and his son, Allan, when Monique had returned home pregnant, she had to fight to win the love and respect of her family who'd finally come around when they fell hard for baby Drew.

Thinking about her friends made Ava change her mind about company, and when she pulled into her driveway, she decided to change clothes and then go have dinner at the diner. She thought that somehow eating alone tonight would not be in her best interest.

Stepping out of the car, Ava's nostrils quivered and her mouth watered at the smells emanating around her. The sounds her stomach made told her that she'd eaten nothing since she had breakfast. This was the first time that food smells other than her own had invaded the air. Surely the wind that was nonexistent couldn't have brought the widow Lansdowne's kitchen efforts wafting down a half a mile, she thought. Her glance went to her neighbor's house where she was startled to see Cole standing on his porch watching her. From the masked look on his face, she couldn't guess what he was thinking.

When she started walking toward her steps, he lifted a hand but he didn't smile. She nodded and waved. "Cole," she said. The last time she'd seen him was yesterday when she'd come home from visiting the sheriff. Then she'd only lifted a hand in a quick greeting, unsure of what to say to the tortured man.

Ava halted her steps and stared into his eyes, the oddest feeling washing over her like a menacing tidal wave. All too crystal clear, she realized that it wasn't the company of strangers in Teddie's diner that she needed—she wanted to be near Cole Dumont. She wanted to feel the strength in those large hands, to buoy her up from her despair. She needed him to be her comfort and her family. But more than that, she desired him!

When she captured his gaze, Cole knew what he'd suspected from the first time they'd locked eyes days ago and to their relief had mercifully dissipated—that Ava, in all her smoothness and denial was a woman in desire . . . for him. What that knowledge did to him just now threatened to take away his resolve to leave her alone—that she wasn't a plaything for his immediate sexual healing.

But just now, in an unguarded moment, she was telling him different. He held her gaze for an interminable moment and then stepped off the porch and came toward her. The second he moved, the spell was broken and she was standing on her porch, hand on the doorknob with him standing beside her.

"Ava," Cole said.

"Hello," she said easily. She had control now, was the master of her voice and body. There was nothing in his manner that told her he had guessed what had been in her mind a second ago. She waved a hand toward his house. "Is that you stirring up my taste buds?"

He nodded, never taking his eyes from hers. "Guilty." She bent her head to unlock her door when he moved closer to keep her from disappearing inside. "Keeping promises and giving thanks. Would you have dinner with me?"

Ava raised her head and looked at him with understanding. "The famous Southern fried chicken?"

"The same," Cole said solemnly. "Along with some supermarket-prepared stuff."

She smiled. "You are nothing if not honest, Cole," she said.

He shrugged. "There's nothing to hide," he said. "I've told you about my limited culinary skills, but you won't find a better-tasting bird, even at Teddie's place."

"You don't have to sell me," Ava said. "I was bought the second my nose came alive. I accept your invitation." It was barely five so she said, "What time were you planning on serving?"

"Now, if you want."

"I want," Ava said, feeling the hunger pangs at the thought of food.

For the first time, Cole smiled at her enthusiasm.

"Then, come on over when you're ready," he said, and started down the steps.

"Can I bring anything?" Ava asked.

He studied her, taking in her smooth bare legs under a short olive-colored skirt with matching vest. A thin white cotton blouse was tucked inside, emphasizing the desirable bulges that he'd imagined fondling in his hands. His eyes snagged hers as he breathed, "Just you." He turned and went lightly down the steps.

Inside her bedroom, undressed and standing in her white cotton underwear and bra, Ava stared at her body in the mirror. She looked at what Cole was trying to uncover with his X-ray vision. Under his intense scrutiny she'd felt her breasts come alive, the buds pushing against the soft fabric of her bra. She lifted her hand and traced the outline of the tiny bulges, still hardened. There was no doubt that she'd longed for his touch, and the feeling was as powerful now as it'd been moments ago. She wondered what feelings she'd have and what thoughts would besiege her as he manipulated and caressed her.

It had been too many years since a man had fondled her, loved her flesh, making it sing like a songbird. Was that what she wanted from Cole? A satisfying romp that would leave her sated? And then what, after the last breathless sigh left them silent, neither knowing what to say or to do? "Same time, my place?" she'd whisper. Or he'd say, "Maybe we can do this again sometime—when I return?"

After washing up and changing into black leather clogs, a short, black denim skirt, and a pale blue scoop-neck top, she left the room. She'd decided to let what will be, be, and not to read anything into anything. She was hungry for sustenance yes, but she was all ready to let Cole Dumont comfort her in the manner she knew she needed and craved. Tomorrow could take care of itself, she reasoned. When she left, she locked the door and tried the knob, thinking about her uninvited intruder. At that moment Winifred's face with its cruel smile floated by and suddenly Ava longed for the strength that Cole's arms would provide.

Cole had set the table with everything he found in the house, and left by Graham. He didn't recognize any of the dishes that he'd known when he was a teenager. He realized that his brother had done a complete refurbishing: new pots and pans, dinnerware, flatware, and appliances. Even the floor had been replaced with a white ceramic tile, and the walls painted a cheery buttery yellow, a complete change from the sky-blue and beige trim his mother had favored. On top of red place mats were place settings for two, with cheery yellow, red and white-patterned dishes. The platter of chicken held center stage while bowls held Southern-style string beans with white potatoes, stewed tomatoes and okra, all from a can, and fresh corn on the cob that he'd just removed from the boiling water.

Just as he wondered if everything would get cold before she arrived, the doorbell rang. Relieved, yet with sudden apprehension, he answered it.

"Come in," Cole said. "Hope your appetite is still with you. Everything's on the table." He led the way to the kitchen while taking from her the bottle of chilled white wine she handed him.

Ava noticed the rearrangement of furniture but refrained from commenting as Cole gestured to a chair. All that she'd heard yesterday reminded her that her neighbor was still tortured by his past and, she thought, staunchly trying to deal with it. She sat and the aroma of the golden-brown chicken made her mouth water. "Are you kidding?" she said. "I hope I'm not going to embarrass myself. Everything looks and smells great."

Cole sat across from her, pleased with her response. He took a deep breath. "Dig in, then," he said.

Ava speared her favorite parts, the thigh and the wing, and the juices flowed and she knew she would be in for some good eating. She filled her plate with the vegetables and began to eat.

Cole watched her while filling his own plate, and when he saw her bite into the juicy thigh he felt his shoulders relax when her eyes squeezed shut. She liked it.

They didn't speak for a while, both hungry and enjoying the deliciously prepared food, when Cole got up and went to the stove and returned with a covered casserole dish. "Forgot this," he said and sat.

Ava lifted the top and the aroma filled her nostrils. "Croquettes, Cole?" she said and smiled her delight.

Cole shrugged as he helped himself. "Something my brother and I picked up from Virginia Thompson. She was always after us to eat better after my mother—well, when we were living here by ourselves." After a moment he said, "Just thought I'd give you a sample of another Dumont specialty while I had the chance," he said.

The past is always present, Ava decided as Cole struggled with anything reminding him of his mother. But she wondered at his choice of words and then realized that Minuet was to be just another blip on the screen of his life. Refusing to let that bit of knowledge dampen her mood, she bit into one of the crisply fried golden-brown balls. "Mmm, potato," Ava said, rolling her tongue around the well-seasoned vegetable, savoring the onion and celery flavors. "Delicious. Reminds me of something my sister used to make when she got busy in the kitchen."

Cole stopped eating and looked at her. This was the first time she'd ever mentioned family. A sister. He wondered how many more siblings she had and what of her parents? Curious. In the days he'd known her, he'd never even wondered about that side of her. Was he only interested in bedding her and to hell with who she was and where she came from?

"Somehow I took you for an only child," Cole said. "You have sisters and brothers?"

"What gave you that impression?" Ava replied as she finished the last of the croquette. She sat back and looked at him. "I'm spoiled, self-centered, and independent?"

"Only one of those," Cole said as he stared back. "You never mentioned family in any of our brief conversations."

"One sister, no brothers." Her eyes slithered away, and then came back to his. "My sister is three years older and has a husband. They have two sons."

The dullness of her voice was a dead giveaway that he was treading on dangerous ground. Still, his investigative instinct made him persist. "Do you visit them often?"

A shudder went through Ava. Why were they talking about her family? she wondered. All she'd wanted to do was enjoy a meal with a handsome sexy man whom she knew wanted her and she wanted him. Feeling sad and unable to reverse the mood, she pushed away from the table, prepared to leave. "Everything was mouth-watering good, Cole," she said. "Thanks for inviting me." She couldn't pull her eyes away from his intense stare and so she sat, glued to her chair.

"Ava?"

"Thirteen years."

"What?"

"I haven't seen my sister, Dahlia, in thirteen years. I've never even met my nephews who are nine and twelve." Her eyes never wavered from his as she said, "When my father died after a massive stroke, I never went to his funeral. Months later my mother suffered a fatal heart attack. I didn't go home for her burial either."

Running. Cole had sensed that from the beginning. *His* mother. *Her* parents. Whew! Could kindred souls really identify one another, he thought? He could feel the warmth and easygoing demeanor evaporating as he noticed her slumped shoulders. She looked the same way as she had when he'd seen her yesterday coming home from work. Whatever had happened at the university had somehow reminded her of her family. What was the connection and what had the people in Georgia done to her?

"Want to talk about it?" he asked, noticing that she was ready to take flight. If anything, he wanted her here with him instead of being alone after he'd been the cause of her sudden change in mood. He *knew* alone.

Talk about being known as a thief? Ava didn't think so, not now and especially not to the man sitting across from her who was still chasing his own ghosts. How could they ever be of help to one another? A case of the hurt tending to the wounded. No, thank you.

Cole saw her close up inside and knew he'd never hear her story—at least for now, he thought. He'd pushed hard and lost the gamble. He stood.

"Cole," Ava said as she watched him begin to clear the table.

"I know," Cole said. "And I understand."

Ava stood and began to help. "You do?" she asked.

"Yeah. Well, almost," he said, and gave her a solemn look. "I'm not exactly what you would call a motor-mouth where family is concerned, you know." They worked in silence until the food was put away and the dishwasher humming. There was more wine left and Cole took the bottle and the glasses and said, "Let's go outside."

It was nearly seven o'clock and the traffic sparse, with most of the commuters already at home.

Ava smiled as she sipped from her glass.

"What?" Cole asked, seeing the twinkle return to her eyes and feeling oddly satisfied.

"Oh, just a thought about Mrs. Lansdowne and what she'd say about the 'newbie' hobnobbing with a long-lost Dumont, drinking in daylight in plain sight."

Cole shrugged. "The old widow keeps herself busy with everybody else's business," he said. "Harmless, though. She's been alone for a long time. Her husband died when I was about twelve. I remember the day when she came running down the road to get my mother. The man had just gotten in from work, said hi, gave her a kiss, and then dropped right in front of her feet." Cole drained his glass. "Her screams in the quiet evening were memorable for a long time." He was silent, remembering some other screams that would be with him until he died. "Except for replacing her dogs, she's been alone in that house for over twenty years."

"A lot of years," Ava murmured. She set her empty glass on the table and looked at Cole. "I thank you again for a delicious dinner. It was what I needed."

"It was?" Cole said, staring at her. He thought about the look that had passed between them not long ago that had had him wondering how this night would end.

"That, and your company," Ava said softly, while holding his gaze. "Yes, my needs were met—for the night."

Cole understood her perfectly. "So, we'll be doing this again," he stated, staring at her.

Ava stood up and watched as he joined her at the steps. "If you want," she said.

"I want," Cole answered. He followed her as she turned and walked down the steps.

She turned to him and said, "I think we should say good-night on your side of the hedges, don't you?"

A hint of a smile touched his lips as Cole stopped where he was and watched her until she reached her front door. Almost amazed when she reached into her skirt pocket and took out a key to unlock the door, he finally smiled.

"Ava?" he called.

"Yes?"

He was back on his porch and his look was unwavering. "Just remember, when you want to talk, I'm here," he said.

"I won't forget, Cole," Ava said, and went inside.

Later, while working at her desk, Ava spied the letter from her sister, reminding her that she'd never responded. Only hours ago she'd been beside herself with hurt and loneliness and was ready to let a stranger love her pain away. Meaningless devouring of the flesh, that's all it would have been, and with a man she'd known for less than a week. But her own blood relative was reaching out to her, to help her heal after all these years. Why couldn't she bring herself to accept the offering—to welcome the love and support from family that she so desperately needed and wanted now? To help erase a painful past—one that should never have been all because of the terrible wrong that a self-righteous man, now long dead, had reaped upon her head.

Ava had no doubt that the days ahead would be filled with fear, pain, and dread. She knew that there was nothing she could do to keep her past from being exposed, because she believed that her friend

Winifred, who had turned on her so viciously, was fighting for her professional career and honor, and that Ava Millington was expendable.

She remembered the way Cole had spoken his last words to her and she thought that as sure as a cat loved cream she would be in his arms seeking the love and closeness that her mind and body craved. But then what would come next? He'd be gone and she'd still be here looking for love in all the wrong places.

Ava took the letter out of the envelope and read it again. When finished, she laid it down. *What better time than to have family in your corner?* she thought. "You've got to try, Ava," she said in a low voice. "Just take a deep breath and give it a shot." But as she pressed in the unfamiliar numbers, she felt the tenseness cramp her stomach and she wondered if staying with Cole would have been the better balm for what ailed her.

"Hello?"

"It's Ava," she said to her sister.

"My, Lord! Sunny?"

Ava was whisked into the past hurtling by a kaleidoscope of resurrected bad dreams that she watched in horror—dreams that she wished she couldn't claim. *Thief!*

But they *were* hers and she gripped the phone as she struggled back to the present. *She shouldn't have called.* Her voice was as brittle as thirteen years of yellowed newsprint. "I haven't been Sunny for aeons, Dahlia."

"You were Sunny to Dad and to all of us, Ava. We still think of you like that. We love you."

"We?" Ava said, her voice rising uncontrollably, bad memories clogging her brain so she couldn't think straight. "Your boys don't know me and you sided with our father and mother along with the rest of the community. So who's the 'we'? I went to my big sister for support and you avoided looking me in the eye for months afterward. You thought Dad was wrong, but you never stood up for me!" *Oh, this is going badly. I shouldn't have called.*

"Ava, stop," Dahlia said sharply.

"Oh, God," Ava breathed as she caught herself, the shrill sound in the room finally coming to a halt. Had that been her? She never thought she could be so venomous. This bottled-up hatred for her family had taken her sanity.

"Ava, you've got to come home. We can talk and end this before it's too late for us as a family," Dahlia said. "Please, Ava, we have to talk."

"Late?" Ava gave a short laugh. "You said you loved me. But you should have loved me then. And home? I am home. Good-bye, Dahlia."

Ava's hand still shook as it rested on the phone. "My God, my God," she murmured. Something had taken hold of her and wouldn't let loose. The cramps in her stomach intensified as her body began to shake worse than her hand. "What's happening to me?" she said as she stood and wrapped her arms around her stomach, as if to squeeze the dull pain away. Her breaths came in gasps and she craved air. She had to get out of here. She hurried to the door and flung it open, and instead of the breeze she expected, the warm evening air smothered her face as she lifted it to the darkening sky. "No," she said, and went back inside. In seconds she had her purse and keys and left again, hurrying down the steps and to her car. She backed into the road and sped away.

Ava had no sense of where she was headed; she just needed to feel the warm wind on her face as she drove. *Oh, what a disaster,* she thought. Why couldn't she have left it alone? After all these years, what did it matter that they were a family estranged? It wasn't her doing after all, now was it? The man who was responsible, her father, was long dead, gone to glory thinking that he'd done the right thing by aiding those who'd branded his youngest child a thief.

It was nearly nine o'clock and dark now and Ava found herself in Hudson, parking in the lot of a popular supper club, a place where she and her friends visited from time to time. Inside, the crowd was small and intimate, a few couples dancing to the slow music provided by CD's, while others talked in low voices at scattered tables. The ambience was pleasant and inviting to those who extended their day with the happy hour the club provided all week. Although Ava didn't know anyone, the waitperson must have recognized her when she nodded and smiled while she took Ava's order of a martini cocktail.

As she sipped, and listened to the music of Luther Vandross singing about his father, Ava felt giddy at her thoughts. So much for seeking out family to help her through this tough time that was going to be far worse than being drummed out of a small community. Here, her career would be on the line. What state would she run to next and how would she support herself? The thought of starting over in yet another strange place was daunting. The image of her being led from the university in handcuffs seemed absurd and brought forth a silly giggle. Oh, no, Ava Millington, a half of a glass of liquor made you sappy? She tapped her glass. "Well, thanks, Mr. Martini, for chasing away the shakes, anyway," she said, and drank some more.

Although the delicious meal she'd had earlier had satisfied her completely, Ava knew she couldn't possibly walk out of the club and drive after downing a second martini. She ordered some food, forcing herself to eat and to drink hot coffee. More than two hours later her head felt clear enough to leave the restaurant. She sat in her car for a long while before pulling off. So much for being a levelheaded, responsible adult, she thought. At the first sign of panic she'd headed for a drink as if that was the end-all and be-all of problem solving. As she drove back to Minuet, she gave some serious thought to her immediate problem: how to convince those that mattered that Winifred Whidby was a fraud and a thief, so that she could continue living in the safe haven she'd built for herself.

It was after eleven o'clock when Ava pulled into her darkened yard. In her haste she'd forgotten to put on the porch light and the quiet was eerie. There was no light coming from her neighbor's porch light either and she was reminded that in the past two years there had been none. She reached her door and inserted the key but the door opened. At first she was alarmed, stepping back as if to run but then realized she hadn't even bothered to lock it in her urgency to get away. Feeling relieved she pushed open the door.

"You forgot."

"What?" Ava's heart pumped as she whirled toward the sound of the quiet voice coming from the shadows of her porch. She saw Cole walking toward her.

"Cole?" she said. "What are you doing here and what did I forget?" Relieved, she reached inside and switched on the light, illuminating the porch and Cole's hard look in soft light.

"That I was here if you wanted to talk."

"Oh," Ava said, remembering. Suddenly weary, she said, "That wasn't what I needed then."

"And now?" Cole asked, still staring at her intently. In the dim light he saw the strain on her face, and as he'd had earlier when he saw her flee, wondered what the hell had happened since their dinner together.

It was all too much, and the sound of his deep voice and the quiet concern shining in his eyes made Ava

think of the comfort she would find against that big
chest. So she simply walked into his arms and said,
"This." She wrapped her arms around his middle and
rested her head against him and closed her eyes. "Just
this," she murmured.

Cole's arms were waiting to enfold her when she
walked into them. He closed his eyes and rested his
cheek atop her hair. She felt as he'd known she
would, soft and warm and smelling clean and fragrant. His arms tightened as he held her close. Her
heart was beating fast and she was murmuring softly,
only one word clear: *family.*

So that was it, he thought. When she'd left him
hours before, family had been on her mind. Something had happened to make her want to escape the
comfort of her own home. He held her until he could
feel her settling down, her heart beating normally
now. But he didn't want to release her, the evidence
of his desire for her undeniable. After days of not
being able to get her out of his head, here she was
his for the taking, vulnerable. Steeling himself against
acting and doing irreparable harm to whatever would
be between them, he stepped away enough to look
into her eyes.

"Okay now?" he asked. He led them to the chairs,
where he eased her into one and he took the other.

Ava shivered, the cool night air chilling her bare
arms. She stared out into the darkness, just watching
the leafy trees and the twinkling of lights through the
dense forest across the road. She thought she'd experienced a time of insanity and wondered at the
catalyst that had sent her into a tailspin. The sound of
her sister's voice; the nickname Sunny that she hadn't
heard in years; the mention of the word *love*: all of
that had led her to want to escape. But here she was,
sitting on her porch, calm, thinking clearly with a

stranger who'd offered his help, which she'd ignored. She'd run only to return to where she started.

Cole watched her. He knew enough about human nature to allow her to make the first move. She'd sought his comfort and he'd given it. It was up to her to say how much more she wanted from him because his body was telling him that he wasn't going to be the one to back away again. He waited.

She glanced at her door and then at him. "You were guarding my house."

"You forgot to lock up."

"You were watching me?"

Cole nodded.

"Why didn't you stop me?"

"I told you that I would be here," Cole answered.

She turned away from his steady look and stared off into the night again. When she looked at him, she stood. "I'm glad that you're here now," Ava said, and held out her hand. When he took it they walked inside the house together.

Chapter Seven

"Something hot or something cold?" Ava asked. She'd already started filling the coffeepot. She needed the hot caffeine. Her brow was furrowed as she thought that after all these years she was about to share her pain. Could she wrap her mouth around the words all that easily? She'd freaked out at just the mere mention of particular words with her sister. How would she fare with a stranger? He hadn't answered her and she turned to see him watching her intently.

"Are you all right?" Cole asked.

"I will be," she answered. "I need some coffee but you're welcome to whatever you like."

"Beer?"

She nodded. "I have that."

They were in her living room. Ava sat on the sofa, coffee mug warming the palms of her hands. Cole sat across from her, waiting and watching.

"I was seventeen, living in Collier, a suburb of Atlanta, Georgia," Ava said. She gestured toward her study. "Everything in that room, that's my whole world now, as it was back then. History, delving into the past, relics, artifacts, I was thirsty to learn all I could about the old, how people lived way back when. I was addicted to knowledge. My parents and my sister thought it was a passing craze. My father finally took me seriously when all throughout high school I claimed the annual Future Historian Award, and in my senior year I was granted a coveted spot as an intern at the prestigious Franklin University. I was beside myself with excitement that such a distinguished scholar as Dr. Henry Biehmer would choose me to be his trusted assistant. When he began discussing his work and his plans for future study I thought I'd died and gone to heaven. He planned to invite me to travel with him the summer I graduated. The trip would become part of my college credits. I couldn't think straight half the time. My father was walking around as a proud peacock telling any and all of his distinguished peers who'd listen about his daughter's accomplishments." Ava paused to drink. The mug was cooling and she set it on the table.

Cole could see the effort she was making in trying to speak unemotionally about the past but knew it was hard. He made no comment but waited for her to continue.

"An artifact went missing," Ava began, but stopped as if thinking about the moment. When she spoke, it was with an awed voice. "Dr. Biehmer accused me." The look she sent Cole was full of pain.

"Why?" Cole asked. "What proof did he have?"

Still living in the moment, Ava shook her head and said, "Because he'd placed it in my hands and told me to lock it up. That was the last he'd seen of it." She clasped her hands in her lap as if silently signifying she'd also kept them to herself back then. Her lips barely moved. "He trusted me."

"That's no proof," Cole said in disgust. "What kind of artifact was it?"

"A manuscript," Ava answered.

"Just a manuscript? Of what?"

His voice, filled with incredulity, made Ava glance at him sadly. "Some manuscripts of old are priceless," she said.

"Granted," Cole said. "But what made this one so special?"

"It was the writings of a modern biographer of African culture, who tried to present a true picture of ancient Africa," Ava answered.

"That's special?"

This time Ava smiled. "Very special," she said. "Plunderers burned and looted the vast, fabulous libraries in many cities, destroying millions of volumes of ancient records. Knowledge of a culture was lost." She made a helpless gesture. "Gone—such precious information about mathematics, science, literature, and technology."

"What was in the manuscript?"

"Mainly it was about a later period, the slave trade and how it began and quickly prospered," Ava said. She grimaced. "The author wrote that all the vile things learned about the blacks were European inventions to justify continuing the abhorrent practices of the newfound trade. He also mentioned the court case of a captain charged with throwing overboard over a hundred slaves." Ava's eyes flashed as she stared at Cole. "Of course, the problem was not the deaths but rather should the captain be held accountable for the financial loss."

Cole swore softly. After a while he said, "Why were you left to lock up the manuscript?"

"Because it was my area of interest. Dr. Biehmer

knew of my desire to learn all that I could about that period in our history and I had only weeks before discovering the slave narratives. So all and anything that pertained to slavery caught my attention."

"Then after you finished your study and locked it up, was anyone else around to verify that?" Cole said.

For a moment Ava didn't answer, but sat as if remembering.

"Ava?" When she raised her eyes to his, he shook his head and breathed a deep breath. "You didn't put it back," he stated.

"Yes," Ava said slowly. "No one was around when I put the manuscript back and locked it up."

Cole looked puzzled. "You put it back," he remarked.

Ava nodded. "I did."

"And then?"

"Dr. Biehmer was away, but he called me. He told me that it was okay to give his archives key to my father." She paused. "For security's sake at that time there were only two keys to keep track of comings and goings and what was being researched and by whom. The curator had the other one."

"Your father?"

"Yes. He was the president of neighboring Melburne University. A very important man." She looked at Cole. "Apparently he made the request to visit the archives for some reason and was granted permission. When he came looking for me I gave it to him." Her brow was puckered. "I seem to remember him saying something about my interest in that document had piqued his and he wanted to study it himself for a future possible lecture."

Cole just stared at her.

"When my father went into the archives he found

that the particular manuscript box that held the folders of papers was disturbed. The manuscript that I had been studying was gone from the folder."

"Gone?"

"Yes," Ava answered.

"You went with him?"

"No," Ava said. "He was shown to the archives by another intern because I was busy working with another professor." She paused. "He said if he missed me, he'd give the key back to Dr. Biehmer who was returning that evening. I said okay."

"So how did you find out about the missing manuscript?"

"My father came hurrying to me, a funny look in his eyes," Ava said slowly while remembering. She glanced at Cole. "He looked—scared. I'd never seen him looking that way before," she said.

"What did he say?"

"He asked me if I was certain that I'd locked up the search room because he and the intern found it unlocked and the manuscript was gone."

"Was that it?" Cole asked.

"What do you mean?"

"Was anything else touched or missing?"

"Yes," Ava answered. "But I found that out later. At that moment all I could think of was that the artifact was my responsibility and now it was gone. I couldn't think straight and all I could do was look at my father like he'd grown two heads. I couldn't believe it. Then when he gave me an accusing look my heart stopped." She stared at Cole. "It was then that I realized why he looked scared. He thought I'd taken it."

"That's dumb," Cole blurted. "For what reason?" he asked, his mouth twisting into a grimace. "Sounds crazy."

"It was," Ava said. "But what happened later was even crazier."

"What was that?"

"Security refused to let me leave," she said. "I was detained at the university until Dr. Biehmer arrived late that evening. He questioned me and my father shot questions at me nonstop until I was exhausted. When I kept insisting I'd returned the manuscript, they sort of threw up their hands and left me in a room by myself."

Cole saw the sudden droop in her shoulders. "Then what?" he asked.

"My father came in to see me alone," Ava said. "He looked sad and I thought he was going to cry. I felt relieved that finally he believed me and was going to take me into his arms and console me. But he didn't. Without any warning he stiffened and his brown eyes were as black coal when he stared at me. He said he thought he would never have seen the day that his daughter would become a thief. He asked me to return the artifact and all would be forgiven and forgotten."

Ava stood. "Excuse me," she said, and left the room.

Cole heard running water, and when she returned he noticed the dampened tendrils framing her forehead and the bright moistness in her eyes.

"'You're a thief and a liar and I never had a clue.'" Ava sat in the same spot on the sofa, sitting back, her arms folded over her stomach. "Those were his words to me," she said in a dull voice. "A thief!"

"That's all he said?"

Ava threw him a look. "There was more," she said, "but that was what I remembered the most. It was what hurt my soul."

"What about the investigation?" Cole asked.

"There wasn't one."

"What?"

"Dr. Biehmer didn't want the publicity a public investigation would warrant. He said it was a private matter since nothing else was stolen and that the incident would be handled in-house." Funny, she thought, how now in her maturity she'd learned that that hadn't been so unusual at all.

"Incredible," Cole murmured.

"Why?" Ava asked.

"I don't get it. Some valuable pieces go missing and it's to be hushed up?" Cole gestured at the air. "Makes no sense. What was the rationale? What about the insurance company wanting an investigation? What about you being accused and your reputation afterward? You were to be held under suspicion with no chance of ever proving yourself innocent?"

"That's the way it was and is, Cole," she said in a dull voice. "In my worldliness now, I've learned that thefts of rare articles are not automatically reported. Some never are. It's a stigma and the institution would rather save face than have to admit vulnerability. Endowments, donations, acquisitions would become nonexistent."

Cole looked bewildered. He finally asked, "What happened next?"

"It was late when my father drove me home," Ava said. "He hardly spoke to me. But when we reached the house we sat in the car. Just sat for a long time. Finally, without looking at me he said, 'Which dealer did you sell it to, Ava? Just tell me how much and we'll get it back.' I nearly fainted from shame. My own father actually thinking that I could do something so dishonest. I thought I was looking at a stranger."

"Dealer?" Cole asked.

She sent him a puzzled look. "You must know about things like that."

"Getting rid of stolen goods? Sure," Cole said impatiently.

"Not just stolen property—antiquities theft. It's always been big. Still is." Ava thought of Winifred and the fraud she'd perpetrated, and she shivered. "Still is," she repeated in a small voice. Then, looking at Cole she said, "Everything after that was a blur. I was living in a dream world for weeks. Dr. Biehmer dismissed me from his staff. My father kept me at a distance after saying how he'd been disgraced by his own daughter. One day he came to my bedroom and just stood there looking at me strangely. Before he left, he said, 'I cleaned up your mess.' That was all. He never spoke to me again about the theft and neither did anyone else. At least not in my presence."

She was silent and Cole tried to digest what he'd heard. How could a father just shut out his daughter like that? he wondered. "Jesus," he murmured. *Just like your mother did.* The inner voice seemed loud in the silence that filled the room and Cole briefly shut his eyes.

"Cole?" She could only guess what he was thinking. "That was long ago," she said.

He looked at her. "Yeah, but it's back again, isn't it?" he asked. "Whatever happened at work is related to your past." When she blinked, he said, "Yeah, I'm right. Want to talk about it now?"

"History is about to repeat itself." Ava thought of what she said and gave a small smile. "My life's work is about to jump up and bite my butt. Ironic, huh?" When he remained silent she said, "I'm going to be accused of theft." Cole looked at her and she saw that he wasn't going to interrupt. She continued.

Both were quiet for a long moment after Ava stopped speaking. Cole was staring out the curtained window, seemingly mesmerized by the occasional flashing light from a passing car. Who said life's a bitch and then you die?

"And that woman you called friend?" He wondered about his own relationships. How many of his colleagues could he call friend? He knew that he had many acquaintances. Even the partners that he'd come close to over the years came but so close. None had ever known about his life in Minuet. As he thought about it, the closest one he could call a friend was his brother, Graham, who'd visited him occasionally in Los Angeles.

Ava shrugged. "As close as I'd let her become," she replied.

"You've never mentioned this to her or anyone? Not even to Teddie?" When he saw her look he said, "I thought so."

"Just like you never mentioned the guilt *you* carry." She stared at him.

Cole nodded in assent. "Just like," he agreed.

Ava moved restlessly on the sofa. She was tired, almost exhausted, as if baring her soul had consumed all her energy. She'd thought that she would feel weightless but she didn't. She still felt burdened by a past that was soon going to be her present—and she didn't have a clue on how to make it all go away. Unless she could somehow convince everyone that Winifred Whidby had pulled the wool over a lot of esteemed eyes.

"What do you want to do next?" Cole's voice startled her and she looked at him. "I think I need a detective," she said.

"You want my help?"

"I need someone to believe in me," Ava answered. She thought of Dr. Biehmer, her father, her mother, and sister. "And someone to trust."

Cole got up and walked to the window. It was late, nearly midnight, and nothing stirred. The few lights that he could see twinkling through the dense brush across the road made him wonder if others were having a life crisis this hour of the night and were awake planning a way out. He walked from the room crossed the hall and stood in the doorway of the study looking around. He felt Ava come up behind him. He smelled her and inhaled slightly. That scent of freshness wafted to his nostrils but he held himself in check. The woman who'd shared her hurt with him was not the woman he intended to love and leave. Those thoughts of bedding her and leaving her to deal with it flew out the window. She was not his plaything. The soft touch to his arm made him shiver and she walked past him into the room and turned to stare at him. "What are you thinking?" she asked.

Cole stared back. "About you." It was the truth wasn't it? he thought.

Ava thought her heart jumped. "What about me?" Why were his eyes so dark and brooding? she wondered. Did she have that effect on him? Or was it her sad tale? "My story is too much for you to handle? You've changed your mind about offering your help?" she said.

Cole gave her a long look. "You're too much for me to handle, Ava." Her pretty brown eyes widened and he turned away from them. After one more look around at her precious treasures, he said, "I need more information from you, but not now. Tomorrow?" When she only nodded he turned and walked to the front door, passing by the foyer closet. He remembered a soft giggle and nearly flinched as he opened the door and left.

It was nearly two in the morning and Cole was still unable to sleep. How in the world could he offer to help someone out of their pain and misery when he didn't have a clue on how to help himself? Now was a time that he wished he still smoked. He needed to do something with his hands and mouth, something that didn't have a thing to do with taking beautiful lips and breasts into his hands and mouth, and sucking them until they cried for mercy.

The next day Ava arrived at the university earlier than usual. She was nervous and on edge but she had to make sure that she hadn't missed anything. Tomorrow was Friday, the day the exhibit was scheduled to arrive. She walked the long hall on the second floor of the building that had been prepared with tables, glass cases, and designated places on the walls for the precious cargo. For months she'd worked along with the curator who was willing to take Ava's suggestions on the best places to exhibit certain items. When the shipment arrived, just she and the curator would have complete involvement in inspecting and verifying the arrival of each piece. She peered at the little pieces of paper taped to the wall and the cases indicating what was to go where. Everything was as she and the curator planned. The only thing left to do now was to wait. She stood silently on the polished wood floor and she whirled at the sudden sharp staccato of footsteps.

"Dr. Thiessen," Ava said breathlessly. "You're here early."

Emily Thiessen smiled. "As you are," the curator said. Ava smiled back at the woman who as far as Ava knew never had a bad day. Her voice was as jovial sounding as her ever-present bright smile and her blue-green eyes were never sad. At five-foot-five, stocky build, great legs, and long brown hair, the forty-some-thing woman always appeared as a breath of fresh air.

"Nervous," Emily said as her eyes darted approvingly at her surroundings. She swiped at a tiny speck of dust drifting through the air, about to land atop the shining glass case. "Now, Ava, I know this can't be your first unveiling," she said, her smile growing wider and her eyes filling with sympathy. "Everything is going to be just fine. Trust me."

"First unveiling, no. Nervous, yes, Emily." Ava splayed a hand. "This traveling exhibit is a first and the president is proud that we were selected to be part of the tour," she said. "The fact that we had a theft from the archives is making him and a lot of us uneasy. You as well, I'm sure. I'm praying nothing goes missing in this exhibit." With a rueful grin she said, "Believe me, I'll be glad when it leaves here." To her surprise, Emily's mouth downturned and gone was the infectious smile.

"A theft. Of Vassa papers?" Emily nearly spat out the words.

"What do you mean?" Ava said. Her stomach began to feel funny.

"Do you really believe that someone came inside here and marched off with *that*?" She swiped the air again. "Sounds mighty suspicious if you ask me."

Ava's heart skipped. "You think it was someone who—works here?" she asked, not really wanting to hear the answer. But she couldn't help herself. "And who do you think it was?"

Emily raised a brow. "With security the way it is? Are you kidding?" She looked directly at her colleague. "Of course it was one of us, and the president is keeping his head in the sand about it."

"But, why?" Ava asked.

The smile was back on Emily's broad mouth. "It's called cleaning up your own mess," she said. "Look, I've got to go, but we'll meet tomorrow around noon. That's when the trucks arrive. See you then, my fellow guard dog." She waved cheerily and her heels made firm, confident sounds as she walked away.

I cleaned up your mess. Her father's words all those years before rang in her ears as though he were standing at her elbow. Ava sagged against the glass case. "What does Emily know and whom does she suspect?" The whispered words sounded loud in the empty hall. But what chilled her through was the vitriolic tone when she'd spoken Vassa's name. Does she know about Winifred's fraud? Had always known? And why hadn't she said anything?

Ava was at a loss. She was in her office pondering over what had just happened. If Emily had always known of the deception, what good was it to keep mum about it, allowing the president and everyone else to think they had something of value—and to have let it go so far as to be included in a cross-country tour? Wouldn't the fraud have been discovered when the exhibit arrived here? Ava pondered over the action or inaction of Dr. Thiessen. Although the woman always had a hearty greeting for her fellow colleagues, she always appeared to be in a hurry, never tarrying long to chew the fat or engage in campus gossip. Ava didn't know whether the woman was married or divorced, in a relationship or looking. She realized that during conversations it was usually all about the university and work, but when it came to private matters it was always Emily doing the drawing out while the other party talked. But since Ava was always hush-mouthed about her own past, no one, including Emily, had learned very much about Ava. Two of a kind, Ava thought. But she still couldn't help but ponder over the woman's silence.

There was a rap on her door and Ava looked to see her colleague standing there with a solemn look. "Hale, what's up?" she asked, seeing the concern etched on his face.

"Did you hear?" Hale asked. He entered the room and sat in the chair across from Ava's desk.

Ava's heart thumped. *What now?* she wondered. "No," she said. "What happened?"

"The exhibit is being held up in Tennessee."

"What?" If Ava had not been sitting, she would have fallen. "What did you say?" This could not be, she thought. Why was she finding this out from a colleague—who was not even in on the planning—and not from Dr. Howell? Her mouth was dry. "I—I didn't know."

"I thought not," Hale said while staring at her thoughtfully. "Why you weren't called in on the early hurry-up meeting this morning is a mystery, especially since you and Dr. Thiessen are so involved. Appeared that Winifred was running the show, though."

"Winifred?" Ava could barely say the name. "But she had nothing at all to do with the coming exhibit," Ava said. She stared at him. "You either, yet you were included?"

Hale nodded. "Yes. It appears that you and Emily were the only two missing."

"But I don't understand," Ava said. She and Hale looked up at the same time at the person who appeared in the doorway.

Winifred was half smiling, half sneering at them.

She didn't enter the room but looked at Hale. "So it didn't take you long to be the bearer of news. Good or bad—however little Miss Brainy wants to take it."

"Winifred," Ava said. "What is going on?"

"Oh, you already heard from the clarion," she said, glaring at Hale. "But, yes, it's true. No exhibit. But I'll let Dr. Howell fill you in. He wants you in his office, by the way. Pronto." After a long look at the astonished woman, she left.

"Witch," Hale muttered. He eyed Ava, who appeared to be shaken. "You gonna be okay?"

His words appeared to be coming from afar. Ava sat numbly, her mind reeling from the utterances of her two colleagues. Her world was spinning out of control and there appeared to be nothing she could do about it. Slowly she stood and moved from behind her desk and walked past Hale while staring at him as though he were a stranger.

"I have to go," she said softly. "I don't understand what's happening."

As she walked to the elevator that would take her up to his fourth-floor office, she wondered why Dr. Howell hadn't called her himself. To send a messenger in the form of Winifred Whidby was degrading, as if she was the bad little girl being summoned to the principal's office by the teacher's pet.

The day had dragged and when Ava left, she felt like a limp dishrag. It was barely four o'clock and Ava wished it was midnight and she was fast asleep, this horrible day a distasteful bit of history and one she would fast forget. Yet she knew that his look, his words were seared in her brain. *We can't be trusted to ensure a safe, secure stay for the artifacts, Dr. Millington. Our secu-*

rity has been breached and the national committee disapproves of keeping us on the tour. We're being bypassed—at least until we've caught the thief. After the private thorough investigation, the committee is really convinced now that the thief had help—on the inside.

On the inside. His penetrating stare had been stultifying. On her way out she'd wondered if his dazed eyeballs had fastened themselves to her back. What could she have said to him? she wondered. Tell him of her suspicions about Winifred? Of course he'd have looked at her as if she'd suddenly lost her mind. And what was the reason for Emily's exclusion? Ava had sought her out, but she was told the curator had left the building for the day. And Winifred—when Ava went to her office, she discovered Winifred had also gone. What did it all mean? She had to get some answers before she really did lose her mind, she thought.

The stigma that was now associated with the university was fast spreading in the small world of historians she guessed and it would be a long time before Floyd Compton University was held in high esteem again. Would she ever be able to walk with her head held high, enjoying the respect and admiration of her peers without seeing doubt in their eyes when they met? Would Dr. Howell ask her to leave—in her best interest, of course? Because as sure as she knew her own name, she couldn't deny that her past was coming at breakneck speed to ruin her present life.

But as she left, waving and greeting friends, she saw her world as it was and what it would become if her secret was revealed. A smoldering ember started in the pit of her belly, and by the time she reached the parking lot it had grown to a conflagration that caused her to try to rub away the pain.

Ava realized that she was going to fight this one. Yes, she was, but how and where was she to begin? It came as no surprise when she found herself not on the road home, but taking the winding streets through the suburbs of Florence, leading to a posh neighborhood of many Victorian-style homes occupied by the town's most affluent doctors, lawyers, and corporate executives. Winifred Whidby's was one of the most palatial.

Ava pulled onto the quiet block where silence was marred by a screech of tires. Someone was in a hurry, she thought. But she dismissed the small car that had barreled away as she noticed Winifred's red Mazda in the driveway.

"Ava?" Winifred's eyes narrowed when she saw her friend-turned-enemy coming up the walk. She'd been watching from the window as her visitor sped away and she wondered if the neighbors had noticed the hurried departure. She glanced in the foyer mirror and smoothed her dark hair, and before greeting her colleague, silently cursed the day she'd ever met the young professor.

"Please tell me," she said a mocking smile on her lips, when she opened the door, "you've been sent by an ecstatic president to inform me of the good news." She noticed her neighbor staring at her from across the street and she stepped back, ushering Ava inside. "Damn nosy folks," she muttered beneath her breath. "The scroll has been found. Thank the Lord!"

Ava watched her friend warily. What reaction had she expected? she wondered. Winifred did not look overly distraught and Ava wondered just what went on in the president's office that had the woman so confident and unperturbed.

"I looked for you," Ava said. They were in the

living room and Ava took a seat in a high-back lime-green brocade chair. "And no, the Vassa paper is still missing." She saw what was almost fear, but the look was so fleeting in the other woman's eyes that Ava was unsure.

"Pity that, isn't it?" Winifred said, a false smile on her lips. "So what does bring you to my part of town then?" Her eyes widened. "Surely you're not going to ramble on with more of your nonsense accusations."

"I'm trying to understand why you perpetrated the fraud initially, Winifred," Ava said softly. "Since the committee and Dr. Howell have agreed that it was an inside job, the stink has just begun and the eventual fallout will touch all of us. Before that happens, why don't you just quietly approach the president with what you've done? I'm certain that given your past performance and the high regard in which they hold you, you'll come out of this with a virtual hand slap. Everyone has skeletons and the scandal will pass."

Winifred's eyes narrowed as she stared thoughtfully at Ava. "Everyone? And do you have skeletons, Ava Millington?"

Her heart skipped as she invisibly shrank from Winifred's penetrating stare. But she said with ease, "I'm human," and hoped that Winifred accepted that response. She knew she'd failed when Winifred spoke.

"Hmm. What a profound truth." After a long look, Winifred stood. "I'm sorry to have to end this little do-gooder mission of yours," she said, "but I have an appointment that I mustn't be late for." She walked to the door and her silent visitor followed.

The false smile that she'd pasted on disappeared once Ava pulled away from the curb. Her look was dark as she walked to the den. A minute later Winifred was staring down at the cause of disruption in her world. The treated parchment, her one claim to fame from its very existence, appeared to taunt her. But she still looked at it proudly, almost as if she'd given birth. Indeed, it was her baby. Her invention. Now it had to be destroyed. Somehow that thought caused her pulse to throb. She'd think about it later she thought, and put it back in the desk drawer.

"Damn, damn, damn," she railed. She stood and paced the room. "What now?" There wasn't a thing she could think of to get out of this predicament. "Damn Ava Millington too!" she exclaimed, inner fury causing her eyes to burn with hate.

She'd been flabbergasted—but then again, knowing Ava she shouldn't have been—when the young woman entered her office confronting her so boldly, and in appearing on her doorstep with her high-falutin' notions.

Winifred had instinctively known that there would be trouble once Vassa's works had been selected as part of the touring exhibit of slave artifacts. She should have guessed that something like this would happen one day. As she was reminded it was she who'd pressed Ava into seeking a position at the school. There had been no alternative but to get rid of the evidence of her colossal fraud.

Fools, she thought. Her reputation at Floyd Compton was sterling and her deception had been so perfect that no one at the school would have suspected her of such dishonesty. The backup research she'd presented with her findings had been accepted without question.

She opened the drawer again and stared at the evidence of her transgression. "Why is this happening?" she whispered in anguish. "It's not fair!" She fingered the paper and then removed her hand before slamming the drawer closed.

She'd paid dearly for that ancient-looking parchment, going through clandestine, discreet measures to assure that the identity of the buyer was never disclosed. *Now, all for what?* she commiserated. To have her life ruined now? Where would she go and what would she do?

Anger surfaced, dissipating her self-pity. After all she'd been through, she wasn't going to let this little setback be her ruin. She'd fought her way out of a little town that time had forgotten in Alabama where, as a toddler, she could still remember the shack she'd lived in with a coal stove, crude plumbing, and a big iron bed that she shared with two other siblings. It had taken her years to quell the smell of the urine-soaked mattress from her nostrils. And that was in the very early sixties when civil rights were beginning to be aggressively addressed across the land.

She'd gotten her civil rights all right and she'd taken them and ran her brain and determination, affording her the opportunities for an excellent education. She hadn't been back to Alabama since. And she wasn't going to be chased from her comfortable world by a conscientious upstart who had the brains to exceed to spectacular heights. Her eyes narrowed. "Not on my back, Ava,"

Something nagged at her and after a moment she sat back drumming her bright red fingernail tips on the polished desk until it hit her. Winifred murmured, "Human, huh?" A tiny smile played about her mouth as her brain raced.

Her face a study of deep concentration, she opened a desk drawer, pulled out a slip of paper, and then punched in a mobile number. "Just hold off," she said through thin lips. "I have a plan." She listened, and then snapped, "I don't *know* how long. Circumstances have changed, in my favor, but believe me, this will work. So much for being human." A brittle laugh escaped as she responded to a question. "You wouldn't understand."

When she disconnected, she dialed 411 for information. "What city?" the metallic voice asked. Winifred smiled.

"Oh, no, what have I done?" Ava was driving slowly toward Minuet and where as before she was sure and confident in going to visit Winifred, now she felt overwhelmed—as if she'd invited a world of troubles by opening Pandora's box.

What she wanted now was a place to escape to, but for some reason, her small isolated house all of a sudden was not the refuge she'd come to know, but rather loomed large as a prison without bars. All her brave thoughts of standing her ground and toughing it out, refusing to be chased away again, were as ghosts that swirled around her head like laughing will-o'-the-wisps.

Miserably Ava whispered, "Where am I going to go? Who am I going to run to?" She had no one. But a small inner voice whispered back, "*Yes, you do.*"

Chapter Eight

Cole was sitting at an outdoor café in Hudson musing at his surroundings. Years before when he and his buddies sneaked off from school acting like toughs in a surrounding unfamiliar to them, it'd seemed like a large cosmopolitan town. Now the bustling city appeared to be the place to come to do big department store shopping and to eat in fine restaurants. It wasn't unlike a popular, busy neighborhood in downtown Los Angeles.

Cole had been in the town since noon, having a fish-and-chips lunch at a place touting its authentic English cuisine. It was six o'clock, and he'd just finished dinner at another upscale place with pale blue linen cloths on the small outdoor tables, and a crowd of tired but contented and successful-looking thirty- and forty-something's. Two-for-one cocktails at the happy hour disappeared and refills appeared magically. Cole appeared to be one of a few who was more interested in filling his belly with food than drink. But he sat sipping on an after-dinner gin-and-tonic as he glanced at his watch again.

She should be home by now, he thought, and he

wondered how she'd fared at work. Last night when he left her, he didn't know what to say or do to help her through her pain. He thought of Jack Thompson's words—*she needs your help*—and he thought of his own silent response. How could he help her when he didn't know how to help himself?

He sipped on his drink and barely tipped his head at the pretty brunette who'd been boldly giving him the eye over the shoulder of her male companion. But he looked away, refusing to be lured into something he wasn't ready for or even entertaining. Instead, sad dark eyes, a sensuous mouth, and tantalizing scents from warm smooth skin mesmerized his senses. Ava had touched something in the core of him, a feeling he hadn't had since he'd thought he'd fallen in love years ago when he was young and on shore leave while in the navy.

After the rebuff from his mother he'd been unconsciously looking for love and had finally found it, or so he'd thought. The cousin of a shipmate had opened his nose to where he thought the sex that they were having was the closest thing to heaven as he'd ever get. A year younger than he, she'd schooled him so thoroughly in the art of a thousand and one ways to do it and she'd done it in such a way that he thought he'd been the one to invent their bed gymnastics. He'd been all set to buy the ring when her cousin told him to grow up—that he'd been expertly played and when the ship pulled out she'd find the next sailor to run the same game on.

Cole remembered punching the guy's lights out, but later, a year and many ports later, after he'd grown up, he saw the lesson he'd learned, and was soon the expert teacher to unsuspecting yet willing nubile females. Once settled in his career in Los Angeles he'd loved and left 'em. No, he'd sexed 'em and left 'em. Love hadn't a thing to do with it.

But in Minuet he knew he wasn't about to run any games on Ava. No, if anything, to get his fix of sex, he'd have to look elsewhere. He knew he'd better act soon because once he got close to Ava the inevitable would happen. All his saintly resolve would disintegrate with the first touch of her skin, not to mention even getting close enough to suck on those sweet lips.

Every city had its red-light district and Hudson was no exception. Even during the daylight hours his keen eye had observed where the action was. Quiet now but once darkness hit, there would be no doubt at what could be had or bought, as the case may be.

While toying with just where he would start, he felt the stare and looked up to see the glare of hot brown eyes on his and he knew the brunette had given herself away with her shameless ogling.

"Damn," Cole muttered in disgust. Trouble couldn't help but sniff him out even as a stranger about his own business. When he saw the man's aquiline nose flare at the tips like some angered bull, he inwardly groaned. He'd come from L.A. to Smalltown to get whaled on again? Not today, he mused, and watched as the average-size man swaggered— or staggered?—toward him.

The man said as he stood over the small table, "What was that, 'bro?"

Now Cole's groan was audible as he stared up at the guy who had trouble standing still so that he pressed the palm of his hand on the table to steady himself. *So much for free drinks,* Cole thought. Liquid doses of braggadocio and chutzpah were a dangerous after-work exercise, he thought. Cole just stared, which seemed to enrage the man further. Cole could

see the guy had second thoughts about encountering
the big silent stranger but because he'd captured an
audience he wasn't about to back down.

"You see something that you want?" the man said,
tossing his head in the direction of the brunette who
was giving Cole smug looks.

Cole's insolent look covered the woman from her
pink-painted toes to her wavy mop of curls and then
swerved sharply back to her man. In a low voice, Cole
said, "Not today."

But the woman had heard the soft reply and her
jaw dropped while her eyes spit fire. Cole hadn't
been packing since he'd arrived in Minuet and instinct made him wonder if he should have. Now he
shifted in his chair to stand and his denim jacket
flapped open and his wallet fell to the floor, opened
with his shield in full view. He bent to pick it up, and
when he straightened he stared at the man whose
mouth went slack. When he moved his hand off the
table, straightening up and taking a step back, Cole
said evenly, "Anything else you want to ask me?"

Minutes later, after paying his bill, Cole was standing beside his car glancing up and down the busy
street. His taste for sampling the wares of Hudson
had soured and after one longer look he climbed
into his car. It was nearly seven and he hoped that
the white Camry was missing from his neighbor's
yard because his willpower had deserted him. He
needed to park, get inside his house, and sit his
behind in a tub of cold water. So much for taking
care of an itch that he couldn't scratch, he thought.

Instead of heading home as he knew he should
have, Cole stopped on a busy street and parked. A
liquor store was what he needed. Drinking at home

was better than risking a ticket, or worse, hurting an innocent stranger with tons of steel.

Leaving the store with bottles of Scotch, wine, and gin and one bottle of champagne for his brother's impending visit, he was stopped by a firm hand on his shoulder.

"No dressing, huh? So I guess that means you're healing fine."

Cole turned his head. "Fiona," he said as the woman came to stand in front of him. She looked at his bag and clucked. He ignored her silent recrimination. "Surprised to see you over here," he said. She was as beautiful as she'd been in high school and he guessed she knew it when with a smile she dismissed the admiring look from a passing male. "You practice in Hudson, too?"

"No," Fiona said, tossing her mane of hair. "My beauty salon is here and I take care of other business. This is a free day for me." She shifted a shopping bag from one hand to the other. "Thank God for evening and a breeze," she said. "That sun was brutal today." Another glance at his bag. "Having company to welcome you home?"

"No," Cole said slowly, an amused smile on his lips. "Just trying to make my house a home again after all these years. Yet, you never know," he drawled.

"Look, can we get out of the way?" Fiona said, after sidestepping another passerby. Without waiting for a response she led the way to a nearby sidewalk café and plopped her bag in a chair and sat in the other. She waved to a chair. "You're not in a hurry, are you?" she said. "Have a drink with me?"

Cole followed her commands and sat after setting his bag on the redbrick pavement beside his chair. When the waiter arrived, Fiona gave her order of merlot and looked at him. "Club soda with a twist," he said, and the waiter nodded and left.

With raised brow, Fiona said, "You're not still on antibiotics, are you?"

He shook his head. "I've eaten and drank, thank you. Anything more can wait."

Fiona took a deep swallow of her wine after the waiter set it before her and then stared at the handsome man sitting across from her. "So, how are you finding the old homestead, Cole? Planning on staying for a while or will you be heading back to that jungle you've been living in for all these years?"

Cole wrapped his hand around the cold glass, liking the sensation against his warm palm. He took a sip before answering. "It's a place to lay my head for now."

She bristled. "A place? Your family loved their home and you did too," she said accusingly. "I know Graham did."

He wondered when his brother's name would touch her lips. "Yes, we all did, Fiona," he said staring at her. "Even Graham."

Fiona flushed as she guessed what he was thinking. "Okay, so don't keep me in suspense, Cole. You know I'm dying to know. Tell me about him please."

Poker-faced, he said, "What would you like to know?"

Crimson nail tips drummed the table. "Is he married?"

He could hear her breathing stop. With a glance at all her rings on the fingers of both hands he said, "I thought *you* married."

A sigh escaped. "That's in the past," Fiona snapped. "Why on earth would I be asking about your brother if I had a man?"

Her hazel eyes were sparking and Cole shrugged.

"It's hard to tell about some women these days. Some just don't give a damn whose marriage they try to bust up."

"Well, I'm not married," Fiona said in a normal voice. She sipped more wine and gave Cole a long look and then sighed as she sat back. "I see you're not going to give up any information unless you're sure of my intentions." When Cole only stared back she said calmly, "He divorced me."

Cole merely looked.

"You remember my parents." It was a statement and she continued. "They still live in town but we don't see each other too much."

"I remember them," Cole said. Mr. and Mrs. Jesse Raymond, stern, churchgoing folk who'd kept a tight rein on their only child.

"Before I went to Meharry I got pregnant," Fiona said dully. "To a guy I didn't love. It was just sex. But I wanted my baby." Her eyes dropped and she stared into the wineglass. "My mother forced me to abort." She looked at Cole. "Long story short, I was looking forward to having more babies when I married Dr. Ronald Fitzgerald, a man I did love. Pregnancy never happened and never will. He wanted a legacy so he left me."

"Where does my brother enter in all of this?" Cole asked quietly.

"The last time I saw Graham was two years ago when he came to look after the house. We got together."

Cole was silent.

"Not in bed," Fiona said irritably. "Though I would have liked to," she added candidly. "He was seeing someone in Ohio and it never happened. But I thought I saw a little of that thing we had in high school and I think I want something to happen between us again."

"What if he wants kids, too?" Cole asked, staring at her expressionless.

"We can adopt. So many people do," Fiona said.

"Graham is not married," Cole said dryly. "The rest you'll have to deal with yourself."

Fiona saw that Cole was ready to drop talk of his brother and be on his way but she wasn't finished. She'd called Graham after he left Minuet but had gotten his machine. He never returned the call and she was too proud to call again. She'd thought that maybe he did marry that woman after all. But now . . .

"So will he be coming to town now that you're here?" she asked, giving Cole a direct look.

Cole dropped some bills on the table and then bent to reach for his bag. When he stood, Fiona had gathered her own bags and was standing watching him. "Graham said he had some time coming and would be driving down. But he didn't say when." His voice held finality and he knew she had gotten the message when she smiled and tossed her head, swinging a wayward curl from her forehead.

"Then I'm sure we'll be running into each other," Fiona said happily as she kissed the air around Cole's cheek. "You take care of yourself, Cole, and I'll be seeing you—soon."

Cole watched her walk jauntily to her turquoise Jaguar, pretending that the admiring male glances went unnoticed. He shook his head as he walked to his car in the next block. The sweet scent left by Fiona lingered somewhere around his chin and he unconsciously lifted a shoulder and swiped, as if that would dispel the smell. What did come to mind was another sweet scent—one that he knew would be with him long after he left Minuet.

* * *

Fiona pinned up her hair for the umpteenth time, playing with the soft tendrils, pulling them around her face, tucking them back, and posing this way and that. Then she would pull the whole thing down, letting the soft fragrant hair tumble about her bare shoulders.

She was standing in front of her bedroom mirror, naked except for scant panties. She dropped her hands to her hips and smoothed them as Graham had done in her bedroom when they were both sixteen. Her parents were at a late church revival meeting and she'd let him in and led him upstairs where they'd undressed each other. It was the second time for them after he'd taken her in the back seat of his car when he learned she'd ditched a boyfriend. Graham loved to play with her hair, entwining his fingers in it, and then he would run his big hands down her neck over her breasts and pinch the soft skin of her belly. He teased her, refusing to touch her there when he knew that's what she wanted, and just kept sliding his hands over her shapely hips. She was doing that now and just thinking of what he used to do to her was turning her on.

Abruptly Fiona dropped her hands and stared at herself. At thirty-five she was still in fine shape and could compete with any woman ten years her junior. The men she dated after her divorce and still dated did nothing to excite her, and ever since she'd seen Graham two years ago, her erotic dreams were filled with his face and touch.

Her glance strayed to her belly and her mouth twisted into a grim slash. When she thought that there would never be another child growing inside of her she felt an inner rage. If she and Graham married she would never feel his seed come to life, eventually bearing his child. All because of her parents, whom she thought of now with distaste.

She moved away from the mirror, and donning a soft short robe she padded barefoot into the kitchen of her condominium apartment and a minute later carried her chilled glass of wine into the living room where she turned on the television. The all-news channel wasn't computing because her thoughts were on her past and what her future could be like if Graham were in it.

What if he wants kids, too? Cole's words brought back a fresh feeling of instant rage toward her parents. After all these years the bitterness was as new as if it'd happened last week. She could laugh sometimes at how foolish she'd been, listening to her parents go on about disgracing them and their good name by bringing an illegitimate child into their home. Those mores had gone out the window years before Fiona was even born and her parents knew it but insisted on keeping up the phony pretense. Sometimes she felt a gnawing ache in her stomach and dreamed of cradling an infant in her arms. When she was in med school she made sure pediatrics wasn't her chosen field. Even now she excluded infants from her practice.

When she'd returned to Minuet after her divorce, she was incensed to learn of the two women who had children out of wedlock and had been accepted by the community, as if having bastard children was the best thing since man walked on the moon.

As a result she'd come to obsess over Monique Anderson and Teddie Perkins, both successful entrepreneurs. Why should they be blessed with children while she would never know motherhood?

Fiona smiled cruelly as she thought of the diner owner. Teddie never did understand why she'd come to be so disliked by Fiona. But Fiona remembered way back when in high school how she'd caught Teddie sending goo-goo eyes toward Graham, who hadn't even noticed the young kid. Even then Fiona was possessive, and she'd made some cruel remark to Teddie, who became embarrassed and fled amongst the titter of Fiona's friends. But now that incident was inconsequential as Fiona's dislike heightened when she'd learned of Teddie's son. She rarely saw the child because Teddie never allowed him in the diner. But on one occasion when Fiona had met him, she thought that he was the handsomest child she'd ever seen. Her dislike for Teddie had intensified after that.

She left the room, and after getting the bottle from the fridge, Fiona returned to her seat and refilled her wineglass. So many thoughts were crowding her mind, and she was too keyed to sleep.

One thing that she knew was that this time when Graham came to visit his recuperating brother, she was going to be on the scene. Now that she learned that he wasn't married, whoever he was seeing back in Ohio had better get ready to move on because she was moving in. Graham was a man after all and she already knew what pushed his buttons. She was sophisticated and mature and when holding her in his arms he'd come to see not the inexperienced teenager but a hot-blooded sensuous woman who knew all about loving him completely.

When Cole was driving, it was dark, past nine o'clock; he wondered just what Fiona had in mind as far as his brother was concerned. He couldn't help but amuse himself with several scenarios once Graham arrived. Thoughts of Teddie and her schoolgirl crush, which Cole believed had been carried over into adulthood, caused him to frown.

What if Graham finally noticed the pretty young woman after all these years and then had to contend with Fiona Fitzgerald? Because sure as midnight appeared each evening, he knew that the beautiful doctor was going to get her hooks in and he was certain it wasn't going to be a pretty thing to watch. He couldn't help but smile and shake his head at the dynamics. Minuet would never be the same and he was glad he'd be gone long before the dust settled.

When he pulled into his yard and parked it was pitch-black. Annoyed that he hadn't thought to leave a porch light on, he climbed out of the car and walked toward the steps when he stopped and looked over at his neighbor's house.

Funny, she always left a light shining and there was none. Not even inside. Yet he could see the shadow of her Camry in the darkness that enveloped her property as well. Feeling uneasy, he walked to the hedges and before stepping through, stopped and listened, allowing his eyes to adjust. Night sounds didn't bother him; it was the absence of human noises that made him alert. As long as he'd been home he'd never seen Ava's lights go out before at least eleven. Even then the night-light was left on.

The soft almost inaudible sound he heard chilled his flesh. Once more he thought about his weapon missing from his hip. Unmoving but listening, he heard the sound again and this time he moved toward the rear of the house praying that he sidestepped any twigs. If the front was dark, the back of the house was pitch-black, and when he stood by the side of the porch he peered into the darkness. Again he heard the sound and it was undeniably a moan. He moved forward and then he saw her.

Ava saw the dark form at the edge of the porch, and when it moved toward her she screamed.

The sound zinged Cole's eardrums, and when he reached her she started to get up and run while flailing her arms wildly. "Get away, get away," she screamed.

Cole caught her hands before she could whack him in the face again. "Ava," he yelled. "It's me, Cole. Ava!"

"Cole?" Ava was bewildered. She sagged against him. "Cole."

"What in hell is wrong with you, sitting out here in the damn dark?" He was holding her and her bare arms were like ice. "How long have you been out here?"

She couldn't stop shaking and he rubbed her arms trying to get the blood flowing. After a while she quieted and lifted her head. "What are you doing here?" she said.

He could have whaled her right then because of the way his heart was pounding. She'd scared him so badly that he didn't even know that he could feel whatever the hell he was feeling right now. If anything had happened to her. . . . He shuddered and then swore while holding her tightly. How had this woman gotten up under his skin so badly that the thought of any harm coming to her had him weak as an infant? Her soft sounds muffled against his chest turned his knees to jelly. All he wanted to do was make it safe; whatever had hurt her he would make go away. Her arms slid beneath his jacket and hugged his waist so hard that he caught a breath.

So many times he'd thought about holding her, feeling her breasts, her silky skin, tasting her, that he was half-nuts with thinking about it. And now here she was holding on for dear life and he wondered if he was dreaming. His voice broke with huskiness as her name on his lips stirred the still air. "Ava."

When she lifted her head, he swore softly and bent toward her. The first touch of her cool lips was as sweet as life-saving elixir to a dying, thirsty man and the shock wave that reached his toes nearly stunned him senseless. "Jesus," he said, and deepened his kiss.

When her mouth opened he found her tongue, so sweet, so warm yet so cool that he savored the taste, as if he'd waited an eternity for such a feast. He alternately explored, ravished, and caressed in response to her soft moans of pleasure. He found one hand moving from her waist sliding slowly upward over her curves just as he'd imagined doing, and when he touched one soft mound he moaned against her mouth. He slipped his hand under her cotton T-shirt, fondling her breast over the satiny fabric of her bra. Even through the thin cloth he felt the hard quivering nub. Craving to taste the ripe berry, in a quick motion he'd bared it to his mouth and tasted.

When his warm, damp, searching mouth closed over her turgid nipple, Ava swooned, straining into him so that he could have more of her. She was on her toes trying to make it easier for him to suckle. "Cole." Was that her? she wondered. The sound was so wanting, hungry, almost wailing in need.

How many times had she thought of being held in his strong arms, seeking the comfort that she craved? To feel those warm sensuous lips on hers, his big hands touching her, making her body sing a tune she hadn't heard in too long. She wanted, needed, everything that he was offering to her. She couldn't stop now if it meant life or death. Being gratified instantly was her only thought.

They didn't know who had started first but in a

flash the clothes began to disappear. Cole's jacket and shirt landed on the porch. Darkness was not a hindrance to what they needed and what they were about. Pants were shed and his shoes kicked away; her shorts and shirt were gone and they were standing in a moonless night, clinging to each other's nakedness. They were slow now as the wonder of what was happening was too profound for words. Touch was the only thing that mattered. They sank down on the cushioned summer lounge chair on the porch, their moans becoming too loud for the still, dark, night. There were no tentative soft whispers of love between lovers, but sounds of pleading from her and murmurs of mercy from him. She wanted to be fulfilled in every way, body and soul, and he wanted to be the one to satisfy her cries of want. In giving he was receiving and he thought he'd died and reached the summit when with one long last thrust into her, he buried his mouth in the soft warm flesh of her neck to muffle his cries. Her soft cries and moans had only increased his ardor beyond anything he could have imagined.

Ava felt his climax at that same instant that her own body jolted with pleasurable pain and then went limp with her own sated release.

It began and it ended. So fast.

Cole heard her soft catch of breath and realized he was squeezing the breath out of her. Reluctant to let go, he swung up and off, easing himself to the floor. In the dark, he reached for her hand and pulled her up. "Can we move inside?" he said gruffly.

Ava shivered. Not from the night that had turned chilly but from his touch. What was wrong with her? She'd lost her good sense. Standing naked with a man she'd wanted from the first moment he stared into her eyes from afar. She wanted him and the thought brought another wave of shivers from her head to her bare toes.

"Ava?"

She moved toward the door and into the house, and was about to turn on the light when she stopped. She was naked and so was he. How would he look at her in the light?

Cole was standing behind her, and as if sensing her fears he said quietly, "You go first. I'll dress here." He stepped back into the darkness and when he saw the hall light go on he began searching for his clothes.

Only after she'd washed and dressed in jeans and a long-sleeve sweater, did Ava stop midstride to go downstairs. No protection! Her body flamed with the consequences of their actions. He was as foolhardy as she. But then they hardly had a chance to discuss their respective health histories. She didn't even entertain the other possibility. She stifled the tiny sound. Too late for recriminations.

Ava found Cole staring out the kitchen window, his hands stuffed in his jeans pockets. He'd put the teakettle on and small spurts of steam hissed quietly from the spout. He turned and leaned against the sink. "I took the liberty. You were freezing," he said, watching her closely.

She entered the room and silently walked to a cabinet where she took down cups. From another cabinet she took a box of teabags and some sugar packets and set them on the counter. "Thank you," she said in a small, tight voice.

A low sound escaped through Cole's clenched lips. He closed the short distance between them and caught her by the shoulders, forcing her to face and look up at him. "Don't," he said harshly.

She stared into his eyes. "Don't what?" she whispered.

"Treat what we did as some dirty little mistake," he said. "Ava, the only thing that I'm sorry for is that I didn't protect you." He gave her shoulders a little shake. "The *only* thing. Do you understand me?" When she continued to stare he said, "I wanted you that bad that I couldn't think beyond the next nanosecond."

After a long moment standing staring at each other, she said, "Me, too."

They sipped their tea at the kitchen table. Ava had warmed some biscuits and thin slices of ham. It was nearly midnight when she glanced up at the wall clock above the refrigerator. She finished the last of her biscuit sandwich and sipped some tea. "It's late," she said.

Cole knew that but he wasn't budging, at least not until they talked, so he didn't answer, just drank the last of his tea, and sat staring at her.

Ava finally looked at him and then after a deep sigh said, "We knew that from the first day, didn't we?"

He didn't play dumb but nodded. "From the first," he agreed. "We both wanted."

Ava played with the spoon resting on her saucer. She didn't speak for a long time and when she did, her voice was firm. "I'm not sorry either, Cole." She looked away for a moment and then said, "Really."

"I'm glad."

She saw him flex his shoulder. "Did I hurt you?" His brow rose and she said, "I felt your scar and I thought I scratched it."

"No," Cole answered. "It's fine."

"Good," she replied.

"Ava?"

"I know," she said, holding up a hand before he could continue. "To answer your question of an hour ago, I fell asleep out there." She shook her head as if in disbelief. "It was warm when I sat down. I'd gone jogging until I exhausted myself. It was barely dusk when I cooled down and then I sat, wanting to think and clear my head, but I must have fallen asleep. I didn't know I'd be out there for hours, and when I opened my eyes it was pitch-black and when I moved, all my muscles screamed in agony at me. I groaned because it hurt to move." She stared at him. "Is that what brought you back there?"

"I was already investigating the unlit house," Cole said. "The sound brought me to the back." He gave her a pointed look. "I was worried about you."

She felt a pang of something she couldn't identify. When was the last time someone had said those words to her? It meant someone cared. "I—I had hoped you were home," she said. "I needed to talk—wanted—needed—you."

His lashes flickered and after a second he said, "So you ran?"

"Yes." She paused. "It felt good, and then I had to come home."

"What happened today, Ava?"

"The university was excluded from hosting the exhibit," she said. "There will be no shipment of artifacts arriving tomorrow." The words sounded alien on her lips and she wondered why she still couldn't believe it.

Cole could hear the dismay in her voice and saw the shadows on her face and he had that feeling again—that odd feeling of wanting to shield her from hurt.

"The Vassa theft?" He guessed that could be the only reason for so drastic an action.

"Yes. It appears that all the evidence indicates that the thief had access to the premises. The conclusion was that it was an inside job."

"Any suspects?" he asked quietly.

"Not yet," Ava answered. "I thought I had a brilliant idea after I left work." Her laugh was brittle. "I visited Winifred at her home, but apparently that was the wrong thing to do." She lifted a helpless hand. "I think I just succeeded in putting the spotlight on myself."

He could hear the annoyance in her voice. "What did you say?"

Ava spoke softly, reliving the events of her day, from the visit to the president's office to her brainstorm of trying to threaten Winifred. The mocking look on her face made Ava shudder. She'd messed up and wondered just how long it would be before her rash action would catch up with her.

Cole listened without interrupting but he knew how much she was berating herself. Without intending to, she'd sent some wheels turning. When Ava sat looking at him waiting for a response he said, "You gave her food for thought."

"I realized that too late."

"Are you certain that you never mentioned what happened to you?"

"I'm sure," Ava said. "You're the only one I've ever told."

He breathed deep. "She knows where you're from?"

Ava thought. "Yes," she said slowly. "When we first met I told her I was from Atlanta."

Cole grimaced.

"She suspects something, doesn't she?"

"You gave her something to chew on because you came on so aggressively." After a moment he said, "That was why you were looking for me."

Ava met his stare. "Yes. I need your help."

"Detecting?"

"Yes."

He pushed away from the table after glancing at the clock. "I'd better go and let you get some sleep." He eyed her. "You are going to work today, aren't you?"

She nodded. "I have to. My historiography class starts Monday. I have things to do." She stood also and watched him gather his jacket and wallet and she spied the shield. "You needed that today?"

"It's a habit," he said, and walked toward the back door. He thought about his earlier encounter. "It came in handy."

Ava knew why he avoided the front of the house. Again she wondered how was this hurting man going to help another hurting soul? She sighed heavily. Maybe doing what he'd been trained to do—helping and caring for others—would be just the balm for his aching heart. Maybe she was put in his path for a reason. After a while he would be healed and what of her? Could he help her shed her own years of hurt and anger?

"What are you thinking?" Cole asked. He was at the back door watching emotions play over her face. He reached up and brushed away a stray hair from her cheek. Very softly he asked, "Are you sorry now?"

Ava's skin tingled from the breezy touch. She looked up at him. "Not then, and not now," she murmured. She thought he wanted to say something but after a brief look he said, "Good night, then," opened the door, and left.

She lingered there for a long time, inhaling his smell and remembering the way her body had responded to his. It was as if she'd been there before, in his sheltering arms and it had felt so real and so right.

You did know where to run, didn't you? The whisper of the inner voice was not mocking but was almost content. And to her bewilderment, so was she. For some unfathomable reason her heart beat easier, the fears of the horrendous day beginning to subside. Somehow though she knew the tough days were still ahead she could face them now. *I was worried about you.* She had someone who cared what happened in her world.

As she turned out the light and went upstairs she didn't think about how long it was going to last; she only knew that having Cole standing with her helping her was what she needed to survive, at least to get her through the dark days to come. She knew without a doubt that she'd thrown Winifred a bone and the angry woman wasn't going to toss it away before gnawing every last bit of meat from it that she could, and if that meant targeting Ava as the thief then so be it.

I was worried about you. A smile was on her lips when Ava closed her eyes.

Chapter Nine

The morning air was sweet with the smell of fresh-cut grass, the drone of the lawn mower heard faintly in the distance as Cole stood on his front porch. It was early and she hadn't left yet. There was no way of telling what time she would leave because she'd driven away at different times almost every day. He was determined not to miss her, so he stepped off his porch and walked toward her house, easing himself through the hedges.

Last night was still a mystery to him, though a pleasant one. He'd surprised the hell out of himself, and her too he'd imagined, but neither as far as he could tell, had regretted their actions. He sure as hell didn't and he wondered where that was coming from. The love 'em and leave 'em man he'd been seemed so long ago. After last night he knew he wasn't ready to leave Minuet or Dr. Ava Millington, least not until he'd decided what he was going to do with his life.

Maybe Ohio, where his brother had been all these years, would be something new and different, and there would be a place for him there. But real estate?

He couldn't see himself sitting behind a desk, trying to sell an anxious couple their dream home that was way out of their means, and considering going into hock because of his expert salesman's spiel. He wondered if Graham were that kind of man. He knew that their father had been one dynamo of a businessman, starting his company from a little hole in the wall and making it grow into one of the best and well-known realty companies in Florence. Cole hadn't that kind of passion for the business and there was no need to pretend that he was his father's son that way. Any legacy was ended when his mother sold the business years before, soon after she moved to Las Vegas. Graham's interest in the field came when he used to spend his summers working with their father. But Cole needed movement, meddling into somebody else's business, trying to save them from their own destructive selves.

Some of his friends on the force had left in sheer disgust, finding new and different ways to earn a living. The wild streets and corruption that was everywhere had soured them to the point of giving up and moving on. Some had become private investigators and others had found prestigious work as heads of security in large corporations. One of the younger guys had even joined up and was now a sergeant in Uncle Sam's army.

As he'd done before, Cole mused about Jack's job offer of deputy sheriff. And then sheriff? From what he'd seen and felt about the town since he'd returned, Cole decided that Minuet was a good place to live. It measured up to any city big or small that he'd seen in his travels. He believed that he could live and work here again. The idea was intriguing, and challenging.

But Cole had to laugh at himself. Here he couldn't even get past a hurt that had kept him from his home all these years, and now he was thinking of saving the world, starting with his hurting neighbor. In front of her door now he thought that at least his meddling would keep him from dwelling on his own problems if only for a short space in time.

The door opened and Ava looked in surprise. She'd seen him coming and wondered. Surely he wasn't coming to offer regrets, was he?

Cole saw the shadow darken her face. "Good morning. Are you all right?"

Ava breathed and a small smile touched her lips. "Yes, but I should be asking you that," she said, concerned. "It's so early. Did something happen?" While she watched him, visions of entangled arms and legs flashed before her and she wondered if the warmth speeding through her would erupt into flames and scare the man away.

You happened, Cole thought. But he said, "How about having breakfast with me?"

"But I didn't even put the coffeepot on. I was planning to get something quick at the diner."

"Nobody ever does something quick at Perk's Diner," he said. "Mind some company?"

"No. I'd like that," Ava said. She stepped back. "Come in while I finish getting ready."

Cole hesitated. He gestured to the chair on the porch. "I'll wait here," he said. "The smell of this fresh morning air has been alien for a long time and I'll miss it."

Ava didn't close the door but left it ajar while she went to get her purse. His words threatened to dampen her mood but she squashed the somber feeling. Didn't she know that Minuet was just a stop on a trail that even he didn't know where it would end? She was determined to make the most of his presence while he was still here.

When she stepped out on to the porch and locked the door, she found him waiting by his car in front of her house. She went down the steps slowly and looked at him with a question.

"I haven't been into Florence yet," he said easily. "After breakfast I'll drive you there and drive you back when you're ready." She looked surprised. "Would that bother you?"

"No, Cole," Ava said. "That wouldn't bother me at all."

She felt strange having someone driving her around. In all the years she'd been on her own, she had done for herself, never wanting or needing anyone to chauffer her about. She loved the freedom of being in control. Once when being escorted to an affair by Hale he had told her that she would never be happy letting a man take the lead. But that night *he* was doing the driving. She remembered being a little affronted by the remark. Was she really as independent as all that? And it showed?

"You didn't tell me the truth." Cole's voice startled her. "Excuse me?" she said.

Cole sent her a quick glance. "You said that you were all right," he said quietly. "You haven't said a word and your right hand is in a fist." Another look. "Are you uncomfortable with me, Ava?"

Musing at his observation she uncurled her hand. The habit was an old one and was done unconsciously when she was thinking. "I'm glad you're here, Cole," she said. He didn't answer. Ava placed a hand over his and smoothed the tense knuckles. "Really." She felt him relax.

As he parked and was about to open the door, she stopped him with a touch to his bare arm. "Does our being together all day mean that we're going to make a plan for your detecting?" A smile played about her mouth. "You'll get to see the scene of the crime."

Cole's relief showed when he smiled. "You're going to do okay as a partner," he said. "That was my intent."

"What?"

He grinned. "I know the security is tight, especially now so I figured walking in with your eminence it would be a snap."

"Oh, you did, did you?" Ava said, laughing at herself, yet happy that she'd brought a smile to his face.

"Come on, lady, let's go eat." Cole was at her door to help her out and when he caught her hand he was reminded of just how much of her he'd held in the late hours of last night. And he wanted her now. She probably guessed where his head was at because she looked at him and smiled, her brown eyes sparkling with pleasure. "I'm really fine, Cole," she whispered. "I was then and I am now." She squeezed his hand. "Now let's go eat."

Inside, the diner was crazy crowded. A hostess was seating guests and Ava and Cole had a few minutes' wait. There were three seats at the counter but they opted to wait for a booth.

They looked at each other and both guessed that their thoughts were on that first morning they'd met in here. Ava thought that it was a long time ago.

She caught the eye of Teddie who was busy across the large room, and when her friend gave her a look, Ava smiled and looked away. When her glance swept across the crowd she met the eyes of Fiona who was staring at her with dropped jaw. And something on her face that she couldn't define. Cole was holding her elbow to keep her from being jostled by exiting customers and she had come to accept his touch as being entirely normal. But obviously that wasn't the case to one particular observer, she mused.

To Cole she said, "I think someone is trying to get your attention."

Cole followed her look and saw Fiona wave to them. She was sitting in "his" place as he'd come to think of the back booth. He waved back and gave his attention to Ava. "Old home week," he said as he waved to other familiar faces. Apparently this was the place for the hospital employees to stop on the way to work. It was just past seven-thirty and many were hurrying through their meal.

"I have a booth for you now," the hostess said. "This way, please."

They were led to the booth just in front of Fiona's who looked from Ava to Cole with an unfathomable stare. She ignored the words of her male companion while she gave the couple the up and down.

"Good morning, Fiona," Ava said as she sat on the side with her back to the doctor.

"Good morning, Fiona," Cole said, nodding to the man who nodded back.

"Cole," Fiona said with a smile on her pretty lips. "You're up early for a man of leisure. I'd think after our day in Hudson yesterday you'd be turning over at this hour." She played with a straying curl at her cheek as she stared up at him.

"You obviously thought wrong, Fiona," Cole said dryly. "Enjoy your day." He sat opposite Ava with a grim look. He had no doubt about Fiona's intent with her words and he snatched up the menu with impatience thinking that his brother was in for the ride of his life whenever he returned. He felt Ava's stare. He put down his menu and caught her hand. "Game playing," he said. "Understand?"

Ava felt the reassuring pressure of his big hand, heard the disgust in his voice and saw the sincerity in his eyes. He wanted her to know that there was nothing in Fiona's remark that could hold water. More than likely she was taking a chance meeting and blowing it into something that it was not—all for Ava's benefit. She'd known deceitful women like that before and Fiona fit the mold perfectly.

"Ava."

She returned the pressure and smiled. "I understand," she said softly. With a final tug she pulled her hand away and picked up her menu. "I'm starved," she said.

Teddie was nearly floored when she saw her friends waiting by the door, and she didn't miss Cole's proprietary hold on Ava. Nor did she miss the quick exchange between Cole and Fiona. She couldn't hear but she read the expressions and the body language and she smiled smugly to herself. Cole had given Fiona the brush-off.

"Hey, you two," she said as the waitress was leaving after taking their order.

"Hey, yourself," Cole said easily, giving her an appreciative look. She sure was a pretty woman, and if his brother didn't pick up on that, he needed serious head attention.

"Good morning, Teddie," Ava said. "How've you been?"

Waving a hand, Teddie said, "Busy. Isn't that great?" She grinned. "Just the way I like it. There's a convention in town and we're getting the overflow every day." To Ava she said, "Sorry I didn't return your call last night but Royce was hyper and was acting up. Had

a time getting him to settle in for the night. Is everything all right? Your voice was a little tense."

"Sure," Ava said. "Just wanted to talk." When she'd
reached home yesterday she needed to talk. There
was no one, so she ran herself into exhaustion. She
felt Cole's stare. "I'm just fine now." She willed her
body to behave.

"Good. I have to go, but why don't you two come by
for dinner tonight? We're having a fish fry. It'll be
fun." She turned to go and was stopped by Fiona's
voice.

"Fish fry, Teddie?" Fiona said. She was sliding out of
the booth. "So old-timey. Why don't you get with the
program like Chauncey's in Hudson? They have lobster night every Friday. You pick your own. I'm sure
you can handle that if you gave it some thought."

Teddie looked at Fiona. "Then I'm sure you can
handle missing Perk's Diner's old-fashioned fry," she
said. "There's something about lobster, though;
sometimes if you don't handle them right, they can
jump up in your face, their claws doing a number on
big mouths. That *would* be a bummer if you couldn't
speak for days. But if you gave it some thought, I'm
sure you can work it out."

Ava turned her smiling face toward the window as
Teddie left and Fiona and her companion walked
away, Fiona leading the way in a huff.

"Whew," Cole said, "was that little Theodora?" He
thought of Graham again and his mouth widened in
a big grin.

"Not the Teddie you knew?" She was curious at his
apparent amusement.

"Hardly," Cole said.

Their food arrived and they began to eat. Cole had
ordered the works and Ava's order was nearly identical,

except for the missing grits. But a stack of pancakes with eggs and ham would satisfy her hunger. As they ate neither spoke of last night but chatted about Florence and how she knew it and the changes that Cole could expect when he began his wanderings. They were comfortable and there was no tenseness about the new relationship. They appeared content and it showed in the easy way that they smiled or laughed at each other's comments.

"You would think it was a Saturday morning, the way I'm dawdling," Ava said. "I'd better get going."

"Okay," Cole said, taking the bill after leaving some money on the table.

They waved to Teddie who smiled and waved back when they walked to the cashier. As he drove, Cole said, "How about it?"

"What?"

"Up for fish tonight? Or you could select a place in Florence after you finish work."

The thought of ending the evening with him was inviting and made Ava satisfyingly warm all over. "Let's play it by ear," she said. "You might see a place that piques your interest."

Cole nodded. "Sounds good," he said after relaxing his body. She *wanted* to be with him, instead of *needing* his company and his detecting prowess. He settled in for the twenty-mile drive. "Sounds excellent," he murmured.

Cole dropped Ava off in the parking lot closest to the administration building where the faculty and president had their offices. He'd waited when she'd given instructions to the guard at the gate that Cole would be driving right back out after driving her to the front door. Identification tags were required, and since Ava had left her car home, she was given a temporary pass, which she put in his front window.

He watched as she walked into the building and then he left parking just outside the black steel gates. Cole settled down and observed. The parking lot had been renovated to make it larger as he noted the number of "monster" vehicles like his. Years ago the space wouldn't have held so many cars. Something must have been torn down to make room for two more parking fields that went beyond his sight in back of the building, but he couldn't remember what. On the other side of the parking field were more buildings that housed classrooms, labs, and a small separate building for the library.

Graham had studied here, and as his contribution to the community, their father, Richard Dumont, had been a guest lecturer on real estate one year, so the place wasn't completely foreign to Cole. When in his junior year, in order to be promoted, he'd had to take a makeup class in math that had only been offered here. His father had driven him each morning until the summer session ended. He'd never known of an archives room and probably wouldn't have cared back then. History wasn't his thing, but catching the eye of a pretty girl was. As he thought about it, college was the furthest thing from his mind, even before the death of his father. Then his mother would gently prod him to think about his future. If he wasn't going to follow in his father's footsteps there must be something that interested him she'd said. There would be times when she'd bring tapes home from work that the high-school students watched in hopes of selecting a career. Nothing had held his interest and he could see his mother doing a slow burn, her patience with him fast on the decline.

The administration building, which had been newly built when he was a teenager, looked the same except that it had been steam-cleaned, and now the stately looking brick preened proudly in its new red dress.

He guessed that because the sessions started Monday there was very little activity. The people arriving of all shapes, sizes and colors, and ages, he assumed were faculty.

Cole watched with a keen eye as people entered, parked and walked or sauntered inside where he could see from the distance another guard just inside the door, checking badges. No one looked the least bit familiar to him, and suddenly Cole felt as the stranger that he was. No one would recognize him either, the teachers he'd met, probably long retired.

An inside job was the determination he thought and they were probably right. As far as he could see from where he was, he couldn't tell if there was a bag search upon exiting. He'd have to ask Ava just how big this piece of parchment was, and, also if the guard would let someone pass on by without a search, depending on his or her status. It had been known to happen he knew and it sometimes resulted in a disaster occurring.

Cole started the car engine. They'd agreed to meet back here for lunch. Ava would introduce him to the vigilant guards as a friend, a visiting police officer from Los Angeles involved in community outreach and interested in culling information to bring back for study. He was always on the lookout for anything that would ignite a spark of interest in the youths. Anything that worked was like finding gold. It was a stretch but she'd promised to get the okay from the president and the curator.

Except for the guard just inside the gate who kept a sharp eye on his surroundings, Cole didn't see another soul. Yet he had the curious sensation of being watched. He flexed his shoulders and was alert to the chill that coursed down his neck. That was what he called his sixth sense. But after another scan of the lot and the building he pulled off, the sensation still with him. He was hesitant in leaving, with Ava alone to face whatever from her peers. The lunch hour couldn't get here too soon for his taste. He slowly pulled off and headed toward downtown.

Winifred had no idea who that was driving that big black SUV. She'd never seen it before. The man hadn't gotten out when he dropped Ava off so she hadn't a clue as to his identity. She just saw a pair of brown hands on the steering wheel and a strong-looking arm resting on the door as he drove through the gates. He'd stayed there for a long time, unmoving, and she'd gotten the queasiest feeling. She'd wished for a pair of binoculars so she could just see who the mystery man was. Ava had never mentioned that she was seeing anyone and the whole scenario came as a shock to her, slamming her with a slew of questions. Was Ava's car disabled all of a sudden? It seemed to be working fine yesterday when the little snippet paid her that unexpected Pollyanna visit.

She wondered if Hale had seen the little to-do and if he would now stop panting after Ava like a silly puppy. He was so obvious in his actions that it was downright annoying to watch, she thought. Months ago when she'd observed his infatuation, she'd been envious of the bachelor's attentions toward the new professor. She'd dismissed the odd inner stirrings as being childish thinking she wasn't a cradle robber. Even if she was, was she piqued because Hale Trotter never gave her a second look?

While she watched the big car move off something nagged at her, and then it hit her: her plan. Suddenly excited, she inhaled deeply and hurried to her desk. Already logged on to her computer, she pulled up the faculty schedule and searched for Ava's name. Since the cancellation of the exhibit, things had changed. Ava was scheduled to attend two meetings, and looking at the roster of windbags, Winifred knew that they were both going to be hours long. Ava also had to go to neighboring Francis Marion University today to interview a student intern, a last-minute replacement who would be working with her this summer.

Not even about to question her good luck, Winifred pushed away from the desk, still staring at the screen. If she moved quickly she would have time to do what she needed to accomplish before Ava left for the day. If she were careful, everything would fall into place. Smiling smugly, she turned off her PC and then reached for her purse.

"Never give up hope," she murmured as she looked into the small pocket mirror, patting a stray hair back into place. Thoughts of Alabama flashed across her mind. Her eyes darkened as she snapped the mirror closed. "*I* will be the survivor out of all this, Ava."

"Are you sure we're in a school cafeteria?" Cole asked. He pushed away his empty plate and finished the last of his ice-cold lemonade. He swore that had been the real thing and not watered down concentrate from a plastic carton.

Ava smiled. "Dining hall," she corrected, and then surveyed the pleasant room. "The alumnus," she said. "We have a great fund-raising team with Dr. Howell at the head. He's the best. But then we have a group of alumnae who insist that this is their baby, and nothing is spared. What the committee asks for, they get. Plus, of course not to leave out the great culinary program that brings students from all over. Our graduates work in prestigious hotels and restaurants all around the country. You just sampled their course work."

"Students?"

She nodded. "All but the master chef who oversees the kitchen operation."

"Are we still going to be here around dinnertime?"

"No," Ava said. "Sorry, but except for beverages and a dessert table later on, the kitchen is closed after lunch during the summer." She looked at his empty plate. "You really enjoyed that, didn't you?"

"What wasn't to like about baked ham in raisin sauce, candied sweets, seasoned *mean* greens to beat the band, and flaky biscuits?" Cole said. "When you said 'cafeteria,' you didn't know what I had in mind. Certainly nothing like this was present in my day."

Ava looked surprised. "You went here? I had no idea you attended college." She thought of her words and was flustered. "I didn't mean that the way it sounded," she said.

"No offense taken, Ava," Cole said. "You know I left Minuet the minute I finished high school." He shrugged. "I got my sheepskin while traveling with the navy." He changed the subject. "So, are we going to take our tour before your next meeting?" he asked.

He looked away from her when he felt a stare and turned to catch a woman looking his way with interest. When she smiled he nodded and then looked at Ava who'd followed his gaze. She waved at the woman. "Who's that?" Cole asked.

"The curator," Ava said. "She'll meet us at the archives and is looking forward to showing you around." As she spoke, Emily got up, waved at them, and left the dining hall.

Cole looked at the retreating figure, and when she disappeared he gazed around the room. His sixth sense had kicked in: he was being watched. Or had been, he mused, staring at the wake of the curator.

The archives room wasn't like anything Cole had envisioned. He couldn't ever remember having visited one. What he'd expected was a small dark room rather than a well-lit very large exhibit area with polished oak floors, several glass cases holding various items from objects to papers, and against the walls more glass-enclosed cases. Many of the cases and much of the wall space was empty and he observed the bareness, realizing that he was looking at the prepared spaces for the coming exhibit that was never to be.

Beyond the space he could see another room that held a reference desk at which no one sat. There were tables and chairs that could hold at least twelve people doing research and shelves stacked with boxes and envelopes. He could see two enclosed separate cubicles with desks filled with papers and all sorts of reading materials. This room was carpeted, muffling footsteps so it was almost reverently quiet. There was no one in the room except Cole and Ava who'd swiped a key card to enter. There was a guard sitting at a desk just

outside the archives door who checked Ava's ID and
Cole's after observing his visitor's pass.

"Where's the curator?" Cole asked, surprised that
they were alone. He'd expected more security than
this, but his sharp eye had taken in the setup even
before he spoke.

"Emily Thiessen," Ava said. "She sent word for me
to do the tour. Something has come up and she had
to leave. She trusts me to do a thorough lecture."

Cole saw that she meant to sound light but he noticed the shadow flicker across her face. They had
walked back into the archives space and his glance
went slowly around the room until it rested on a
small waist-high rectangular case. Its top was slanted
on an angle so that the contents could be viewed
without having to bend over. It was empty.

Ava saw his look. "No, this didn't house the Vassa
document, but another piece of history that was important in Florence's beginnings," she said, walking
toward it. Standing in front of it she looked down in
deep thought. "The Vassa paper was back there." She
gestured to the search room that they had just left.

After a minute Cole said, "What are you thinking?"

"Since I started working here, I've been on this
floor and in these rooms but twice, except for when
I was down here with the curator planning for the
exhibit. I never knew that this institution had acquired such important documents. I was only intent
on whatever project had brought me here for further research and just gave a perfunctory glance at
everything else around." She shrugged. "Some historian. So into my own world I didn't have time to
stop and study the place where I intended to make
my home. That's like building your glass house on

the edge of a golf course; a wayward ball shatters a pane and the whole thing tumbles in on you."

Cole was thoughtful. "Only twice?"

She nodded and looked at him curiously. "Why?"

"Then how were you to give me an expert tour if you're unfamiliar with the things that are in here?"

Ava made a helpless gesture with her hands.

"Who was it that gave you the tour?"

"Winifred," Ava said slowly as she remembered that first time. "She opened the door and waved her arm around and said, 'Well, this is it, honey. Not what you're used to after all your grand travels.'" Ava's eyes narrowed as she thought about that day. She looked at Cole. "I just followed her lead and looked around the room, and when we strolled to something that she wanted me to see she spent the rest of the time explaining what else was in the room and where I'd find stuff if ever I needed to research something else." Ava led Cole back into the reference area and the search room and pointed beyond some shelving. "Around that wall are more acid-treated manuscript boxes holding folders and papers filled with research materials."

"And the second time?" Cole asked already guessing the answer.

"Winifred accompanied me again, showed me what I needed, and then proceeded to take some materials of her own to study, saying that she'd put it off long enough."

"You didn't think that odd?"

"Not really," Ava said and lifted a hand. "Winifred was always putting off things until the last moment. She liked living on the edge. She called it saying that she performed best under duress."

"She never left you alone?"

"No, although I was seated at one carrel and she was at the other where we could both see the other." She saw his look and pointed to the two cluttered desks. "Carrels," she explained, "is where the curator and her staff can work quietly. Sometimes the space is given to a visitor who needs enclosed quiet away from the other tables. We finished together and left." Ava frowned. "Funny how you don't put stock in some things until you're forced to," she said.

"Like what?"

"How she kept coming into my carrel to see that I was still bent on my subject," Ava said. "You know, making excuses for being nosy?"

"I know the feeling," Cole said. Then, "Why wasn't the curator your guide?"

"Emily was at an out-of-town seminar."

"You never had the need to visit the room again?"

Ava shook her head. "No. I always had it in the back of my mind to spend some time in here but in these two years I never got around to it." She grimaced. "I've had a good look now," she said.

"So where was the Vassa document kept if not on full view, given its importance?" he said dryly.

She gestured to the stacks. "In one of the cataloged boxes with other documented historical letters of the period."

"Serious?"

Ava laughed. "Serious," she said. "Can you imagine if everything of importance had its own glass case? Curators and archivists use these acid–treated boxes and envelopes, all specially made to hold certain size papers, and they're categorized in kind."

He shook his head in bewilderment. "What's the point?" He smiled. "Don't even start to explain," he said. Cole wanted to touch her lips just then, and he did, bending his head quickly before she could object. He tasted and then made a small greedy sound. "I couldn't resist," he whispered, and then said softly, "Don't worry, no one saw. Your rep is safe." He tweaked her nose before moving away.

Ava wanted more and she knew he knew it when he gave her a knowing look—with a promise attached—and then he turned serious and walked around the room silently surveying the layout. She watched as he studied this and that, walking around the bend and staying there for about five minutes before walking back to where she was standing. He was so into what he was doing that he was almost impervious to her presence.

She watched his strong hands run over the cold glass and she thought of how they had handled her the night before: so gently, yet hungrily, giving her what she needed to feel sane again. It was almost as if she was telling him the places to touch, to kiss, to linger, each time making her swoon like a dying swan. He'd known her body like he'd loved it all her life. His voice startled her out of her remembrances.

He looked at her curiously when she didn't respond. "What's wrong?" he asked.

"I'm sorry," Ava said. "What did you say?"

"Just that Winifred must have been in stroke territory while she was watching you in here," Cole said. "I can't even imagine her not doing away with the evidence of her deceit once she knew you were going to be working here."

"I know," Ava agreed. "I couldn't understand that either."

A sound of disgust escaped. "I don't think that she's sitting around twiddling her thumbs since your crusading visit yesterday," he said. Cole cocked his head. "If you want my opinion, I think the woman just stuck it in her briefcase and marched right out with it." He gestured. "Just look at the security," he said dryly. He gave her a direct look. "Have you heard from her since you've been here today?"

"No," Ava answered, wondering why there had been no sign of the woman. She was certain that the buzz was all about when she'd brought Cole into the dining hall. Winifred would most certainly have put in an appearance if only to look over Ava Millington's lunch date. Even Hale had stopped by this morning curious to know what had happened to her car. He'd been fishing and Ava had to smile at his crestfallen look at the mention of "just a friend."

After they left the archives Ava walked with Cole to the entrance where they parted and she went to her meeting. The university was providing a car to shuttle her to and from her appointment at Francis Marion and she told Cole that they would be ready to leave for the day around five-thirty or six o'clock.

When he drove off Ava had the strangest feeling that something was about to happen. All the fears of the past week surfaced to make her skin crawl. It wasn't like Winifred to be silent about Ava's unexpected demand and Ava believed that Cole was right: Winifred wasn't sitting around watching soap operas; she was up to something, and Ava began to worry. She appeared to be the picture of confidence when she walked briskly down the hall to the elevator, but her knees were weak and her breathing shallow and she wished that this day was long gone.

Later, at six-thirty, Ava and Cole were having dinner in a seafood restaurant, Cole had scoped out earlier. It was a place that Ava had eaten in several times and the food was always delicious. She could never pass up the lump crab cakes that were the real thing and not crammed with bread fillers. Cole was enjoying a whole fried catfish.

"You think Teddie will forgive us this time?" Cole asked, thoroughly satisfied with his meal. "I think she was expecting our appearance at her fish fry."

"I think she will," Ava answered. "She's probably so busy she won't even miss us. There'll be others, I'm sure. It's summer and she does well with the gimmick."

"Then I'll pick you up about six next Friday?" Cole said easily.

Ava didn't answer right away but finished the last of a buttery biscuit and sipped some ginger ale. "Is your wound healing nicely, Cole?" she asked.

Puzzled, Cole looked at her sharply and then said, "Why, Ava?"

"I think you said something about leaving when you were better, that you would be going back home." She wasn't smiling when she said, "Will you even be here next Friday?"

His eyes darkened and his body tensed, his hands balled on his thighs. "What are you getting at?" he said in a low voice.

"That last night was, well, last night," she said, meeting his unwavering stare. "You agreed to help me expose Winifred and now, after you've seen the scene of the crime, I expect you have something concrete to tell me so that I can finally relay my suspicions to Dr. Howell. That shouldn't take but a few days I imagine, long before next Friday gets here." She lifted her shoulders. "And then you'll be gone. I don't expect anything else just because of what we—well, because of last night."

"Are you finished?" Cole's voice was as icy as his eyes.

"I have nothing else to add," Ava said with a lift of her chin.

His glance flickered to the tables around him filled with hungry diners who appeared to be minding their own business, but Cole knew how voices carried. "You picked now to ask me that and you want an answer, here?" he asked softly.

Ava suddenly wasn't as bold, and no, she didn't want his answer here where she'd be mortified by smirking diners. She said as calmly as she could, "No."

"Then let's go," Cole said, signaling for the check.

When they were in his car there were at least five minutes of silence before either spoke. Cole's voice was husky when he said, "I was feeling you last night, Ava. There's no denying that, wouldn't you say?"

In the dark Ava nodded and said, "Yes, I could say that."

"And you could feel me too," he stated.

"I definitely felt you too," she murmured.

"Then why in hell did you think I took so long in making a move on you?" he said harshly. "I didn't want to, because yes, I *was* getting out of here as fast as I could. I also knew that you weren't the one-night stand that I would probably wind up having before I left Minuet. I've wanted you since I first saw you flash those big beautiful anger-filled eyes at me. I've had you and it was just a teaser. I want more of you. Even now. Do you think when you opened that door this morning that I didn't want a repeat of last night? Being near you is killing me." He braked when he pulled up too close to another car.

"Christ." He slowed and then pulled onto the shoulder. "I would have been better saying my piece in front of the restaurant," he said gruffly. He glanced at her and she was staring at him with bewilderment, her lips parted slightly.

"Oh, hell," he said, and unbuckled his seat belt, and in an instant had pulled her to him. His mouth closed over hers hungrily, tasting her sweetness, and when she responded his kiss deepened as though it was to last for a lifetime.

Ava met his onslaught with all the passion she'd felt last night while in his arms. She was kidding herself big-time when she thought it was a passing moment, something that she thought she needed to ease her anguish. No, she realized that she wanted him for all the right reasons. She was falling in love with a stranger who'd touched her heart from the first day they'd met. There was no denying what her mind was telling her and her body was feeling. She welcomed his probing tongue and his hands on her breasts and she strained into him, wishing she could feel all of him.

A car horn blared as it passed and Cole groaned, releasing her reluctantly. "There must be a state law against doing this kind of thing out here," he said huskily.

"There is," Ava whispered as she straightened her dress.

"Then, is there something that we can do about it?" he asked, staring at her before starting the engine again.

"Yes, and I know of a place," Ava said, her breathing coming a little easier now. "We can be there in another fifteen minutes."

Cole buckled up. His voice sounded hoarse when he said, "I think I can make it in ten."

Chapter Ten

"Let me," Cole said in a hushed voice. He wasn't hurried now as he rained gentle kisses on the nape of her neck. He held her with her back to him as he unzipped her dress, one hand wrapped around her, fondling the fabric-covered mound, while anticipating in seconds its nakedness. The dress fell to the floor between them and he felt her squirming to face him. "Let me hold you like this, Ava," he whispered. She quieted, a small sigh escaping. He was holding her bare waist now and, reluctant to stop fondling her breast, he used both hands to unhook her brassiere. When it dropped, his hands slid to her panties and he eased them down and over her hips and they landed with barely a sound at their feet. He was holding her now, tightly against his chest; his eyes closed, and chin resting on her head. Her hair had tumbled down and covered her neck and he pushed the soft mass away with his mouth and nuzzled her there.

"Cole," Ava murmured. Her arms were immobilized beneath him and it was all she could do to contain the scream forming in her throat. His slow hand was torturing her beyond comprehension. Cole was naked except for his underwear, and when her fingers skimmed his bare muscled thighs and his chest hairs tickled her back she thought her passion would overflow. When she felt his fingers touch the heated place between her thighs the fire inside her became a bubbling seething volcano on the verge of erupting.

They were standing between the bed and the dresser and Cole, without releasing her, turned so that they faced the mirror in the lighted room. He moved his hands to her shoulders, and when her eyes met his in the glass he said, "See how beautiful you are?" he rasped. "I had only imagined it when I first saw you. And last night in the dark my hands told me what I already suspected." He kissed the tip of her ear. "And now I know." He said huskily.

Ava could feel the warmth in her groin speed to heat her face. No one had ever called her beautiful before. Her heart swelled with desire for this man who hid this gentle side of him. She caught his hand and still staring at him through the mirror she said, "Love me, Cole."

Unable to resist the soft plea in her voice and her eyes, Cole groaned and easily lifted her up in his arms and carried her the few short steps to her bed. He removed his underwear and kicked them aside. Uttering a soft oath, lest he mess up again, he quickly retrieved his pants, found what he wanted, and was back by the bed in seconds. He sheathed himself and with one look at her parted lips, her hair flowing against the pillow, her expectant look, with a small grunt he eased himself on top of her. "You're my beauty," he whispered.

"Oh," Ava exclaimed as he settled over her, his

hands doing their magic again all over her body while his mouth was busy caressing her eyes, her ears, her nose. And when he took her nipple between his lips she bucked against him. He'd known her sensitive spot and was milking it greedily. "Cole," she murmured, "you're killing me." She was jolted when in answer, with his fingers, he entered her private place and slowly massaged. Last night he'd been explosive and now he was gentle and pleasing, trying to give her all the pleasure. She wanted him inside to quell the fires that were white-hot with her passion. Ava touched his penis, and when he jumped and swore, she guided him inside of her and thrust her hips upward. "Now, Cole."

There was no mistaking that demand and with Ava's legs wrapped around his thighs, Cole thrust. The sound that burst from his lips was almost primal when his deep penetration brought a wanton response from her. He thought he'd never been to where she was taking him in her uninhibited passion. His name on her lips was like balm to a hurting soul—his. Though unspoken, he knew what was in her heart and it scared him but he selfishly accepted all she was offering and he gave her what she pleaded for; he loved her.

It was ending and Ava could feel it. She felt as though she were falling out of the heavens as her body went limp. But even as her legs fell away from him, her arms stayed clasped around his chest. Unmindful of his bulk, she wanted the wet warmth of his body to cloak her forever. She felt safe here. Yet something in her brain told her that this, as was last night, was a fleeting moment; there would be no more. Not like this. She'd given him her all and he'd known it because after a brief hesitant moment he went wild inside of her. Could their minds have linked and he'd caught her thought that she was falling in love with him? She didn't want to believe he'd push her away now, but her gut was never wrong. She felt him sag against her with a last deep shudder.

Cole was lying full-length against her, his hands caressing her cheeks while he stared down at her. She stared back, and what she never said he saw in her eyes, although briefly, for she blinked and it was gone. But he knew.

"Hey," he said softly. "Did I hurt you?" He guessed that she hadn't been with anyone in a long while. When she softly denied it, he eased himself to her side.

Cole was silent as he finally looked around his surroundings. Earlier, when he'd parked, and was about to walk up the front steps, emotions had swirled inside of him like a ball of confusion. He'd thought that her "place" was full of ghosts that threatened to rob him of his passion once he entered. But then he'd looked over at *his* place and thought of the ghosts in there too. Where could he love her in peace? he'd thought. She'd seen his uncertainty and had murmured, "It will be okay, Cole. We can use the back door." He'd looked at her, and something had surged inside of him that he'd never felt before, even when he thought he'd been in love all those years ago. He'd bent and kissed her lips and then took her hand. "The front door," he'd said.

But the front door and the foyer closet didn't cover it. He and Graham had chased little Curtis all over this old unwanted house. The toddler's soft calls and giggles were everywhere, in every room of this house. He shuttered his eyes and sighed. Was there no escape? he asked himself.

He felt Ava's hand take his in hers. She squeezed. Then she touched his cheek and murmured sleepily. "It will be okay, Cole."

When she burrowed into him her head nestled in the crook of his arm, he saw the easy rise and fall of her chest. She was asleep.

After a few moments, Cole left the bed and went into the bathroom where he dashed cold water over his face. He stared at himself in the mirror for a long time. He returned to the room and stood watching her sleep as he pulled on his underwear and slipped his T-shirt over his head. There was a chair in the room and he sat in it after glancing at the clock. It was just past eleven and she would probably wake up before morning. How would she feel if he'd spent the night in her bed?

Cole had had sex with women in their "places." He'd spent the night at one of them but once, and he'd never brought them to his home. There was something about having intercourse and then waking up beside a stranger that left him feeling sour.

But as he looked at Ava he knew that this was different. If he got back in that bed he would never want to leave it—or her. And that wasn't in his plans. He wanted to love her, needed to love her in order to keep his sanity, but what demons he carried inside of him was nothing to offer someone that he loved. The thought jolted him. Yeah, he thought, he'd fallen for the thoroughly loved woman sleeping just steps away.

Quietly he finished dressing and when he was tying his shoes he heard her.

"Cole," Ava murmured. "You're leaving?"

He walked to the bed and sat beside her, and bent to kiss her lips. "Go back to sleep, honey," he said.

"I'll see you in the morning." He kissed her again and left.

"In the morning," Ava said dreamily and closed her eyes.

Saturday morning at seven-thirty Ava was in her backyard doing cool-down stretches. Instead of taking her usual route into town and ending with breakfast at Perk's Diner, she'd gone in the opposite direction and had run for only twenty minutes. She'd foregone her first cup of coffee before starting out and now she was starving and craving that initial jolt of caffeine. A he-man's meal was in order for her expected guest, and the thought brought a small smile to her lips. She remembered his whispered words: *I'll see you in the morning.*

She'd awakened before dawn and had lain in bed for a long time, thinking about last night. She'd made incredible love to an incredible man. And he'd loved her back. If she ever had to pick a moment in time to regret it certainly it wouldn't be this one. Never. Even when—and she knew he would—Cole Dumont decided that Minuet held too many ghosts for him to stay and plant roots again, and left all that they would have shared, she'd especially hold the last hours dear to her heart until the day she died.

Breathing hard from her workout, she unlocked the back door and went inside. She put the coffeepot on and went upstairs to shower. Twenty minutes later she was in the kitchen frying bacon, and when the doorbell rang her heart skipped a beat. The hungry man had arrived, she thought as she went to the door.

"Teddie?" Ava stepped back to let her friend in.

She quickly lost the happy smile. "What's wrong?" she said, seeing the look on Teddie's face. "Come on back. I have bacon on."

"Smells good," Teddie said as she followed Ava. She walked to the cupboard and got a mug and filled it with the hot coffee. She sat at the table and drank the brew black. "Still rivals mine," she said appreciatively, and staring at the meat that was now on a platter, she said, "That's a whole lot of bacon for little old you. Who else is coming?"

Ava sipped from her own mug as she joined her friend. "My neighbor," she said.

"Mrs. Lansdowne?" Teddie sputtered. "Since when—" She stopped when she saw her friend's tiny smile. "Cole?" At Ava's nod, she said, "Well, I'll be!"

Ava said, "Will you stay?"

"Not on your life, sweetie. Don't let it be said that I was the one to stop something before it got started." She looked suspiciously at Ava who took that moment to bring the big mug to her face. Teddie grinned. "Uh-huh."

"Never mind," Ava said, a little embarrassed that her sharp-eyed friend had guessed what was up. "Now's not the time, okay?"

"You made an excellent choice," Teddie said softly. "You won't be sorry."

"I won't be," Ava said simply. But then she gave a worried look to Teddie. "Something brought you out here this early. Is Royce okay?" she asked.

Teddie nodded. "He's great," she said.

"Tell me," Ava said, gently.

"Remember the guy I told you about from Fashion Avenue in New York City?" Teddie said. Ava nodded. "Well, he's here."

"What?" Ava had known for over a year that

Teddie's clothing designs that she sold through Monique's shop had been doing serious business. One of her biggest buyers was from a successful designer with a famous house. As a matter of fact he *was* the house.

"He showed up last night unexpectedly at my fish fry," Teddie said. She looked suspiciously at Ava. "I missed you and Cole," she said coyly and then grinned again. But the smile quickly disappeared. "He wants me to come to work for him."

Ava almost dropped her mug. "What?"

"True. All true."

"I don't know what to say," Ava said. "I—I'm happy for you but . . ."

"You think it would be a mistake," Teddie finished for her.

"No, no, no," Ava said. "How could you even think that? For goodness' sake, you have a talent that's been buried here for years and you desire to create more than anything." Ava had mixed emotions. "I'm thinking of myself. I would miss you like crazy. What would I do without you?" A lump caught in her throat and she turned away because her eyes were stinging. Her world was changing, she thought, and so rapidly. Her academic career was in jeopardy. She was falling in love with a man who would love her and leave her. Her best friend would embark on a new career in a faraway place. She closed her eyes briefly, as if that would put back everything the way it was.

"Ava," Teddie said when she saw the anguish. "I haven't gone yet." She tried to make it light but her voice was tight. "I don't know what to do," she said. "My life has always been here. Royce doesn't know anything else. I have no one in New York City. No family or friends to look out for us. What if Royce gets sick? I'd be scared to death for both of us in that great cavern of a place." Her voice broke. "Minuet is our home."

Ava felt her indecision and she reached over and held her hand. "But it's something you've dreamed of, Teddie," she said. "It's an opportunity of a lifetime. If after a year the man comes begging to your doorstep to offer you a job, he's not just puffing smoke, is he?"

"No. He's for real. I've seen the contract, the perks, and the money offer. I'll even have an apartment for a year until I'm settled into a place of my own."

"You've been discovered, girl." Ava squeezed her hand.

Teddie looked miserable. "Gee, thanks," she said with a weak smile. "All this time I've been happy just doing my thing, sending a design to Monique's, and forgetting about it. I was happy doing that because I never dreamed it would turn into something too big for me to comprehend. Or to change my life so drastically! Why should I have to leave town to become a name?"

Ava smiled. "Because you'll be in the environment where you can make fantastic things happen. You'll be seen and become a fixture on Seventh Avenue. It will be your only job without worrying about keeping the diner afloat. Besides, you've got the business to the point where Roonie and Allan can run it sleepwalking."

Teddie laughed. "I can just see that now."

"Look," Ava said, "why don't you think about it some more before making a decision? If this is something you really want, we can do a think-tank thing—you know, do a pro and con for all the reasons you'll accept and decline the offer. What do you say?"

"Sounds like a plan," Teddie said. She stood. "You know, Robert will be coming by the diner tonight. Why don't you stop in? I'd like for you to meet him. Monique has been doing business with him for over a year and now that she's met him she feels he's the real deal." She put her mug in the sink. "I really would like that. Do you think you can make it?"

"I'll be there. Just tell me what time."

"Seven is good." Teddie heard the footsteps on the back porch and she looked curiously at Ava. "Cole?" she asked.

"Yes," she said, without explanation and went to the fridge. "I'd better get these eggs on. Sure you don't want to stay and eat with us?"

"No," Teddie said. "I've got to get going." She waited while Ava went to open the door for Cole. When he entered the kitchen she said, "Hi."

"Saw your car," Cole said. "Everything all right?"

"Sure. Just had to run something by my friend here," Teddie said, and glanced at Ava. "Tell him for me, will you, please? I've gotta go." She smiled at the handsome man who was looking mystified. She gently touched his arm. "I'm glad you've come home, Cole." As she walked down the hall to the front door, she called back, "Maybe I'll see you tonight?"

Cole watched Ava deftly crack open eggs and whisk them before pouring them into the hot frying pan. He couldn't help but stare at the woman who'd been in his thoughts since he'd left her. She was in his mind in his heart and she was making him crazy. "Can I help?" he asked softly.

Ava flushed from his bold stare. "No, everything is ready," she said, moving quickly from the stove to the table, setting dishes down and pouring coffee.

Cole went to her and caught her hand. "Good

morning," he said. He pulled her close and held her. Then he kissed her lips, first gently then hungrily seeking until he found her tongue and feasted.

Ava's arms tightened around his waist as she leaned into him. "Good morning," she managed against his kisses.

"Did you sleep well?" Cole asked while holding her cheeks in his hands. His eyes were probing.

"The best in years," she whispered, and then flushed.

Cole kissed her again and then released her. "Me too," he said simply. And that was the truth, he thought. For the first time since he'd arrived he'd passed through the big silent house thinking of nothing but the soul-stirring experience he'd had. He'd fallen into bed and slept soundly until the sound of Teddie's car awakened him. He thought that maybe, just maybe there could be a life for him here in Minuet. He sure as hell wanted it to be because he realized that hurting Ava would tear a hole in his heart.

After they'd eaten and on second mugs of coffee, Cole gave her a curious look. "What did Teddie mean?" he said. "Is something going on?"

"A lot," Ava said. "Can we sit outside?" she asked. He nodded and they settled themselves in the chairs on the back porch.

The early-morning stillness was what Ava cherished about her space. Times spent back here watching the tiny creatures begin their day, the trees unfurl from a night of rest and the sun boldly pushing its rays to earth to wake up the world was rejuvenation for her and she felt at peace. Although she wondered if her heartache would ever ease. But now Ava felt similarly apprehensive and content. What a contradiction and an upheaval to the nervous system, she thought. It was almost laughable. Change had happened in her life in the short span of time from one weekend to the next. And she had no idea what the status of her life would be come next weekend.

"You were going to tell me about Teddie," Cole said quietly. He'd been watching her but said nothing to disturb her silent musings. He of all people understood the turmoil within. He was respectful of that.

"She's thinking of leaving Minuet and going to work in New York City," Ava said bluntly without looking at Cole. "She was looking for advice."

Cole was instantly floored. "Leave?" He let out a low whistle. "After all these years?" he said. After a moment he added, "Starting a restaurant business in such a big city isn't as easy as all that. Where is that coming from?" he asked.

"Not food," Ava said. "Clothes. She's a designer."

Cole looked surprised and listened as Ava spoke. When she finished he was astounded and proud. Theodora Perkins, a hot-shot designer from a small town in the Carolinas turning the fashion world on its head. "And this guy, the designer, he's here to convince her to go back with him?"

"That's his aim," Ava said dryly. She looked at Cole. "That's what she meant when she said maybe she'll see you later. I think she wants you to come to the diner tonight too."

"You'll be there?" Cole asked. When she nodded he said, "Do you mind if I drive?"

"No, Cole," she said. "That would be fine."

After a moment, he said, "What of her son?"

"What do you mean?"

"It couldn't be all that easy for the father to give

up visiting his child without having to traipse to New York City to do it," he said.

"She's concerned about uprooting Royce," Ava said. And then she frowned. "She's never spoken about Royce's father. As long as I've known her she's the only parent in his life. There are no grandparents in town either. I think Roonie takes that place. But something she said once led me to believe that the father doesn't live in Minuet or even in the state."

Cole looked thoughtful. "Then I guess she's free to do what she thinks best for herself and her son," he said easily. "The best we can do is listen and then encourage her to make up her own mind." He thought of the many single parents he'd encountered in his job in L.A. The young street-smart toughs boasted about how many babies they'd had as if that proved their manhood. The young girls were content to have the babies just to hold on to their man. It all seemed so callous and wasteful of their youth. All the counseling he'd done to make them see that was a big joke. The moment they were out of his sight they went and continued to do their own pointless thing. What he felt was sympathy for the babies. They had nothing and no stable future.

"I think that with his mother being a successful designer, Royce would have the things he'd never have if she turned the offer down."

"And all that materialism is supposed to bring him happiness?" Ava said. "Do you really think that he doesn't feel happy now?"

Cole glanced at her. "You would really miss her, wouldn't you?" he said.

"She's my best friend," Ava said softly. "Yes, I would miss her terribly." When she stared at Cole, something in the way he cocked his head and wrinkled his brow made her think of someone else. Sheriff Jack had a similar motion when he was thoughtful. Even Roonie had the same look when he was fussing with one of his cooks. She dismissed the feeling. *Must be an affliction of a Minuet man,* she thought.

When Teddie drove away from Ava's she was happy that she'd decided to leave Royce with his sitter, Renee. With no expectation of seeing Cole this morning she'd had a feeling. What if he'd seen Royce? There would be no doubt in her mind what Cole would have thought. Now she really was in turmoil. Robert Jacobs showing up in town so suddenly was like a bombshell exploding in the pit of her stomach. He wanted her in New York as soon as she could, to be specific, like yesterday. He was working on a terrific new line for next spring and the addition of some of her designs would "knock 'em dead," as he'd put it.

But how long could she go around with her heart in her mouth avoiding places where Cole might run into her and Royce? And tonight she'd planned on leaving him with Monique and Drew but remembered that Monique would be having dinner with them also. So that meant she'd have to impose on Monique's parents to keep Royce as well since Renee wouldn't be available tonight. Besides, she hated to impose on the woman's good nature.

Change had never bothered Teddie before. Not even when she had had Royce and she lived her life in peace and without outside interference with her son. But now, the change that was bothering her the most was Cole Dumont. She'd meant what she'd said about having him come home. But now his presence would be the factor in whether she was going to change her and her son's life.

Later, while she and Cole were driving to the diner, Ava thought about her day. She'd been able to relegate her own problems to the background while she pondered on Teddie's plight. What would *she* do if her child's future changed because of her actions? Who would it benefit the most? Her or the child? The questions nagged her and she still didn't know what kind of advice she would offer her friend. Maybe after she met this Robert Jacobs person she could better make up her mind and make some wise statement that would help Teddie to decide. Something had been nagging at her during the day and she couldn't identify it but now she thought: just how long had Teddie been on a first-name basis with the famous designer from New York?

As usual, the diner was crowded. Teddie had arranged a table for five in the back of the restaurant where there was less traffic. Ava spied Monique, who waved. The man, who was sitting between her and Teddie, stood up when Ava and Cole reached them.

After the introductions were made, Ava was flanked by Cole and Robert Jacobs. When orders were taken and drinks served, Ava couldn't help but notice a quiet Cole observing the designer as the conversation turned to general talk with Robert Jacobs leading with very pointed questions about the town of Minuet.

"Are you thinking of bringing couture to town, then, Robert?" Cole said easily to the man who'd insisted on first names.

Surprised, Robert said, his sandy brown brows raised a notch, "Actually, no, Cole," he said just as easily. "I think competing with Monique would hardly be fair since I'm aiming to steal an important part of her business away." His pale brown eyes shifted to Teddie's and after a moment he glanced back at Cole. "But once Teddie is established up north we'll still be doing business in the south, with Monique, of course."

"Of course," Cole said. He looked at Monique, whom he'd just met. She was pretty with berry-brown skin and sloe eyes that appeared to look right through you. They were dark and intelligent and she was returning Cole's look with curiosity. "How does that sit with you, Monique?" he asked. "I mean, you and Teddie really have something going, haven't you?" He shrugged. "Why be so ready to change a good thing?"

Monique thought that she would like Cole from the minute he took her hand in a firm handshake. His eyes were honest. And he was forthright. She smiled. "It's not up to me after all, is it, Cole?" she said. "I don't know that if an opportunity like that came my way that I wouldn't pull up stakes and go."

Cole's reply was interrupted when the food arrived, and when he caught Teddie's look, he decided to let it drop. But he wasn't at all convinced that she was making a sound decision, now that he'd met the designer. Just what it was he couldn't figure but he wasn't impressed or comfortable with what he saw. Yet, Teddie was grown now and not the youngster he once knew. So much for trying to take care of the world and he'd do well to mind his own business on this one, he thought.

During dinner, Ava didn't miss Robert's attention to Teddie and her friend's response. She concluded that Teddie didn't mind in the least being in his company. Without understanding the reason why,

Ava wished that Teddie had never met the designer who was trying to change her life.

After dessert and coffee, Cole excused himself. He was feeling restless and thought that if this little get-together was for Teddie to help make a decision he feared it'd been a bust. Conversation had lagged only because Robert had hogged the spotlight. Always the topic of conversation turned back to him and New York. Cole could see that even Monique was bored and Ava was trying hard not to yawn.

On his way back to the dining room Cole met Roonie in the hallway. All those years ago when the older man worked with Hank Perkins, Cole had thought the man was old then when of course he was probably only in his forties. But now the man seemed tired, and Cole wondered just how long he could go on helping Teddie run her business.

"Cole Dumont," Roonie said, clapping Cole on his good shoulder. "You haven't changed a bit, just taller and bigger. Still got those angry-looking eyes, though." His deep voice softened. "But we're all glad you've come back home. Everything's going to be all right."

Cole smiled at the old man. "Thanks, Roonie." They both knew what was meant by the remark. Not ready to discuss old times, he surveyed the space. "Teddie certainly made some changes," he said. "Nothing like I remember at all. Didn't realize there was so much space back here."

"Oh, that girl has some great ideas," Roonie said, admiration showing all over his lined face. "Enlarged the galley, made herself an office." He clucked proudly. "Come see for yourself." He caught Cole's elbow. "Come on."

Cole was surprised to see the changes. Years ago,

old Hank wouldn't think nothing of sending a kid
in the back to fetch new bottles of ketchup or getting
more containers of milk from the big commercial refrigerator. He looked approvingly at the space Teddie
set up for an office. Then his roving eyes stopped.

"Some setup, huh?" Roonie said.

"Who's that?" Cole said in a strained voice.

Following his gaze to a framed picture on the desk,
Roonie said, "Royce. Teddie's son. He's only five but
is smart as a ten-year-old and handsome as a movie
star. That boy is going to be somebody. Sure is."

Cole stood as though he'd been turned to stone.
Curtis.

"You okay, man?" Roonie said, concern in his
voice. "You look drained. That wound not healed up
yet?"

Cole walked closer to the desk and picked up the
frame. Those eyes were mesmerizing and Cole thought
that he was looking in the mirror. He turned at the
sound of her steps.

Teddie's mouth was dry and her heart was pounding so loud she thought surely it would jump through
her chest. She couldn't speak but only stared at the
question in Cole's eyes. Roonie had gone and just she
and Cole stood there staring at each other.

Cole put the frame back down on the desk. He felt
hot and cold and wanted to do something, anything
but stand here and look at the ghost of his baby
brother. What the hell was going on? he wondered.
Without looking at the picture again he just waved a
hand toward it while his eyes begged her for an
explanation.

Teddie's hand was pressed against her bosom as
she looked at the stricken man who'd guessed her

secret. Her voice was but a whisper when she said, "I can't, Cole. Not here. Not now."

He walked by her without another glance and left the room.

Ava saw Cole coming and she gasped. Something was wrong.

"Let's go, Ava."

Monique had gone and Ava said a hasty goodnight to Robert and followed behind Cole.

They drove in silence.

Cole parked behind her car and walked her to her steps. In the dim light from her porch light she could see that whatever was eating him up inside was still there. She touched his arm. "When you want to talk about it, Cole, I'm here," she said.

Cole nodded and watched her unlock her door. When she was safely inside he backed out of the driveway and pulled into his own yard.

It was a long time before he went inside the house. He sat on the porch in the dark just staring. Now there really was no place to run, he thought.

Chapter Eleven

It was early the next morning, barely nine, when Cole parked his car behind Teddie's. He stood looking around at the house that he hardly remembered from years ago. He couldn't recall what color it had been but he saw signs of fresh paint, updated vinyl windows, and new lumber on the modernized porch. The shrubbery was landscaped and flowers were in abundance in the beds along the front of the house. He didn't remember the profusion of color back then. Billie Perkins was always away at the diner and he guessed she didn't have the slightest interest in gardening.

Memories, he thought. More memories. He or Graham would drop Curtis off here, just dump him when they were on their way to a game or off with their friends. Teddie would babysit him until they or their mother picked him up. He shuttered his eyes against the visions and closed his ears against the giggles of a toddler ready to play games with the laughing young girl who was tickling his stomach.

He looked when he heard the door open and saw

Teddie standing there. She closed the door softly behind her and came down the steps.

"I expected you," she said softly. On the side of the house were more flowers and a bench. She led him there and they sat.

Cole didn't speak, just sat and inhaled the clean smell of the quiet Sunday-morning air. Cars drove by slowly as if not to mar the peace. Churchgoers he thought. He wondered if they would leave the place fulfilled and rejuvenated, ready to shed their problems. Maybe he should follow them.

Finally he turned to the silent woman sitting beside him. "He's my nephew."

"Yes," Teddie said quietly.

He looked away again. "Graham never told me," he said in a bewildered, hurt, voice.

"Graham doesn't know."

Her lightning-bolt words made him jerk his head back toward her. He gaped. "What?" Then a slow spiral of anger wormed its way to his throat. In a raspy voice he said, "My brother is a father and doesn't know it?"

Teddie didn't speak but she turned from the fury in his eyes, her own beginning to mist. At last she said, "I didn't want your brother that way."

The lump in Cole's throat hurt. When he could swallow he said, "Talk to me, Teddie."

"That old schoolgirl crush I had on Graham Dumont just grew right along with me," she said softly.

He didn't speak.

"Graham came home one year to look after the place as he did sometimes. He was his usual self, a smile and a listening ear to everyone who stopped by to chat. He even listened to me bemoaning my fate, stuck with a diner that was stealing my dream of

studying fashion design. He consoled me telling me
I'd done wonders with the place and not to be sorry.
Before he left Minuet he told me to take some time
off. If I came to Ohio he'd show me what a big city
was like and that I wasn't missing out on a thing."

She was quiet and Cole said, without looking at
her, "You went."

"For a week that turned into two," Teddie said. A
smile touched her lips. "I fell in love."

"Did he?"

Teddie faced him. "I don't know," she said. "But
what we had, what we shared, I hoped he was feeling
the same." She toyed with the hem of her white
shorts. "But when he never came back, I knew his
feelings weren't the same." Her eyes misted. "Then
I learned about Royce coming. I knew without a
doubt that I was keeping him. No slinking around,
holding my head down with shame. I was in love with
my baby's father and that child was made in love—at
least on my part."

"But he's been back here since then," Cole said.
"What happened? He never saw Royce?"

"He was distant," Teddie said. "He'd heard I'd had
a baby even before he returned. And when we met,
he treated me like I was fourteen again, a schoolgirl
with a crush. He was pleasant enough but we didn't
speak about my trip to Ohio or the lovers we'd been
for such a short time. I let him think that I was having
a fling." She smiled and looked off in the distance. "I
believe that's what he wanted to think himself."

"Christ, Teddie," Cole blurted. He stretched his
jeans-clad legs out and folded his arms across his
belly. The enormity of it all was mind-blowing. His
brother had a kid. He had a nephew that was the
spitting image of Curtis Dumont!

He looked at her. "Is that why you didn't want me to take you out for dinner that night? I might have seen your son?"

"Yes."

He shook his head. "Then how long were you going to play that game of hide-and-seek? Especially if I planned to stick around?"

She shrugged. "I don't know," she said simply.

Thoughtfully Cole said, "Graham will be coming here soon."

"I'm not surprised," Teddie answered.

"What will you do?"

"If he doesn't find out before I'm ready, then I hope to be gone," Teddie answered. She let out a sigh. "I guess all that indecision I was going through went out the window as soon as you saw that picture."

His eyes narrowed. "What do you mean?"

"I have a job and an apartment waiting for me in New York," Teddie answered. She looked at Cole. "I'm not giving my son up to Graham."

"Damn. You would keep a man away from his son?" Cole exclaimed. "Why, Teddie?"

"Because Graham is rich and I'm not," she said hotly. "If it came to a court battle, his lawyers would see to it that my son would be living half the year in Ohio with a man he doesn't even know. I'm not going to put my son through that."

When she quieted, she gave Cole a look. "Are you going to tell him?"

Cole just stared at her. What he saw was a mother lion guarding her cub and ready to take on the fight of her life to save him. He looked away. Finally he said, "I think that should fall on you." When he looked at her again, he said, "But don't take my nephew away without telling Graham. Then I will butt in."

"Mommy, are you out here?"

Cole's chest constricted. If the picture had sent him into a tailspin last night, what was the real deal going to do to him?

"I'm here, baby," Teddie called.

Royce appeared, tousled hair and sleepy eyes, and bare feet. Rubbing his droopy eyelids he said, "I'm not a baby, Mommy." He climbed into his mother's lap while staring at the stranger. "Hello," he said sleepily but then continued to stare.

"Royce I want you to meet your . . . to meet Mr. Cole." Teddie looked at her son who was staring so hard at the visitor that she said firmly, "It's rude to stare, honey."

"Hello, Royce," Cole said. The little boy held out his hand and he was almost afraid to grasp it. But when he took it, the soft fingers clasped in his big palm almost made him lose it. "How ya doing this morning?"

"I'm fine, Mr. Cole," Royce answered. He turned from the visitor and looked at his mother. "Mommy, Mr. Cole has a face like mine."

Teddie drew in a breath and looked fearfully at her son's uncle.

He saw the panic on her face. Was now the time to whip something like this on the little guy? God! What could he say? But Royce solved the problem when he said, "Are you going to eat breakfast with us Mr. Cole?"

Cole breathed easy. "No, I can't, Royce," he said. "I have to be somewhere in about fifteen minutes and I should be on my way. But we'll meet again real soon, okay?"

"Sure. Do you have a little boy that I can play with? I have a friend named Drew but he doesn't come too much because his mommy works a lot."

"No," Cole answered. "But what if I came one day and took you to where a lot of little fellows your age play. That is if your mommy will let us go. What about it?"

Teddie looked at her son and a lump formed in her throat. Royce smiled for the first time and his big round deep brown eyes sparkled when he looked at her. "Can I, Mommy? Please?" he said.

Cole was staring at Teddie.

She kissed her son on his cheek. "I think that would be okay," she said. She lifted him off her lap. "Now come on inside so we can get some breakfast." She threw a grateful look at Cole.

"Bye, Mr. Cole," Royce said, and raced into the house.

There was a short silence, which Cole broke. "How are you going to handle that?"

She sighed. "I will have to tell him," she said. "I guess I knew this day would come, especially since you've returned. There's no mistaking the resemblance, and others are sure to notice now. I guess it's time."

"It's time," Cole said as he was about to get in his car. He looked at her. "Ava doesn't know?"

She shook her head. "No one does," she said. "I think Roonie suspected once Royce got to be a toddler. He knew I'd gone to Ohio on my vacation. But he never said a word."

He nodded. "Yeah," he said, "it's time."

"Cole," Teddie said, watching him closely, "are you okay?" She'd seen the shock on his face when Royce appeared, and the tightness in his chest when he

held his nephew's hand. "You wanted to hug him, I
know," she said softly. "He is so much like Curtis."

"I don't think I could have handled it very well,"
Cole said tightly. "I would've scared the little guy out
of his skin." He gave her a direct look. "I'll take a
rain check on that, though."

Teddie nodded. "I promise."

He started the engine and then said thoughtfully,
"The name you gave your designs, RC Fashions—is
that Royce Curtis?"

"Yes," Teddie answered.

Cole nodded and drove off. Five minutes later, he
reached the intersection that would have taken him
left to Pine Road and home but he crossed it and
kept driving.

Around two Ava was sitting on the front porch. It
wasn't like she was watching for him she thought,
but the sound of a car had her looking toward the
road again. *Oh, stop it, girl* she admonished herself.
Since when is he supposed to report his schedule to you?

She didn't like the look on his face when they'd
parted last night and she knew something had happened at the diner. She sighed. She supposed that
when Cole was ready he'd let her know what was on
his mind. At the sound of another approaching car
she looked again and this time she was surprised to
see Teddie pull up in her late-model black Maxima.

"Hello, Miss Ava," Royce said as soon as he unbuckled himself from his seat belt. "Mommy said we
would be a surprise. Are we?" He hugged her once
he bounded up the steps.

Ava smiled and returned the squeeze to his little
body. "You sure are, sweetie," she said. "And what a

nice surprise too. Are you going to have Sunday dinner with me?" She looked at her friend and her eyes narrowed. *Something really did happen at that diner last night,* she thought. "Come on inside and let me get you a big glass of lemonade and a cookie," she said to Royce. "What about it?"

He giggled. "What about it?" he repeated. "That's what Mr. Cole said." He opened the door and bounced inside.

Ava looked at Teddie who said, "We'll talk."

Over an hour later, Ava and Teddie were sitting on the back porch. Royce had been sleeping for almost a half hour after Ava had read him a story from one of the many books she kept for him.

Teddie had spoken softly and Ava didn't interrupt. The two friends sat quietly, their faces turned to the welcoming warm breezes that touched their damp skin. It was another hot day and they looked forward to the setting of the sun.

We all have secrets, Ava thought. She wondered what her friend would say once her own secret life was exposed because she knew deep down that that time was near. But she pushed that thought away. Teddie was hurting and tensed about what was happening in her life and it was her time for attention.

"What does Royce know about his father?" Ava asked quietly.

Teddie shuttered her eyes briefly. "No, I never told him that he was dead, if you had that thought," she said. "I told Royce that his father had moved far away because of his job."

Ava was listening.

"Oh, I know that was lame," Teddie said "but I had hope that one day . . ."

"That was it?" Ava said with a frown.

"Oh, I added more when he got older. I told him that his father had been hurt badly in an accident and the scars all over his face and body prevented him from walking and talking properly," Teddie said. "And that he was afraid we wouldn't love him anymore so he left us."

"Oh, no, Teddie," Ava murmured.

Neither could speak.

"Cole was freaked last night," Teddie finally said. "But this morning it was worse after seeing Royce. I wish I could have said or done something that could have made the hurt go away." She looked at Ava. "He didn't come back home?"

"I haven't seen him." After a while she said, "Did you really decide to leave Minuet?"

"I'm seriously thinking about the job offer," Teddie said.

"But you promised to tell Graham," Ava said. "What good is leaving then?"

"Suppose he wants to return?" Teddie said with a frown marring her forehead. "I don't know that I can live so near to him and not be with him. You understand?"

"You still love him?"

"Yes." She smiled. "Don't you think that I've tried to forget him? To find a father for Royce? Well, it just didn't happen. Maybe with a new life in a different place my fortune will change. Once Graham gets over his fury at me, we can be friends and establish visiting rights. Maybe that will be my life."

Early Monday morning, Ava drove to work with great trepidation. Her feelings of uneasiness were still with her. That and the fact that Cole's car was still missing from his yard, made for a foreboding that was hard to shake. She couldn't help but wonder where he'd gone. Who was helping him through a rough period. Would he return?

Even as she parked in her space, her head wasn't where it should have been. Teaching her favorite topic had always been a joy for her and now she had to give herself pep talks to bring life to ancient history.

Winifred watched Ava arrive and the set of the younger woman's shoulders told her that it hadn't been a good weekend for the professor. A smug smile on her face, Winifred returned to her desk. She wondered if the fun was going to begin today, or was the very reserved Charles Howell going to wait a day or two. No matter, she thought. If he wanted to verify her story so be it. She was certain that the news she'd called him with at home, disturbing his Sunday evening, had been a bombshell. Well, she'd set the ball rolling. All she need do was sit and wait and then watch with pleasure when it finally dropped in Ava's lap.

The lecture class on Ava's schedule was over. When she'd entered the classroom, she'd surprised herself once she got started. The students were interested and that made her job twice as easy. She sailed through the assignments, making comments on the various research projects some had selected. When one smart young woman bubbled over about her choice, she marveled that her project revolved around Gustavus Vassa and wasn't it something that that very man was the topic of all the excitement in the last week. Ava had nearly lost her cool but kept it together as she gave her suggestions on how to continue with the research.

At last the day was over and Ava was headed home. She felt something akin to relief when she got in her car and drove off. The day had been uneventful. There had been no sign of Winifred and the president had been away for most of the day, she'd heard. But something was in the air; she could feel it and it just wasn't the sudden darkening of the sky foretelling of an evening of rain.

It was nearly seven o'clock when Ava turned on the dishwasher and left the kitchen carrying a mug of green tea to the back porch. She rested on the same lounge chair where she and Cole had made love four nights ago. The memory was so vivid that she started thinking that she'd heard his gentle whispers. But it was only the sounds of the night.

Earlier she'd been surprised when she saw that his car was still missing. Surely he would have pulled it together by now, she'd thought. She felt left out after what they'd shared; she thought that he would've sought her out to talk.

The rain had been steady for hours now and though she was sitting far back, the soft occasional spray reached her. Ava was content here. She liked the feel of the warm rain intermittently accompanied by a warm wind that cooled her skin. Peaceful moments like this were becoming rare in her suddenly disordered world.

The sound on the side of the house at first didn't bother her. There were so many woodland creatures surrounding her property that she was used to their scurrying about. But when she heard the click-click of nonhuman feet on the bricked walk beside her flower beds, she sat up straight and set her mug on the table. Looking over the side of the house toward the woods, she saw eyes gleaming in the dark and she stood, her heart pounding fiercely.

"Twister!"

Ellen Lansdowne appeared peering from beneath a huge plaid umbrella, holding a leash in her hand. The soaking wet cocker spaniel was dancing alongside her, dodging the hand that would trap him. He ran up on the porch to where Ava was standing and started barking.

Ava didn't know whether to feel relieved or mad at the animal that had probably trampled her flowers with his romping.

"Mrs. Lansdowne," Ava said, "come on up out of that rain."

"Shoot, it ain't the rain that's bothering me," the vexed woman said. "This is the second time I had to come down here after that dog. I was expecting you to come calling once you got home Friday night. But guess it was so late and dark you didn't notice the damage he'd done." She'd closed the umbrella and was on the porch busying herself with leashing the dog who was jumping and yapping at Ava.

"Friday?" Ava said. She knew very well what she'd been doing Friday night and she wondered if her face were flaming. "What time was that?" she asked.

"Oh, I don't know," Ellen said, impatiently trying to quiet her dog who was straining at the leash. "Must have been midday when I noticed the gate was open and he was gone. By the time I started looking up and down the road I heard his yippin' and yappin' coming from down your way. I was halfway down here, then there comes a car just bounding on to the road and going like sixty."

"From here?" Ava asked.

"Don't know whose yard it came from. Couldn't see that good 'cause it was already out on the road by the time I saw it," she said. "Since you were at work I guess it was somebody looking up young Cole now that he's back. But he sure didn't have to raise Cain leaving. That's what had Twister all in a dither, I'll bet. A stranger that was in your yard or Cole's." She sniffed. "But I did see that Twister had been all over those flowers and I'm sorry about that."

She didn't tell the woman that on Friday, Cole had been in Florence all day. And who would have come by to see her at that time of day? Ava wondered.

"Never mind, Mrs. Lansdowne," she said. "I can fix up whatever Twister ruined. Don't worry about it." She watched as the woman opened her big umbrella and walked down the steps with her dog straining to be gone.

After the fussing woman and her dog left, Ava shivered and rubbed her arms. Who had that been? she wondered. As far as she knew, Cole had kept to himself the short time he'd been home. But maybe an old friend came visiting anyway, she thought. Or could it have been Winifred? No, she decided; the woman had been at the university, and anyway, why would she subject herself to more of her accusations? Perplexed and now nervous about the whole thing, she went inside. Then on a hunch she went into the spare room and stared at the space around the window. Someone had gotten in here before, she knew, and just maybe . . . She walked to the window and stood staring. Nothing had been disturbed. The window was secure and the statues and other items she'd placed just beneath the window on the floor were in their place. She'd done that only as an afterthought once Cole had said that that had been the point of entry for her intruder. If there was a next time she surely would notice.

Ava left the room and began a search of her home. She tried all the window locks, peering closely at possibly jimmied windows. Upstairs and downstairs, she found nothing amiss. Feeling satisfied that no one had gotten inside, she went to the study where she sat at her desk. If there had been an intruder then the outside evidence of that had been washed away by the rain.

With that ominous thought, Ava opened her folder, ready to prepare her lecture for her next class, but half an hour later she closed it. Instead of concentrating, she'd been listening for the sound of a car pulling into the next yard. At the window she saw the lights of an occasional vehicle, hopeful that it would turn into the driveway.

She dropped the curtain and turned away. In the living room she sat quietly, but her mind was churning with dire thoughts.

When on Thursday, Cole pulled into his yard and parked, before going up the steps he stood and looked at the place of his childhood. Unlike when he'd first arrived, now he let the memories wash over him willingly and without fear. He let himself see his family as it was back then before the tragedies happened that had changed their lives. He saw his father, usually a reserved man, chasing his wife around the house with a bucket of water after she'd doused him with the hose he'd been using to wash his car. He heard their laughter and the giggles of Curtis and his and Graham's chuckles as they watched the grown-ups act so silly. They'd been a happy family then. Pushing off the car, Cole walked around the house letting more memories bathe him. He looked at the woods behind the house where many times he and Graham had hid, playing hide-and-seek with their little brother. His gaze landed on the small house next door and more memories came, and this time he did not close his eyes against the hurt but cherished the sound of a toddler's laughter.

He turned away and went inside. There he stood seeing the house as it had been back then. In the kitchen he intentionally stared at the spot he'd dreaded, the place where he'd found Curtis gasping his last breaths, his mother and brother screaming and crying the little boy's name. Then his mother had turned on him, fury making her eyes and face demonlike. For an instant he closed his eyes, shying away from that moment but he recovered. That was then, a horrible moment in his life that would never go away. It had changed and consumed him all his adult life so that he was a scarred individual unable to forgive himself. He knew what he had to do and he would, very soon. He left the room and went upstairs.

On the landing he stood looking at the closed door of his old bedroom. He opened it and just stood there, the visions coming swiftly. He was lying there in a stupor, his arms cradling the toddler begging him to be still and go to sleep. Instead, *he'd* fallen asleep. What came next he'd always chased from his mind and brain, but now he faced the cries and the words of hate and anger. When the cacophony subsided, he left the door open and left the room, knowing he'd be back.

In the bathroom, Cole looked at himself in the mirror. He hadn't shaved since Sunday, and he looked like a grizzled man just down from the mountains.

Later, after a shave and a long soak in the bathtub, Cole dressed in tan shorts and a navy T-shirt and without hesitation went to work in his bedroom. The windows were opened wide. Then he stripped the linen, grimacing at his old full-size bed. Furniture shopping was in order, he thought. With the linen changed, he emptied the dressers and the clothes closet, tossing everything left of his youth into large trash bags. When he finished, the room was clean and smelling fresh, the curtains blowing softly from the warm breeze. He stood back and looked. He left, and when he returned he was carrying his luggage and clothes and began filling his dressers and closet. He was moving in.

Before tackling downstairs, Cole kicked off his shoes and lay on the bed, his head resting on his palms, feeling a sense of peace that had eluded him all these years.

On Sunday, after leaving Teddie's in a fog, he'd driven out of Minuet past Hudson, and when he stopped hours later he was in North Carolina. Too exhausted to continue, he'd rented a motel room and there he'd stayed for four nights. That first night he remembered not being able to sleep; yet when he did, he saw Curtis and Royce in his fitful dreams. He saw the two of them together, laughing, talking, and being little devils like they hadn't a care in the world.

The next few days he'd walked and driven around the small town he was in, living and reliving the nightmares that had kept him from his birth home. But the picture in his mind of his little nephew kept chasing all the bad dreams away. And then in a stark moment, he could see. It was almost as if Curtis was standing before him with his stern little face, pointing his finger and giving Cole a lecture about being a grown-up, something that Cole had done many times when Curtis was acting like a baby. And in the next instant his nephew's face took the place of his dead brother's. Royce was smiling.

Cole had always believed in the here and now, but he understood that something out of his ken had broken through; his wounded spirit was healing. He somehow knew that he was meant to be here in his old home at this time in his life, and young Royce's. The youngster was going to learn of his uncle and his father. Deep down Cole knew that he was to be a presence in the boy's future. He didn't know about Graham but it didn't matter; *he* would be here for Royce Curtis Perkins. Cole knew that it was dangerous, that he would always look for Curtis in his young nephew, but he prayed that he would let the little boy grow into his own personality. Never would he think that Royce was a replacement for what had been lost, but Cole knew that he would love that little boy like he was his own. There would never be another Curtis but he would not be forgotten either. One day he would make sure that Royce knew of his uncle who never had the chance to grow up.

He closed his eyes and his words were but a whisper: "Curtis, little guy. I love you and I'm so sorry. Please forgive me."

Cole got up and went downstairs and began his work in the kitchen. When he finished, he looked around. Gone was the feeling that ghosts hovered over him, causing him to rush out of this room, filled with guilt. His heart was beating normally and he was able to walk over the spot without trepidation. He wasn't trampling over his brother's spirit.

It was after six o'clock when Cole left the house. He'd thrown out all the rotten food in the fridge and a trip to the market was in order. After so many days of eating just enough to keep from starving he was ravenous.

A glance at his neighbor's empty driveway brought a frown. *Ava should be home by now,* he thought. But then a tiny smile touched his lips. When he returned he knew where he would be stopping.

During all of his soul-searching and his decision to stay in Minuet, he knew that Ava Millington was in that plan. There would be no happy future without her in his life. He was going to let her know that as soon as he laid eyes on her. And for a man who wasn't given to praying, as he drove, he said a silent prayer that she would let him in.

Let her help you, Cole. Those were the words of Jack Thompson, at what seemed ages ago. "She already has, Jack," Cole murmured as he thought of the beautiful woman who'd touched his heart and his soul. Now he was open and ready to help her heal *her* wounds and prayed that she wouldn't turn him away.

It was with a smile on his lips that he drove past the old widow Lansdowne who was standing at her gate looking at him with a curious expression. He returned her wave and couldn't help thinking that, yeah, it was great to be home.

Chapter Twelve

One more day, Ava thought as she unlocked her door and stepped inside out of the oppressive heat. Immediately after turning on the air conditioner, she began shedding her clothes. It was nearly seven and the sun seemed like it was never going to set. Yet another over-ninety-degree day was predicted for tomorrow and relief wasn't in sight until midweek. She dreaded the oppressive heat of the coming July. Now was a time she wished she'd decided to travel instead of taking on a summer lecture series; she could have been lolling in the cool waves in the Mediterranean.

Stripped down to her undies, she was sitting in the kitchen drinking a glass of ice-cold water. She sucked on an ice cube, allowing the frozen water to deliciously cool the insides of her mouth. Too tired and lazy to even pull something out of the freezer to zap in the microwave she took her glass to the living room and lay down on the couch. She closed her eyes thinking that after tomorrow she'd have two worry-free days. All week she'd had the feeling that the earth was going to drop out from under her feet. She'd seen Dr. Howell and he had been so engrossed in his thoughts, he'd only nodded at her and kept on going. She could have sworn he was muttering to himself. Hale had been missing all week filling in as a guest lecturer at the community college. Winifred passed by, giving frosty greetings, and Emily Thiessen had taken some time off, since the exhibit was no longer a factor. Ava had tried her best to keep her mind on her work but had found it an uphill battle.

Ava knew that each morning that she left she'd expected to see the big car sitting in its usual spot, and when it wasn't there, she'd arrive at work a real mess. Where was he? she wondered. Why hadn't he reached out to her? So many doubts entered her mind about the lovemaking they'd shared that she was second-guessing her own actions.

When he returned, was Cole going to just ignore the new relationship that they'd begun and go on about his business as though nothing had happened? She kept pushing that morbid thought out of her mind because she didn't know what she'd do if that were so. How in the world do you continue to be a casual neighbor to the man who'd stolen your heart? There was no practical answer to that question, she decided. Yet, after four days the possibility of him returning and picking up where they'd left off was so remote. She now believed that her fatigue was nothing more than the weight of a heavy heart.

Cole stopped ringing the bell and began banging on the door, his thoughts going in every direction. She had to be in there. Her car was parked and she would have better sense than to go running. He'd already been around the back and the door was locked. Nothing had been disturbed as far as he'd observed. Could she have had an accident? He banged louder, and just as he was about to go and peer through the windows, he heard her. His heart quieted and he waited.

"What? Who's there?" Ava said in a panic. She jumped off the couch with a start and looked at her watch. Seven-forty? She'd fallen asleep. Someone was banging on her door to beat the band and she rushed to the foyer. Without thinking she opened the door.

"Cole?" Her pounding heart leaped into her throat and her eyes stung. "You're okay," she whispered.

He had been dreaming of holding her naked skin against him, hardly able to think straight most of the time. Here she was barely clothed, her smooth golden skin damp and inviting. Her eyes were wide in panic for him. He could have kicked himself for putting her through that. The door was flung wide and he stepped toward her.

"Christ!" The guttural sound coming from his throat was a raw cry of pent-up emotions. "Ava," he said as he wrapped his arms around her. She was still shaking and he held her close. "Shh, sweetheart," he whispered against the soft skin of her neck. "It's okay. I'm okay," he murmured. He felt her arms around his waist and she was squeezing him so tightly that he could feel her heartbeat.

Ava clutched his shirt in her fists as if to keep him from slipping from her grasp. It was as if she were trying to save herself from drowning. He was the buoy that was keeping her afloat. He just held her crooning softly in her ear until the waves of fear subsided. When she was breathing normally she lifted her head and stared at him. They looked at each other in silence. After a while Ava said in a faint voice, "You *are* okay."

"I am," Cole said. He kissed her forehead. "Yes, I am." And he breathed deeply at hearing his admission. He'd known that, but uttering the words was like being stamped with a seal of approval for a new beginning.

Ava had never felt such delight. It was only when his eyes drank in the rest of her and his hands were gliding smoothly over her bare skin, that she realized her state of dress—or undress—she thought giddily. After he'd kicked the door closed without releasing her, she gave him a quick hug and moved away.

"Let me get some clothes on," she said. "I'll be right back."

Reluctant to let her go, Cole said, "Hurry back."

Minutes later, dressed in shorts and a cotton sleeveless pullover, Ava joined Cole, who was sitting in the living room on the couch. He held out his arms and she snuggled into them, her head resting on his shoulder. She ran her hand up and down his strong, muscled arm. He was rubbing his knuckles softly against her cheek. She closed her eyes and breathed another prayer that he'd finally come home.

"I'm sorry," Cole murmured as he bent to plant a kiss on her head.

"Don't," Ava said. "You did what you had to do. I'm just grateful that you've worked it out." Her hand stopped moving. "And I'm happy that you've come back home." For she knew he had.

"It was a heavy four days," Cole said. "Enlightening, but heavy." He knew that she wanted to know but was waiting for him. He took a breath. "It was Royce," he said.

"I guessed," Ava said quietly. She said nothing else.

Cole talked for a long time, almost reliving every moment from the time he spotted the picture in the diner, telling her his thoughts and feelings and finally his revelation.

"And all the time," he said, "I was praying for this, to have you in my arms."

Ava closed her eyes and gave thanks that her own prayers had been answered. She'd almost lost faith when she began to believe in her own inadequacies.

Holding her and not having her was driving him a little crazy. He wanted to love her, to keep her close and never let go. Gently he shifted until she was sitting and he was holding her hand. "You know I want to love you, don't you?" he said. Before she answered he stood and pulled her up with him. "Come with me—I want to show you something," he said softly.

He watched as she locked her door and then he led her through the hedges and up the steps to his house. She looked at him when he opened the door. It wasn't locked.

Cole smiled sheepishly. "I know. I thought I was coming right back." Inside, he led her to the kitchen.

Ava noticed the rearranged table, and she was beginning to see. With a frog in her throat she said, "I understand, Cole."

He took her hand and led her upstairs and stopped at the opened door nearest the landing.

Ava stepped inside and turned to give him a querulous look.

"This is my bedroom," Cole said quietly. "I just moved back in it today." When her beautiful brown eyes showed her love, his heart turned over. "As downstairs, there are no more ghosts in here," he said quietly. "This is where I want to make love with you now. I'm really back home."

"Oh, Cole." Ava slipped into his arms. She wound her arms around his neck and brought his mouth down to hers. She kissed him hungrily, greedily, inhaling his clean, lime-scented skin. "Yes, yes," she managed to whisper as his response to her onslaught made her blood race.

Cole's cry of relief came from the bowels of his soul as fire met fire. Crushed in his embrace, he devoured her lips, her eyes, and captured her darting tongue. "Ava, sweetheart, my love," he whispered as he tasted the sweetness of her soft throat. He tugged at the hem of her pullover to feel her heated skin, but she removed it and then quickly unhooked her bra, releasing the pulsating mounds to his exploring hands. "God," he moaned as he dipped his head and tasted the perfumed buds that quivered in his mouth. Her moans and her hands moving over his buttocks sent a jolt of electricity through him.

Ava cried her frustration at not getting what she craved. She couldn't undo the button of his shorts and the zipper was stuck and she yearned to touch him, to feel him in her hands again. Memories of a time before made her breath quicken in anticipation. "Cole, please," she murmured.

Her plea was answered when Cole stepped away and was instantly naked, standing before her. He undid her shorts and they fell to the floor. When he slid her panties down and they too dropped with a whisper, he looked. And just as he was about to swoop her up into his arms he remembered. "Wait," he whispered, and bent to get his wallet from his pants. Soon he was ready after removing the paper from the condom. "Now," he said husky-voiced. She was on her back waiting, her eyes roving over him. The tip of her tongue darted out to lick her lips and he groaned, falling on her with moans of anticipation.

Ava reached for him, and as if she'd never stopped, began loving him as she'd done before. But there was sweetness, a permanency, almost possessiveness in her as she guided his penis into her throbbing secret place. Magically, as before, she was swept away.

Cole fitted himself to her as if she was made just for him. With the thought that he was at home at last, his deep penetration brought a cry of joy from her lips as her hips rose to meet his.

Delightful shivers enveloped Ava as her legs, like steel vines entwining his thighs, trapped him in a vise. Intoxicated by his male musk, she was overwhelmed with increased desire as she loved him with all her being.

Their loving was fierce and prolonged as they reached new heights only to descend and rise again with renewed, greedy exclamations of want and need. Then it ended, each sated, and with closed eyes, wondering what had taken hold of them.

With panting breath, Cole opened his eyes and stared down at her, and as always his heart turned over with joy. Was he so deserving of all this? he wondered. He touched her lips with his and nuzzled her nose. "I love you, Ava Millington," he said hoarsely, kissing her eyelids and tasting her salty, damp neck.

Ava looked deep into his eyes and saw the truth. She wondered if he could see the truth in hers. "I love you, Cole," she said simply.

Cole positioned himself so that his elbows were holding his weight. He didn't want to move from her. They lay like that for a long time while he murmured his love. She laughed when he tickled her legs with his toes and she got him back by kneading and squeezing his nipples. He yelped and moved against her and she felt him rising. She was turned on again and wanted him. He read her thoughts because he prepared himself anew and they were again lifted to heights she thought were impossible. She swooned, asking herself if she hadn't been there already. This time they were slow and steady, feeling and touching as if committing each precious part to memory. They explored, and found their likes and discomforts, with Cole discovering that the spot behind her neck was an erogenous zone for her and he milked it until she yelled for mercy.

Cole reluctantly slid from her and lay panting. He didn't speak for fear of spouting gibberish. God, he loved this woman so much that his soul ached.

It was dark and the breeze lifting the curtains was a welcoming cool now. Cole felt Ava's hand go limp and fall from his stomach. He looked to see that she'd fallen asleep in the middle of the small bed. She seemed so at peace that he was reluctant to wake her. He frowned because moving was going to be an exercise in agility. He was on the edge of the bed, and if he moved wrong he'd fall flat on his butt.

As he maneuvered expertly, swinging his legs over and planting his feet on the floor, he knew definitely a shopping trip was on the agenda, like yesterday.

Later, in the kitchen, he was heating the prepared foods he'd purchased. It had been his intent to invite her to dinner but those plans had been sidelined. Was he complaining? Cole grinned and fixed two plates, leaving one in the microwave. Spoilage was chancy because she just might sleep till morning. Now that was a thought that tickled his fancy. Waking up beside her was a dream long anticipated.

* * *

Ava awoke quietly, looking around the unfamiliar surroundings. The smile that appeared came with the memories of where she was. She lay contentedly, savoring the warm bed and the cool breeze that fanned her face. Noises from downstairs and the smell of food tickled her palate and she remembered she'd eaten nothing for hours. Before getting up she buried her face in his pillow and inhaled. *Dear, sweet Cole,* she thought, *how I do love you.*

He was squatting, searching for something in the fridge. Ava stood watching, smiling at the movement of his firm, rounded buttocks, remembering how it'd felt beneath her hands.

Without turning, Cole smiled and said, "I know you're there." He found the tub of margarine and stood. The intake of his breath was sharp as he turned and looked at her. *So much good fortune,* he thought. *Is it here to stay?* he wondered.

They met in the center of the room and she slid easily into his arms. "Hey," Ava said, kissing his lips lightly. "You heard me?" she asked.

Cole shook his head. "You were quiet as a mouse," he said. "I felt you." He held her close for a moment and then released her. "Hungry?"

"Starved." Ava eyed his plate of food. "Where did that come from?" she said. "It smells divine."

"That's because you're hungry," Cole said. He checked the plate in the microwave and then zapped it for a few seconds. When he placed it on the table he said, "Compliments of Prudhomme's Home Cooking."

Rotisserie chicken, mashed potatoes and okra with

tomatoes graced their plates. Cornbread and iced tea completed the meal. They ate in silence for a while.

"Mmm, this is sinful eating like this so late," Ava said. "I'll never be able to sleep." She swallowed the last of the delicious cornbread and drank some tea.

"We can always find something to do to keep you awake until your stomach is settled," Cole said easily with an innocent stare.

She felt her face flaming. But she reached over and caught his hand. "You don't need excuses to make love to me, Cole," she said softly. "I want to be with you."

Cole returned the squeeze, but couldn't speak as they held each other's gaze.

By the time they left the tidied kitchen it was after ten o'clock. Neither wanted to say good-night but the pressure of another workday for Ava meant she should get some sleep. But they lingered in a long embrace and finally, reluctant to end the night, they sat on his porch, hands entwined.

Ava's voice was soft when she spoke. "Cole, I think Teddie really wants to leave Minuet. She's fearful that your brother will fight for their son."

Cole drew in a breath. "I know," he said, thinking of what was to come. "I'm hoping that Graham will listen first and act afterward, but it's going to take some doing." He shook his head. "Five years is a lot of time not to be in the life of your child." He tensed. "So much missed," he murmured.

She soothed his hand until it relaxed. The pain was still great inside and she understood. "Such a decision," Ava said. "It's a chance for her dream to come true, to design her fashions under the tutelage of someone who believes in her."

Cole's eyes narrowed when he thought of Robert

Jacobs. "Are you certain that's all that Jacobs wants?" he asked.

Ava hesitated. "I know what you mean," she said thoughtfully. "I sensed he had a hidden agenda, too." And then, "I don't think Teddie is fully aware, though. I didn't get that impression that she was ready to go that way. She still loves your brother."

"I don't want my nephew raised by that man," he said tersely. Cole felt time was imminent. Graham had to come home.

After a while, Cole said, "You haven't mentioned work. Has anything happened yet?"

Ava's peaceful state of mind dissipated. "No," she finally said. "I'm still waiting."

"Winifred is making herself scarce?"

"To me she is, but she goes about her business as though everything is all right. The only change is me. I keep looking over my shoulder."

Cole knew that something was going to break and he wished he could be there for her when it did. He felt so helpless, not knowing where to begin.

"I wish there was something that I could do to bring this to a head," he told her. "You probably feel like you're in a pressure cooker."

"Whatever comes will be easier now," Ava said. "I'm glad you're here." She leaned over and kissed his cheek.

Cole wanted more and he pulled her from her chair into his lap and embraced her. His kiss was long and deep. It was a long while before the night ended.

Over two weeks had passed since that night Cole had returned. On this Monday, Ava's step was jaunty as she entered her office. She couldn't believe that for the first time in weeks her feelings of doom and gloom had finally disappeared. Nothing in the president's manner or Winifred's cool demeanor told her that Ava's secret had been discovered. She was feeling her old self and relished giving her lectures. The students' response to her was gratifying and she gave each research project her all. She smiled with sheer joy.

"Now that's more like it," Hale said as he came and sat by her desk.

Ava looked. "What are you talking about?" she asked as she put her purse away and then turned on her computer.

"That smile has been missing for a mighty long time around here," he said. "And you even act differently." Hale's eyes narrowed as he studied her. After a few seconds he groaned loudly. "I've missed the boat, haven't I?" he finally said. "You've gone and fallen in love." When he saw her flush he groaned again. "I knew it."

Does it show? she wondered, unable to prevent the smile that touched her lips. "Don't you have somewhere you have to be, Hale?" she said as she read her e-mail.

"I guess I'd better find a new hangout," he grumbled. "Try my charms elsewhere."

Ava laughed. "Now you know you're the fabled confirmed bachelor," she said. "If you were really serious about settling down you would have given all your attention to Dr. Gloria Francis, by now. Everyone can see she's interested."

"Oh, is that why you haven't met me halfway?" he said with amusement. "Being gracious and noble for the other woman?" He stood, his exaggerated sighs making great noises. At the door, he turned serious. "Be happy, Ava."

Oh, I am, Hale, she thought after he'd gone. "I am," she murmured.

She answered the phone on the first ring, listened, and then, "Certainly, Dr. Howell," she said. "I'm on my way." *What a time to call an impromptu meeting,* she thought impatiently. It was almost time to leave the building for her class.

Ava was in her car trying not to speed. Her head was hurting, filled with Dr. Howell's words, yet she tried to ignore them but couldn't. She wondered how much of a head start they had and would they wait for her or did they have the right to break in? She took deep breaths to calm herself. Killing someone or herself would solve nothing.

Anger taking control over panic, Ava thought about what came next—that is if she were given a chance to even act on her own behalf.

Cole stood at the window watching the delivery truck pull off and then he turned to look satisfyingly at his new queen-size bed. It appeared to dwarf the bedroom, he thought, but oh, how much more space he had to make love to his lady.

Two weeks ago when he'd gone to order the bed he thought he'd drive away with it, but had to be content until the store did a computer search and finally found his choice on the floor in New York's North Carolina Showroom and had it shipped. He was about to make up the bed with new linen when he stopped at the sound of a car in Ava's driveway.

No, more than one car, he thought as he went to the window. His heart raced as he stared, and in seconds he was downstairs and out the door. Three police vehicles. Where was Ava?

Cole was staring at the cars when a fourth pulled up. Jack Thompson got out.

"Cole," Jack said.

"Jack, what the hell's going on, here? Where's Ava?" Cole looked when Ava pulled up but had to park on the road. There was no room in her yard.

When the officers saw Ava they left their vehicles and stood waiting. The spokesman, Officer Kirkland, approached her. "Ma'am, we have a warrant to search your premises."

Ava nodded. Cole was by her side and she slipped her hand in his. "Dr. Howell believes the scroll is in my house," she said calmly. "They have a search warrant." She looked at Sheriff Thompson. "You knew?"

"Called me as a courtesy, since this is my jurisdiction," Jack said, concealing his anger at the preposterous situation.

"Am I allowed to stay?" Ava said once they were all inside. Lord, how many of them did it take, she thought? So Hollywood! At least nine men crowded into her home, and seeing them walking around, disappearing into different rooms, panic began to crowd her throat as it had in the president's office. But anger overtook the fear, and at that moment she hated Winifred Whidby.

"Yes, ma'am," Officer Kirkland answered, and he began to methodically search her living room.

Cole was standing with Ava. "What happened this morning?" he asked in a low voice.

"Based on information that he received, Charles

Howell believes that I stole the Gustavus Vassa scroll."

"Information?" Cole scowled. "Winifred?"

"Of course that was confidential," Ava said with a grimace.

Cole followed behind Jack and Ava, silently cursing the stupid man who could have believed the lies about his dedicated professor. *Idiot!* he fumed. They had left the living room and were almost finished in the spare room. He could see the frustration on the faces of the two men and he almost laughed aloud. When they finally finished and left the room, he followed, passing by another pair that were on their way upstairs.

Ava was standing up against the wall in the hallway just outside the kitchen. When she looked at Cole he stared back and the message in his eyes gave her strength. She smiled at him.

Jack didn't miss the interchange of unspoken words between the two and he kept his council. He'd seen them going around town together and he knew then that he'd been right; they were a pair that needed each other.

Time passed slowly. The horde of men continued to meticulously search every room and every closet, drawer, box or container of every shape or form.

Some were upstairs while others had even gone outside to her gardening shed. A few were silently pawing through closets and cabinets and bathrooms. Ava was beginning to feel weary.

"Officer Kirkland, in here," one of the officers called.

Cole and Ava shared a perplexed look and followed some of the other men who were crowded around her study door. Ava pushed through and peered inside.

"What is that?" Ava said, staring at the unfamiliar cream-colored rectangular card the man was holding. The vellum-type paper certainly didn't resemble an aged scroll. Even they must see that, she thought.

Officer Kirkland took the item from his colleague and placed it in a large plastic bag. "Where was it?" he asked his officer.

"Under the glass," the young officer replied. "An edge of it was protruding from beneath some of the other papers you see there."

"What is that?" Ava cried again, her eyes wide in disbelief.

"This is part of what we were looking for, ma'am," he said.

"Exactly what is that, Officer Kirkland?" Jack said mildly. "Dr. Millington apparently has never seen it before."

"Just part of the warrant, Sheriff Thompson," the younger man responded. "We're going to have to ask Dr. Millington to come with us for further questioning."

"What?" Cole exploded. "What kind of sense does that make?"

"And who are you, sir?" Officer Kirkland said, eyeing the tall, angry stranger.

"Detective Cole Dumont, L.A.P.D.," he said heatedly.

"You're a long way from your jurisdiction," the officer responded easily.

Jack stepped up. "Easy, Cole." To Kirkland he said, "She's under arrest?"

"Only if she refuses to cooperate and come in for further questioning," he said. He added, "We have a

warrant for that too." He turned, and they all watched
as he reached up under the protective glass covering
on her desk and pulled more papers out as if hoping
to find more evidence. Satisfied that nothing else of
importance was there he let the glass down softly.

"Christ!" Cole said.

Ava went limp and stared in disbelief at her cluttered desk. How long had that "evidence" been lying
cleverly hidden beneath that glass by mounds of her
research work? she wondered. She shuddered. How
Winifred had managed that, she couldn't fathom.
And when?

"Ma'am?" the officer said, looking at Ava.

"If I refuse to go, I'm under arrest?" Ava asked
Jack. He nodded. "Then I'll go," she said simply.

Outside, Cole walked beside Ava. "I'll be right
behind you, sweetheart," he said. He kissed her
lightly on her lips. "Heads up."

Cole and Jack watched the cars pull off, with Cole
holding Ava's stare until the car disappeared from
view.

"I'll be damned if she's spending the night in jail,"
he told Jack. Cole moved to slam lock Ava's door and
then said, "You know any lawyers?"

Jack nodded. "One of the best, a friend of your
father's. Name's Lester Donlevy."

Cole was on his porch already pulling off his shirt.
"I'll be out of here in a minute. Can you get him on
the phone, tell him what's happening? I'll take care
of everything. Tell him to meet me at the police station." He stopped. "Jack." The sheriff looked at him.
"Is he good?"

"I told you, he's the best."

"Okay," Cole said and rushed inside.

In minutes he'd changed, grabbed his wallet with

his shield, and sprinted downstairs and out the door.
If he had anything to do with it, Ava would be sleeping in her own bed tonight. The fear and disbelief in
her eyes made him cringe with anger. He'd wanted
to punch somebody. But as he drove, he quieted.
She'd been there for him and now it was his turn to
be there for her. He wasn't going to blow it by spouting off and causing her more grief. With calm came
a clear head that sent his brain to working.

After a while he said, "Winifred Whidby, how'd
you do that?"

Chapter Thirteen

Ava awoke when Cole stopped the car and shut off the engine. The digital dash clock told her it was after midnight. Her bones were aching and screaming for relief. She could barely unbuckle her seat belt, and while fumbling with it she felt Cole's strong hands close over hers and the belt snapped loose.

"Come on," Cole said, holding out his hand. Taking it, Ava held on while walking to her door.

"Thanks again," Ava murmured, too weary to think and talk straight. Surely she'd said that so many times in this one day.

She felt unclean after spending hours in the police station. She'd wondered where Cole was. He'd promised to follow her. But then a lawyer, a Lester Donlevy, had miraculously appeared, telling her that Cole was waiting for her. With the lawyer sitting beside her, she'd been questioned for hours. She'd never seen such patience in a man. Where she would have an outburst of anger, tired of hearing the same questions over and over again, he would shush her, talk quietly to her, and then wait silently while they battered her with more questions. A few times he interrupted, telling her that she didn't have to answer. Mercifully it ended and she was allowed to leave, but only after Mr. Donlevy stood and said detaining her any longer was absurd—either charge her and make an arrest or let her go. Once outside, seeing Cole on the court building steps brought tears to her eyes. It was the only time that day she'd wanted to cry.

Cole was holding out his hand. "Your key?"

"I—in my purse," Ava murmured as she opened it and began searching. "B-but I had it when I let them in this morning." She stared frantically at the space around her feet. "Maybe I dropped it or left it inside."

Hearing the beginnings of panic in her voice, Cole caught her by the shoulders. "It will turn up," he said sharply. "Wait here." He released her and went around the side of the house. In minutes, the door opened from the inside.

Ava started. "The window," she murmured.

He saw her shudder and glance fearfully down the hall from where he'd come. "There's no one hanging around in here now, Ava. They've already accomplished what they wanted." He took her by the elbow. "You hear me?" God help the person who'd done this to her, he thought. He'd never seen her so beaten.

Trembling, she wrapped her arms around her waist but was startled when Cole's arms came around her, clasping her tightly to his chest.

"Stop this, Ava," he said against the crown of her head. "It's over for tonight. Over. I'm here with you."

Ava closed her eyes and leaned into his granite length. He was so strong and she culled some of his strength, taking it into her own body until she was breathing easier. She could feel the freeness taking hold and she was beginning to come alive. She straightened and eased out of his arms.

Cole looked at her, feeling the change. She was coming around. "Can I get you anything?"

"I want to wash," Ava said quietly.

He understood. Police stations had that effect on a body at times. "Coffee will be waiting," he said. "Or would you like iced tea?"

"Coffee, please," Ava answered, already at the foot of the stairs. "Do you need help finding things?"

"No. Go on, now. Don't be long." He watched her go and felt her every heavy step until she disappeared around the curve at the top of the stairs.

The warm water cascaded down Ava's head tumbling to her shoulders and soaking her body as she soaped and soaped again with the soft loofah. She tilted her head back, letting the water pelt her eyes as her hand followed the silky flow over her throat, down her breasts and to her hips, smoothing the peach-scented shower gel in dizzying circles over her skin. At last when she could scrub no more, she rinsed her body and ended the soothing stream of water. Drying her hair in the mirror she studied her image. She was alive now. Her eyes told her so. Her body tingled with life and expectancy. Not because she was squeaky clean but because he was waiting.

Cole was there and he would be there throughout. She knew that. Ava thought of hours earlier when she'd been driven away with him standing there speaking to her with his eyes telling her not to worry. Even hours later, when they continued to question her endlessly with their repetitive questions, she'd thought of him. No thoughts of her family, of Dahlia her only close relative: she'd only thought of Cole the one person she knew without a doubt who would be there for her. He was all the family that she knew. She felt peaceful, knowing that Minuet was truly her home now.

"Mmm, smells delicious," she said, inhaling the pungent coffee aroma as she entered the kitchen. "Thanks."

Cole caught her in his arms and kissed her lips. "I don't want to hear that word another time tonight," he said firmly.

Ava eased away and seconds later was sipping the hot brew. "You must know how I feel, so you also know that I can't help myself. When that lawyer walked in, well I . . ." She shrugged. "How can I not be so grateful?"

Cole listened as he drank. "I know you are," he said. "I understand."

His tone made her study him closely. "You've done this before," she stated. "Your job in L.A.?"

"Not exactly like this," he said, a smile appearing. "But, yes, every once in a while a kid came along who wanted to be saved." His eyes shut briefly. "I did whatever I could."

The enormity of the help he must have given in all those years swept her, and she suddenly realized why he'd chosen to work with the youth gangs. Curtis. He was trying to give life to a stranger in memory of his baby brother. Yet in the end one of them had tried to kill him. She closed her eyes against the pain and sense of betrayal he must have felt.

He saw her eyelids flutter and he cursed himself as he stood and put the mugs in the sink. "You must be exhausted," he said. "You should get some rest."

Ava stood and took his hand. "No," she said, leading him into the living room. "I want to talk."

Cole sat beside her on the couch, holding her

hand and waiting. He knew the feeling, he thought. Wanting, needing someone to talk to, to help you figure out what was going on in your brain. He understood. He waited.

"It's just all so crazy," Ava said.

"Sounds like it to me," Cole agreed in a tight voice. "Just what *was* that that she planted in there?" For he knew that it could only have been the she-devil, Winifred.

A laugh filled with incredulity escaped Ava's lips. "When they finally showed me the 'evidence' I nearly went wild on them," she said. "I think I actually scared one of those big guys."

"What did it mean?"

"You know how when you're looking in a museum and you see all these descriptive cards tacked to the wall beside an item? Well, sometimes the card is in the case with the object. What you saw was a nice-looking card, expensively done with fancy script, describing the history and the origin of the Gustavus Vassa letter."

"That's it?" Cole said.

"Uh-huh," she answered. "It's so ridiculous that it's scary that anyone could be held on so flimsy a charge, and worse, eventually arrested. But since the two were stolen together it's assumed that I'd already sold the letter to an unscrupulous dealer and for whatever zany reason kept the card." She felt her temper rising again. "Stupid, stupid people," she fumed. "Why would I do that?" She made a face. "If anything, the description would have gone along with the parchment. If it exists, the buyer would always want that description so he could know more about the piece he was illegally purchasing."

"Did you tell them that?"

"Of course, but who would listen? Mr. Donlevy as much as told them that they were treading on thin ice, that they had no case." She paused. "He's a good guy, knows his stuff."

"Jack said he was the best," Cole answered. "He was a friend of my father's, but I'd never met him before. He seems confident in what he's doing."

Minutes passed when Cole said, "I think you're overdue for some sleep. You'll never be able to get up in the morning." He stood and pulled her up with him.

Ava leaned into him. "Now there's a thought," she said dreamily, caressing his cheek. "That is, if you'll stay with me tonight."

He put on a solemn face. "I was planning on something altogether different," he said, and then smiled. "But there'll be tomorrow."

They were walking arm in arm when, in the hall, Ava looked apprehensively about, shivered and rubbed the gooseflesh that suddenly appeared.

"What's wrong?" He'd thought that she was recovered, but now he had doubts. "You're not afraid, are you?"

"Just worried," Ava said. "I really can't imagine how or when someone got in here without leaving behind some kind of sign." Thoughtfully she began to walk up the stairs. "I truly believe that Winifred did this, but how? It would be just like her warped thinking to put that thing right under my nose, knowing my littered desk would be the perfect hideaway, yet with a thorough search would be discovered. Just enough of an edge to be peeking out from beneath other papers, to be noticed by an observant eye." She frowned. "She was at the university the same as I was these last weeks, so she couldn't have been here. Do you think she had someone to do it for her?"

"But who?" Cole said. "And why? You'd think she'd go to some lengths to keep her dirty little secret." He paused as they entered her bedroom. "I'm still stumped at why she didn't leave the letter itself," he said. "What sense does it make to keep it when she wanted to put the theft off on you?"

"That's just it," Ava said. "She doesn't want the letter to be found."

He looked puzzled.

"It's a fake, Cole," Ava said. "Once discovered and returned, it's bound to be noticed by the archives staff. Maybe." She thought about the curator and her hardly there, minimal staff.

"Damn," Cole said. "Then that means the letter will probably never see the light of day again. She certainly had to have destroyed it by now."

"I believe that," Ava agreed with a solemn nod.

Cole was holding her by the waist and he pulled her closer to him. "This whole scenario is so ridiculous, like a bad play that will just die on its feet the first night out," he said in anger. He felt her shiver and prayed that he was right. His breathing heightened at her nearness and the control he'd been exercising since he'd put her in his car earlier was about to burst. She was so soft, smelling like a ripe, juicy peach, and he wouldn't agonize another minute of not tasting her. The low sound he heard was coming from his throat and before he scared her out of her wits, he acted. He turned her to him, and grasped her tightly. "Ava," he murmured, "I was scared, sweetheart. Thank God, you're here now." His mouth clamped down on her parted lips. She was as sweet as he'd remembered and his kiss deepened as his tongue went on an exploratory mission of its own.

"Oh." Ava was literally swooning in his arms at his fiery kisses. Her arms went around his neck as her feet left the floor in his bear hug. Quivering at the feel of his hard body as she slid down the length of him, her feet touching the floor once more, she succumbed to the torrents of desire sweeping through her. Her soft moans became his name as she moved her mouth over his, savoring every delicious thrust of his tongue. His hand was on her breast and her body responded with ribbons of fire shooting through her.

Cole found what he was seeking when his hand touched bare flesh beneath her bra. He was burgeoning against her when she touched his erection, and an ocean of stars exploded before him.

Almost of one mind they reluctantly separated and quickly undressed. Ava felt his movements and knew he was preparing to love her. She was waiting when he came to her bed. With looks of love and in silence they joined, each with their own thoughts of love causing great shivers of desire to rock them. The stillness of the night was punctured with their cries of delight and awe as the two naked bodies were driven to new heights of passion.

A surprised sound was torn from Ava's throat as she sank back down to the mattress.

Cole couldn't help but look at her in disbelief because like her, he had no words. He was lying beside her stroking her damp belly. "I didn't think so either," he finally said.

"What, love?" Ava asked dreamily.

"That there was something more to discover and to feel," he said, his body still basking in the warm glow of heated passion.

"I know," Ava said, her eyelids beginning to droop in the aftermath of good loving. She wanted to be still, to fall asleep relishing his feel.

Cole felt that deep sigh and he looked to see that she'd fallen asleep. He smiled, thinking that this was a pattern that he would definitely never object to. He didn't care in the least whether she fell asleep on him after loving, he thought, as long as she awoke in his arms.

Cole was falling off to sleep himself when he opened his eyes. Just the faintest sound caused him to tense. The room was dark, the door was open, and there was no light shining from downstairs. He sat up and left the bed, watching a sleeping Ava turn over, arm flung out over the edge of the bed.

On the landing he stood and listened. It was nearly 3:00 A.M. and any loud noise would have been an aberration to the quiet.

As he stood unmoving, he thought of years before. The empty-house smell of so long ago was gone. Filled with furniture and rugs, it was a home offering peace and comfort. His mind's-eye images of little sneaker-clad feet racing around the place, only to have muffled giggles give away a hiding place, brought a smile. Weeks ago he wouldn't have been able to walk through this house much less spend a night here. But Cole knew that a whole new life was about to happen to him. He would cherish the memories now, the pleasant ones of his brothers and his parents.

Downstairs, Cole was in the spare room securing the window again. He went from room to room studying and wondering just how the intruder was able to enter and leave with no sign of forced entry. At the study window he pushed aside the curtain and stood staring over at his house. There was nothing moving in the darkness, though uneasy, he watched and waited. He left the room still perplexed, then after prodding his brain he finally guessed: Ava had probably left a door unlocked.

During these last weeks that they'd spent so much time together, he had chided her several times on the bad habit. She'd laughed and said that she was definitely going to do better. He hadn't found it so funny. Now he shuddered to think what if she'd been at home when her visitor called? Especially if Winifred had sent a thug to do her dirty work, which was highly likely since Ava said the woman was almost always at the administration building. But what of the hours Ava was away in another building? he thought. She couldn't possibly keep track of Winifred's comings and goings.

At last satisfied that he'd heard just the ramblings of a night creature, he returned to find Ava still asleep. He slid into her bed and when she stirred he took the moment to nestle her in his arms.

Ten minutes later, a frustrated Cole was still awake. He knew that he should sleep because in a few hours reality was going to hit big-time and he needed to be alert and ready to go after the one who had stolen his love's joy.

Ava awoke at the same time as she would have if she were going to work. The smell of brewed coffee reached her nostrils. She sat up, pleased that he hadn't left her.

With mug in hand she found him out on the back porch sipping his own brew. When he heard her he looked up and held out his arm. She went to him.

"Good morning," she said, kissing him on the mouth.

Cole allowed his kiss to linger. When he released her he said, "You're moving slow."

"Yes."

He couldn't detect the odd note in her voice. "Aren't you going in?" he asked, giving her a long look.

Ava looked thoughtful. "No, I don't think so."

"Why not?" he asked, wondering what she was thinking. "You know you weren't charged with a crime, so there should be no harm as far as your job is concerned."

She relaxed against the chair, drinking her coffee and inhaling the fresh morning air. "Yes, I know," she said, a tinge of sadness in her voice.

"Tell me what's on your mind," Cole said.

She shrugged. "You know, while I was washing up just now, thinking how late I was going to be, I stopped and looked at myself," she said slowly. "My life has changed just like I knew it would from the moment I learned of the theft." She made a sound of disbelief. "I didn't know what I'd do once it came to this, that I was somehow involved or even thought to be the thief." She glanced at him and then turned away. "But I know now that if I entered that building I would be looking over my shoulder again, trying not to see the speculation in my colleagues' eyes, them wondering why I'd made such a stupid career-ending move."

"But it's over," Cole said, offering consolation.

She glanced at Cole and shook her head. "I'm found out," she said, the sadness entering her voice again.

"Someone knows about Georgia?" Cole asked.

"Charles Howell."

"What did he say?"

"He wasn't threatening or ranting when he told me," Ava said, curious about that. "He said he'd gotten information about my past and he wanted to hear it from me whether it was true or not. Said he wasn't one to act rashly on unfounded hunches about people. He knew all about the accusations against me. He had names and dates and knew that in that case the artifact was never found." She lifted a hand helplessly. "The information was all there— everything," Ava said. "I told him my side of the story and he listened, with more attention than anyone concerned gave way back then." She gave Cole a surprised glance. "I didn't expect that from him and I was taken aback, and grateful."

Cole wondered if she were really as calm as she appeared or if it was just her way of holding it all together before she burst from the shock. "Did he ask you to stay away while the investigation continues?" he asked.

"No, he didn't," Ava answered. That was another surprise, she thought, and wondered why he'd gone against his initial decision to keep the theft an in-house matter.

"What are you going to do?"

"I'll call Dr. Howell—tell him to find a replacement. I'm not going to continue the class."

"Replacement? For you?" He feigned horror.

Ava laughed. "Thanks," she said, feeling warm inside at his attempt to ease the hurt.

"Why, Ava?" He'd turned serious.

"Oh, I just think that I don't want to be there right now, not under the circumstances," she said. "I can't live under the suspicion like I did before. It hurts too much." She shrugged. "If it means that I have to start over elsewhere, I'll do what I must."

He stared at her. "Start over? You mean away from Minuet?" He couldn't, wouldn't let the little quiver in the pit of his stomach turn into an earthquake.

Ava held his gaze. "No, Cole," she said, with warmth, "I'm not going to leave Minuet. You're here. This is my home now." She reached out and took his hand. "I mean my work, my job. I'll have to find another place where I can be at peace with myself and my colleagues."

Cole brought her hand to his lips and kissed the soft palm. There was an ache in his chest and they sat, silent, thinking of what lie ahead.

After a while, he said, "We're going to solve this thing." Returning her squeeze to his hand, he murmured, "I promise you."

Hours after they parted, Cole was still puzzled over what had happened. He was almost certain that the person entering Ava's house had done so without having to break in. But when? he wondered. He was almost always around and would have heard or seen a car coming and going. No, that's not true, he berated himself. There were those four days that he'd been gone, left her, practically dropping from society. But he knew it had been his lifesaver and he didn't regret it. There was still the question that somehow someone had paid a visit to her unsuspectingly. The phone interrupted his thoughts. He answered it.

"Hey," he said, "what's up?"

"Business, man, business," Graham said. "I thought I'd be able to get away by now but it looks iffy even for the next couple of weeks. I'm sorry about that, man. How's the back?"

"Like new," Cole said, wondering if that was a note of insincerity he heard. "Working you to death, huh? I thought the boss could always take off, whenever."

"You civil servants always think that about us hard-working stiffs," Graham said.

"Yeah, and you know what we say to that," Cole drawled.

Simultaneously they said, "Hardly working." They both laughed.

Graham hesitated. "Uh, how's everyone in the old place? Jack and Virginia? Have you run into Fiona yet? You know she's a doctor, don't you? What's everybody else into?"

Cole listened with his third ear. "You mean everybody like old widow Lansdowne and her mutts?" Cole said easily. Then, "Like Teddie and her son?"

Graham was silent for a second. "Yeah, all of them," he finally breathed.

"Oh, well, the mutts are now a shepherd and a spaniel," Cole began, "named Scout and Twister . . ."

"Damn, Cole," Graham said.

"What?" Cole said innocently. "You asked about everybody. Was there someone specific you had in mind? Well, Fiona's laying for you I think, so watch out. I wouldn't be surprised if she wanted to be boyfriend and girlfriend again. You know, the old high school thing." He paused. "And little Theodora Perkins is a stunner. Don't know how she's survived all this time without someone snagging her. But I think there might be something going on there. I don't know."

"What do you mean? Teddie's getting married?" Graham asked.

"Well, not yet," Cole said thoughtfully.

"What's that supposed to mean?"

"Just what I said, not yet."

Abruptly Graham said, "So when are you leaving for L.A.? The job is calling?"

"I'll go back, but not to stay," Cole said. "There are some things I have to clear up, and then I'll return."

"You mean you're staying in Minuet?"

Cole heard the disbelief and he wasn't surprised. "Yes," he answered. "I'm staying home." That sounded good to his ears and he couldn't help but smile.

"Then . . . then everything is okay?"

Cole's breathing was easy as he said, "Yeah, Graham, I'm okay." Silence.

"Hey, you fall asleep on me?" Cole asked, wondering what had just happened. He'd heard the soft sound. "You okay?"

"Sure," Graham answered. "Just wondering what happened to make you do such an about-face after all these years, but I'm happy for you, man. Hey, how's the neighbor; the lady Doc? If I recall she wasn't all that friendly toward you. Did she make nice yet?"

Cole cleared his throat. "Uh, she's just fine," he said. He grew warm thinking about this morning when he and Ava left her back porch. He felt himself squirming.

"Hmm," Graham said. "She's fine, huh? Maybe I will try like the devil to find some time to get down there. Is she single?"

"For the time being," Cole said easily.

"She's involved?"

"Something like that."

"You?"

"Me," Cole answered.

"Damn!"

After a moment Cole said, "I think you need to come home—soon." His voice had grown quiet.

"What is it?" Graham asked in a lowered tone.

"There are things that need your attention before it's too late."

"Too late?"

"Just come home, Graham," Cole said, and hung up.

Toward the end of the day, Graham dropped what he was doing and pushed away from his desk. Since he'd called his brother he'd been restless and uneasy. Something had happened and it wasn't only the old business, the haunting ghosts in Cole's head that had miraculously vanished after all these years; no, it was something else just as important to his brother. He'd heard it in his voice. Cole wasn't a man who played games.

Graham called his assistant. He said when she picked up, "Check my calendar, and see what can be rescheduled for sometime in the future." He listened. "No," he answered. "Not for next week. I might be gone for a month."

Cole had nearly broken his promise to Teddie. Yet a gnawing in his gut was a sign that things were going to come to a head sooner rather than later. It wasn't difficult to remember the attentions of Robert Jacobs toward Teddie, and the pressure of just his appearance with a fabulous offer, could be almost too much for a woman who held such inner turmoil.

He knew that he was right to put some doubt in

his brother's head, because if Graham didn't come and see what was here waiting for him, he'd be on the verge of losing it forever. Cole knew all about letting time pass by.

But one thing he was certain of, he wasn't going to let Teddie take Royce out of his life so soon, not without the fight of his life. His nephew's bright, laughing eyes floated before him. It had been at least two days since they'd been together last and he was missing him, missing the laughter and the big hugs from those little arms. They'd been spending time together and he would fill up with pride whenever they were out and Royce would clutch his hand. He picked up the phone.

"Hi," Teddie said. "Is everything okay?"

"Things are fine." He hesitated. "Are you all busy tonight?" He wondered if he was becoming a bit overbearing, insinuating himself in their lives every chance he got.

Teddie understood. "No, as a matter of fact can you come for dinner tonight. Around six? Royce and I would love to see you."

He swallowed. "Six is fine. Would you like me to bring anything?"

"No," she answered. "Royce is always looking for you." She paused. "He cares, Cole, and it's long past time that he learned to love you . . . his uncle." She hung up with a soft click.

"Past time," Cole echoed. He thought of his brother and wondered if Graham had gotten the message.

Chapter Fourteen

The next morning, Ava was in the supermarket. She meant to go about her life as normally as possible, and cooking and eating were necessary to stabilizing her life, though Cole Dumont was an excellent stabilizer, she thought, smiling and thinking about last night. Yes, he was the strength she needed right now.

Charles Howell hadn't been too surprised when she'd called. He'd sounded saddened by the whole unfortunate mess, but he understood. He'd told her that maybe it was best for her because he'd been approached by the board, something about a moral clause in the school's policy. But he'd offered her encouragement and promised that when the matter was finished she was certainly welcome to take up her old duties again. He also said, after she'd inquired, that Emily Thiessen was willing to act in her stead until he found someone else to fill Ava's shoes.

Ava had been surprised at that news but felt gratified. She was wanted. It was with a start that she came out of her daydream while loading her trunk with her groceries.

"Ava," Fiona said, watching her with a smile.

"Fiona," Ava said dryly, taking note of the falseness exuding from the woman. Now she understood the reason for the doctor's goading of Teddie Perkins. Fiona was reliving her youth thinking that they were still teenagers vying for the affections of the school jock. *Oh, how wrong you are, Fiona Fitzgerald,* Ava thought. *Teddie's got something more precious than you will ever get from Graham Dumont.*

"I heard about your arrest," Fiona said with feigned sympathy. "What in the world happened? I thought when I heard that there must have been a dreadful mistake."

Ava got in her car. "I don't know what you heard, Fiona, but you're certainly entitled to your own thoughts about what's happening in my life." She turned on the engine. "As a matter of fact, why don't you do that yourself?"

"Do what?" Fiona said impatiently.

"Get a life of your own." Ava backed out of the lot without another glance at the woman.

At home, she was putting the groceries away when the doorbell rang. She opened the door and surprised, she stepped back. "Hale? Did anything happen?"

"That's what I want to know," he said, stepping inside. "For God's sake, Ava, what's going on? What in hell is the real story?"

She led him into the kitchen where she finished her chore and then offered him an iced tea, which he accepted. "Aren't you supposed to be working?" Ava asked once they were settled on the front porch.

"You are too. The place won't be the same without you," Hale said in a mild voice. "I heard rumors. Now I want to hear the truth. Why were you a suspect in the theft of the Vassa document?"

"Because I was accused of the same kind of thievery

when I was seventeen," Ava said. "Looks like once a thief, always a thief." Her laugh was brittle.

"Don't do that, Ava," he said.

"Oh, Hale, don't look so worried," she said after seeing that he was not amused. She sighed heavily and sipped her tea. "Ever since the theft I was treading water, expecting the inevitable to happen, and it did." She then told her side of the story, including her suspicions about Winifred and the document, their confrontation, and finally the ordeal at the police station. "That's the truth of it all. Now all I need is a solution. Do you have any?"

Hale whistled. "A fake?" he said. "How in the world did she manage that? Damn!"

Ava smiled. "That's what I say."

"Well, I'm glad you can lighten up about it," he said. "But I know no one else in their right mind believes that crap." Hale's brow was furrowed when he asked, "What can I do to help?"

"Help?" Ava said. "I don't think you'd better get involved in this mess, Hale. It's like trying to get rid of gum stuck to the bottom of your shoe. Keeps you mired."

"You honestly believe that I would turn my back on you?" he said.

She saw she'd insulted him. "I'm sorry, Hale. I just don't want my friends to fall under suspicion, and that can easily happen. Association, you know. You must know that the document will never be found, so there will always be that doubt. You don't need that." She smiled. "After all, you might chase Gloria Francis away if you're too close to even a hint of a scandal." She saw his frown deepen. "What's the matter?"

"I'm thinking that Winifred can't get away with this," he said thoughtfully. "There must be a way to prove her fraud."

"We're working on it," she said.

"We?" He saw her face flame. "Oh, the guy who stole your heart," he said. "Well, I hope he can come up with some ideas."

"We're doing our best," Ava said.

Hale stood. "Then let me know if there's anything I can do. Anything," he said.

They both looked at the vehicle that pulled into the next yard, and when Cole got out and waved, Ava beckoned to him and he came through the hedges. She watched as the two men sized each other up.

"Hale, this is Detective Cole Dumont. Cole this is my colleague, Professor Hale Trotter."

Hale gripped Cole's hand firmly. "Detective?" he said. "Great. Ava tells me that you two are working on this mess. Anything I can do, don't hesitate to call."

Satisfied with his instant assessment of the man, Cole said after releasing his hand, "You work at the university?" He looked thoughtful.

Hale nodded. "I'm at the community college for the next few weeks but yes, I work at Floyd Compton with Ava." He saw the other man's frown. "Why?"

"Do you know anything about Winifred Whidby?"

"Not much of the personal, if that's what you mean."

"That's what I mean."

Hale could see where this was going. "Anything I can find out, I'll pass along."

"Appreciate it."

After Hale left, Ava leaned against Cole who'd slipped his arm around her waist. "I don't think anything will come of Hale sidling up to Winifred," Ava said. "She's too closemouthed about her private life and Hale suddenly trying to get next to her will send up a red flag. Don't you think?"

Cole hugged her. "Maybe," he said. "But we have a man on the inside now." He kissed her cheek. "One way or another, that woman is going to let her guard down, and I'm hoping that it will trip her up." He turned her toward him and looked into her eyes. "You know your colleague likes you," he said.

"Hale?" Ava said. She smiled. "I know."

Cole raised a brow. "Should I be worried?"

Ava leaned into him and reached up to caress his cheek. "Never, my love," she murmured. "Hale's always been just a friend."

"*Friends* are good." Cole was holding her close, and when he felt her hand glide over his nipples and squeeze, he burgeoned against her. "Ava." He gasped. "Look where we are, sweetheart," he managed before she captured his mouth with hers. Her teasing manipulations to his body caused him to writhe in sweet agony.

"Yes, I know," she whispered, and then reluctantly pulled away. "Later, then, I guess." Her hand slipped, brushing his erection.

Jolted by the lightning touch, Cole rasped, "Later?" He quickly ushered her inside and slammed the door shut. He pulled her to him and kissed her forehead. "Too much sun, I think," he muttered. When he kissed the back of her neck, it was all over for both of them.

Much later, Ava and Cole were having dinner in Hudson. The seafood was excellent and they'd stuffed themselves on lobster and snow crabs until neither could savor another bite.

"Oh," Ava groaned. "I hate doing that, cheating myself out of that key lime pie." She stared at the dessert being eaten by another patron. "Ooh, that's simply torture."

Cole smiled. "That's torture?" he said, mildly giving her a look.

Ava flushed. Her skin still tingled from his earlier

magnificent ministrations to her body. She brushed the spot on her nape where he'd tortured her unmercifully. "Of the culinary kind," she said, knowing her face was aflame.

He brushed her hand lightly and smiled. "Okay, sweetheart, no more teasing," he said. "At least not here." A wicked smile touched his lips.

Cole sat back and sipped some more cognac. After a moment he said, "I'm thinking that Jack made a good point."

Ava thought about their late-afternoon visit to the sheriff. "He made a lot of sense in what he said," Ava remarked. "What point are you referring to?"

"About going back to the source," Cole answered.

"You mean to Georgia?" Her stomach felt queasy with the thought of revisiting her past. "That's the one thing I disagree with."

"I know," he said, feeling her fear. He knew about going back. But in his case he was being given a new life—that included her. "That's something that will come later," Cole said. "First, I think I'd like to know who is helping Winifred. I want to start there."

"But, how?" Ava asked. She felt clueless as to where to begin. "Do you really believe that she would even tell anyone else about what she did?" She shook her head. "The woman is too clever to let that out. Besides, what would be the point especially after taking such pains to create that thing? It must have cost her a fortune to boot."

Cole shrugged. "People make mistakes but they don't know it until they're caught. I'm going to find where she messed up."

"You're so certain?" Ava said.

"Yes." He made a sound of disgust. "There's got to be something and it's probably right under my nose." He signaled for the check.

During the drive home they played the events over and over, trying to hit on something they might have missed.

"This all looks so hopeless," Ava said in exasperation.

"It does—for now," Cole answered.

They were passing by Mrs. Lansdowne's and the dogs barked. Ava frowned, and she touched his arm. "Cole, I remember something. Twister."

"That's the noisy one," Cole said. "What did he do now? Get into your flowers again?"

"Yes," Ava answered slowly.

Cole looked at her face but didn't answer until after he parked in his yard. When they were sitting on his steps, he said, "Tell me."

"It was one day while you were gone," she said. "The day it rained so hard and into the night. It was a muggy warm rain and I was out back wondering where you were and if you were all right." He caught her hand and held it tight. She continued. "Then Twister came, scared the devil out of me because he was silent at first, tipping along the side of the house. When he saw me sitting in the dark, he began barking and Mrs. Lansdowne came right behind him fussing like she does as if at a naughty child."

"What happened?"

"She apologized for him messing up the flowers, and that I probably hadn't even repaired the damage from his previous foraging."

"Apparently she needs a better lock on her gate," Cole said.

"She realizes that, but she was just so annoyed that she had to come looking for him again in all that bad weather. That's when she mentioned that a few days before Twister had probably scared the people who drove like crazy out of your yard—or my yard."

Cole stiffened. "What do you mean?"

"That's just it," Ava said. "When she realized where his barking was coming from, she started down this way and that's when she saw the car barreling out of one of our drives. She couldn't say which one. She thought that it was one of your old friends visiting after hearing you're back."

"She didn't get a good look at who it was?" he asked.

"No. She was too far away. The only reason she thought about it was because they were driving so fast from a runt of a dog who couldn't get at them. She thought it was strange."

"Agreed," Cole said, although he wouldn't like to be on the receiving end of those sharp canine teeth. Still holding her hand, he stood. "Come on, I think we'd better call it a night." When they were on her porch, he bent and kissed her, long and lingeringly.

Ava held him, reluctant to let him go, but she realized he was respectful of her need to rest. "I'll see you tomorrow?" she asked, planting light kisses on his neck.

"Bet on it," Cole said, inhaling sharply. "But late. I'm going to look into a few things." He watched her unlock her door and push it open. "Want me to take a look?" he asked, watching her hesitate.

"No," she answered. "I'm okay."

"Ava?" Cole said quietly.

"Yes?"

"Have you called your sister about any of this?"

Ava was silent for the barest second. "No."

"Will you?"

"No." Her voice was bitter. "She wasn't there for me years ago, so why should she bother now?" Ava kissed his lips and then said, "Good night, love. Tomorrow night?" She closed the door gently, knowing he was waiting to hear the click of the lock. When she heard him walk down the steps, she went upstairs, trying hard to push Georgia and her sister out of her mind.

Winifred was in the dining hall finishing a lunch of a cool, crisp salad and lemon iced tea. The July fourth holiday had come and gone and the heat was still relentless, bringing out the crabbiness in everyone. That entire hullabaloo that took place with Dr. Ava Millington was but a memory. Winifred had scoffed along with others when her name had come up in all that mess, but it was laughed away as being ridiculous. Though Charles Howell was still angry and perplexed, the theft was no longer news and people were looking for the next big happening in their small world. Fools, she thought. But she smiled, thinking that now that her life was unfettered, all the fear and apprehension gone, she was anxious to get away and start her vacation. Once again she could live the life she'd struggled to attain. She was respected in her world, and where she came from that was all that mattered.

Her glance around the room centered on the curious couple who were talking softly to each other. Gloria Francis rose, smiled at her lunch companion, and then walked from the room. Hale caught her gaze and she nodded. She watched as he stood and walked toward her.

"Winifred," Hale said, not waiting to be asked, but sat down across from her.

Looking surprised but not offended by the attention of the handsome man, she said. "Hale." She cocked an eyebrow. "So, is there something budding there?" she asked.

"Uh-uh, not you too," Hale answered. "One lunch a relationship does not make, Winifred. You should know that. Look at where we are." He flashed his most charming smile. This was not the first time he'd tried to approach her, and was surprised by her welcome.

Winifred sniffed as though the air had suddenly become odorous. "Men," she clucked as though chastising a child. "One chickadee leaves in disgrace, but there's always another to take her place," she said.

Hale tensed but held his temper. If he wanted something from this woman he certainly wouldn't get it with curdled cream. "Gloria is a wonderful person and an excellent instructor, Winifred. Have you ever really chatted with her?" This time the smile widened.

"Oh, and what of Ava? Off your mind so quickly?" she drawled. "Well, I don't blame you. No one likes to be tainted by a scandal." *Damn, he's a handsome man,* she thought. Her glance flickered over his lips and she busied herself with sipping her tea. Why in the world Ava played so hard to get was beyond her. She squelched the sigh, thinking thoughts that she shouldn't have. But, she thought, just maybe . . . He had to be forty and she was going to be fifty on her next natal day. Hmm, there were worse age differences than that, she mused.

Hale was taking in every movement, flicker of eye and tone of voice that Winifred made. He had always been a good judge of people and he could almost see the conversation she was having with herself. He almost groaned with what was to come but he'd promised to do what he could to help a friend. Ava Millington was no more a thief than the Man of Steel. And too much time had already passed. Wondering how to broach the subject, he was given an out when a colleague approached.

"Winifred, Hale," John Brady, greeted them. "Man, I'm sure glad the spotlight has been taken off this place." To Hale, he said, "I've been meaning to catch up with you. How's Ava? Have you seen her, talked to her about all this? Damn shame, but if she took the damn thing well, she's got to know people have to pay for their mistakes." He pursed his lips in dismay. "A fine, intelligent woman, like that."

Hale saw Winifred's stare. "No," he said. "Haven't seen her and it sure beats the heck out of me too why she'd do such a thing," he commiserated with the upset math professor. "You just never know who you're dealing with."

"Yeah, never know. Okay, I'm off. See you two around." He left, still shaking his head.

Hale put on his own show of disbelief after the man left. "Isn't that the truth," he said in a puzzled voice. "You never know." He looked at Winifred who was eying him closely. "You two are pretty tight," he said easily. "What about it? Why do you think she did it?"

She gave him a reproving look when she said, "I have no idea what was in Ava's head."

Careful, Hale, he breathed. "Just what *is* something like that worth on the black market? You know, with the exception of your fascinating discovery, I never dreamed that we housed such priceless artifacts." He looked embarrassed. "I admit I've never visited the archives."

"Then you've missed quite a lot," Winifred said airily. "Floyd Compton has a very impressive collection of acquired manuscripts. You're doing yourself a disservice not to know what we house."

"Then I'm at your service Dr. Whidby," Hale said. "You will give me a private guided tour, won't you?"

Winifred fussed with gathering her things from the chair next to her. His emphasis on private was not missed and she wondered if she was receiving the correct signals. A quick glance at his handsome face made her drop her eyes again.

Well, well, she thought, if he chooses to close his eyes to their age difference, why in the world should she stress it?

"What's your schedule like later today?" Winifred asked. "The archives are empty after five."

"A clean slate," Hale said. "If the tour isn't that long maybe we can have dinner together? That is if your schedule permits," he added.

"We'll see," Winifred said. "At five-thirty, then."

Hale was still standing, watching her walk, head held proudly in that way she had, greeting people and passing them by as though they were her subjects.

Spending an evening with her needed fortifying and he hoped he had the stamina. There was something about the woman that had turned him off from the day they'd met and he could never put his finger on it. Her imperious air was one thing, but there was something else. Like a clock striking the hour he got it—furtive. That was it. She had that secretive quality that bordered on sneakiness.

There were about four hours left before his meeting with Winifred and he had work to do. Leaving the dining room, he went downstairs to the main floor. When he stopped at the frosted glass door he wondered who was on duty. Hoping it was a friend, he opened it and stepped inside. His smile was engaging. "Hi, there."

"Hello, Dr. Trotter. How can the personnel department help you today?"

* * *

Frustrated, Cole hung up the phone. For days he'd been calling, hunting down information for the littlest clue. If he never knew anything about antiquities and the black market before, he certainly did now. What a business. He scowled. If anyone thought that Ava had gotten rich off this one bit of thievery they needed a head exam. As Ava suggested, the Gustavus Vassa document—if a thing ever existed— was long gone, like a puff of smoke carried away with the wind.

It was midday and he hadn't eaten since breakfast. His food stock was limited, but leaving the house now would interrupt his momentum and it was getting late. He found a can of tuna and after the hastily prepared lunch he was on the phone again.

It was an hour later that he hung up, his brow furrowed. Impossible, he thought. He kept staring at the phone as if the instrument was going to speak to him. But he was certain that he'd heard right. The private detective, now retired, didn't have a thing to lose by telling the truth. Why would he lie about a long-forgotten unsolved case?

Cole stood, closing the book where he'd jotted down his notes. There were quite a few filled pages in the little notepad and he put it in his shirt pocket.

The sun was hot but he left the air-conditioned house to sit outside on the porch, where he began mentally mapping out his plan. The decision had already been made to leave for Georgia, but how much of what he'd learned was he going to share with Ava?

He hated to leave Ava alone in Minuet, but he didn't want her with him on his investigative trip. Not now. He glanced up when she pulled into her drive. When she saw him she smiled and waved, and he stood.

Cole thought that he would never tire of looking at her, watching her walk, talk, smile, and the way she balled her fist when she was angry, or thinking. He loved that woman and the thought of harm coming to her in any form was hard to take.

"Hey," he said when they met. "Had fun?"

"Mmm," Ava answered, returning his kiss. She held on to him for a second before plopping down on the chair. "Beat, but I enjoyed myself. We didn't stay as long as expected because the sun was too brutal. The kids even got tired standing in line for the next ride." She made a face.

"The day-care teacher liked the way Renee and I handled the kids and she invited us back for their next day trip to a different theme park in Nameoke," she said. Ava had been apprehensive about doing first-time chaperone duties with Royce's day-care center. But when the center director, a friend of Renee's, had pleaded for more volunteers, Teddie had given her consent for Royce to attend the outing. It was Renee who'd invited Ava to volunteer.

"You were a natural with them huh?" Cole said.

"They're a handful, but what a cute bunch. You can't stay mad at them for long," Ava said with a smile. "Royce is such a joy to be around," she added. She glanced at him and saw his smile. "But you already know that, don't you?"

Cole nodded. "That, I do," he answered. It seemed so long ago since he'd started bonding with his nephew. The little guy was inquisitive, full of questions about where Cole lived and what did he do and why he stayed away from home for so long. Learning that he was a detective had made Royce bubble up with excitement, and even more questions tumbled from his mouth. Cole would drop by some evenings and they'd go for a short drive to the park and walk around the pond. Sometimes Teddie would pack a basket and Royce, Cole, and Teddie would eat their supper wherever they happened to stop.

"Have you heard any more from Graham?" Ava asked quietly. She thought that he'd be here by now to see about his brother. She often wondered if his absence was because of Teddie. Maybe he did really love her and didn't want to experience rejection, especially since he believed she'd had a child by another man.

"No," Cole answered, and shrugged. "I'm guessing he'll show up though before long." He glanced at her. "Are you too tired to go out for dinner?"

"Oh, yes," Ava said, reaching down and massaging her legs. "Would you like to try potluck from my freezer?"

"From *your* freezer?" Cole laughed. "Any day," he said, and stood. "Come on. I barely remember the taste of that tuna sandwich, and my stomach is talking to me." He caught her hand and pulled her up, stealing a kiss from her delectable lips. "Mmm, you taste good," he murmured against her. He nuzzled her face, and with a slight maneuver he found the spot that he loved to tease. When she moaned, he grinned, pleased that it worked every time. "I see somebody is as starved as me," he whispered in her ear.

Later, when they were at her door enjoying a long kiss good night, Ava clung to him. Finally, lifting her head she said, "How long will you be gone?" she asked again. She couldn't believe that she wouldn't wake up to see his car or watch him come through the hedges with that sexy grin. It'd taken Cole a long time to allow a smile to come so naturally. But with all that'd happened in his life so recently, she knew that he was the happiest that he'd been in a long time.

"I don't know," Cole answered. "Maybe two or three days. Depending on how cooperative this guy is and if he'll give me any more leads."

"I still don't get it, though," Ava said. "How is what happened to me in Georgia so long ago tied to the theft of the Vassa letter?" She was perplexed.

"Sounds muddled but it makes sense at the same time," Cole said. "That black-market underground is vast. People know things, and in that shadowy world someone is bound to make a deal to line his pockets just by giving a name or two. And if you believe that Winifred Whidby had it created, that could lead me to another name. You never know. Slim leads often turn out to be linchpins."

Ava sighed. "Well, if you believe the trip is necessary. But can you try to finish up in a day? I'm going to miss you."

"I'll do my damnedest, sweetheart," Cole said, engulfing her once more in his arms, releasing her reluctantly. "Lock up now," he said gruffly. "I'll call you when I get settled."

After Cole left, Ava kept busy by gardening, and cooking and studying. Though the dog days of July were killing, she still ran in the early mornings, sweating all the evil thoughts from her head. They only served to cloud her thinking. She knew there had to be a way out of this mess, something that would implicate Winifred, because that was the only way Ava would be exonerated in everyone's eyes.

Cole had been gone for a night and she knew she'd miss him but not so achingly. It was barely two months that she had laid eyes on the man and had fallen in love as swiftly as a shooting star. Her resolve to remain put, not to run again, centered on her being absolved of any theft, otherwise the happiness she would have with Cole would always hold shadows.

She was in her study, poring over the notes she'd printed out. They were step-by-step events leading from the time she learned of the traveling slave exhibit and Winifred's "discovery" to her present situation. Earlier, she had called her source, her mentor—the person who'd confirmed that Winifred's letter was indeed a fabrication and had led to Ava's confronting Winifred about her classic deception. He'd been astounded at her predicament and ranted over the unjustness of it all. But he did give Ava the names of respected individuals who could have validated Winifred's find. Now she had something to do even if it turned into a dead end, but everything was worth looking into. She looked at the time and made a face. She made a note to make that call later.

As she studied the pages over and over again, something continued to nag her. When her eyes lit up at an item she murmured, "Could this be something?" But her thoughts were interrupted. She picked up the phone.

"Hi," she said. "I was going to call you later."

"Thought of something?" Hale asked.

"Yes," Ava said. "Winifred's letter was authenticated. Would the name of the expert be listed in some file somewhere at the university?"

"Hmm, it might be," Hale answered. "I'll check it out. It should be listed as general information in the archives. That shouldn't be a problem to get since they know me now. I can probably ask for Emily's assistance."

"Thanks," Ava said. "You've been a great help in all of this, Hale. I'm grateful."

"Not a problem," he answered, and then laughed. "Well, now I'm lying about that. To get all that information that I gave you about Winifred's past, took more than one dinner out." He paused. "Was any of that helpful?" he asked. "Given where she came from, it's not hard to understand that she'll do anything to keep her standing in her small world."

"But not at the expense of others, Hale," Ava said, trying to keep the heat out of her voice. "She committed a criminal act and that shouldn't be rewarded."

"True," Hale said. "You know, this place is not the same without you. I hear some of the students dropped your class with hopes of taking it when you return."

After a second, Ava said, "Thanks for that, Hale."

"Well, look, let's hope Cole found that info useful. How's it going on that end, anyway?"

"Puzzling," Ava answered. "But I agree. I hope he turns something up soon."

When they hung up, Ava turned back to the marked item on her paper. It bothered her until finally she got up thinking that it wouldn't hurt to just ask.

A short time later, Ava was walking with a purpose down Pine Road. When she stopped, there were no dogs barking and no Mrs. Lansdowne in sight. Frustrated, she wondered how in the world the woman received visitors or even deliveries with those two guard dogs making a frightening ruckus at every sound. Hesitant to just push open the gate and walk up to the door, she was about to walk back home when she saw the old widow beckoning to her from an upstairs window. Still unsure of where the silent dogs were, she didn't move, but when her neighbor began beckoning with vigor, and mouthing something that she couldn't hear, she unlocked the gate and stepped inside the yard.

When she got close to the house, she could hear. "Ava, come in. Come upstairs." Curious to find the door unlocked, Ava went in.

She'd never stepped foot in the yard, much less the house, Ava thought. To the casual observer, the old two-story house with its freshly painted exterior was the picture of quiet small-town country charm. The interior was immaculate and smelled as if it had just been scrubbed with lemon-scented cleansers. The décor was simple: pale yellow walls with beige trim and furniture reminiscent of Ava's early childhood in her parents' country-decorated home. Later her mother had gone more contemporary, but Ava saw that the big overstuffed sofa and chairs with baby blue and brown plaid covering were old but still looked good and serviceable. Colorful shawls were sprawled over the backs of two of the chairs. The floor was covered in a deep navy carpet that was fairly new.

From where she stood, Ava could see the stairs leading to the second level and down the hall, the kitchen. Listening for the dogs, she stood still.

"Ava, come upstairs. The dogs are not here."

Surprised and suddenly concerned at the weakness in the woman's voice, Ava found her way to the bedroom where she saw the widow sitting in a rocking chair by the window.

"Mrs. Lansdowne, what's wrong?" Ava had never seen the big woman look so small huddled beneath a huge comforter, her long braid loosened allowing her thick white hair to fall limply to her shoulders. "Are you ill?" Ava went to her.

A wan smile touched her lips. "Girl, I can't remember the last time I was laid up like this," Ellen said. She could barely speak through her parched lips.

"What is it?" Ava asked. "You look feverish." It was

a hot day and the house was an oven without any air conditioning, yet the woman was bundled up and shivering as if it was midwinter.

"Been like this since yesterday morning, ever since I took the mutts to the vet. I felt something coming on and I took some aspirin and lay down. It was near midnight before I woke up, and could hardly move."

"My goodness," Ava said. "You've been like this all that time? Why didn't you call someone?"

Ellen only looked away out of the window. "No one to call. Besides, no phone in here. No need since I'm only in here to sleep. Tried to make it downstairs but got dizzy and nearly toppled over so I made it back in here. I must have dozed again because I awoke and found it was midday. I sat by the window hoping that I'd hail the mailman for help but I guess I missed him."

Ava could see the effort the woman made in making her long speech. She felt her forehead. "You've got something," she said. Without a word she pulled off the comforter. "Come on. Let's get you back in bed and then I'm going to call the doctor. And you must be starving. You haven't had anything to eat since breakfast yesterday?"

"That'd be about right," Ellen said weakly. She didn't balk at Ava's help but willingly settled her aching body in the bed, pulling the covers over her.

"Is the phone in the kitchen?" Ava asked. When Ellen nodded, she asked, "Who's your doctor?"

"Doc Tomlinson." Ellen sniffed. "He's about as old as me," she said in her raspy voice. "I don't know about him making any house calls."

Ava left the room and in the kitchen found the phone directory. After reaching the medical clinic she was assured that Dr. Tomlinson or an associate would come. She hung up and began searching the fridge and the cupboards. A half an hour later, Ava was carrying a tray upstairs. She made space on the dresser for it and said, "I'll be right back." She returned with a washbasin and toiletries.

"I think you'll be more comfortable in a few minutes," she said. After helping her to wash and brush her teeth, Ava brushed the long hair and tied it back with a ribbon she found on the dresser. "There," she said. "Now let's get some of this soup in your stomach."

When Ava returned after taking the tray downstairs, Ellen looked at her neighbor. "Thanks," she said, her voice not as weak as it'd been, but she was still cold. "Guess I caught the bug," she said.

"I'm thinking that it's one of those foreign things," Ava said. "But I'm sure the doctor will be able to treat it." She frowned. "You know it might be a good idea to have a phone installed up here. You never know when an emergency will arise like this again."

"Something to think about," Ellen said. Her body ached and she wished she could fall asleep, but the chills and headache kept her awake and feeling downright miserable. "I'm glad you stopped by, Ava. Were you coming to see me?"

Ava looked in surprise. Was that a plaintive plea she heard? She realized that the widow must really be lonely, especially now when she had no one to call, to drop in to see about her. Ava wondered if she hadn't stopped by, just how long the woman would have remained here, sick and in trouble. She shuddered at what could've happened.

"Actually, I was coming to ask you a question about that car you saw a few weeks ago. The one coming from our driveways? I was wondering if you could possibly remember anything about it. The color, the plates. I know it was a distance, but the least little thing might be important."

Ellen closed her eyes briefly and with an effort said, "Young Cole came by asking the same thing," she said. "He was real serious and looked like he would wrestle a bear to get what he was looking for." She stopped to catch her breath. "I know the trouble you're having," she said. "I sure wish I could be of some help, but like I told him, it was so fast."

"Not even the color?" Ava asked. Cole had been so frustrated when he'd told her that his visit to the widow had yielded zilch.

Ellen frowned. "Appeared that it was a dark color," she said. "You know, not black, not blue but something in between. I didn't want to say because I'm just not sure. And it looked small, I think, not like these tanks people drive these days, not American-looking." Her forehead puckered again. "Sort of reminded me of that old car Donnie Gordon had souped up a while back. But don't ask me what make it was. Don't know."

Foreign, Ava thought. "That's something, Mrs. Lansdowne," she said. "More than we had to go on. Just maybe that person or persons could be responsible for all my troubles. And thanks for your concern. I appreciate it." There was a flicker of the old woman's eyes. "Is there something else?" She held her breath. *Oh, please,* she prayed.

"You know there was something about that tag. Even from the distance I could see it wasn't one of ours. Matter of fact, it looked like nothing I ever saw before."

"What do you mean?"

"Looked like a fake," Ellen said. She closed her eyes.

Ava could see the effort of talking had taken its toll and she wondered what was keeping the doctor.

"You and Cole getting married?" Ellen asked suddenly, opening her eyes to give Ava a stare.

Ava felt the warmth in her face. "I think you're feeling better already," she said briskly. The sound of a car sent her to the door. "Your doctor is here," she said. "I'll go down to let him in. And just in case you need a prescription filled, I'll wait. Even if it's delivered you won't be able to answer the door." She thought she saw the glimmer of tears in the woman's eyes and she turned quickly and left the room. *She really is lonely,* Ava thought. She couldn't help wonder what her future would have been like if a handsome man hadn't moved next door and stolen her heart.

When she opened the door she stepped back in surprise. "Fiona?"

Chapter Fifteen

"Ava!" Recovering quickly, Fiona stepped inside. "So besides romancing a fabulous Dumont, you've taken to nursing? My, what undiscovered talents you're exhibiting lately."

Holding on to her temper, Ava gestured toward the stairs. "Your patient is upstairs, Fiona," she said dryly, and went outside to wait on the porch.

After she calmed down, her thoughts went to the sick woman. Curious, she never paid attention to who came and went in this house. But then again, she was hardly that close by to watch the widow's activities. She would see her in town occasionally walking along Center Street peering in the shop windows or passing gossip with other women. Yet to hear of visitors just coming to look in on her, she was in the dark. Mrs. Lansdowne had always given the impression that she was totally independent and wanted or needed no one, though she was known to be a busybody. How she managed that without constant traffic in her yard was a mystery.

Ava thought that maybe she should start paying a little more attention to the elderly woman. She was willing to bet that that gruff act of hers was just that—all an act.

"Still here?" Fiona said, appearing on the porch. She gave Ava a piece of paper. "She said that you would take care of this for her."

"What's wrong with her?" Ava asked, taking the prescription.

"Stomach virus," Fiona answered. "She'll be fine in a day or so with bed rest and fluids. She's dehydrated." She walked down the steps and then turned before she got into her car, giving Ava a long stare. "Tell me something, Ava," she said.

"What do you want to know now, Fiona?"

"I was wondering, now that you've lost your job, when are you planning on leaving Minuet?"

"My plans are to stay right here, Fiona," Ava said softly. "Does that bother you?"

"Not in the least," Fiona said with a crooked smile. "It's just that when a man like Cole gets tired of playing and leaves for L.A., you'll be the one looking like a fool because he's played you like a bass viol." Her eyes narrowed and the smile vanished. "I just don't want you to think that his brother will be your consolation prize once he gets here because you're only steps from *his* bed," Fiona said in a hard voice.

Ava grimaced. "You're a sick woman." Then her heart raced. "You've heard from Graham?"

Fiona laughed. "That's my business," she said. Still laughing, she got in the car and backed out of the drive.

Teddie, Ava thought. Graham's returning to see Fiona? Staring at the prescription in her hand, she turned and went back into the house.

* * *

"What the hell," Graham said, staring at the phone as if it was something come alive. He pressed the replay button and listened again. It hadn't changed and he remembered his last visit home when she'd used that sultry voice to try to take him to a place where he refused to go.

"Graham, it's been too long since you've been home." She paused. "But I think you'd better come—and soon. There's something you've got to see for yourself. Soon now."

Listening to Fiona, Graham remembered that Cole had used almost those same words. *Come home soon.* He pushed away from the desk, his brow furrowed. "What the hell is happening in Minuet?" he said to the empty room.

A few weeks ago when he'd cleared his calendar to travel home, he'd changed his plans because he just didn't know whether he could face his brother in good conscience. Especially not after what he'd learned that had given him a one-two punch in the gut. What would it do to Cole now? he wondered. His brother was back home and sounding content at last. Should he mess all that up for him now?

Wearily he rubbed his forehead as if that would solve his dilemma. Then, he pressed the intercom and, grim-voiced, spoke to his assistant. "Get my mother for me please," he said. Graham closed his eyes, praying he was doing what was best.

The faster she drove, the more Fiona wanted to hit something, namely Ava Millington. She slowed but was still fuming when she reached the clinic.

After fifteen minutes of uninterrupted quiet she

had finally pulled it together. Seeing that woman so unexpectedly had been a jolt to her nervous system, especially since Ava had been on her mind for the last few weeks, and not in a pleasant way. Fiona had to admit that she was jealous of the professor who had moved to town and in just two years had become a welcome addition. Fiona had grown up here, and when she returned, a successful doctor, old-timers and former school friends still kept their reserved, respectful distances from her. No warmth, just respect. But she saw how they greeted Ava, like old friends, even though Ava was considered to be something of a loner, keeping to herself in that isolated house with no one for a neighbor except an old woman and her dogs—and lately Cole Dumont.

When Fiona had seen the unmistakable romance between the two she had been more than surprised— and envious. Cole had lost that dark, haunted look in his eyes that had appeared when sweet, little Curtis had died so tragically. Even then as a teenager, those few months that he stayed around after his mother had abandoned him and his brother he had changed from happy and carefree to a young brooding stranger, daring anyone to try and console him. She and Graham had done their best to make him snap out of it, but he'd brushed them off too.

Fiona felt herself getting tense again and she breathed deeply. The first time that she'd seen Cole with Teddie's son, Royce, she had wondered why she hadn't seen it before. Why no one had ever guessed. Royce Perkins was the mirror image of Cole Dumont. There was no doubt that Royce was a Dumont. But which Dumont? she'd wondered. She eliminated Cole almost immediately when she remembered that

Teddie had traveled to Ohio almost six years ago. And Royce was five. That realization had hit her like an exploding bomb. Graham and Teddie? Visions of the lovesick young teenager came back in living color.

So, she'd thought, Teddie had finally gotten her wish; she'd slept with Graham Dumont. But Fiona didn't panic. If there was something even remotely like love, Graham would have been back here to be with his woman. Since he was still in Ohio she knew that he didn't care one iota about Teddie Perkins. They'd had a fling and that was the end of it.

All except for Royce. She knew that Graham wasn't the kind of man that would abandon his child, so he obviously was ignorant to the fact that he was a father. The one thing she knew was that Teddie wasn't going to have him. Not again.

Graham was her old love and she meant to have him even now after all these years. The call she'd made to his office was just the start. Once he got here and saw how Teddie had deceived him, keeping his child a secret, the would-be fashion designer would be history. That would leave her in Minuet with Graham—and his son who would become part of her life.

Her eyes misted. A child to hold and to love. She wondered what her parents would think about that. A harsh laugh escaped as old memories surfaced. *Dear old Mom and Dad*, she thought, *you made me kill your own flesh and blood, but now you'll have to accept a bastard step-grandchild in your life. Won't* that *be something to live down!*

After seeing that Mrs. Lansdowne was settled with her medication and had eaten small portions of toast and soft-scrambled eggs, Ava left, promising to look in on her in the morning. She walked home deep in thought, wondering what she should do. Approach Teddie? But with what information? That Fiona had been in touch with Graham? Were they an item?

It was late almost eight o'clock but Ava decided the time was right. Teddie should be getting Royce ready for bed and they'd be free to talk. She changed from her perspiration-soaked clothes into a fresh navy short-sleeve pullover and white baggy cargo pants and sneakers. Then she called.

Teddie saw her friend coming and opened the door. "It's still hot," she said, still standing in the doorway.

"Yeah, it's going to be that way until the spell breaks," Ava replied in the same quiet voice. "You okay?"

"For now," Teddie answered, and then gestured. "Do you want the air or the warm breeze?"

"Let's sit outside," Ava said, and Teddie closed the door, and then they walked to sit on the bench on the side of the house.

They were quiet for a little bit until Teddie said, "She's going to make trouble, isn't she?" Her voice was calm.

Ava sighed. "I'm afraid so." She caught Teddie's stare. "What will you do?"

A slight shrug of the shoulders. "Graham doesn't love me."

"He did once and you have a child as a result."

"I told you. It was sex for him and love for me."

"Then you'll sit and do nothing while he rekindles something that's been long dead between them?

And watch while she tries to steal the affection of your child?"

Teddie's eyes hardened. "That'll never happen," she said harshly.

"Stranger things," Ava murmured. Something in her friend's manner scared her. "You've decided, haven't you?" she said in a bleak voice.

"I've thought about it," Teddie said. "Yes, I've made up my mind."

"Why?" Ava asked.

"Because I can't stay here and watch the two of them. It would have been bad enough just to have Graham so near, but to see them together as lovers with my son in between like they're emulating Damon Wayans and his TV family . . ." She looked away. "No, that would be too painful."

"And what of Royce?" Ava asked. "Once he learns about his father, you would deprive him of that relationship?"

"He's young," Teddie said. "We'll manage together."

"With Robert Jacobs?" Ava blurted. "Oh, Lord," she said. "Forget that I even said that. It's none of my business."

"No, you weren't seeing things when he was here," Teddie said with a slight smile. "I know he likes me and is hoping for a relationship once I get to New York, but I don't feel the same. He's not going to be in my son's life like that."

"When will you leave?"

"Before Graham gets here," Teddie answered. "Apparently Fiona has been in touch, and I have a feeling that he'll show up soon. It'll take me about a week to get things together with the diner and all. Hopefully that will be enough time."

"You promised Cole that you'd tell Graham," Ava reminded her.

"I know," Teddie said. "But it's a promise I can't keep now."

The two friends contemplated in silence.

"I'm going to miss you," Ava said. "You've been a great friend to me."

"I'm going to miss you too, Ava." Teddie caught her friend's hand. "And I'm glad you've found someone. Cole is a wonderful man and I hope it turns into something permanent." She laughed. "Don't make it sound like I'm going underground. We'll keep in touch, if only because I have to keep trying to turn you into a fashion maven." She made a face at Ava's pants. "I'm going to get you out of those things yet. You look as if you're ready to go on safari, except that you're missing the vest and the big elephant gun." She turned serious. "But I wouldn't change anything else about you." She studied Ava's face. "All except for those shadows in your eyes," she said. "I hope that when Cole returns he'll have news that will end this big mess once and for all."

When she returned home Ava picked up the message. Cole had called. She felt a twinge of loneliness for she had hoped that he would be on his way back home. She called his number.

"Hey, sweetheart," Cole said. "How's it going?"

"Hot in Minuet," Ava said, happy to hear his voice.

Cole laughed. "I'm afraid this heat wave is sweeping the country, I think I heard something about hail in the Sahara. Now *that's* scary."

"Wondrous," Ava replied. "I miss you, love. Are you almost done there?"

Cole hesitated. "I left Atlanta and I'm in Collier now, Ava," he said.

She stilled. After a second she said, "Why?"

"The information the private investigator gave me led to more questions and a lead that needs following up." He paused. "I need to talk to your sister."

"Dahlia," Ava said woodenly. "What can she tell you other than call me a thief as they all did." She sighed. "Why did you call me? Just do what you have to do."

"I wanted you to know," Cole said quietly. "If she called you before I returned, I didn't want it to look like I was insensitive to your feelings. But I think she can shed some light on a few things."

Dear sweet Cole, she thought, feeling more loved than she had been since she was a child. He cared about her, deeply.

"Ava?"

"Yes, Cole, go ahead with your plans," Ava said. "And thanks for letting me know."

"Love you, Ava," Cole said.

"I love you back. Hurry home."

The following Monday morning Ava was up at six and running. She'd tossed all night, finding it hard to sleep with all the commotion in her head. She'd felt like jumping up and fleeing the house into the darkness joining all the nocturnal creatures that were going about their mysterious existence. The straight route into town was a stretch of lonely dense forest on either side of her. Many drivers passed her on the

way to the turnoff that would take them to the highway and their jobs. She almost felt like making the
turn with them instead of continuing her usual run
into town. Halfway there, Ava stopped and turned
around. She didn't want to see or talk to anyone, especially Teddie. The sadness in her friend's eyes
was almost too much to bear. Ava wondered if her
friend would even stop and take the time to come say
good-bye before she left. Deep down she knew that
Teddie wouldn't, because running into Cole was too
chancy.

Passing by Mrs. Lansdowne's, she saw that all was
quiet, and made a note to look in later as she'd done
for the past two days. The dogs were still at the vet's
and were to remain there until the widow was on her
feet. Ava had made the arrangements. The information that the woman had shared replayed in her
head, and Ava was still mystified about who had been
snooping around in her yard. The sketchy description of the car was one that she was unfamiliar with,
belonging to no one that she knew, at least not in
Minuet.

Once inside and showered and dressed in a casual
skirt and top, Ava slipped into sandals, got her purse,
and went downstairs. It was still early but she had all
day to do what she needed to do. Downing a quick
breakfast she left the house, and after the promised
visit to the elderly woman she was soon driving the
familiar route to Florence.

Later, more than two hours had passed with Ava sitting in her car in an inconspicuous spot in the
parking lot. As staff drove in and parked, Ava eyed
each vehicle with an observant eye, dismissing those
that were the wrong size and color. She didn't realize

just how many big SUVs of all shapes and hues
hogged the roads. It was easy to keep an eye out for
the car of Mrs. Lansdowne's recollection. At ten,
when the traffic had slowed, Ava felt tired and de-
spondent. Her bright idea had panned into nothing.
Hungry and miserable she pulled out of the lot,
waving to the guard who gave her an understanding
nod, and waved back. Ava realized that that little gesture saddened her. She was missed and she missed
her life here, yet she had chosen to give it up because
of her thin skin.

"What now, little Miss Detective?" she said in frustration. She tooled the car toward downtown and
before long since it was barely eleven o'clock, she
was seated in a restaurant having another breakfast
of eggs and hash browns. She looked around wondering what to do next. She had been almost certain
that given the time and the chance, she would spot
something that looked vaguely familiar, because she
knew that whoever had been in her yard had been
sent by Winifred. There could be no other explanation. And that person had planted the evidence in
her house.

Ava counted out Winifred because the woman's
bright red Mazda was parked in its spot in the lot
on that particular day, and surely Mrs. Lansdowne
couldn't have confused that color with any other.

Feeling beaten, Ava finished her meal but sat staring at nothing, unable to move. She had nowhere to
go and nothing to do. There was nothing else that
she could think of that would help her in her quest
to absolve herself of any wrongdoing. *Whatever
happened to just telling the truth?* she wondered. She
almost laughed at that, considering that the twenty-

first century in its infancy was steeped in lies and deception.

As she sat mulling over her future, she thought of something that suddenly gave her hope. Why she hadn't asked the woman at the time she'd never know, but there had to be something there, Ava thought.

In her car Ava was undecided. Should she go to the university or just make a call? After a moment, she decided a call would be better. The woman might not even be on the grounds. She pressed the numbers for the school and waited to be connected. At the sound of the cheery voice she said, "Hi, this is Ava."

Emily Thiessen said, "Ava?"

"That's me," Ava said. "How are you doing with my students?" she asked tongue-in-cheek, remembering the bad report. "Are they as bright as I think they are?"

Emily hesitated and then said, "I had to give that up after the first week. They replaced me with a sub just here for the summer. I'm sure they'll be okay. Besides, this is the last week anyway." She paused. "So how's it going for you? Do you think you'll be back in the fall?"

"I'm hoping so," Ava answered. "I just don't want to return with that cloud hanging over my head. It'll work best for all concerned that way."

"I hear a question, but it's not coming," Emily said with laughter in her voice. "What's up?"

"I was wondering about something that's been nagging me and maybe you can clear it up in my mind."

"Shoot. Anything to help."

"Remember when we were setting up for the exhibit?"

"Seems so long ago but yes," Emily replied. "What about it?"

Ava had to laugh. "You know, Emily, Gustavus Vassa would probably be filled with mirth at the stir he's caused centuries after his death."

"I'm sure, but what exactly would be so funny?"

"You sort of indicated that the document that was stolen was not authentic and I was wondering about that."

"I did?" Emily said. "How'd I do that?"

"Your manner and what you didn't say when I mentioned the theft," Ava said. "You remember? It seemed as though you suspected that the letter was a fraud and so what if the truth never be told."

Emily said, "I wasn't aware that I was sending out vibes like that. I'd think that if I did suspect such a fraud I'd have enough sense and integrity to make my suspicions known."

Ava heard the censure and had mixed feelings about it. Apologizing now for her thoughts was too late; she was on a mission to clear her name and wasn't ready to deal with hurt feelings. "I agree," Ava replied. "But my feelings were pretty strong, and in leaving nothing uncovered I had to ask." Changing the subject she said, "Have you heard whether the university will be considered in the future for the exhibit?"

"No, I haven't heard a word," Emily said. Her voice lightened. "Something like that you should ask Charles. I'm certain he would be more than happy to keep *you* abreast of what's happening."

She wasn't surprised by the sarcasm. She'd stepped on the woman's toes. "Well, maybe I'll do just that," Ava answered. They disconnected and she was more depressed than before she'd made the call. What had that accomplished?

She'd learned nothing and was at a loss at what to do next. The only thing she could do now was to wait and see what Cole turned up. For the first time since he'd told her about visiting Collier, she thought of Dahlia. She wondered just what her sister would say and would she suspect how important the handsome detective was in Ava's life.

With thoughts of Cole and how she would feel once in his arms again, she pushed the ugly thoughts away and started her car. Home was the only place she wanted to be right now, her amateur-ish detecting skills deserving a big razz. What did she think she was going to accomplish? Even if she thought she could spot a car that probably didn't even exist, what was she going to do? She could just see herself accosting the driver and being looked at as if she were an alien gone berserk. She probably would have wound up in the police station again this time for harassing a citizen who would proba-bly press charges and she would really be arrested then.

Ava was surprised as once before instead of heading home she found herself in Winifred's neighborhood. Subconsciously she knew the answer to her problems lay in that house. She was sitting in her car a block away from the impressive-looking structure, waiting for what, she hadn't a clue. But something bothered her and she couldn't grasp what it was for the life of her. She had to smile at that because it *was* her life that was at stake here. All that she'd sweated and studied for and had finally achieved, was disintegrating and she was helpless to stop it.

Giddy, she wondered how does one break and enter. How did they break into her house? That was a no-brainer, she thought; her unlocked door was the perfect invitation. Would Winifred be so careless? Not a chance, Ava brooded. But she knew that inside there was a clue to what Winifred had done. Maybe she'd kept the letter, tried to preserve it somehow as a testament to what had brought her such respect and admiration from her peers. No, she'd hardly be that vain and dumb, Ava thought. She was too clever.

With nothing to gain by sitting alone in her car on a deserted block she started the car and slowly drove by Winifred's still house. Then it clicked; she remembered.

That day that she had so boldly confronted her former friend, when Ava was pulling onto the block she'd seen a car practically spin its wheels, pulling away from the curb. She'd remembered how the shrill noise had disturbed the peace in the quiet upscale community. Had that person been visiting Winifred or her next-door neighbor?

Her mouth went dry as she saw in her mind's eye what she'd been searching for all day long. The car had been dark, a blue or black or something in between; Mrs. Lansdowne's uncertain observation of a car that had moved too swiftly from view!

Too excited to continue to drive, Ava pulled over two blocks away from the house. "I was right!" she said, bewildered yet elated. Winifred did have help. The car being driven so erratically had been a blue-green. A small dark green car.

* * *

Winifred was sitting at her desk drumming her bright red lacquered nails on the desk. She'd been sitting there for more than an hour unable to concentrate on the mound of papers on her desk ever since she'd stood at her window staring out at the parking lot. Ava had sat unmoving in her car, just watching as each vehicle entered the gates. Did the woman think that she was inconspicuous?

She was seething inside. Just what was Ava up to now? she wondered. Thinking that the mess was well behind her, Winifred was on the verge of exploding. What or who had Ava been looking for?

Winifred played back in her mind the planning that had gone into getting that paper into Ava's house. As far as she knew nothing had gone wrong. The events following had played out like clockwork. Her visit to Howell; planting a bug in his ear; his investigation, though in her opinion it had taken the man too long to act; the discovery of the evidence. Winifred frowned. The only thing that she hadn't planned on was that Ava wasn't charged and arrested for theft. That smart Lester Donlevy had represented her well, knowing his stuff down to the last letter, she thought.

And even though her name had been mentioned, it had been dismissed almost as a joke. No one had believed Ava's wild accusations. None of that slime had even touched her and now Winifred smiled. But it was soon replaced with a frown.

If Ava was on to something else with her dogged search for evidence to implicate Winifred Whidby, she wanted to know about it. She wasn't one for being taken by surprise.

Winifred picked up the phone and after a second

said, "Ava's up to something. Find out what she's about." She listened and a bitter laugh escaped. "For *your* future as well as mine," she said, slamming down the phone in disgust.

Chapter Sixteen

Cole was grim-faced as he drove steadily toward home. *Home.* Every time he thought of Minuet as home, something tugged at his insides. In all these years, buried in his subconscious that he could never go home again, was the thought that life was so unfair. As a boy and later as a teenager—before his father died—he thought that he'd lived in a world that could do him no harm. Even as his friends were applying to colleges all over the globe to get away from their small-town existence, he'd never given the slightest thought to moving away. He grimaced. Choices had forced him to change on that point because he had joined the navy and had done just that—seen the world.

Then life in South Central L.A. had given him another hard knock on the door of reality. He'd seen all that he ever wanted to see of seedy underworlds. Big cities such as Casablanca, Paris, London—they all had their seamier faces that were generally overlooked by the traveling public. So L.A. was hardly the worst nor the most notorious of them all.

But one thing he'd learned during those years was

that human nature was a bitch. You thought that you had found a friend to trust and discovered that a betrayal could drop one in your gut that forever sullied your faith in human beings, although you could compromise and think: *That was a stranger, not my blood.*

He shook his head and he felt his lips twist in a hard line. When it came to family, how were you supposed to react to betrayal? Do what he did? Follow his mother's example and run away from it all? If the whole world did that then where would the sacred family structure be?

His stomach was twisted in knots, same as it had been after he'd left the Jenrettes. Ava's sister, Dahlia, and her husband, James, had at first been reticent; neither had wanted to talk to him about the past. He'd met their two sons, nephews Ava had never laid eyes on. Such a parallel his and Ava's lives were, Cole thought. He felt the frowns fade when the image of Royce filled his vision, and then return.

How was he going to tell Ava the truth? It would kill the final shred of hope that she unconsciously harbored of ever reuniting with the last of her family. To be able to do that meant that she would have to put the past behind her, forever accepting that she'd been branded a thief, never being able to prove her innocence, all because she wanted to live in peace for the rest of her life with family. Before leaving he'd extracted a promise from them that if they called Ava, they were to tell her no details of his visit.

Now all Cole wanted to do was to hold her, to love her, never wanting harm to come to the woman that he'd fallen for so hard and fast. He was feeling as the male species of old, that he was the one to offer solace and protection to the female. That he would always be there to understand and to mend wounds.

The drive seemed to be taking forever. Too many long hours had been spent without her. Depriving him of the smell of her after sex, after her shower, after kissing her in the morning, a taste of coffee on her lips, the way she walked around her kitchen moving quickly and efficiently from one appliance to another, her long legs and tight butt making him ache to take her where she stood. He'd done that too, making her flustered, sneaking up behind her, finding that spot on the back of her neck that drove her wild. She'd pretend annoyance, but then she'd let herself go, flooring him with the intensity of her response to him. He loved that in her, that honest display of emotions when she loved or wanted loving. She was almost saying "I'm giving you my all and I'm taking what I want of you." And he'd let her.

Pressing the pedal, Cole arrived in Minuet close to midnight. He pulled into his yard, the flickering light from his porch illuminating the darkness. That flicker was signaling an impending burnout and he made a mental note to change the bulb. Ava had seen to the place not looking deserted in his absence.

After a second's hesitation Cole slipped through the hedges. He wanted to make love to Ava. A smile touched his lips. Sometimes, when she was asleep, he'd love her awake and in the dream she thought she was having she was so uninhibited that the mind-blowing sex was incredible. He could feel his arousal just thinking about it. In no time he was on her porch.

* * *

Ava was sleepy but for some reason she couldn't go upstairs to bed. She missed Cole so badly that thoughts of him were so strong that it scared her. What if something was wrong and he couldn't contact her?

Since he'd told her of visiting Dahlia and James, she'd been dreading that call from her sister. What had Dahlia told Cole? Would she have told him how she'd aligned with their father and mother, who'd shown their disgust at having bred a thief? Ava couldn't imagine Cole sitting there taking all of that in, believing those lies about her. But she'd told Cole the truth. What if he came away with different thoughts of her now? Would he now begin to question the Vassa theft and her involvement in it? What would become of his confession of love to her? Would it survive the lies he'd heard?

Now she wished she hadn't been so cowardly. She should have called Dahlia, even if to hear from her own mouth the lies she'd told Cole.

She was sitting at the kitchen table gripping a cold mug long emptied of tea, which had served to warm and still the butterflies in her belly. She couldn't help but wonder where she was going . . . what her future was going to be. Would another job such as she had be forthcoming or would she have to move away to continue doing what she loved? Could there be the possibility that she could return to the university and life would go on as before? She was getting a headache just thinking. Her life had become a giant question mark.

At a loss of what to do next, Ava rose and put her mug in the sink. Maybe with the dawning of a new day fresh ideas would come. Sleep would probably come if she just went and lay down and closed her eyes, she thought. She made a face thinking that sleep would be elusive; Cole's scent was there. She turned out the light and left the room.

In the hallway, Ava jumped at the muffled sound on her porch. Footsteps? She held her chest as if to hold her heart in place as she stared down the hall. Then came the soft knock on the door and her blood warmed. An intruder wouldn't knock, she thought giddily, and hurried to the door and unlocked it. When it swung open Cole was standing there.

"Cole," Ava breathed, launching herself into his arms. "Cole, Cole," she murmured, kissing him all over his face, his neck, his eyelids, suddenly laughing, thinking that her intense thoughts had conjured him up. She clung to him, her arms wrapped around his waist.

"Shh, honey," Cole said softly as he moved them inside and with his foot kicked the door closed. "Ava, it's all right," he murmured against the top of her head. She was shivering so violently that he frowned, wondering what had scared her so badly. He held her, waiting until her body settled down. Something had happened, he thought. Visions of another clandestine visitor brought dark thoughts. His hold tightened, and his lips thinned. If she'd been frightened out of her wits by Winifred and her gang, someone was going to pay. He tilted her head and kissed the tears that glistened on her eyelids. Staring into the watery dark depths of her eyes he wasn't sure whether he was seeing fright, confusion or hopelessness.

Then all the thoughts he'd had while driving to her pelted his senses and the arousal that had started was now pressed hard against her soft body. He took

her face in his hands and bent to taste her lips. A
shudder shook him and he wanted to savor the feeling, unhurriedly exploring the inner warmth of her
mouth that he'd come to know so well. His kisses
were slow, deliberate, masking the urgent need that
quivered in the regions of his groin. His thumbs caressed the softness of her cheeks and brushed the
damp eyelids. He kissed them tasting the salt of her
tears. His lips left hers to nibble at the pulsing hollow
of her throat, her moans of pleasure inciting him to
continue his slow study of her facial contours. He was
drowning in the womanly scent of her knowing she
was ready for him to love her.

"Ava, sweetheart," he rasped, "I want you."

She was experiencing wave after wave of desire,
and taunted by his soft touches, his whispers of love,
she wanted him too, to feel the familiar nakedness
that her body would never forget. Her hands slid
down his taut frame to where the rock-hard bulge
straining against the fabric of his pants drew animal
sounds from her throat.

"Yes, my love," she whispered. Shivers of delight
raced through her when he pulled away and began
leading her up the stairs.

In her bedroom where she would have undressed
in the dark he switched on the light and stood gazing
at her.

"Let me look at you," Cole said in a gravelly voice.
"God, I've missed you, sweetheart." He unbuttoned
the soft white cotton blouse she was wearing and
when it hung open he pushed it off her shoulders.
The soft pink lacy bra covered what he desired and
he reached behind her and unhooked it, releasing
her breasts to his hungry gaze. "Damn," he said, and

bent to swirl his tongue around the tiny brown berries. He closed his lips over them and suckled until he heard her gasp. He unzipped her jeans and pushed them away, baring the sexy pink lace panties. When she stepped out of her jeans and moved to strip away her panties, he stilled her hands. "Let me," he rasped. He did it slowly, and when she was naked his eyes devoured the female mound that pulsed with need. He touched her there with one strong, thick finger and felt her damp. She jumped and arched her body into the invasion.

"Cole," Ava said in a whisper of a voice, "you're taking too long." She squeezed her thighs, capturing the intrusive finger that was still slowly, excruciatingly, massaging the quivering nub and she strained even farther into it. Her desire was overflowing and she pleaded, "I can't wait," she cried. "Please . . ."

Cole pushed inside of her and was quickly rewarded with the flood of her love. Her cries rent the room and when she collapsed against his chest he held her quivering body.

"You shouldn't have," Ava said nearly breathless. "I wanted to love you."

"You did, sweetheart," Cole said. "You gave me what I needed. Your love." She was undoing his belt and pushing away his pants and when she finished she tugged at the hem of his shirt and he helped her pull it over his head.

Ava took his hand and guided him to her bed. She saw him reach for his pants and when he came to her, naked and protected, she was ready for him. She held out her arms. When their bare bodies came together, Ava sighed. "I love you, Cole Dumont," she whispered. "Let me show you how much."

At last, he thought, as he laid his full length atop her, he was where he wanted to be after longing for her for so many hours. He wanted to get inside of her, satisfying his greedy need. When she moved, quickly sliding from beneath him and fitting her body on top he squirmed when she grasped his erection and bent to tickle his nipples with her warm moist tongue.

"Ava," he groaned, bucking at the sweet sensation that enveloped his body, sending fiery flames down to his toes.

"Shh," she whispered against his chest as she continued to nuzzle, gently pulling at his chest hairs with her mouth.

"Oh, man," he groaned. "That's torture, Ava." He opened his eyes to see her wicked grin.

"I love doing this to you," she said, her voice filled with sexy desire. "You squirm under me so sexily as if you want to melt right into me." A tiny laugh escaped as she bent her head to suckle his swollen nipples again. She was moaning and licking, delighting in her bold act of possessiveness.

"Oh, is that right," Cole rasped. When he would explode he felt her guide his penis into her and when she sank down taking him fully he yelped. "God."

Ava, head flung back, hair swirling around her shoulders, moved her hips slowly as if time were of no importance. She was kneading his nipples and as he writhed, she was quickening the pace until with one wild arch of his hips she saw the proverbial stars as she released her liquid love. While floating to earth she felt herself land swiftly on her back and then was lost as she was swept away in the tide of his loving, feeling him as he exploded inside of her.

Cole couldn't do anything about his gnawing need except to give her all that he had. His love for her was consuming him like an unfulfilled dream. He had to take his fill of her, to soothe and still the fires in his groin. His hunger was insatiable and he fed it with all the power that was in him. Her soft moans and warm hands touching, kneading, soothing his heated flesh, kept sending him spiraling into higher planes. Then, it was over as he sank with uncontrollable shudders overtaking his body.

Their bodies still moist from their lovemaking, they lay panting and breathless, Cole beside her with one arm outstretched beneath her head. Ava snuggled close, eyes closed, basking in the afterglow of mind-searing love. She'd longed to have him home and he appeared almost at her will. How magical was that? she thought dreamily, feeling pretty much like a sorceress.

Cole felt her drifting into sleep. "Sweetheart?" he said. Her answering response was a murmur as she turned into him, her lips brushing the tender skin of his rib cage. "Damn," he said, squirming, never knowing what a sensual spot that was for him.

She was still sleeping deeply when Cole returned from the bathroom. He slid into bed beside her, covering their bodies with the lightweight blanket. His skin, his whole body was alive from the loving it'd gotten and he was too keyed to sleep.

As he lay thinking about what he'd learned over the last few days, he felt the bitter mood return. How was he going to tell her? *Was* he going to tell her? After all these years, he rationalized, why must she know? Yet he feared Dahlia's sudden guilt trip would be the catalyst that could send Ava into a tailspin from which he would be helpless to rescue her. He could only pray that the Jenrettes would keep the past in the past.

Cole brushed his lips against his sleeping love. What he needed to do now was to bring some closure to her present dilemma. That would bring exoneration and eventual peace. He was determined to give her back her precious life, the serenity that she had before an evil woman had crossed her path. He hoped that then maybe she would think about sharing the rest of her life with him.

A cold sweat enveloped him. What if the evidence was never found, and the theft would always be associated with Ava? Would she go into herself and begin to exclude him? He shuddered, drawing the blanket up closer. His eyes closed as if trying to shut out the unthinkable—his life in Minuet without Ava.

The next morning Ava awoke slowly, stretching and purring like a satisfied feline. Cole's arm across her waist had her trapped.

Cole had been watching her. He'd awakened and found her nestled like a kitten, her cute rounded butt burrowed against him. He'd found himself rising, wanting her all over again.

"Good morning, love," Ava murmured. She lifted his arm and planted a kiss in the crook of it, inhaling his warm male smell. With her lips she pulled on the prickly hairs and wiggled into him when he yelped and flipped her over onto his belly.

"You don't want to start that," he growled, giving her a warning look. "You'll never get out of this house today."

Ava grinned and began kneading his nipples. "Like that would be the biggest problem of my life," she said as she dipped her head and kissed his eyelids. She let her body go limp against him, her head resting on his chest. "I love you, Cole," she murmured.

"Love you back," Cole said, holding her tightly against him. "Next time I go sleuthing, you're tagging along with me," he said. "I missed the hell out of you."

Ava smiled at a thought. "Mmm," she said, "maybe we can open up a detective agency together. Ma and Pa Sleuths at your service. You can teach me all the tricks I need to know to be the best partner you've ever had."

"Ma and Pa, huh," Cole said. Ava had slid off his belly and was propped on one elbow, looking at him with impish eyes. "Do you know what that implies?" he asked.

"Uh-uh. What?" Ava said as she twirled a finger around his cheek making tiny circles.

"That we're parents," he said seriously, watching her.

Ava stilled her hand. "Oh," she said. She adjusted herself and lay on her back staring up at the ceiling.

Cole, not expecting that response, watched her intensely. "That doesn't appeal to you?" he asked quietly. "To have my children?"

"Whew!" Ava said, blinking her eyes rapidly. "Cole, what are you asking me?"

"To become my wife and the mother of my children," he said in that quiet voice. He had no idea that those words were going to flow from his mouth. But he was only speaking what was in his heart. Had he spoken too soon, scaring her witless?

Ava sat up. "Wow." She shook hair out of her eyes and pulled her legs up until she was hugging her knees. Then she said, "Excuse me," and hurried from the room.

Cole heard water splashing in the bathroom and he couldn't imagine what she was feeling or thinking. Had she never considered the possibility of sharing the rest of her life with him? he wondered. Whenever he'd ever thought what life would be like without waking up beside her every morning, it seemed the only natural thing to do was to be together every day for the rest of their lives. So wouldn't she want to marry him? It was quiet now and he heard nothing. He lay still, waiting—worrying.

Ava dried her face and the damp ends of her hair and stared at her shocked image in the mirror. Marriage! She sat down on the edge of the tub. What was wrong with her? she wondered. Why did she react like that? She knew that if the unthinkable happened and Cole left her, she would think it was the end of her life. So why shouldn't she want to be with him for the rest of it? Wasn't marriage and kids the next progression when you were so madly in love that a mere few days of separation was like being on a tether?

But how could she willingly give herself to him forever when she had such baggage? She made a face as she hugged her bare arms. What would the future be like for Mr. and Mrs. Cole Dumont? Or rather, Sheriff Cole Dumont? He had spoken to her of his conversation with Jack Thompson and the sheriff's wish that Cole run for his job in the future. The campaign slurs would be nasty and mean. Overcoming that, would the new sheriff's wife always be looked upon as a thief and therefore untrustworthy? He'd probably be suspect in certain dealings and actions. What kind of role model would that be? she thought.

Cole heard the door open and he couldn't stop the thudding of his heart. He knew she'd made a decision and he remained still, eyes closed waiting for his world to plummet.

She saw his still form, naked beneath the covers, and she knew she'd hurt him. Ava slid into the bed, her bare flesh touching his, and as always her body reacted with warmth flooding her. But she needed to talk so she held herself in check. She kissed his eyelids and he opened his eyes. "I love you," she whispered, kissing his lips.

Cole forced himself to look into her eyes. "That's funny," he said in a voice that was barely a whisper. "I thought that that was why two people became man and wife." He adjusted himself until he was sitting arms folded against his chest. "Want to tell me why I would think that? Has the world changed that much while I was living into myself all these years?"

"No, love," Ava said, doing her best to keep from touching him. She saw that his body language didn't want that. He was struggling with his emotions and she was saddened at what she had to say.

"Cole, just look at what you'd be getting," she said in a hushed voice. "You've spent all your adult life living with such guilt and pain that it nearly ruined you forever. You're on your way to healing." She shut her eyes briefly against his stoic face. "I, on the other hand, have this cloud hanging over my head like some dark specter that will follow me forever, because we both know that the fake document will never be found." She gave a harsh laugh. "I almost wish that I had been accused, arrested, and served my time, and then I would feel that at last I was exonerated in the eyes of the law and my colleagues. Even you," she said.

Cole looked incredulous. "Me?" he rasped.

Ava said, "Yes." Then she went on to explain her reasoning, and when she finished he was looking at her like she'd grown antlers in front of his eyes.

"Sheriff, be damned," Cole exploded. "What kind of man do you think I am?" His dark look snagged her eyes as he could only will himself to keep calm and not take her and shake some sense into her.

They were both silent with the high emotions encapsulating them.

It was Cole who spoke first, finally taking her hand in his and holding on tight. "Ava," he said, "I love you. I don't want us to be separated by some hedges. That's not the way I want to spend my life here in Minuet. I want to marry you, to take care of you, and if we're lucky enough to have children, then I want that too. I want everything that I never had, but only if you're with me sharing in it all." She was about to speak when he leaned over and brushed her lips with his. "Shh," he said. After a moment he continued. "I'm going to do my damnedest to get to the bottom of that staged theft at the university, and I won't stop even if it turns into the great unsolved mystery of the century. And if that is the only thing that is keeping you from marrying me, then I know damned well it won't take me that long." He tilted her chin and made her look at him. "You understand what I'm saying?" When she nodded, he seemed satisfied. "Then I won't ask you again," he said. "Not until I've done what I have to do." He kissed her lips. "Then

you'd better get ready to have Teddie start designing
your wedding dress."

Ava had tears in her eyes and her heart was overflowing. She kissed him, long and lingeringly. "I'm
so lucky to have bought this house," she said dreamily. "I knew it was meant for me. I hate to think of
what of my life if I'd settled in Marrakech or somewhere far from Minuet," she said. "Then I would
never have found you."

Cole caught her in his arms and bent to caress her
nape. When she sighed and squirmed against him,
his breath was ragged when he said, "Unthinkable,
sweetheart."

Later, much later, Ava and Cole were sitting on the
back porch where they'd just finished a very late
breakfast. They'd slept, showered, and spent the
quiet hours talking about the years he'd spent in
L.A. He would have to go back, he'd told her, to
clear up a few things. There was his condo to put
up for sale and to empty out. His resignation from
the force he wanted to do in person.

"You know you're coming with me, don't you?"
Cole said mildly while giving her a look.

Ava smiled. "Just try leaving me behind," she said.

He grinned. "You're going to make a very good
partner, Detective," he said. "Seriously, though, I
know you've probably been there several times in
your travels but I'd like you to see it with me." He
smiled. "There are some great places to visit and the
restaurants are among some of the finest," he said.

"Once," she said. "And I was so stuck into my studies I hardly saw the light of day."

"Well, we'll have to change that," Cole said.

They fell into a comfortable silence when Ava stirred. She sucked in a breath.

"What?" Cole asked.

"I told you about Mrs. Lansdowne being sick," she said. He nodded. "I've been thinking about something she remembered about that car."

Cole sat up and he stared at her. "The car that she saw leaving here?" He was alert, his senses beginning to tingle. "What did she recall that she couldn't tell me when I asked?"

"It has to be foreign. And it's probably dark green," Ava said.

"How does she come up with that?" Cole said impatiently. "Small doesn't translate into foreign and blue or black doesn't turn into green."

"But it's the way she described it," Ava said. "And why couldn't it be a dark green if not black or dark navy blue?"

Cole conceded. "Okay, we'll go with the dark green," he said. "But that's it?"

"She said it reminded her of one that used to disturb her peace a while back but she hasn't seen or heard a car like it in some time, probably not since last summer."

"Bad muffler?" he asked, suddenly very interested.

"No, I don't think that's what she meant," Ava said, mulling it over. "More like a revved-up motor."

"Anything else?" Lord, what else hadn't that woman told him? he wondered, trying not to explode inside. So much time was wasted.

"Just that she thought that even from the distance the tag looked different, but she couldn't put her finger on it."

Cole was standing and he was slipping his feet into

his backless sandals. He stopped when he saw the frown on her face. "More?" he breathed.

"There's something else," Ava said, now standing beside him. "I went back to Winifred's house yesterday."

"You what?"

"I remembered something." She'd followed Cole into the house where he was getting his shield and his wallet where he'd placed them on the living room table.

"Go on," Cole said, anxious to be on his way.

"The first time I went there, something bothered me about the noise a car made when it was speeding from Winifred's block. I only caught a glimpse of it because it was so far down the street, but I think it was dark green," she said.

"Christ, Ava," Cole said, hurrying to the front door. "Why didn't you tell me all this?" he said in exasperation.

"I think I had other things on my mind last night, Detective," she said, clinging to his hand as he pulled her with him.

Cole stopped and clasped her to him in a bear hug. He kissed her mouth—hard. When he released her he said, "Well, amateur, I've got a lot to teach you about gathering and sharing the evidence while it's fresh." He cocked his head and grinned. "But now that I think of it, I'm sure glad that I didn't start the lessons before last night because I wouldn't have been otherwise occupied." He kissed her and watched her squirm. "And not making you feel like this," he whispered in her ear. He opened the door and blew her a kiss. "Got work to do. Lock up, sweetheart."

At home and in less than ten minutes, Cole had

changed into fresh clothes and was out the door. He drove quickly but cautiously from his drive, frowns now replacing the smiles he'd had for his love. Cole only hoped that solving this part of her mystery and bringing an evil woman to justice, would absolve him from telling Ava about the foulness he dug up in her past. *Maybe, just maybe,* he thought, *she'll never have to know.*

Chapter Seventeen

Jack Thompson swiveled back and forth in his chair while he listened without interrupting a very intense Cole. As the younger man talked, Jack realized that he'd been right about the professor. Ava Millington had secrets. But that didn't change his impression of the young woman who'd brought an old friend back to life. He'd seen that she'd had a serene goodness in her, one that was essential in dealing so effectively with a wounded soul. And, he thought with amusement, falling in love hadn't hurt the two young people either. His visitor had finished his story and was waiting, watchful of his reaction.

"Sounds like Ellen was holding on to an important piece of information," Jack said and then frowned. "But then again, people don't always place any significance on what we law officers do," he said. The wrinkles increased. "Last summer, huh?"

"About then, yes," Cole answered while trying not to appear too hopeful. "Any clue as to what or even who she was talking about?"

"Trying to think," Jack said. "Sounds like a hotrodder. The deputies have had their hands full of that sort of thing and mainly in the hot months when the boys want to show off their rides, impress the girls. You know about that." His brows rose and he looked ready to smile at an old memory.

"Yeah, only too familiar," Cole said, a grin cracking his lips. When he rolled his shoulder, he was grateful that it'd healed without further problems. "So what do you think?" he asked. "Anything ring a bell?"

"Not to me, but maybe one of my staff remembers something about bringing somebody in for speeding and disturbing the peace." He pressed the intercom and called in one of his deputies.

"Deputy Bobbie Nichols, Cole Dumont," Jack said, introducing the young woman.

"Hello, Cole. Nice to see you again," she said shyly.

Cole looked in surprise at the pretty young woman who apparently knew him. "Deputy," he said, standing and taking her hand. "I'm sorry. From school?" he asked. He couldn't place her face. He sat back down.

She smiled and shook her head. "You wouldn't remember me, but everyone knew the Dumont brothers. I'm the youngest in the Nichols clan. Two of my brothers played with Graham on the football team. I was still in grade school."

"Oh," Cole said, and smiled when he recalled the family. There had been a bunch of them, about six boys and three girls. Ray-Ray and Otis Nichols had been two terror running backs on the team and had helped to win many a game. "I remember," Cole said. "How are they doing?" he asked the deputy.

"Good," Bobbie Nichols answered. "They, like most of my brothers, moved away, all except for the one next to me, Mitch, who is a mechanic here in Minuet."

Cole looked at Jack who returned the look with satisfaction.

"Deputy," Jack said, "we're interested in any souped-up cars that have been disturbing the peace, especially last summer. Mitch still fixing up those cars for the boys?" he asked mildly.

Deputy Nichols looked annoyed. "Sure is, Sheriff Thompson," she said. "I had to tell Mitch about that one day last year when I was nearly plowed into by one of his jobs when I was on patrol." She shook her head. "I pulled Donnie Gordon in here and then gave Mitch a piece of my mind. It didn't do any good because now Donnie is away. He was driving that thing drunk and he hit a pedestrian. I wasn't on the scene but heard that he smelled as if he'd been soaked in a beer barrel, he reeked so badly. Thank God the man is fine, but he could have been killed."

Cole said, "Do you remember anything about the car? The make or model?"

"Sure," the deputy answered. "I was interested in how a teenager was able to get and maintain that Jaguar." She shrugged. "But then, that wasn't too hard to figure out," she said. "His parents give their kids anything they can afford and they can afford a lot. They own their own software firm in Florence."

"I wonder what their money is doing for Donnie now," Cole mused.

"Deputy," Jack said, "would Donnie have been racing up and down Pine Road at any time that you can recall?"

Bobbie nodded. "Sure, that's where he nearly snagged me," she said. "Not far from the widow Lansdowne's place." She looked relieved. "Since Donnie nearly killed that man, I notice the hot rods are few and far between. Not too many complaints from the citizenry about the cars disturbing the peace."

"Since last summer?" Cole asked.

"That'd be about right," Bobbie answered thoughtfully. "As a matter of fact, this summer has been peaceful so far."

"Thanks, Deputy Nichols," Jack said. "You've shed a lot of light on the problem."

Before she left, Cole said, "Deputy, have you noticed any other Jags around town lately, say in the last couple of months or so?"

Bobbie thought and then said, "Not in town, no. But I was on patrol on Pine Road a few weeks back when I saw a car that reminded me of Donnie's, but of course it wasn't him. Then again, I observed the temp plates and knew it wasn't his."

"Where was this?" Cole asked.

"Not too far from your place on Pine Road, Cole. I was on my way into town and the Jag was coming toward me at a fast clip but not noticeably over the speed limit." She smiled. "I think when I was spotted, the driver slowed down but I couldn't be sure."

"What color was it?" Cole asked.

"Same as Donnie's. Dark green."

Cole nearly held his breath. "Are you sure they were temp plates?" Cole asked.

"Definitely. From my rearview mirror, I saw the white paper taped to the inside back window with a temporary number. The fake plate itself was one of those garishly colored advertisement things touting the dealer's name."

Cole's eyes narrowed. "Did you get a look at the driver?"

"Just a quick glimpse of the profile as she passed,"

Bobbie said. "She didn't glance at the patrol car and kept her eyes straight ahead."

"Anything else?" Cole said.

"No, nothing unusual."

"Well, thanks, Deputy," Jack said. "That'll be all."

When the door closed, Jack said, "I think we can make something out of all that, don't you?" He picked up the phone and after a second said, "Get me Motor Vehicles." He winked at Cole. "We're on our way," he said.

Well, of course there wouldn't be anything unusual, Cole thought as he was driving back home more than an hour later. In this day and age there were so many diverse communities that no one looked out of place unless they were sporting green skin and blood-red eyes. Jack had patiently made calls and listened to information he'd garnered from other agencies. He'd passed the information to Cole with a look that said there were a lot of rotten apples in the barrel and they all weren't at the bottom either.

Cole hoped Ava was still home because he wanted to drive into Florence as soon as he could. From Jack's office he'd also spoken to Hale. The brother had been helpful in the past weeks getting that info on Winifred's past, and hopefully he could tell him what he needed to know now. Cole made a face. No wonder the woman did whatever she could to make a name for herself so as to rise to the top of her game. He just couldn't understand people who did things like that. It was obvious the woman had a decent brain and was already respected among her peers and colleagues. But for some, a brass ring was never enough; they wanted the sky sprinkled with diamonds, he thought.

Cole found Ava on the side of the house messing in her flower garden. She was on her knees so engrossed in pulling some weeds that she frowned, and he could have sworn she was muttering to herself. He smiled, letting his eyes drink in all of her—the cute rounded firm buttocks and her strong thighs and shapely legs. He could feel them wrapped around him in a love vise, and his body reacted. This wouldn't do, he thought as he began walking toward her. They had business to attend to, but later he would hold her and do his utmost to love her hurt away. He wondered if the news would make her sad or happy that it was finally coming to an end.

"Hey, sweetheart," he said when he reached her. He knelt on one knee and stared at her wilting flowers. "Couldn't save them all, huh?" he said with sympathy. He brushed her cheek in a light kiss.

"Hi, love," Ava said, turning her head so that his kiss turned into a deeper one on her mouth. "Nope," she said. "The weather did them in, but I'm trying to salvage what I can." She sadly pulled a wilted day-lily that was too far gone. Cole caught her hand and pulled her up with him. "So," she said, "did you solve my mystery for me, love? You were gone a long time."

Cole heard the pathos behind the light voice and saw the wariness in her eyes. He was still holding her hand and started walking toward the back door. "Come on, get washed and changed. We're going into Florence." Once inside he said, "Hale will be calling you anytime now. Want me to get it if you're still getting ready?"

"Hale?" Ava said. "Why?" She was already going up the steps when she turned and looked at him. "He's found out something?"

"I'll tell you when you come back down," Cole said quietly.

His tone was grim and after a second, she said, "I'll hurry. And yes, please get the phone."

By the time Ava was ready and downstairs the phone hadn't rang and Cole was worried. What was taking so long? he wondered.

"Why don't you just tell me?" Ava said in a quiet tone. "Maybe it would be better to find out while I can still throw things. In the car all I'll be able to hit is you," she tried to joke.

Cole smiled. "I think you're right." They were sitting in the kitchen and Ava had poured cold soft drinks for them. He took a sip and set the glass down.

"The car Mrs. Lansdowne half described was a dark green Jaguar," Cole said. "It belongs to Emily Thiessen."

Ava looked blank, yet her mind went into a tailspin. "Emily? The curator? What in the world does she have to do with this?" She gave Cole an incredulous look. "She and Winifred? They barely speak. Winifred doesn't deal with people she considers beneath her level. She doesn't even respect Emily's field!" Ava was bewildered. "What's going on?"

"Your Dr. Whidby has a lot of talents," Cole said grimly. "She and Emily have a history together."

"What do you mean?" Ava said while trying to keep a clear mind.

"Winifred was one of Emily's character references when Emily applied for her present position," Cole said.

"What?" Ava was puzzled. "I don't understand," she said, looking at Cole in consternation. "How do you know all of this?"

The phone interrupted Cole and he looked at her. "Probably Hale," he said, and gestured for her to answer. When she picked up the receiver, he waited.

"Hale," Ava said. She listened. "Yes, I just found out," she breathed. "Yes, he's right here." She paused. "Sure, I'll put him on the speakerphone." She set the speaker and then said, "What happened?"

"I called Sheriff Thompson. He said that he would alert the Florence authorities so that the proper warrents could be obtained."

"What have you found out?" Ava asked.

Hale said, "I was able to get into personnel records again and you were on point. Emily listed as one of her references a Dr. Melvin Codling. It was the same name listed as the authenticator of Winifred's great find."

Ava stared wide-eyed at Cole who gave her a quizzical look. "Codling?" she said. "That man's been a disgrace to the profession for years," she said. "Incompetent, dishonest, and has lost face with several of his esteemed colleagues. I learned that while in my senior year of college. The last I heard he'd retired into the woodwork because he was on the verge of doing some time because of his black-market dealings, but with little or no proof and turning rat, the authorities let him off the hook with the proviso that he make himself scarce." She was shaking her head in amazement at Cole. "How could his name have been accepted as an authority in such a thought-to-be important discovery? Unbelievable." She was leaning on the counter, hand on hip, and now she gestured helplessly into the air. "What was Dr. Howell thinking? Has he tried to contact Codling about this?"

Hale laughed. "Please, Ava," he said. "Howell is all

into the fund-raising thing, you know that. Probably never even knew about Codling's history." He paused. "Besides, it won't do any good even if he did get his head out of the sand and try to question Codling. Unfortunately, he'd have to do that through a medium."

"Codling's dead?" Ava said in anguish. She met Cole's sympathetic look.

"Heart attack, soon after Emily started work here," Hale said.

Cole was by Ava's side and he gestured for the phone, and she gave him the receiver. She turned off the speakerphone. "Thanks, man," Cole said. "Is she there?"

"No," Hale answered in disgust. "Not in today. Winifred either. I tried Winifred at home but she's not picking up."

"I'm not surprised," Cole said. "Do you think they're on to your snooping? They could be trying to clean up any mess they left behind." He scowled at the phone.

"Could be," Hale said. "Let's just hope the judge believes and is signing those warrants."

They spoke for a few more minutes and when Cole disconnected he saw that Ava had left the kitchen. He found her sitting on the back porch staring at nothing.

"Ava." When she looked at him, his heart dropped to his shoes. Deceived again. How could he even think of telling her what he'd learned in Georgia? he wondered.

"What's going on, Cole? What else did you and Sheriff Jack come up with?" Ava held out her hand and Cole came and sat beside her.

Cole's thumb was running back and forth on her palm and he felt her squirm. He stopped because he knew that was a turn-on for her so he just clasped her hand in his big palm.

"Emily was associated with known smugglers of precious artifacts from Italy and Egypt," Cole said. "Years ago, early in her career and before she became an established curator, she was questioned in a theft of a picture carving, a cracked slab from a tomb in Cairo. She was small potatoes and was let go without being charged with anything. Later, the history professor who had been her mentor was arrested and charged with the theft. It was found that he had for years, reproduced some of the supposed-to-be-finds from some of the great tombs of Egypt. In his home they found stuff ready to be marketed to eager tourists who thought they were buying a bit of history. Pure junk it all was. What did him in was that he had kept a couple of the real deals for himself."

"Black-market stuff," Ava said in disgust. She looked puzzled. "How in the world did Winifred hook up with her?"

"They met in Rome one year and soon afterward Emily was employed at Floyd Compton, and not too long after that, Winifred made her 'find.' "

Rome. Ava couldn't help but think of the city where she first met Winifred. Must be something about that climate, she thought bitterly, wondering if fate had played a cruel joke on her. She said, "So I guess Emily had burned her bridges everywhere else and was looking for a place to plant her feet." *Just like me,* Ava thought.

"Apparently," Cole said. "We think that Emily helped Winifred plan this whole scheme, making you the mark." He stood. "I think we should go now. We want to be around when this thing comes to a head before the day is over."

Ava stood, her body feeling like she'd been punched in the gut and then thrown on the ground and stomped on just as if she were competing for the title of champion wrestler of the year. Silently she went through the motions of gathering her purse and locking up and following Cole to his car.

As they drove, Ava said, "So do you think that the artifacts will be found with Emily? She's gone back to her old tricks?"

"That's what we're hoping for," Cole said. "When I was doing my investigating, calling in some favors from some buddies, I was able to find out that nothing is floating around underground, like the objects stolen from the university. It just might be a possibility that she hasn't made a bona fide contact yet." He shrugged. "Who knows? Maybe she's holding out for her price, whatever that might be. Anyway, I hope she doesn't smell a rat with Hale's sudden friendliness toward her friend."

"I was worried about that. That was definitely a red herring," Ava said, and then sighed heavily. "Poor Hale. What he must have gone through. He can't stomach Winifred."

Cole glanced at her. "Like I said, he likes you."

She caught his sideways look. "That doesn't bother you, does it, Cole?" she said.

He waited a second and then said, "I'm glad he's your friend, sweetheart." He felt her stare and he gave her a quick look. "And I'm glad I'm the lucky guy." Cole smiled when he felt her hand on his thigh, squeezing it gently. He caught her hand and brought it to his lips. He thought of his life before she entered it and then said huskily, "The luckiest guy around."

They were close to Florence when she spoke. "You

did such a tremendous amount of detecting in such a short amount of time, Detective," she said to Cole. "You hardly needed me as your partner," she tried to joke.

Cole reached over and ran his knuckles over her cheek and then tugged on a wayward strand of her hair. "I had ulterior motives," he said softly. "I have a question that's been searing my tongue just waiting to be asked."

Ava felt a blush warm her cheeks. "I know," she said in a soft voice. "I know."

Cole's cell phone rang. It was Hale. "Everything good to go?" Cole asked.

Hale swore. "No, I guess you and Ava can forget about anything happening tonight," he said. "I'm at the police station and I just found out that the judge isn't acting on what he's heard. Wants more proof." He paused. "Sorry about that."

"Damn," Cole said, and disconnected. After a quick look at Ava's face he gripped the steering wheel, staring straight ahead. He felt as helpless as a drunk trying to clear his head after a binge.

Ava saw the look of frustration on Cole's face after he'd disconnected. Her head began to hurt when she guessed there were no warrants. Where was all this going to end, she thought. "We lost?" she said.

Cole turned to Ava, and seeing her look of hopelessness, caught her hand. "No," he said firmly, shaking off his bad mood. "Just this round." He caressed her cheek. "Not the whole match, sweetheart."

* * *

"For God's sake, Emily," Winifred groused. "I told you not to start your mess as long as you were at Compton." She glared at the woman and then got up and began pacing the living room floor. "Howell was hardly subtle today with his questions!"

"Don't start, darling," Emily said smoothly. "I'm not in the mood for your take-pity-on-me act. I wasn't the one to invite an expert on slave narratives to move into the very place where you had your dirty work on display for the world to see." Her voice was pleasant but her face was a grim mask. "Besides, how would it have looked if only that worthless piece of paper was stolen? Just think about it," she said, and made a sound of disgust. "Those other artifacts I took are invaluable. I don't even know how they were acquired for this hole-in-the-wall place. Whoever comes to look at them?" She threw a look of disgust at the angry woman. "Your learned faculty is so ignorant of what is housed in that building." She smirked. "I saw the opportunity and I took it," she said.

"Yeah, and where did it get you?" Winifred said. "You haven't even been able to unload all of it like you thought you would. So easy, you said," she spat, as if her tongue burned with bile. Then she turned on her heel and advanced on the woman who sat up straight staring at her with apprehension. "You're so stupid! Anybody knows from watching those silly cop shows that you don't flaunt your wealth right after doing your dirty work. Anticipating your riches you just had to get rid of your ancient heap and go and buy that old Jag, didn't you? Why couldn't you wait until you got the hell out of town?" She looked down in anger at the woman and balled her fists as if to keep from striking her.

"Oh, chill out, Winifred," Emily said disgustedly. "How the devil is anyone going to associate my Jag with any of this? Now you're getting paranoid."

Winifred looked heavenward. "Well, I should be!

Little Miss Expert wasn't sitting in that parking lot nearly all damn day looking for a lost lamb. She must have had a clue as to what she was looking for. And you couldn't even find out why!" Her eyes narrowed. "And you swore that no one saw you at that isolated house that day."

"No one did," Emily said blandly. She stood and gathered her shoulder bag. "In any case, I'm not sticking around," she said. "I don't feel right about Howell's suspicions and especially how Ava's lovesick friend has taken a sudden interest in you when he hadn't a clue that you ever existed," she said with a laugh. "Do you really flatter yourself that he's actually besotted? You'd better check yourself out, darling." She walked to the door. "I've already decided to move on, and after removing one more iron from the fire, I'm on my way and you should be thinking about doing the same, Winifred." Emily grinned at the stupefied woman. "Yes," she said. "It looks like you're about to lose your pedestal in your little world. Too bad, isn't it?"

Winifred watched Emily pull off with the same clatter she always did, as if she were driving the Indy 500. She turned away from the door, and glancing in the gold-framed mirror, stared at her face. She stood there for a long time. After a while she reached up and with her fingers explored the area around her eyes as if trying to smooth away the wrinkles. Finally her painted red mouth twisted into a smirk. "You fool," she said.

* * *

It was nearly eleven o'clock when the taxi dropped Graham off. He stood in the yard of the house where he'd lived as a child. Surprised not to see Cole's car, he walked toward the dark house. The darkness was unrelieved even from some light from the neighboring house. There was a car parked in the drive and he supposed the professor that his brother was enamored with was already asleep.

Graham used his key and opened the door. When he reached inside and flipped the switch for the porch light, nothing happened. Annoyed, he shut the door and walked into the dark house. In the kitchen there was light and he felt relieved.

"Cole?" he called. Even before he called his brother's name he knew the house was empty. He turned out the light and went upstairs, where he turned on the hall light and went in to his old room. In the dark, he put his one suitcase down on the floor and removed his jacket and shoes and fell across the bed, bone-tired, and closed his eyes.

"Feeling better?" Cole asked. He glanced at Ava who'd been more upbeat on the drive home from Florence where they'd stayed all day and evening. Since they'd been so close they had continued on after Hale's call and had made a day of it, trying to take their minds off of the present dilemma. After a movie they'd had dinner and then went to a jazz club where local artists were allowed to sit in with the professionals.

Ava said, "The day turned out not to be all doom and gloom. Tomorrow will be here all too soon to start worrying again." She touched his thigh and squeezed. "Thanks for making today bearable."

"I wish it was all over," Cole said. "But let's hope that judge wakes up tomorrow and sees the light," he said tightly.

"Yes." Ava glanced at Cole and then looked away. All day, ever since Hale's call with the disappointing news, she'd felt a change in Cole but couldn't figure out what was bothering him. He'd done all the right things, said all the right things, laughed in all the right places when she tried to make jokes, yet she felt that he was on the verge of saying something and then catching himself up. She couldn't help feeling that he was keeping something from her, and she wondered if Hale had come upon something. It would be just like men to decide what a female could or couldn't handle, she thought.

The silence was not a comfortable one and Cole wondered what thoughts she was suddenly having. A quick look at her face told him that her mind had traveled somewhere else.

"Ava, this is going to come out in your favor," he said. "You'll have your life back before you know it." He only wished that that were true and prayed that he would be able to help her through it.

"Will I, Cole?" Ava said softly.

"Why wouldn't you, after the shock of Winifred and Emily wears off?" he said.

"I can't help feeling that there's something you're not telling me," she said. Then she smiled. "Trust me, love, I can field as many monkey wrenches that are left to be thrown into my life. With you helping me to play catch, how can I not?"

"I'll always be here for you, Ava," Cole said.

Curious at the seriousness of his tone, she didn't answer, yet felt even more deeply that Cole had a secret.

When Cole pulled into his dark yard and parked, ready to walk Ava to her door, he stopped and stared at his house.

Ava said, "We didn't leave any lights on. Guess we forgot in our haste getting out of here." She saw how still Cole was. "What's wrong?"

He inclined his head toward the house. "No porch lights," he said. Then, "Damn. I knew that bulb was on its way out," Cole said in disgust. "Meant to change it but guess I had other things on my mind." He frowned. "A light is on in there somewhere. There's a shadow around the side," he said, gesturing toward the far side of the house.

"Wait here," he said, and his hand went to his hip. "Damn!" He wasn't packing.

"Cole," Ava whispered. "I'm coming with you." She was close to his back in the darkness. "You're not leaving me behind."

Unable to see, he knew that her jaw was set firmly. "Okay," he whispered, and quietly turned his key in the lock. Uncertain as to whether a prowler was in the house, he decided to leave off the lights. He knew the place better than any intruder and the darkness was on his side. Stealthily he made his way inside and gestured for Ava to stay close behind him. Listening for sounds, he heard none coming from his immediate vicinity. The house was eerily quiet. He saw that the light was coming from the upstairs landing.

A quick but silent inspection told him that the first floor was undisturbed. On the stairs he paused and mouthed to Ava to stay put. She remained halfway up the stairs while he continued.

The door to Cole's bedroom was closed and as he stood looking down the hallway, a relieved sigh escaped as he walked toward the opened bedroom door. He stared.

Feeling something had disturbed his sleep, Graham

awoke quickly. He turned over and saw the still form in the doorway. "Slaw?" he said.

"Crackers," Cole answered. He shook his head. "Where the hell's your car?"

Chapter Eighteen

Cole had seen a tired and surprised Ava safely into her house after making the introductions between her and his brother. He'd held her close, promising an early-morning visit. Now he sat at the table, patiently waiting for the interrogation into his love life.

Graham pushed away the empty plate after devouring the cold chicken sandwich and was on his second bottle of Pepsi. He looked around the kitchen and then turned his attention to his brother. "You *are* all right," he observed with his penetrating stare.

"I am," Cole answered easily while returning the probing look.

"That's some of the best news I've heard lately, Slaw," Graham said in an emotion-filled tone. He cleared his throat and looked away.

Cole smiled at the use of the old nickname and didn't answer right away, giving his brother a chance to collect himself. Early on before they were preteens they'd joked about the names their parents had selected for them, laughing that their mother probably had food cravings. Graham crackers was her staple when she was pregnant with Graham and coleslaw was the food of the day when Cole was in the oven, they'd decided. They would crack up at their mother's reaction when they started ragging on themselves by using the nicknames to her consternation. As they grew up, the names were used rarely.

"She's beautiful," Graham said softly, noticing the look of contentment about his brother. He thought he was looking at a stranger a far cry from the hurt and angry man he'd left in a hospital bed in Los Angeles. "And she's in love."

"She is, and she is," Cole answered, wondering just how long Ava would remain in love with him.

Noticing how easily Cole moved about the house, and seeing the changes he'd made, Graham said, "You're thinking about making it permanent?"

"If she'll have me," Cole answered quietly.

"You've asked?"

"Yes."

"I don't want to get all up in your business, but she doesn't look like she's getting ready to take flight anytime soon."

"There are issues," Cole said heavily.

"Anything you want to share?"

Cole talked for a long time, his brother refraining from making comments. Somehow after he'd finished, Cole felt relieved, as if a burden had been lifted. *Must be something to confession,* he thought. *Good for what ails you, and all that,* he mused.

"That's heavy, man," Graham said after a while.

"I know," Cole answered.

"You think she'll never be the same once you tell her?"

Cole shrugged. "I'm hoping she won't change and

will let me stick around. She's going to need somebody and I hope that somebody is me."

Graham saw that his brother was a man in love and he was happy for him. He'd thought that the woman in Cole's life would be there to pick up the pieces once Graham revealed his own secret, but now he thought she would hardly be in a position to console his brother while she was falling apart herself. *What a damn mess,* he thought with anguish.

Cole saw the weariness suddenly overtake his brother. "Guess you want to hit the sack again, huh, man?" He grimaced. "Two flats? Unheard of," he said. "But the wait was worth it, though. Changing a flat on that dark highway wasn't the safest thing to do, and getting a tow into town was the best way out. I'll drive you in tomorrow to pick your car up from Mitch's place."

"That's a bet," Graham said, standing and discarding his Pepsi bottles. "Not too early though. I'm dead on my feet. That traffic was nothing like I ever remember. Makes me wonder if that town I once knew still exists." They were on the landing, and before Graham entered his room he said, "So I guess you're waiting until I'm wide-awake before hitting me with some news, huh?" He gave his brother a curious look.

Cole thought about his promise. There was still time, he thought. "I think you should see Teddie Perkins first thing," he said. "Tomorrow."

Graham studied his brother's serious face. "If not sooner, huh?"

"Something like that. Good night, Graham."

Before six in the morning, Cole was in Ava's bed. He'd hoped he wasn't scaring the devil out of her ringing the doorbell at five o'clock. When she welcomed him with tousled hair and warm, rose-scented skin, he'd had all he could do not to take her right there in the foyer. She was lying, snuggled in the crook of his arm.

"Mmm, love," Ava murmured. "You sure do know how to make the world stop for me." She was twirling her finger in circles in the hairs on his chest. "You won't lose that magic thing that you do, will you?"

Cole laughed softly. "Magic? Merlin, I'm not," he said. "You're the sorceress." He caught her hand and slowly moved it down to his aroused state and held it there. "See?" he said. "I can't make this kind of magic all by myself." He tightened his buttocks and groaned when she gripped him tightly and then slowly began caressing his pulsing penis in sure, fleeting touches. "Sweetheart," he moaned.

"Shh, let me," Ava said in a throaty voice. "I need you again." She propped herself up on one elbow while kneading his erection. He had his eyes closed and she kissed his eyelids. "Look at me," she whispered. "I love to see your eyes when you're on the brink. They're like melted chocolate, and I can't get enough of losing myself in them. I feel like I want to live in that warm sweet comfort and never come out. It's so safe." His hand was fondling her breasts and when he squeezed the hardened nipples she moaned her pleasure, feeling the liquid love dampening the warm place between her thighs. She wanted him inside of her, loving her until she begged for mercy. She had to smile at that thought because as long as she lived she would never ever think of asking him to stop taking her heart to places only he could.

"Ava," Cole uttered, his body responding to her manipulations so swiftly that he thought he would explode. She was on top now writhing slowly against his erection. He was stroking her buttocks; the smooth firm skin was aflame. Unable to stand the delightful agony, he flipped her over and was on top and inside of her. "Ava, you're the love I've never had," he whispered while looking her in the eyes. "I'll love you forever. Don't ever leave me." He thrust, and watched her eyes glisten with love for him. He thrust again as if dotting the i's and crossing the t's. And then he was lost as he allowed her sweet moans and arching hips to take him to unexplored heights in their lovemaking.

Too soon, when all was silent in the room except for their deep breaths that soon quieted to satisfied murmurs, they began to speak in soft tones. Ava had her arm flung across his middle while Cole basked in the knowledge that he had a beautiful woman who loved him. There was no way in the world that he wouldn't do all in his power to keep it that way.

"I'm sorry," he said, missing what she'd just said.

"I said, you're almost as good-looking as he is," Ava said.

"Oh, is that right?" Cole grumbled as he tweaked her ear.

A soft laugh escaped. "Just kidding," she said, leaning over to plant a light kiss on his lips. Her voice was subdued when she said, "Do you think Graham will go see her today?"

Cole was grim-faced. "I'll be driving him to town to pick up his car," he said. "I'll make sure he stops by the diner." He frowned. "By the time we get there I'm sure Teddie and everybody else will know he's home."

"Do you think Teddie will try to avoid him?" Ava asked. "She really is making plans to leave in a few days. Graham showing up now will really be traumatic for her. Will she leave before she's ready?"

"You mean to run away?"

"Yes."

"That won't happen," Cole said firmly. "I promise you that. My brother is going to know he's a father. Soon."

"I'm afraid for them," Ava said, suddenly fearful for her friend and her son. "What if it doesn't go well because Graham has someone already? And then there's Fiona just waiting to move in and wreak havoc."

"None of that's going to happen."

Ava smiled and caressed his cheek. "You're going to see to that, my love?"

"I'm going to do my damnedest," Cole said tightly. He felt his chest constrict and he wondered if his words were just wishful thinking.

Later that morning, Ava waved to Cole and Graham as they drove off. She'd declined Cole's invitation to accompany them. Whatever happened, she didn't want to be there to witness Teddie's pain if Graham reacted negatively to her confession. She'd rather be on the other end, being a friend when Teddie needed her.

She busied herself puttering around her house that didn't need cleaning, wondering what was happening back in Florence, and the judge's mind. Before she knew it, she was in the kitchen looking in the freezer and the cupboards. She had the sudden urge to cook. Who knows, she thought, maybe after this day she'd be the one who would need a friend.

She smiled, knowing that she had Cole. He would always be there for her.

Teddie arrived at the diner at seven in the morning and by eight-thirty was leaving after seeing that Roonie and Allan and another manager had everything under control. She was apprehensive at first but then laughed at herself. Wasn't the operation already set up to run smoothly in her absence? So why couldn't she leave everything today, she thought as she hurried out the door. In her car she looked fearfully around her and satisfied drove quickly toward her home.

Somehow she'd had a feeling that her plans were going to go awry, and sure enough it was happening. The first thing she heard this morning after she'd arrived was the buzz that Graham Dumont was in town. The story had spread when one of Mitch's mechanics stopped by for breakfast around six and the chatter was still going on an hour later. Her head had started to spin and she didn't know whether to run or stay and face him, because as sure as the sun rose every morning, he was going to stop by the diner with Cole. She'd decided to run. She wasn't ready for him.

Cole and Graham arrived at Perk's Diner around ten when the crowd was thin and service was quick. Just as they'd done with him, Roonie and his son, Allan, heartily greeted Graham while Cole watched. When they were seated in a booth, Cole looked around, and when he still didn't spot Teddie he asked and raised a brow when he was told that she'd come and gone.

When the waitress left after bringing their food, Graham said, "The word got around quickly, didn't it? Guess you want me to see Teddie more than she wants to see me." He dug into the stack of pancakes and sausages.

Cole didn't like the feel of that. He ate his Western omelet and chewed on crisp toast, mulling over what he wanted to do. The dire thought of Teddie taking off like a fugitive was clouding his mind. She couldn't, wouldn't do that, he thought. He ate hurriedly, unmindful of the taste of the deliciously prepared food.

"What's up?" Graham had been watching his brother go through some sort of deep soul-searching. When it was over he knew something heavy was going down.

"We have to leave," Cole said while giving Graham a straight look. "Don't ask me any questions because I made a promise," he said gruffly.

Many times, Graham had seen that look one of near-desperation during those months after Curtis died. Whatever was going on was affecting his brother deeply, and if it was enough to bring that look back he would do whatever he could to make things normal again. He drained his coffee mug. "Okay," he said simply, and signaled for the check.

Outside, Cole said, "I'll take you to get your car. Then we're going to Teddie's."

Graham got in the car without saying a word. They drove to the garage in silence and when he paid Mitch, he pulled off behind Cole's SUV. *A promise is a promise,* he thought but wondered what was driving his brother.

When Cole reached Teddie's house, he didn't pull into the drive behind her car but let Graham do that. He was going back home. If Teddie had had the idea of taking off before seeing Graham she was too late. The two of them would now have to deal with whatever was to come, but at least it would be in person and not long distance with Graham chasing after her to the jungles of New York City. He knew Teddie would be spitting nails for what he'd done, but if it meant Royce was not going to get hurt he'd do it again. Cole consoled himself with the fact that he'd kept his promise; he hadn't uttered a word to Graham about his being a father.

Graham was out of the car walking with a bewildered expression toward Cole who was still sitting in his car. He grinned. "Cuttin' out on me?" he said.

Cole nodded. "I'll see you back at the house," he said, and reached for the ignition key, but he stopped at the sound of the front screen door banging shut and Teddie's loud scream.

"Royce, come back here!"

Both men turned to see a young body come racing down the drive toward Cole's car.

"Mr. Cole, are you coming to take me out?" Royce yelled gleefully. He stopped to look at the other tall man who was talking to his friend. He looked from Cole who'd gotten out of the car, to the stranger, and back at Cole. "Mr. Cole," Royce said with a puzzled look on his face. "That man has a face like yours and mine." Then he giggled.

Teddie was standing on the porch, holding her chest to still her beating heart. "Oh, my God," she whispered. "My God."

"Oh, no, not like this," Cole said through clenched teeth while watching in horror Graham's shocked look. "This is not happening!"

Royce took Cole's hand, trying to pull him toward the house, and said, "Come on in. My mommy said we're going on a trip and she said we didn't have time to say good-bye to everybody. But you can come say it now, can't you?"

Graham was staring at the little person who was the image of another little guy who'd died so long ago. And of his brother who was standing beside him. Graham tore his gaze away from Royce and looked at Cole who didn't have to say a word. One look at Teddie who appeared to have been turned into stone, told him the truth.

"You knew?" Graham rasped, catching his brother's look.

Cole flinched at the cold sound barely leaving his brother's lips. "The night I told you to come home, that was the same day I found out," Cole said. "I promised Teddie that I'd let her tell you first."

"Royce, come into the house now," Teddie called. "But, Mommy . . ."

"Now, Royce." Teddie was holding on to the porch railing and her gaze was on Graham. "Oh, God, how can I handle this?" she whispered.

Royce dropped Cole's hand and ran toward his mother.

Graham stood with clenched fists watching his son say something to his mother and then disappear inside. Teddie was walking toward them. He hadn't seen her in two years, not since the last time he'd stopped in the diner, and she'd barely had a word for him. Even then she'd looked as desirable as he'd found her the time she visited him and they became lovers for two weeks. And they'd made a child that she'd kept from him. He felt the blood rush to his head and he wanted to hit something. But he waited, walking to his car and leaning against it.

Teddie stood looking at the two handsome men.

One she loved and the other, whose neck she wanted to wring right now.

"I thought you were running away, Teddie," Cole said simply. "I'm sorry. I didn't think it would go down like this."

"You kept your promise?" Teddie was calm.

Cole nodded.

"Then you couldn't help what just happened. I'll talk to you later?"

"Yes, later," Cole answered. He looked at a tight-lipped Graham. "I'll see you later." His brother only nodded and Cole got in his car hoping that Graham wouldn't mess up. He saw the way Teddie had looked at Graham and how Graham caught his breath just looking at her. As he drove he knew that given time they could work it out. There was a little guy who needed that to happen.

Graham, with arms folded across his chest, could only stare at the beautiful woman who was looking at him with a blank expression. He couldn't tell what she was thinking. As he stared, his thoughts went back to a time where he'd thought he was in love.

"He's about five?" he finally said.

Teddie nodded.

"Royce is his name?"

"Royce Curtis Perkins."

"Perkins."

"Yes."

"We're going to change that, aren't we?" he said softly.

Teddie lifted her chin. "Why?"

Graham felt calm enough to move closer to her, and when he did he felt familiar warmth envelop him. He breathed deeply. "Why did you do that to us?" he asked softly, spearing her with his sharp gaze. "My son doesn't even know me!" The word sounded alien on his lips and he felt his stomach do a somersault. He was a father! "God, Teddie, why did you do that?"

Teddie heard the sob catch in his throat and she swallowed the lump in her own. She reached out her hand. "Come, Graham. It's time to meet your son," she said softly. When he took it and held on tight, she felt those same feelings that had made her lie with him and make a baby. She still loved this man and she wondered why she'd let so much time pass by without declaring her love and making him a part of her life and their son's.

They were at the door and Graham hesitated, but entered when Teddie tugged on his hand. His heart jumped when Royce appeared and was staring at him.

Teddie held out her hand to her son. "Come here, Royce," she said. "I want you to meet someone." When he was standing in front of them staring up at Graham, her eyes misted. They were father and son.

"Royce, sweetie, remember when I told you about your daddy and how he had to live far away from us?"

"Yes, Mommy," Royce said.

"Well, your daddy has come home to see you," Teddie said. "Say hello to your father."

Royce looked from his mother to his father. He said, "Daddy, do you love us again?" He was holding out his hand.

Graham choked as he took his son's hand in his. His voice was merely a rasp when he spoke. "Yes, Royce. Your daddy loves you." He knelt down on one knee. "Can I get a hug?" he said, trying hard to keep it together. When his son's arms went around his neck, Graham clasped him, burying his chin in the boy's soft curls. He looked up to see Teddie with tears rolling down her cheeks. "Your daddy loves you and your mommy again," he whispered, never taking his gaze from Teddie's.

"Thank you, Dr. Howell," Ava said. "That's good news." She listened and then said, "I think that's an excellent idea. Perhaps the committee can make Compton the last to exhibit at the end of the tour next year. Yes, so do I." She paused. "The lecture series was a success, I heard. Of course, I'll see you in the fall. Thanks for letting me know. Bye."

Ava sat down on a kitchen chair, her mind in a daze. The warrants for Winifred and Emily had been issued and were being served as they spoke. "Lord, please let it be over now," she said with closed eyes.

She wondered just what Winifred's face would look like when she was arrested. And Emily? Why had they done this to her? Ava tried hard not to feel hatred for the two women who had disrupted her peaceful world all because of their greed and deception. She prayed that there would be enough evidence to find the women guilty so that they could be punished for making her life hell. There was no way that she could return to the university only to run into Winifred on a daily basis. Ava knew that she would never return under those circumstances.

As she finished wrapping her food and putting it in the fridge and covering the pan of cornbread, she frowned. What if they couldn't find anything in Winifred's house? she wondered. Suppose the detectives didn't know what to look for? Her skin began to crawl with the horror that would come of that. She could see the sneer on Winifred's face. Oh, no, that couldn't happen. Making a decision, she left the kitchen and went upstairs. She hurriedly washed and changed and in fifteen minutes she was driving from her yard. Maybe, just maybe, she could be of some assistance.

But while driving, Ava had the anxious thought that she wouldn't be allowed near the place much less go inside Winifred's house. Why should whoever was conducting the search let her insinuate herself into the proceedings? "I have to be there," she said, her stomach doing a somersault. Suppose they overlook what might appear to be an innocuous-looking piece of paper? she thought. Her mood lightened when she remembered the very thorough search that turned up that doctored card that could have turned out very badly for her. She blessed Cole for sending her Donlevy.

"Thank God," Ava murmured as she parked several houses away from Winifred's. Law-enforcement vehicles took up most of the space on the block. She left her car and prayed that she was in time.

She was stopped at the door by a serious-faced officer who gave her a stern look. "You can't enter, ma'am," her said.

Ava said, "Please, I think that I can be of some help." She racked her brain for anything that would gain her entry, when Winifred appeared in the foyer with another stern-looking officer hovering at her shoulder. When she saw Ava, a cruel smile made a slash of her mouth. "It's gone, isn't it?" Ava said almost fearfully to the defiant-looking woman.

After a long, steady look at her colleague, Winifred shrugged. Before turning away from the woman she'd come to despise, she gave a short laugh and then walked from the foyer with the officer following.

Ava turned away and was walking despondently down the walkway when she heard her name. She glanced to see Officer Kirkland giving her a surprised look.

"Dr. Millington," Officer Kirkland said as he walked toward her. He saw her staring at the large plastic bag in his gloved hand.

"Officer Kirkland," Ava acknowledged him. "You've finished pretty quickly," she said, her eyes glued to the bag.

"We had a pretty good idea what we were looking for," he said, drolly.

Ava said, "Do you mind if I get a good look at it?" Her heart pitter-pattered with excitement and disbelief at what she could see through the plastic.

After a curious look at the professor, the officer opened the bag and with a tweezers that he removed from his pocket, he lifted out the parchment for Ava's inspection, careful that she didn't touch it.

Ava stared at the piece of paper. It had been a bane in her side, but she couldn't help but begrudgingly admire the work. Even without intense study she knew what she was looking at and realized that Winifred had paid dearly for this magnificent fraud. But for the fact that Ava knew that such a letter as this never existed, she would have had a hard time proving this piece of parchment a fake. Whoever had done the work had given it the authenticity of black ink fading to brown over a long period of time. The chemicals used had even burned into the paper, giving it a lacy effect.

"Officer, would you let me see the back of it please?" Ava saw that the acid had migrated to the back of the paper. "Wonderful work," she muttered. She saw Officer Kirkland give his colleague a look, and she smiled at them. "Thanks," she said. "Yes, this is what you're looking for."

Walking away, Ava couldn't help wondering about Winifred's vanity. Why hadn't she just destroyed the evidence instead of keeping it as some sort of testament to her success? She'd hated the woman for bringing such chaos to her life and now she only pitied her.

Ava was fairly skipping. Life was beautiful, she thought, as she drove to her peaceful home and to the man she loved.

Cole hung up the phone. Ava had sounded like she was going to burst with excitement and relief when she explained where she'd gone and what had happened. He was feeling her and he couldn't stop smiling as she related the events of the afternoon.

At six o'clock he was lounging on the back porch waiting for her to arrive. He'd wanted to go out to dinner to celebrate the occasion but she declined telling him she'd cooked entirely too much food and it shouldn't be wasted. He took another look at his watch. It'd been hours since he drove from Teddie's, leaving her and his brother to resolve their differences. Graham hadn't come home nor had he called and Cole assumed that they were at least talking.

For the first time since he'd found out he was an uncle, and now that Graham knew he was a father, Cole felt unfettered and ready to begin a new life. Mentally he started planning the time when he'd take the necessary trip back home to close that chapter in his life. He stopped himself with a grin. He *was* home.

The sound of a car in the front and the slam of the door told him Graham had returned. "I'm back here," Cole yelled.

"Hey, man," Graham said when he settled his frame in a chair by the table.

Cole searched his brother's face and then nodded. "It went okay," he stated.

"Yeah," Graham answered. "It went okay."

There was silence.

"I never knew about that part of her life," Graham said in amazement. "A sought-after designer." He swallowed. "She's staying," he said. "For now, anyway."

"And later?" Cole asked.

He shrugged. "She wants what's best for Royce, and right now that's getting to know me. She thinks that can best be accomplished in Minuet rather than in New York City."

Cole thought about that. "So she's putting her career on hold—again," he said.

"No. She'll still do what she's been doing with Monique, only on a larger scale. She saw how the diner can get along without her so she's giving it up full-time."

"Anything else?" Cole asked casually.

Graham grinned. "A lot else," he said.

"But nothing you want to talk about?"

"Only that you're right—she's a beautiful woman." He looked disgusted. "How I took a chance on letting her fall into some other guy's arms is sheer stupidity and pride."

"Moving back?"

"Plan to," Graham answered. "It'll take some work getting the Dumont firm established again, but in time it'll work."

"There's a lot of development going on," Cole said. "You might think about setting up in Hudson instead of in Florence."

They talked for a while, Cole telling Graham about Ava's good news.

"Man, that's great," Graham said. "She seems like a wonderful person. I'm happy for her."

"Me, too," Cole said, wondering what was taking Ava so long to get home. He saw a shadow cross his brother's face. "What?" he said.

Graham stood and paced the porch, finally sitting on a railing, arms folded across his chest.

"What's wrong, Crackers?" Cole asked a sudden chill coursing through his body. Unseemly, with the air still warm from a day of hot sun. He waited.

"Look, Cole," Graham started, "I have something to tell you." He closed his eyes briefly. "Apparently this is a day for secrets to be routed from their hiding places and for all concerned to put the past in the past."

Cole went stiff. "Tell me," he said his voice steely and his body braced for the worst.

"Before I went to see you in the hospital in Los Angeles I went to see our mother in Las Vegas. I begged her to come with me, to make peace with you since you were in such an unstable state. It might have been the l-last time," he stuttered.

Cole didn't want to hear about his mother when he was feeling so great with the world, but he said, "What's the secret?" His voice was dry.

"Damn," Graham said as he brushed a hand over his head.

"Just tell me, Graham," Cole said. He felt the anguish, and suddenly realized that whatever it was had been tearing his brother up.

"You did nothing wrong," Graham said, the words spoken with great difficulty. "The pills that Curtis swallowed and the ones that killed him belonged to our mother, not you. You were zonked out for a long time from your own fever and meds. The little guy apparently was bored to tears and had to have been wandering around the house for a good while when he found Mama's pills. You know all the antidepressants she was taking since Dad was killed. That's what he swallowed."

Cole was still as a statue as he tried to make sense of what Graham was saying. His head moved from side to side as if in denial. "No, that's not right," he said, and his voice sounded foreign to his ears. "*I* saw my pills on the kitchen floor. *You* saw them. *Mama* saw them. What are you talking about?"

"The medical report," Graham said, holding on to his anger. "Mama showed me the autopsy report that she's had all these years."

Cole looked at Graham with tears in his eyes. He couldn't speak.

Graham's throat tightened up but he continued. "When she found out, she was still feeling so bitter toward you that she kept it a secret. She hated looking at you, and she said she felt some sort of vindication that since Curtis was dead and you were alive, you didn't need to feel happy and live a contented life. She wanted you to suffer like she would for the rest of her life." Graham couldn't hold back the tears. He pounded his fist into the wood. "God, Slaw, I'm sorry," he said, husky-voiced.

It was a long time before Cole spoke. "What does she look like?" Cole asked in a quiet voice.

"What?"

"Our mother. What does she look like?"

Graham cleared his throat. "Old," he finally said. "Very old, with dead eyes."

Cole sat for a moment and then he stood. "Would you ever have told me?" he asked in a low voice.

"I don't know," Graham said. "I toyed with the idea, but when I saw how happy you were with Ava and finding Royce, I thought that it wouldn't serve any purpose to tell you."

Cole nodded and left the porch and went upstairs. Before going into his room he continued to the end of the hall where the master bedroom was and opened the door. He stood looking around the big room where his parents had lived their wedded lives. There were memories in here and he closed his eyes briefly against them. When he looked again he imagined his little brother gleefully finding the pills that he ate like candy and that would eventually end his young life.

Neither Graham nor he had ever moved into this room even after Patrice Dumont abandoned the house to her sons. Though unspoken between them, he and his brother felt that the memories were best left as just memories. He closed the door softly and went to his own room and closed the door. He lay on his back, staring up at the ceiling for a long time. After a while he turned over on his side and the bed shook with his deep sobs.

Chapter Nineteen

Ava pulled into her drive, and when she parked she noted with satisfaction that both cars were in the Dumont yard. She was going to have Graham to dinner and would finally get to know the man that Teddie had fallen in love with. She hoped that the unsuspecting man had met his son this morning with open arms and a heart full of love.

She moved lightly as she got her purchases from the backseat and began walking toward the house. She hadn't meant to stay out so long, but she was feeling high with happiness after her trip to Florence. Seeing Winifred's face made her feel euphoric with new freedom. She'd passed Minuet and continued to Hudson where she'd had her hair washed and styled, had a manicure and a pedicure. Afterward, she visited a perfumery where she bought a new fragrance, delighted with the scent of jasmine that she knew would please Cole. He loved to bury his nose in her neck and nuzzle, inhaling her warm scented skin. Then she shopped for champagne. With Graham home she was hoping that he would break bread with her and Cole tonight. Lord knows she'd cooked enough food for a gaggle. Laden with fresh-cut flowers and several bottles of champagne, she reached the porch. She almost wished the night was ended so she could lie in Cole's arms snuggled against him after some serious loving.

A movement on the porch next door caught her eye. She saw Graham who stood, and after waving started her way.

"Hello," Ava said, balancing her bundles while trying to unlock her door.

"May I help?" Graham said, already reaching for the bag of champagne bottles.

"Thanks," Ava said once they were inside and the packages on the table. "That would have been a disaster had they gone flying," she said with a smile. Once the bottles were in the fridge, she looked at Graham who appeared a bit subdued, far from the smiling, happy man she'd met briefly this morning before he left with his brother for Perk's Diner. He was tall, besting his brother by at least a half an inch. They had the same shade of beautiful copper-colored skin, and the same angular face. Graham's eyebrows were a bit thicker and darker and he had beautiful brown eyes, but not as round and deep chocolate as Royce's and Cole's.

Graham was watching Ava under cover of helping her. She seemed so happy, yet he knew what he had to tell her was going to bring more sadness to her eyes. He felt angry suddenly that something that had happened so long ago could still bring heartache.

"I hope you haven't eaten yet," Ava said. "I'd like you to join me and Cole." She was smiling as she began to take the herbed roasted chicken from the refrigerator, and was about to turn on the oven when she stopped to stare at his serious face. "Cole is home, isn't he?" she said, suddenly apprehensive.

He nodded. "He's home."

Intuitively Ava dismissed the food and sat down at the table. "What happened?" she asked, knowing that all was not well. The thought that she didn't have a right to happiness passed fleetingly through her mind. Trying to shake off the feeling of impending doom, she gave Graham a straight look. "Does it concern me?" she asked.

Graham took a seat opposite her. He answered her question. "Not directly,"

"That's not an acceptable answer," she said almost woodenly. "Indirect, direct—whatever concerns Cole, concerns me. We love each other." She held Graham's gaze.

"I know and I hope that whatever's going on in his mind right now, you'll be there for him even if he tries to push you away. I saw him with you. He's the happiest I've ever seen him."

"You're scaring me, Graham. What happened today?"

"I told him that he was not responsible for causing Curtis's death," Graham said. "Our mother was."

Ava felt her body go numb as her brain stopped working. The words she heard seemed to come from the mouth of an alien who sat there looking at her with a black, angry look. She could only sit and listen as Graham continued to talk, not in the voice of an alien but making sounds like an emotionally drained human being. When the voice stopped the only sound in the kitchen was the hum of the refrigerator motor going through its tedious cycles.

"He's been in his room since I told him," Graham ended with frustration. "I imagine he's going through some changes." She was looking at him now and he said, "He'll come out of it." His voice dropped. "I felt like I was the steamroller doing him in this time."

Ava found her voice. "My going to him won't help, will it?" She sounded very weary.

"Not yet," Graham answered with a shake of his head. "He probably doesn't even want to look at me either." He shrugged. "Let's hope he's just trying to bury the anger instead of taking it out on all of us."

"Burying it is what he's done all those years," Ava said. "I doubt that that's the way to handle this latest blow. It took something traumatic like seeing his nephew to bring him out from under that cloud. What's it going to take now—your mother showing up and throwing herself in his arms, asking him for forgiveness?" she spat. "I don't think that's going to happen! Do you?"

Graham saw and understood her anger and didn't fault her for it. "Give him time, Ava," he said. "I doubt that he's going to throw away what you two have going for you."

She heard the plea in his voice, and feeling her anger subsiding she slumped back against the chair. "Time," she said softly. "I have plenty of that now." She stirred. "It's getting late," she said, looking at the wall clock. It was after seven. "You must be hungry. Would you like to eat something? It's not a problem."

"No, thanks, Ava." Graham stood and walked toward the front door. "I'm going back to Teddie's. We have a lot to talk about. Renee is going to babysit while we go out."

They were on the porch and Ava looked for a long moment at the man who seemed determined to accomplish a mission. "Teddie loves you," she said bluntly.

Graham studied her face. "I know," he said. "I fell in love with her in Ohio. I was just too proud to beg. I'm going to try and change that," he said simply. He saw her doubtful look. "Trust me," he said softly.

Ava looked doubtful. "I think I trust you, Graham, but I think you've got an uphill battle on your hands trying to prove to someone else in town that you're not up for grabs."

Instantly Fiona's strange telephone call came to his mind and Graham frowned. "I think I know what you mean," he said. "Fiona Fitzgerald is not in the picture." As if conjuring the beautiful doctor up, a car pulled into the Dumont yard. Both Ava and Graham looked as Fiona, noticing the two people on the porch, walked through the hedges.

"Graham, darlin'," Fiona said, a bright smile on her face. "I'd heard you were home and I couldn't wait another minute to see you." She was on Ava's porch and she leaned into the handsome man and planted a kiss on his lips. "It's been a long time, stranger." Over Graham's shoulder she gave Ava a smug but evil look.

Ava stood, mouth twisted in a grimace at the gall of the bold female. She was silent, waiting for Graham's reaction.

Graham stepped easily out of Fiona's embrace, moving an obvious distance away from her. "Fiona," he said. "This isn't high school. That was so long ago I can't even remember why we were an item for a brief time. It just might have been the beautiful cheerleader, hot superjock kind of thing going on," he mused. "We're all grown up now and I don't care to go back in time. I've moved on, and I think it would be a good thing if you did too." He gave her a patient look. "But I want to thank you for your call.

I did need to come home to finally meet my son—
and to see his mother again." His tone gave her no
chance to misconstrue his meaning.

Fiona stepped back as if slapped. She looked from
Graham to Ava and back to Graham. She saw the look
of finality on his face, and after one more hateful look
at Ava she backed away and then turned and hurried
down the steps. She backed out of the driveway in less
time than it took to say her name, and sped away.

Ava spoke first. "Do you think it'll do any good?"
she asked the quiet man.

"Fiona's not a happy person," Graham said. "Never
was. She needed attention and affection that was with-
held by her parents. Maybe one day she'll find
someone who will give her what she needs." He
looked at Ava. "I'm not that man."

After she watched Graham drive away in his BMW,
she sat on the porch for a long time waiting and
watching for Cole to emerge from his sorrow. When
that didn't happen, she got up and went into the
house. It was already dark, after nine, and very late to
have a heavy meal. She opened a bottle, poured herself a flute of the Mumm champagne, and carried it
upstairs to her bedroom. There she looked in the
mirror and saluted herself with the sparkling liquid.

"To Ava," she murmured, "who deserves some happiness herself."

"Oh, stop. You don't believe that any more than I
do," Teddie said to her friend. But even she sounded
skeptical as she looked at Ava's face. "Cole loves you
and he will be back to tell you that himself. The idea
of him going off to carouse with hootchie mamas, is
a bit far-fetched, don't you think?"

Ava shrugged and glanced at Royce who was sitting under a tree, dutifully looking at his book. She smiled at the little boy who was fidgeting, anxiously waiting for his father who was coming to take him out.

"What am I to think, Teddie?" Ava said. "Is our life together, if there will be such a thing, always going to be like this—with him running off to seek solitude when he runs head-on into an obstacle? What am I in his life?"

After Graham had left her, she'd fallen asleep that night and had awakened from a dream where she thought Cole was loving her awake, but it was just the lingering scent of him in her bed that had aroused her. The next day she had busied herself in her garden, had visited the widow Lansdowne, and then had driven to Hudson where she window-shopped. She just knew that she'd return to find her lover sitting on her porch waiting to welcome her into his arms. Befuddled, she'd gone to bed wondering if her world had finally spun to a dead stop.

In the early-morning hours, her bruised heart and ego threatening to shred every last bit of pride as she kept listening for the sound of his Tahoe, she left the house driving with no known destination in mind. It was close to one o'clock when she found herself at Teddie's.

Now Ava rose from the bench where she and her friend were sitting and fished her car keys from the pocket of her shorts. "I'm leaving before Graham gets here," she said, and then smiled. "I want you guys to have all the time to yourselves." She eyed her friend. "It's working out, isn't it?" she asked, and knew the answer when Teddie blushed.

"Yes," Teddie answered with a small smile. "I think we're going to be all right."

"I'm glad you've changed your mind about leaving," Ava said, feeling tremendous relief that she would still have her friend nearby. At her car they hugged. "I'll be in touch."

At home the quiet that Ava so loved was deafening and closing in on her. If someone had told her that she'd be feeling this way, she would have called them all kinds of prevaricators. She loved her isolated space at least until a big black car had brought its owner into her life. Now she couldn't think of time and space in the future without Cole.

One day she'd awakened to the sound of a motor and had found Cole shearing back the hedges on either side. He'd made a perfect squared natural thoroughfare so the bushes didn't slap at them as they passed from one yard to the other.

So much for making permanency a part of their lives, Ava mused. Restless, she was in her study packing away her notes and books for her lecture series. A lot of work and planning had gone into what had promised to be an interesting and stimulating summer project. Thinking that she'd be able to use some of the materials for next year, she didn't regret the concentrated effort she'd made in pulling the series together.

An envelope slipped from between all the paper and she stared at the letter from her sister. She didn't bother to read it again; she remembered every word. She set it aside and then opened a drawer and put it inside as if closing the door on her past.

Not once since Cole had returned from Georgia, did Ava think about her sister and the lies she must have told him about her. She didn't want to know, and the farther she pushed it to the back of her mind, the better off she'd be. She had decided that all the family she needed was right here with Cole and Teddie and Royce.

Her eyes clouded. Her future, a future with Cole in it was not so certain, she thought. Did that mean that she would have to move? Or would Cole do the gentlemanly thing and make himself scarce? She could hardly believe that they would start a new life, each going their separate ways under the nose of the other. Ava laughed at the absurdity of the scenario.

When at last she'd cleared away the mess on her desk and she could actually see the well-worn deep walnut wood through the thick glass covering, she sat back admiring her handiwork. Ruefully she thought that if she'd kept a neater workspace Emily would have had to use some brain power to hide that letter more cleverly. As if to look for another task, that would occupy another hour of her day she was about to get up when the phone rang. She looked at the display and her face twisted into a grimace as she wondered if her thoughts had conjured up the devil.

"Hello," Ava said in an emotionless voice.

"Ava, I'm glad I caught you." Dahlia's voice was hesitant.

"Glad?" Ava said. "Why? Is there something you forgot to tell Cole Dumont? Maybe it's him you should be calling."

"Ava, I knew you would be bitter after you heard, but I thought I'd waited enough time before calling you, to let it run its course through your system." She hesitated. "I thought it was time to tell you myself I'm sorry for what we did."

Ava frowned at the receiver. "What you did? You've got that a little backward, haven't you?" she said with a mirthless laugh. "I was the young seventeen-year-old who suffered that last year at home being looked at as something you wiped off your shoe. What was it that *you* did except turn your back on me?"

There was a short silence.

"He didn't tell you," Dahlia said in a sad voice.

The sudden throbbing in her temples threatened to make Ava shout out in agony as she steeled herself for more words of pain.

"Cole didn't tell me what?" she said in a hushed voice.

"Your friend uncovered the truth from that retired private investigator he visited in Atlanta," Dahlia said. "He came to me with it to verify it for himself."

"Truth? What truth?" Her heart was pounding now.

"Dad lied, Ava. He stole the parchment from the archives after you'd put it back."

"What are you saying?" Ava whispered. She was standing now, walking around the room as if looking for a way out. She was suffocating. She found herself on the back porch going down the stairs and walking in circles around the expansive yard. The phone signal was weakening and she walked closer to the house where she plopped down on the bottom step of the porch. "Tell me," she rasped.

"Our father was a thief," Dahlia said in a dry voice. "He was a big important educator, respected in his community, but he was a thief. That parchment he stole and blamed on you for stealing was not the first thing he had stolen to sell to a private collector." She gave a short laugh. "That big beautiful house on the hill that we lived in had been bought years before with dirty money. Every time he needed more he would engineer the theft of another precious object or valuable manuscript map, or letters written between famous people. Remember all those times he would be away from home traveling to Europe and Africa under the guise of study? Under aliases he would visit various repositories posing as a professor doing research on whatever document or manuscript he wanted to steal." She swore. "That's how he was tripped up by that investigator. It only took someone as diligent and crafty as he was to put the times and places together. Dad was always away from home when the thefts occurred."

"I don't understand," Ava finally said. "That entire time Mother knew about what he was doing? *You* knew?"

"No!" Dahlia said with emphasis. "I never knew, but Mother did. She finally told me years later after you left home and it was clear that you hated us and were never coming back. She regretted not standing up to him and speaking up." She paused. "When she was dying, she asked me to find you and beg for your forgiveness. Dad had asked the same thing before he died in that nursing home. His last stroke had left him immobile and practically speechless."

Ava's stomach hurt and she was holding it as if to keep the cramps from exploding like a bomb and splattering her to kingdom come.

"But why me?" she finally managed. "His daughter? What made him do that to me," she cried.

"To save face for him, the university, and all concerned. When he suspected that they were on to his last deal, he got the idea to throw them off by making you the suspect. But it didn't work. They were going to expose him when he made a deal with Dr. Biehmer. If he gave you up in return for non-involvement of the university and he named names in previous dealings, then he would be exonerated, keep his job and standing in the community. All that would happen was that he would have a daughter who was suspected of being a thief." She paused. "In his world that was stigma enough."

"But the artifact was never found," Ava said.

"No, it wasn't. That wouldn't have worked if you were no longer suspect. Then the whole bag of dirty laundry would be opened again to smell up his world in academia," Dahlia said in a wry voice. "You probably know that in that world any theft is anathema to an institution. They would rather lose insurance money than to admit that they had been victims. That's why all those involved agreed to handle it the way they did." She paused. "It's suspected that it is sitting in the private collection of a very important man," she said. Her sister was quiet and Dahlia said, "Ava, I'm sorry."

"Sorry?" Ava whispered. "That I lived all my adult life under that horrible cloud of suspicion? Suppose it had kept me from living my life and supporting myself in a career that I love?" She kept the tears at bay as her eyes burned with the hot liquid about to fall and scorch her cheeks. "My sister, and my mother and father, hating me for besmirching their world? Why would you be sorry now? I can't believe that a mother could love a man so much that she'd give up her child for him like that."

Dahlia made a sound. "Love it wasn't, Ava," she said in disgust.

"What?" Ava couldn't believe that there was more she had to know.

"Mother hated Father. She was on the verge of leaving him many times, but he threatened to make her life hell if she left and took us with her. He would get custody too because he had proof of her extramarital affairs. A man of his stature, divorced, children taken from him—his ego couldn't handle the scandal."

"What are you saying?" Ava said. "Affairs? How could I not know that, not see any of what you're telling me?"

Dahlia's voice was soft when she said, "Ava, you were always in another world filled with lore of yesteryear. You just didn't see a lot of what anybody else saw."

Ava listened and suddenly felt tired. Her voice was bitter when she spoke. "So he made his youngest child his martyr." She didn't want to hear any more. She wanted to shut out her sister's voice.

"Dahlia, I can't talk to you anymore. My head is too filled up."

"Will you at least think of us and maybe come to visit, Ava?" Her voice was full of hope. "I still love you," she said. "You're my sister."

Ava hung up without answering. She sat on the wooden step for a long time, the receiver still in her hand weighing about a hundred pounds. It was almost as heavy as the weight on her heart.

Nightfall had fallen pretty and she thought that August would arrive in fabulous fashion. Ava had watched the sun set, the gold and the reds and the oranges melting together into a vast molten ball in the sky, playing trippingly on the horizon.

She had eaten a dinner of a cold ham sandwich and iced tea and was enjoying the warm breeze on the back porch, with a glass of wine.

After Dahlia's call hours before, she'd tried to act like a normal person doing whatever it was that normal people do after a bombshell of a confession. She didn't think that her betrayal by Winifred and Emily had hurt so much after learning what her own father had done to her. Had she been so unloved, so unwanted, that even her mother had been so willing to go along with the preposterous lie?

She thought of Cole's absence and how he must have felt after listening to Graham's confession. Now she didn't fault the man she still loved for wanting to run away as far as he could get from the sound of his brother's voice and the place where the deception had occurred. She wanted to do the same thing after cutting off her sister's voice. But her practical mind butted in and she scrapped the thought. Besides, she'd done the running thing and knew that it wasn't going to take away her hurt and sorrow of the past.

And just where was she going to find solace and in whose arm's? she wondered. She'd known love in Cole's arms and knew there would never be another man like him. That person didn't exist and she felt it to her core.

The only sad part of it, she thought, was that Cole hadn't sought her out, to take refuge in her arms. She was here and would always be there for him. She just regretted that he didn't know that. She also knew the reason that he'd kept his Georgia findings a secret; he wanted to protect her from the evil that had touched her way back then, especially from a parent.

The warm breezes had turned chilly, and before going in, she reached to the floor to pick up her empty glass of wine that had warmed her insides. Perhaps the night would go fast and she would sleep till morning. Sensing movement, she was startled by the shadowy figure at the side of her house.

"Don't be frightened, Ava," Cole said in a quiet tone as he walked toward her. He stood at the bottom of the steps and looked up at her.

Ava caught her breath. Frightened? she thought giddily. "Hello, Cole," she said, trying to guess what was on his mind. He sounded so subdued. As much as she wanted to strangle him for causing her such pain, she wanted to love him at the same time. But she needed a cue from him. She waited as he continued to stare at her.

"Can I come up?" Cole asked, his hands at his sides.

"Yes," she murmured, and sat up straight in the lounge chair. It was the same chair that they'd first made love on outdoors. There had been many other times but that first time was one of those precious moments that one forever cherished.

Cole was beside her now, looking down at her. "I want you to know that I didn't desert you," he said quietly. "I would never do that in life." He held out his hand. "Can we go inside? I want to see your eyes."

She placed her hand in his and that long-yearned-for touch made her gasp. His grasp was strong as he pulled her up, and when she was standing, he caught her briefly against his chest and then released her.

Cole's heart was thumping nearly out of his chest as he prayed that he still had the love of this woman who had become the source of his life. He only hoped that she would forgive his silence for the last two days. They were in the living room and Ava was seated next to him on the sofa. They were still holding hands and she was looking at him expectantly.

"Are you leaving me, Cole?" Ava asked softly as she looked intently into his eyes.

"What?" Cole croaked. "Oh, my God, no. Is that what you've been thinking?" He caught her to him and held her tightly, burying his nose in her hair, nuzzling her neck, and tears dampening his eyes as he held on.

His chest was tight when he released her, but he still clasped her hand in his. "You are my life, sweetheart," Cole said. "If you don't want me, then it's all over for me."

Ava couldn't stop the sudden gush of warmth that rushed through her body like a whirlpool. "Oh, Cole, I do love you. How can I not want you?" she murmured in a choked voice. "You've brought more meaning to my life than I could ever have imagined. I would find it the most difficult act in my life to start all over again without you by my side."

They were silent as their words were digested, and if as one, their minds and body relaxed.

Cole tilted her chin so that he could look into her beautiful eyes. "I went away not because I was hurt and sulking and had nowhere to turn," he said. "I knew you were here and would be my strength." He paused. "Graham's revelation hurt like the dickens," he said. "But I dealt with it, and before I left the house after all those hours of soul-searching, I got past what my mother did. She's living with all that pain all these years so her running away couldn't have helped her either. Just like mine never helped me. I was still an angry, bitter man. Until you and Royce happened in my life. Now I ask for nothing more."

"But you left," Ava said softly.

"I know, sweetheart," Cole answered as he caressed her soft cheek with his knuckles. "I had a question to ask you and this time I wanted to be prepared." His eyes clouded briefly. "And there was something that I had to tell you." His voice was husky. "I didn't tell you everything that I learned while I was investigating in Georgia," he said as he cleared his throat.

Ava knew but was silent.

"I didn't want to bring more hurt to you. The meanness inflicted upon you by Winifred was despicable. You shouldn't have had to experience more deception, so I exacted a promise from your sister not to call you to say a word about what she'd told me, although I wanted like hell to spare you. As you can see, the words wouldn't come—there was no right time to tell you."

Ava caressed his cheek, and then with the pad of her thumb touched his mouth exploring the outline of his lips that she longed to taste.

"Shh," she said in a hushed voice. "I know, love."

Cole's eyes narrowed. "She called you?" *Oh, my God,* he thought, *she knows?*

"Yes. Earlier today."

"Lord, and I wasn't here!" His voice was full of anguish. "Ava, sweetheart," he said. "I'm sorry."

"I know, I know," Ava said. "I've had hours to think about it and I feel like a caged bird that's been freed and allowed to fly away." She saw his frustration and sought to assuage his guilt. "Maybe when you would have revealed the truth, I wouldn't have been strong enough to handle it," she said. "But things happen for a reason when they do. Maybe I needed to feel good about Winifred being found out first before I could deal with my father's unbelievable act of hatred toward me." Strangely she didn't feel the need to cry at the thought of her father, or her mother's curious position. Or of Dahlia's long silence, even after their parents' deaths. She supposed that in time all the hurt would be a faded memory.

"Ah, sweetheart," Cole said in an emotional voice. "I love you madly." He kissed her then, a long lingering kiss where he tongued open her lips and greedily sought the warmth and sweetness of the inner recesses of her mouth. He suckled and tasted her tongue, nearly drugging himself in his heady explorations as her response sent swirls of desire through him. He couldn't waste any more time without thoroughly loving her.

"Cole," Ava murmured against his lips as he feverishly sought to feel his bare skin against hers. "I do love you," she whispered as she tugged his shirt from his pants. His chest was bare and she sought her prize, feeling and kneading his male nipples that were already taut with his desire for her. She dipped her head and tasted, catching one of the stiffened buds between her lips and pressed gently, evoking a yelp of sheer pleasured agony from his lips.

"Ava," Cole gasped.

She was where she'd yearned to be and she was relishing every moment. As if there would never be another time, like a masochist she wanted to prolong the release of love. But when he pushed up her bra and his lips found the berries of her breasts she squirmed in his arms and threw her head back in a moment of ecstasy. He was suckling with his lips on one while his hand caressed the other. Her senses went haywire. "Cole," she gasped. "That's torture, love." Her shorts were down around her knees and she kicked them off. When his hand slipped inside of her panties and cupped her quivering mound she squirmed into him. "My God," she whispered, her eyes closed against the onslaught. She could feel the damp between her legs threaten to cascade like a flowing river.

"I'm feeling you, honey," Cole rasped. "Soon." He moved swiftly kicking off his sneakers and pushing away his pants but not before retrieving the condom from his pocket. She'd unhooked her bra and he pushed it away. After shedding his shirt they were both naked.

Ava couldn't feel the length of him like she wanted and cried out her frustration. "No, Cole, please, not here." She caught his hands and neither would later remember how fast they came to be lying in her bed with his length atop her.

"I know," Cole said, and grinned. "I wasn't getting enough of you either." He gave her a mischievous look. "And I missed doing this to you, too," he whispered, and then bent and with an adroit maneuver tickled her nape with his tongue. His body jolted with her reaction as she arched into him. "Oh, yes, sweetheart, yes," he rasped.

Ava moaned and grasped his erect penis, the shaft so hard, throbbing with want that she nearly exploded from anticipation. "Now," she managed as she guided him into her deep velvet dampness. She thrust her hips upward to meet his sudden plunge. "Cole!"

"I'm here." And he was as he entered her deeply into her core, giving her all the loving that she craved and that he'd missed. He'd promised her once before that they would never be separated again and this time it was a promise he meant to keep.

Ava felt his unbridled passion as he loved her body and soul and she reveled in it. With all that she possessed she loved him. Her identical desire and passion for him was like a demon unleashed as the

electricity they generated coursed through them like
fiery ribbons. Her body vibrated from the current
and almost as quickly as it had started, the ebbing
flames were as a cooling, gentle fan as she drifted
back to Earth. The sigh she emitted was one of total,
love-satisfied exhaustion. She wondered just how
many orgasms she'd had but dared not to count as
she basked in the warmth of his love.

Cole was still shaking from the experience. He was
on top of her and he couldn't move because he was
encased in her arms and legs and Ava didn't appear
to mind. He didn't want to move but knew his weight
must be crushing.

"Ava. Let go," he said in her ear. "I must be hurting you."

Opening her eyes, Ava looked at him with a mock
ferocious stare. "Let go? Are you mad, lover?" She
tightened her legs around his thighs and her hands
began to move over the taut muscles in his back.
"I'm never letting you go," she growled in a bad im-
itation of a mother lion.

Cole's belly shook with laughter. "You're my crazy,
sweet nut," he said. "But if I don't move now there'll
be nothing left of you for me to love, sweetheart."
Moving swiftly, he unfolded himself from her grasp
and slid to her side. He kissed her nose. "You don't
have to entrap me because you'll always have me—
mind, body, and soul. I'm not going anywhere." He
kissed her again and then slipped from the bed and
left the room.

Ava was smiling in the dark and she reached over
to turn on the light. She ran her hands over the in-
dentation in his pillow. She remembered the nights
she didn't want to go to bed because his scent would

envelop her. No more separations, she thought. Never.

Cole returned and she watched him as he walked toward her, his magnificent, muscled body gleaming with love-sweat. His thick thighs that she'd enfolded were inviting her to touch again. His heavy penis was nearly erect again and she swallowed just thinking about how she'd accepted him into her so easily. She'd always thought that and it never ceased to amaze her that they fit so well together. It just was to be, she thought.

"Hey," Cole said, not missing her introspection of his body. He loved that she loved it and him and hoped she'd never tire of looking at him with that look in her beautiful dark eyes. He got in bed beside her and as she was, propped himself up against the pillows. "I had to get something from my pocket," he said, and opened the envelope he'd been holding.

They were touching shoulder to shoulder and their bare skin was like a lightning rod to explore each other again. But Cole resisted, even if it was for a little while.

"Do you remember the question you never answered for me, sweetheart?"

"Yes," Ava said, remembering the proposal she'd turned down.

"I said I wouldn't ask you again until I solved the case against you," Cole said in a serious voice. "Well, as it turned out, I had little to do in solving it. You did." He hesitated but still held her gaze. "That didn't stop me from going ahead with my plan."

"Plan?" Ava was curious at what more there was to know.

"Yes. I wanted to ask you again but I wanted to symbolize it with something special. That's where I was." He let out a sheepish laugh. "I know you think it was a crazy thing to do, but when I couldn't find what I wanted in Minuet or Hudson, I drove to Bremington." He seemed excited when he said, "I think I found something that would make you happy." He opened the envelope and spilled the brochures on the bed.

Ava looked in amazement at the assortment of big houses, some mansionlike in every style and a carousel of colors. "What's this?" she said, completely taken aback.

Cole picked up one brochure and said, "This is really the one I could see you in." With it clutched in his hand, he took both hands in hers and stared into her eyes. "I love you, Ava, and I want you to be my wife. Will you marry me and make my life complete? I want to make a present of one of these to you to symbolize my love for you."

All she could do was to stare from him to the brochure and back again. His eyes were shining with the love he had for her and her heart nearly broke.

Cole couldn't understand her silence and he felt as though his world were collapsing. "Ava?" His voice was but a shadow of its deep baritone.

"This is in Bremington," Ava said. "Nearly thirty miles away. You want to live in Bremington?"

"I want to live anywhere you want to live, Ava," Cole said in a hoarse voice. He frowned. "Anyplace where you'll be happy." He could see the sadness come into her eyes as swiftly as a current carrying minnows downstream. "What is it? If that doesn't suit you, there are hundreds of others you can select from." A thought stopped him cold. "Does this mean that you don't want to marry me?" He didn't know how he got those words past his lips.

"Oh, Cole, Cole," Ava said with a soft cry. "Yes, I'll marry you." She caressed his eyelids with her fingers to chase away the sudden bleak look in his eyes.

"You will?" The tenseness left his body as he sagged against the pillows. Then he looked at her and kissed her mouth in a long lingering kiss. "You know how to lead a guy to stroke city, don't you?" he said, tweaking her nose. Then he looked at the scattered papers. "I thought that you would like to start a new life away from all this," he said, and waved a hand as if to encompass her house and the one next door. "So many memories. We don't need to start off like that. It would be a new beginning for us."

Ava smiled. "A new beginning is wherever we are, love. My home is here. Your home is in Minuet. Royce is here." She ran her fingers over his cheek. "You know thirty miles would be too much distance between the two of you. Both of you would pester each other to no end until you could get together." She emitted a soft sound. "I want to stay here in Minuet," she said. "Do you mind?"

Cole thought about that, and before he answered he gathered up the papers and tossed them to the floor. "No, I don't mind, sweetheart."

"But?" Ava said, seeing his hesitation.

"This house is too small for us," he said. "My house, well . . ."

Ava thought she understood. The master bedroom. She snuggled down against him. "I think this little house will be a nice fit for us, love," she said. "At least until late next spring."

"Next spring?" Cole was puzzled. "Why? What will be happening then?" And he yelped as her fingers began roaming over his love-swollen nipples.

"Because I want to make love to you again," she murmured as she bent to taste the hardened buds.

Cole gasped. "Aargh, sweetheart," he said. "As I want you." He was more than ready for her as he reached inside the drawer where he kept a stash of condoms. "And what will be happening next spring?" he rasped as her hand manipulated him into a throbbing frenzy. "God, Ava!"

A soft laugh escaped as Ava took the condom from him and tossed it to the floor. "Just that our precious little cargo should arrive by then," she said. "The one that we're going to make now." She stilled for a moment. "You do want our children, don't you, love?"

"What?" Cole was atop her in a flash. He kissed her lips and whispered against them. "How about a double order on this try, sweetheart?"

"Twins!" Ava moaned as she arched her hips, surrendering to his adept ministrations all over her body. She was being swept away by his firm, deep entry. As always, she felt safe and cherished, and the thought of having Cole's babies brought a smile to her lips. Twins, she thought, as she swooned when a powerful move sent her over the edge, and Ava giddily wondered if her lover really had the secret recipe! We can only see, she thought as she succumbed again. We can only see!

Epilogue

Late spring

Cole looked in wonder at the little bundle cradled in his wife's arms. He hadn't held his son yet, still awed by the creation.

"He's little," Ava said to her husband. "But he won't bite. Take him, honey." Cole was sitting on the edge of her hospital bed and she maneuvered the baby into his father's arms. "See, he fits perfectly," she said, loving the look of father and son together.

"Unbelievable," Cole murmured. "He smells brand-new." He remembered when he'd first met Ava, the clean smell that had wafted to his nostrils and that had sent him bonkers. He looked at her. "You're so beautiful."

Ava reached up to caress his cheek. "You two are too," she said and smiled at her family. *My family*, she thought. After all these years, she had her own real family. She touched the baby's cheek. "Are you really happy with his name?" she asked her husband, not for the first time.

"Richard Curtis Dumont is a strong-sounding

name, sweetheart," Cole said, frowning down at his precious issue. "But he's so little!"

Ava laughed. "He's not going to be seven pounds forever, love," she said. "He'll grow into his name. We can call him Rick if that'll make you feel better."

"Rick's a fine name, Daddy," Graham said as he walked into the room. He clapped his brother on the back after Cole gave Rick back to his mother. He was grinning from ear to ear.

Cole grinned and said to Ava. "Will you look at that face? What a difference a day makes." To Graham he said, "How's it feel, Daddy? Got used to your daughter yet?" It was only yesterday that he had driven Graham and Teddie to Minuet Hospital where their daughter was born late last night. Only hours later in the wee morning hours it was Graham driving Cole and Ava back to the hospital where Rick was born at dawn.

Graham beamed. "She's tiny," he said "but little Alison Renee Dumont is already my princess."

Ava watched the two brothers who'd reclaimed their former bond with each other. After Graham had closed his Ohio office, he was now successfully established in Hudson. He and Teddie had married only weeks before her and Cole, unaware that their second child was on the way.

The problem of the two houses had been settled almost immediately after the brothers had proposed marriage. Both houses were gutted and rebuilt into homes for large families. Cole was ferocious about keeping the opening in the natural hedges as he never tired of Royce's visits to see his uncle Cole. The little boy had fallen in love with his father and was ecstatic about becoming a big brother.

Cole and Ava had honeymooned in Los Angeles

where he used the opportunity to close the chapter on his life there. The plan to continue to Las Vegas was canceled when Patrice Dumont failed to return Cole's calls. Cole refused to let it dampen his spirits and promised Ava that one day they would try again.

Ava and Teddie were probably the only people in Minuet who weren't surprised at the sudden departure of Fiona Fitzgerald the day of Teddie and Graham's wedding.

Cole, alone with his wife and son after Graham went back to his own family down the hall, smiled at his wife. "Happy, sweetheart?" he asked.

"Perfectly," Ava answered. She reached up and caressed his cheek as she loved to do. "Is Jack giving you as much time as you need to get used to all of this, Daddy?" she asked with a teasing look.

"Deputy Sheriff Dumont doesn't have to report for duty for three weeks," Cole said. "So says our newly elected sheriff for the umpteenth time." They both laughed at Jack Thompson's mythical retirement, and then Cole turned serious. "Do you think you'll call her now, sweetheart?" he asked. "I think she'd like to know that she's an aunt."

Ava looked at her son and gently touched his cheek. Her heart was filled with love, and when she looked at Cole her eyes were misty. "It's time, isn't it?" she said slowly. "Time to share our love with Dahlia. We are a family after all, aren't we?"

Cole bent to kiss his wife, the woman he would always cherish. "Yes, we are." Then he said thoughtfully, "And while we're at it, I'll give Las Vegas another try."

Ava thought of Graham's children as she looked at her precious baby. Such beautiful grandchildren they are. "I think you'll win out this time, love."

Dear Reader,

Ava and Cole found each other after many years of thinking that emotional love would forever be elusive. Their story is meant to be encouraging to all who have experienced betrayal or heartbreak in one form or another from those dear to them, and hopefully can look toward a brighter future.

It is also a message to all to remain diligent and responsible in safeguarding our little ones from adult negligence. They are our future.

To all who have sent heartwarming responses to *Hello Again*, I thank you. I have no plans to give Wesley his story as many have requested, but it is food for thought.

Thanks for sharing,

Doris Johnson
P.O. Box 130370
Springfield Gardens, NY 11413

Email: Bessdj@aol.com

Look For These Other
Dafina Novels

Check Out These Other
Dafina Novels

Grab These Other
Dafina Novels
(trade paperback editions)